ACADEMY
GIRLS

ALSO BY NORA CARROLL

The Color of Water in July

ACADEMY GIRLS

nora carroll

LAKE UNION
PUBLISHING

Published by Lake Union Publishing, Seattle

www.apub.com

Amazon, the Amazon logo, and Lake Union Publishing are trademarks of Amazon.com, Inc., or its affiliates.

ISBN-13: 9781503947443
ISBN-10: 1503947440

Cover design by Connie Gabbert

Printed in the United States of America

This book is dedicated to the memory of Audrey Sheats, who taught me to memorize poetry and to Thomas Geilfuss who encouraged me to write some of my own.

This was in the white of the year,
That was in the green,
Drifts were as difficult then to think
As daisies now to be seen.

Looking back is best that is left,
Or if it be before,
Retrospection is prospect's half,
Sometimes almost more

—*Emily Dickinson*

PART ONE
NOW

1

At the Grove Academy, we learned three immutable lessons: literature is a kind of religion, only failures get married, and though we would eventually leave the academy, the spirit of the Grove would always stay with us.

In those days, we were careless about the way we discussed our futures, the three of us: Kat, the poet; Lissa, the beauty; and me, who I guess was supposed to be the serious one. We held fast to ideas—truth, good manners, and beauty. And to far-flung destinations—Tangiers, Nantucket, and Shanghai. As Grove girls, we armed ourselves with lines of poetry, never thinking that we might need something more practical to fall back on later in life.

Sometimes, when our English teacher, Miss Amanda Pymstead, would tread past us, trailing her long lavender scarves and air of barely veiled misfortune, we'd say, "And of course there's always the fallback position . . ." From where we sat, the future seemed like a hazy shadow of anticipated continuing good fortune, impossible to picture in any concrete form. One thing we *could* picture, at least, was to stand where

Miss Pymstead now stood at the chalkboard, presiding over an endless loop of Vermont seasons, bored girls, and poetry.

When our time was up, we hastened out through the Grove's stone gates without a single look back. But all of us assumed that the Grove would open her arms to welcome us again, if ever the need should arise.

Thirty-five years later, it was late August, and the stone pillars that marked the opening to the Grove's long driveway delineated the precise space between present and past. Up until now, rattling down back roads in my worn-out Subaru, I'd kept focused on the present, but as I rounded the corner and saw the twin stone gates, I had a sudden rushing sense of where I was going. I braked, unconsciously, and then glanced in my rearview mirror, where I could see my son, Charlie, lifting his head, puzzled, before looking back down at his phone. He was fifteen, tousle haired, and good-looking—immersed in the conversation he was rapidly tapping out with his thumbs. He didn't know it, but he was the reason I had returned to a place that common sense suggested I should avoid at all costs. I had a secret. But then, I told myself, didn't we all?

As soon as the car rolled between the two pillars, I entered the past. The paint on the buildings was a little brighter; the grounds seemed better kept; but the brick-and-stone edifices, and how they were situated in the landscape, threw me back in time.

We emerged from the woods and rounded the curve in front of Loomis Hall. The broad playing fields that we called Siberia came into view and the entire campus spread out in front of us.

Charlie looked up and murmured, "Sweet!"

A moment later, we passed a steep grassy hillside that dropped precipitously to the left, just beyond the campus's chapel. My hands were sweating on the steering wheel as my stomach seemed to skitter over the precipice. I heard a voice telling me to turn around and leave while I still could, but Charlie's presence in the backseat reminded me what little choice I had. My son, my reason for living, did not understand the stakes, but I did. This was a last stop. If I screwed this up, we would have nothing. I had developed a habit of not trusting myself—and being here, at the Grove, only reinforced this feeling.

Words once memorized came back to me: *the more things stay the same, the more they change.* A line among many lines I was led to believe would be worthwhile to remember. But that was a long time ago, when I was a girl in a circle of girls. When all of us believed that words mattered as much as money, flesh, and blood.

In the trunk, there were a couple of suitcases, my battered copy of Emily Dickinson, my old Grove yearbook, and a spiral notebook that Kat, Lissa, and I had kept during our senior year. Beyond these few possessions, I carried a much weightier burden—the heft of memory.

As for the three lessons?

Here's what they should have taught us. First: *don't believe what they tell you in books.* Second: *marry money.* Third . . . well, as for the third lesson, the spirits that haunted the edges of my memory of the Grove had always stayed with me. So, maybe the third lesson was right after all.

I looked around, and I could almost smell the faint odor of clove cigarettes and hear the sound of Neil Young wafting through the open windows. I could almost see the students, dressed in their hippie prints—kaffiyeh scarves or bandanas wrapped around their heads— and I felt a deep rushing, like being caught in a fast-flowing river heading straight toward the rapids. I could almost hear the sound of Miss Pymstead's voice reciting the words of Emily Dickinson.

I was a divorced mother of one, a failed novelist, broke, and had been given a one-year position to teach English to seniors at the Grove. The position was "probationary," as I had no relevant experience. I was under no illusions that I would keep the job if my performance was not up to par. I was not proud that I was only given the position after my former roommate, Lissa, who is married to TV producer Martin Edelstein, intervened on my behalf to get me the job—the fallback position. My old Subaru Outback, a '92, barely made the trip up from New Jersey, but at least it was paid for, and as I pulled up in front of Gould Cottage, which was now an administration building, it sighed to a stop.

There was a name for what I was doing here. It was called a last chance.

2

The framed diplomas on the walls of Elaine Farber-Johnson's office were certain to soothe any prospective parents who wondered whether they would get their money's worth at the Grove. And Elaine Farber-Johnson herself, who stood when I entered and greeted me with a firm handshake, was such a perfect specimen of a Grove girl grown up that I was filled with a sense of recognition and perhaps even comfort.

"Welcome, Ms. Milton," she said. "How was your trip up? Not too difficult, I trust." Hitchcock chairs emblazoned with the Grove insignia surrounded her desk, and the diplomas demonstrated her perfect prep-school pedigree: Grove, Wellesley, Harvard School of Education. The picture windows behind Dr. Farber-Johnson's desk looked out over Siberia.

"The school is looking quite spruce," I said. "I had remembered it as being more rundown."

"Some of our alumnae have been very generous." She smiled. "Besides the changes in the physical plant, I'm sure you'll find that the spirit of the place is much the same."

"Well, of course, I'm not used to seeing boys on campus," I said.

Since I had graduated, thirty-five years earlier, the Grove Academy was no longer a school for girls. It had merged with the Hardley School across the river and become the Hardley-Grove Academy. The Grove Academy for Girls had gone coed.

"Yes, of course," she said. "The old girls always find that quite disconcerting. You'll be used to it before you know it."

I had no objection to the school's decision to go coed. I remembered the hothouse environment of the Grove—hopefully, that had improved somewhat.

"If you don't mind my asking, what drew you to the field of teaching? This marks quite a *departure* for you, doesn't it?"

I pictured my big house in the suburbs—the kitchen with granite countertops, my office upstairs where I whiled away my time, supposedly writing but more often looking at Facebook. I blinked. All that was gone now. No point in dwelling on it.

I wasn't sure how much Lissa had shared with the administration about my personal situation, but since I had been given a job for which I was wholly unqualified, I was sure that she must have given some indication about how desperate my predicament was.

"I love literature. I hope to impart that love to my students, just as my teachers did for me when I was here."

I saw a faint crease appear between Dr. Farber-Johnson's eyebrows.

"Eighty percent of the faculty here at the Grove have advanced degrees," she was saying. "Twenty percent have published papers in their subject field. Fifteen percent have been awarded grants for travel or further study."

"Of course," I murmured, my face hot.

"You," she said, "did not meet the same stringent requirements that are usually expected of our new hires." She clasped her hands in front of her. "But I'm sure you know that."

I nodded. The litany of my own shortcomings was one verse I had committed to memory.

"If what has brought you here is some misguided fantasy of *Dead Poets Society*, with yourself in the starring role, then I'm afraid you will have to think otherwise. Teaching is much more about preparation than inspiration."

"Preparation. Yes, of course." I tried to keep a straight face, but blood was rushing through my ears like a raging river after a storm— and I was hoping to keep my mind off dead poets entirely. Was it sheer coincidence that she had mentioned such a thing?

"I need to tell you that there has been a change of plans since we offered you the position." I felt the room telescoping in around me. I was so close to the limit on my charge card that I couldn't even buy gas to get back to New Jersey—not that there was anyplace to return to. Charlie was counting on me. I really and truly did understand that this was a last-ditch effort, and I could not afford to screw it up. Nothing but my concern for Charlie's welfare could have dragged me back to this place.

"A change?" I said. I tried to sound calm. I did not feel comfortable discussing my financial situation—Grove girls did not *ever* discuss money.

"Our housemother for Abbott North has just been diagnosed with cancer. I need to replace her. It's quite unexpected, of course."

"Of course."

"Normally, a coed placement is strictly against our policy."

I was still standing. Dr. Farber-Johnson had not yet gestured for me to be seated. I was scrambling to keep up with her, my mind not yet unclouded from road fog, and from the unfamiliar sensation of finding myself once again inside the confines of the Grove, a place I once swore I'd never set foot in again—and for a very good reason that I was trying hard not to think about at that moment. I pressed my sweaty palms against my skirt.

"And it will require the utmost, shall we say, circumspection, and um, vigilance, on your part."

I said nothing.

"But I knew that, as a Grove girl, you would understand that when we need to make do, we make do."

I smiled. I tried not to let on that I wasn't quite sure what she was talking about.

"That boy of yours. Charlie, is it?"

I nodded. *Charlie.*

"I assume he's reliable."

Through the window, I could just see the side of the Subaru. I could see his form slouched in the backseat, one arm out the window, his hand rat-a-tatting on the side of the car.

"Oh, very," I said. "Absolutely."

My memory of the Grove had no boys in it—well, no ordinary memories of boys, no pedestrian memories of boys who were slouched against cars, boys who were there for no reason, boys who were there just the way a tree or a lamppost was there. Boys snuck in and snuck out. We hid them. But there were never just regular boys out in the open.

"Well, he will need to be reliable," she said. "It's less than ideal to put a teenage boy in a dorm full of girls. He'll need to use the utmost self-restraint. You'll see to it that he does. I'm assuming, of course, that he's quiet and well mannered."

It was beginning to sink in.

"I'm going to be housemother of Abbott North?"

"I'm so grateful," Elaine Farber-Johnson said. "You've made things ever so much easier for us. But of course I can always count on a Grove girl to be a pinch hitter. Now, let me get Nate to show you to your new quarters. Once you're settled, we can meet to discuss your responsibilities."

Dr. Farber-Johnson lowered her voice and looked discreetly around the room, as though to make it clear that it pained her to be required to discuss such a matter.

"Lissa Edelstein has shared a bit about your . . . *personal situation*. As housemother, all of your meals will be included. You will join the children for three meals a day in Commons."

She placed her hands on her desktop and leaned forward. "When our Grove sisters return to us in *straitened* circumstances, we find that taking meals in Commons can be a welcome respite." She stood up again. "Faculty children, of course, are expected to set the standard for good manners."

I looked at Dr. Farber-Johnson, took in her healthy complexion, smooth chestnut-colored hair, and the assurance that came from decades of prep-school breeding. I wanted to ask her about money. Maybe the extra responsibilities came with extra pay—but I figured maybe I shouldn't press my luck right away.

"I'm deeply grateful for the opportunity," I said. "It's lovely to be back at the Grove."

Dr. Farber-Johnson held out her hand to me.

"I wish you the best of luck. You'll find things much changed, but nothing that isn't still best handled by tact and common sense. And remember, I'm here for you if you need me."

I understood that I had been dismissed. Apparently in the universe of Dr. Elaine Farber-Johnson, head of the school, you had to earn the right to be seated.

Abbott North was the first of a line of four cottage dormitories lined up along the hill facing Siberia. It was also the largest, followed by Lane North, Lane South, and Abbott South. It was a short walk across Siberia from Gould Cottage, which had once been a classroom building, to Cottage Row, but in the Subaru, I had to follow the pavement, which took me all the way around, in front of Pencott Library and Underhill House. Up on the hill, Whittaker Chapel sat like the jewel in a crown, its rose window sparkling in the late-summer sun. As the pavement rounded a corner, I could see the walls of the boathouse—red like dried blood, with the sweep of the Connecticut River just beyond it—and my breath sucked in, blood rushing to my wrists. I could feel Charlie shifting in the backseat, ballast. I pressed on the accelerator a little.

As we rounded another bend, Commons came into view, sitting up on the hill, like the Parthenon, with its Doric columns. No wonder we were all so thin back then, Grove girls with our famous willowy figures. We had to trudge up that giant hill every time we wanted to eat. As though he were reading my mind, Charlie spoke up from the backseat.

"Hey, Mom, I'm hungry. Can we get something to eat?"

"There are still some sandwiches in the cooler," I said.

"They're disgusting. They're all hot, and stale."

"Well, then," I said. "You'll have to wait."

Charlie had pulled out his cell phone and was fiddling around with it. It was our one extravagance. I hadn't had the heart to take it away from him yet. The next phone bill, it was going to get cut off, but Charlie didn't know that yet.

Then, suddenly, like a mirage out of place, a big building appeared where I remembered there used to be nothing but some underused playing fields. It was spiffy-looking. Brick, and very sophisticated—in the style of the cottages and the library, only this was new, with nice bright paint. There was a large painted sign across the front: "Edelstein Student Center." Inside, through the big plate-glass windows, I could see a wing with exercise equipment; in another wing there was something that looked like a food court, and I admit, my heart sank when I saw a Starbucks sign.

Charlie sat up in the backseat. "Hey, Starbucks. You think that's open?"

I didn't get a chance to answer. There was a big fellow, balding, with a ruddy wind-burned face, standing in front of the building, waving me down. I rolled down my window.

"Jane Milton?"

I nodded.

"Good to see you. Nate Hodges. You don't remember me?"

I stared at his face. There was something about him that made me uncomfortable. "You are *that* Jane Milton, aren't you?" he asked.

I felt a trace of heat pass over my face. I had just remembered who he was.

The girls wouldn't be arriving for another day, and so Abbott North was peculiarly devoid of personality. The walls inside had been repainted, and the floors had been scrubbed with industrial soap. The stairways, with their fire-regulation doors and red light-up exit signs seemed cold and institutional. Charlie and I traipsed upstairs with our few belongings. I declined Nate's offer to help, not wanting to let him see how few possessions we had brought with us.

The housemother's quarters were cramped, up under the eaves and deathly hot. The windows were all propped open, the air stirred limply by one ancient Western Electric fan. It was nothing more than a glorified senior girls' suite: two small bedrooms off a central common room. It hit me what close quarters Charlie and I would now be sharing. I glanced with dismay at the toilet, anticipating a year's worth of seat-up/seat-down wars. In truth, I had expected that Charlie's free tuition would include lodging in the boys' dormitory. But I had grown used to dashed dreams. One bedroom looked out over the boathouse and the river, and beyond to the campus that used to be the Hardley School for Boys; the other looked the opposite way, toward the chapel and Commons. There was a nod to a kitchenette—a half fridge, a sink, and a cupboard. Inside the cupboard: a couple of Grove mugs, a box of Lipton tea bags, a drawer with a few bent utensils, a few chipped pieces of crockery. Charlie had gone off in search of the Starbucks, even though I had warned him it would likely be closed since no students were about.

I thought of all Charlie had given up in the past year—his father in prison, his home sold off to pay our debts. I had never wanted the extravagant things my ex had procured for us—the big home, the nice cars—but I had never complained, or suggested that we do less. I asked myself, countless times, if deep down I suspected the worst—did I willingly turn a blind eye to our problems? I could have gone out to look for a real job to help support the family, but instead I had played around, writing novels, not understanding that my husband was driving our family deeper and deeper into debt. When the fraud caught up with him, my signature was all over the bad debt. Pleading ignorance, my lawyer *just* managed to keep me out of jail. I had to work, but soon learned that my only skill—words and how to string them together—was not much of a marketable skill.

"Are you finding everything all right?"

I whirled around to find a woman standing in the doorway, her approach so quiet she seemed to have materialized from nowhere. I felt the hair stand up on the back of my neck. But she looked harmless enough. Rather small in stature, thick through the middle, somewhat mannish-looking, with her shoe-polish-black hair pulled back in an off-kilter bun.

"Yes, thank you."

The woman came in without asking. She looked around as she did so, but my own belongings were so sparse they hadn't added much to the surroundings.

"You have a son."

"I'm Jane Milton," I said, hoping to cut short her inquiries.

"Abigail Von Platte. Chemistry. Lane North." She pointed toward the open windows. "We're neighbors. Right through the window. You can just scream if you need help." She laughed a laugh that sounded more like a caw. "Although the distress calls don't work as well once the girls get here and they turn the air conditioners on."

"Oh, the dorms aren't air-conditioned," I said, a touch too breezily, because I immediately had to clamp my mouth shut while I watched Abigail Von Platte tap her stubby finger on what was obviously a thermostat on the wall.

"Well, I'll be," I said. Air-conditioned dorms? At the Grove we had always worn our Puritanism with a weary courage.

"Things have changed, Jane Milton," Abigail Von Platte said. "Things have changed quite a lot. Being Jane Milton won't make you so special anymore."

I did not have a chance to tell her that being Jane Milton certainly didn't make me feel special anymore—quite the opposite. She left as suddenly as she had come, but it wasn't until I could only just hear her footsteps in the hallway that it came back to me—the fat girl who roomed alone down at the end of the hallway. The one who used to have Oreo crumbs on her shirtfront when she came out of study hall in the evenings, the one that we only talked to now and then when one of us needed help with math. Now, I could remember the girl's name: Abigail Von Platte.

3

When Charlie discovered that we had no television, he fell into his other favorite occupation—sleep. The moon was out over the river, and Siberia was as bright as half daylight. Charlie shifted on his bed, the room already filled with his boy smell. Through the open doorway, I could see that he had staked his territory with a scattering of discarded clothes. I had worried myself sick about what this move might do to him, but thus far I couldn't tell. I think he was hedging his bets: when you're young, the empty shells of buildings tell you nothing. When you're older, you come to believe that they can tell the whole story.

It was hot in my room. I closed the door and sat on my narrow bed, holding an old shoebox on my knees. Inside were a spiral-bound Mead notebook, now brittle with age, and a small white box. The front cover of the notebook was inscribed in my handwriting, *CLUE NOTEBOOK*. The small box contained a gold Grove class ring tied to a stiff leather thong.

I opened the notebook and leafed through the pages. Some were covered with notes in my schoolgirl cursive; others had items stapled in—old photographs, copied poems, and the like. My old friend Kat's handwriting, once scribbled around the margins in pencil, had mostly faded to the point of illegibility. Two typed manuscript pages were stapled to the back cover, the erasable bond turned yellowed with age. The top of each sheet had a watermark, and the second page was spotted with three old coffee splashes faded to a color that could have been dried blood. An image of Kat's face flashed in front of me, her hazel eyes rimmed with kohl that smudged in the corners. Kat had written a book. A book about us. Nothing remained of it except these two pages—the first page, and the one that read: *The End*. I did not know what had become of the pages in between, but I knew that those pages contained the tale of our senior year.

The past seemed so close, so vivid in my mind's eye, but the stiff yellowed paper told the truth: it was so long ago. When we arrived at the Grove, Lissa and I were only fourteen, and Kat, always the precocious one, was just thirteen. Kat liked to brag about how she was always the youngest at everything because she was born prematurely. We had felt so grown-up, off on our own, the world of our school so vast, and mysterious. There were no TVs at the Grove, and no Internet back in those days. It was a world apart. It was the whole world. We believed that it had its own logic, and its own rules.

I ran my fingertip along the typeface, feeling the slight indentations made by the old manual typewriter, the one that used to skip the crosses on the *t*'s and leave the tails off the *y*'s. I scanned the familiar text.

The Boathouse

The purpose of this book is to write down every single thing that happened before we forget and paint over it and decide that it wasn't really that way at all. I've read The Catcher in the Rye, and A Separate Peace, and I'm in a boarding school too, but that's where the similarity ends. You see, I'm a girl, and girls' stories are different. There were three of us, the pretty one, the smart one, and the crazy one. I'll explain all this to you—but not yet. Right now, this is just the story of how the three of us stole out late one night and found some lines of poetry written on the side of a boathouse.

That's how our story began.

Lane North, my old dorm, was next door to Abbott. The room I lived in during my senior year was on the second floor. I had my flashlight in my pocket. It would only take a moment to pop in and out of my former room. The idea that I was going to look for something in a room I had not inhabited in thirty-five years was clearly absurd, yet I knew I would not rest easy until I looked.

I did not want to attract the attention of Abigail Von Platte, who lived on the third floor of Lane North, so I circled outside, calculating which door was farthest from her apartment. I had no desire to explain my mission to her, especially since I hardly knew what I was after myself. Entering the north doorway, I tried to step softly, but it was little use. The stairs in Lane squeaked with each footfall.

When I reached the second-floor landing, for a moment I stopped dead, startled by how little my old dormitory had changed. It seemed that the girls who had once lived there—Emma Doerr, Jo Dawson, Katie Cornwell—might pop out from behind each one of those doors.

The light filtering through the tall dormer windows at each end of the hallway made my skin appear ghostly. I shoved my hand in my pocket and felt the reassuring solidity of the flashlight. At the end of the hallway, I saw the doorway to my old room: 2B. Slowly, I pushed the door open. Inside, it was a standard-issue Grove Academy room. I saw a metal-frame bunk bed with ticking-striped mattresses, top and bottom, both now bare; a pair of mismatched dressers; two battered desks; and two wooden chairs.

Right now, washed out in the moonlight, the room looked barren. I struggled to imagine that this cramped and ordinary space had once served as the crucible for our fevered imaginations. In my mind, I could see Kat standing on one of the chairs, a scarf draped around her thin arched neck, declaiming lines of poetry, one arm stretched in front of her as if she were in a ballerina pose. A thumping sound from the floor above startled me back into the present. I heard footsteps, then a clunky shuffling—most likely Abigail Von Platte. I needed to stop thinking and look, and then get out of there.

There were two closets, but I was disoriented and couldn't remember which had been mine and which Kat's. I opened the door of the one closest to me: it looked as if the interior hadn't been painted in years, if ever. I shone my flashlight around. Inside the door, there was a slab of wood, bolted on, with two wooden pegs painted a faded black. Behind that wooden slab, Kat and I had discovered a small opening, just the right size for leaving folded-up notes. We had exchanged many hidden messages this way, but I knew that on my last day at the Grove, I departed without ever knowing if she had left me one final message. For thirty-five years I had wondered. I wanted to know. But could I ever know? Was it possible that for thirty-five years no other girl had ever thought to look there?

I heard footsteps again, but this time I wasn't sure they were coming from overhead—and then I thought I saw a light flashing outside. I ran my fingers along the ridge where we used to tuck our notes, expecting nothing, but when my fingers caught on a ridge of folded-up paper, I knew exactly what I was feeling. I shimmied it out carefully, afraid that the paper might tear. Finally, it slid free, and I held the tightly folded piece of paper cupped in my palms. As I unfolded it, my hands were trembling so violently that I couldn't read the words. But finally, I managed to steady myself and hold the paper up to the moonlit window.

My cheeks flushed hot as I recognized Kat's handwriting and saw the Emily Dickinson verse:

> *I died for beauty, but was scarce*
> *Adjusted in the tomb,*
> *When one who died for truth was lain*
> *In an adjoining room.*
>
> *He questioned softly why I failed?*
> *"For beauty," I replied.*
> *"And I for truth,—the two are one;*
> *We brethren are," he said.*
>
> *And so, as kinsmen met a night,*
> *We talked between the rooms,*
> *Until the moss had reached our lips,*
> *And covered up our names.*

Had I come all this way, and found a final clue, only to understand nothing? After thirty-five years, I still did not know.

I crumpled the brittle old paper in the palm of my hand. The door to 2B squeaked open and a beam of light blinded me.

"Visiting old haunts?" a male voice said. I couldn't place the voice, but when the flashlight was lowered and I blinked a few times, through the purple spots before my eyes, I recognized the broad frame of Nate.

"Shoulda figured it was you, Jane Milton . . . ," Nate said.

The crumpled paper still clutched in my hand felt hot and obvious.

"I was, uh, just . . ." I stammered, trying to think of some explanation for my presence there.

"Oh, you don't need to say nothin'," he said. "The old Grove girls, they all do it. This was your room, wasn't it?"

"Surely you don't remember . . . ," I said.

His smile was sly. "I don't forget much." We both turned at the sound of approaching footsteps in the hallway.

"Shh . . . better let me handle this." He stepped out of the room.

I heard Abigail Von Platte's loud voice. "Anything amiss here, Nate?"

"Nope, just doing routine rounds. Nothing out of the ordinary. Nope. Nobody 'round here Miz Von Platte, now just go on up to your room and don't you worry about a thing."

A few minutes passed and then he popped his head back into the room.

"Coast is clear," he whispered. "But, hey. If you're smart, you'll watch out for that one." He jerked his head toward the darkened stairway that led up toward Abigail Von Platte's rooms. I could just hear the low murmur of her television set.

I waited for him to say more, but he added nothing, so I followed his bobbing flashlight beam back down the stairs. We parted with a nod when we reached the front walk; I was furious that Nate Hodges had managed to make himself my accomplice.

4

In the bright August sunshine of the next morning—as SUVs and
minivans started pulling through the gates, disgorging students and an
almost unimaginable quantity of belongings—it was no longer possible
to mistake then for now. In the presence of Tahoes and Suburbans, the
buildings seemed scaled down, chastened even, and I was struck that the
place felt resortlike, with the brightly painted buildings, the flags fluttering on their poles, and the long-legged students, all of whom appeared
to have spent the summer acquiring perfectly even tans.

Around the periphery of groups of girls, I heard familiar snippets
of conversations about their summers: Martha's Vineyard, Wyoming,
London, and the Outer Banks. Abbott North quickly grew small again,
filled with piles of stuff: laptops, alpine skis, Bose speakers, suitcases and
trunks, Abercrombie shopping bags and boxes with *Pottery Barn* emblazoned that looked as though they would scarcely fit through Abbott's
narrow New England doors.

I stood at the doorway, dressed in a manner that I hoped was suitable to being the housemother of Abbott North: a khaki skirt and a
blue-pinstriped blouse.

Around the corner of the building came a woman about my age, her hair gathered up in a messy bun, a halo of escaped curls framing her face.

"Jane Milton?"

"That's me."

She stuck her hand out and grinned. "Jessica Foster. Biology. I'm supposed to be helping you." She whispered. "The onslaught. No fun. Don't know which I hate more. The parents. Or the stuff."

"It is a little . . . overwhelming . . ."

"Thank God they're required to be off the grounds by three p.m."

I glanced at my watch. It was only ten.

"Excuse me?" A thin woman with blond hair interrupted us. She was holding a large flat-screen TV box in one hand and a cell phone, still pressed against her ear, in the other. Her car, a black Escalade with Massachusetts plates, was parked in a way that blocked anyone else from entering or leaving the building. Beside her stood a very bored-looking daughter, immersed in something on her phone. Not long ago, I would have found the mother ordinary, a wealthy suburban helicopter mom, just like a lot of the people who lived in our old neighborhood; but now, as I gazed at her across a chasm of differing circumstances, this well-dressed woman seemed like an alien species. Without meaning to, I nervously smoothed my dowdy skirt.

"Yes?" I said, with what I hoped was a helpful tone.

"Kaitlyn doesn't like her room. She wants the room across the hall."

Jessica looked at me. I could see the levity lighting up her eyes, but she didn't say anything.

"I'm sorry, but the rooms have already been assigned."

"We'd like the room across the hall."

I smiled diplomatically. "I wouldn't worry about it. All the rooms in Abbott North are more or less interchangeable."

The woman frowned. Just a little crease appeared between her perfectly plucked and penciled brows, but I could see she was used to getting her own way.

I glanced at Jessica with a look that I hoped said, "What now?"

"Why don't you tell Kaitlyn to put her things there temporarily, Mrs. Corsyn," Jessica said. "We'll get Dr. Farber-Johnson to make sure everything gets straightened out for Kaitlyn just as soon as she comes around. Now, I'd like you to meet Jane Milton. She's our new English teacher."

Mrs. Corsyn looked as if she was unsure whether she was going to be mollified, but Kaitlyn had already found something more interesting than another room—and I noticed that the something in question was none other than Charlie, who was gallantly offering to carry her myriad boxes and shopping bags for her.

Mrs. Corsyn looked over at her daughter and saw the way that Charlie was hefting a large trunk up on his back. Kaitlyn giggled. Mrs. Corsyn sniffed, then leaned in, as if preparing to impart an important secret.

"Kaitlyn is very gifted," Mrs. Corsyn said. "She gets bored if the work isn't challenging enough for a student of her caliber . . . *English* is her best subject."

Kaitlyn turned full around, and I could see from the arch of her eyebrows that she found her mother ridiculous. The mother was interchangeable with a thousand other suburban wives, but the daughter was another matter. She was an exceptional beauty, with a look in her eyes that made it clear I would have to watch out for her. "Above the ninety-ninth percentile," her mother said.

"I wouldn't doubt that at all," I said.

As the Escalade pulled away, Jessica leaned in and whispered, "You need to be careful with that one. Farber-Johnson will want us to try to be accommodating. The Corsyns are . . ."

"The Corsyns are what?" I said. I could think of several choice adjectives to describe them, but I held my tongue, for the moment.

"You'll learn," she said. "We have a way of doing things around here."

The dining hall of the Grove Academy seemed to have been built all out of proportion to the number of students. I looked around and spotted Jessica Foster, who was wearing jeans and white Keds. Perhaps Grove faculty members were not expected to dress like preppy clones of Dr. Farber-Johnson.

"Hi," she said, waving me over.

"We don't have to sit with the students?"

"What students?" she asked.

I looked around and it was true that the hall, which normally looked half-empty, was almost completely empty. Did Grove girls no longer eat breakfast?

"Where is everybody?"

"Are you kidding? They're not going to drink this warmed-over stuff"—she swirled the dregs in her enamel coffee cup—"when they can get a latte down at the Starbucks in the student center . . ."

I took a sip of my coffee, which tasted like dishwater.

"Since when has there been a Starbucks and a snack bar here?"

"Since the Edelstein Center went up, a few years back. I heard some of the old girls weren't too happy about it. There was a big fight and people took sides—that's when Farber-Johnson came in and railroaded it through. Not everybody likes her, but I wouldn't cross her. So, how did she rope you into being housemother? I hope she's paying you a lot?"

I set my cup down.

"Paying me a lot?"

"Well, yeah . . ." She looked at me quizzically. "Oh no—I mean, you didn't fall for any of that 'I can always count on a Grove girl' crap, did you?"

I stared down at the table.

"Oh no," she said again. "You need to stick up for yourself. That position comes with an additional stipend. I swear. Sometimes I wonder what the hell they put in the water to brainwash the old girls. Not healthy. Definitely not healthy."

"Are you—?"

"A Grove girl?" She laughed. "God no! Worcester High School. I love teaching up here though. I really do. We get some bright ones, among the spoiled brats. But you know, the spoiled brats, they turn up everywhere. And it's pretty, and . . ."

"So, what brought you here?" I asked.

"Oh, I . . . ," she said. "I didn't start out as a teacher. I was a field and stream biologist. My husband wanted to come here. He just couldn't stay away . . . What about you?"

"It's a long story," I said.

"Go ahead," she said. "I'm listening."

"Well, for one thing, my ex is in jail," I said.

She cocked an eyebrow. "Tax fraud," I whispered. "He had a gambling problem."

"Oh, that's not good."

"He gambled away our life right in front of my eyes. I wasn't paying close enough attention. I cosigned some of the loans. So, here I am. This is the only job I could get. I've never taught before, but I just can't afford to screw this up."

"Jane, don't worry," she said. "You can do this." She gave my arm a friendly squeeze. I could tell we were going to be friends.

The only manuals I had read about teaching, up until this point, were. *The Prime of Miss Jean Brodie*, *Jane Eyre*, and *Good-Bye, Mr. Chips*. I thought I could teach senior English at the Grove Academy. But I was counting on receiving some degree of instruction in how *exactly* to go about the task.

My meeting with Dr. Farber-Johnson to discuss my "responsibilities," as she had put it, was scheduled for Monday morning, with classes to begin that afternoon. We met in her office, where she slid a depressingly slim manila folder across the clean surface of her desk.

"Your predecessor, Miss Nelson, decided to pursue a different career," she said.

"Oh?"

"River guide," Dr. Farber-Johnson said. "In Montana."

I opened the folder, and in it I saw a typed-up syllabus with a list of books to be read, and beneath that were some handwritten notes. In short, not much there—it looked depressingly similar to the contents of Charlie's English notebooks shortly before final exam time.

Dr. Farber-Johnson must have caught the quizzical look on my face. "Miss Nelson was a fabulous lacrosse coach," she said. "But perhaps not fully committed to the teaching profession . . . Not all are suited to the role."

She looked at me appraisingly. I swallowed, screwing up my courage.

"Since you have given me the added responsibility of taking over as dorm mother, I'd like to know what the extra compensation will be."

Dr. Farber-Johnson appeared unruffled by my question. "Under normal circumstances, yes, that position does carry an additional stipend, but I'm afraid that in your case, we've budgeted that money for a faculty mentor, from the English department. You will be working with a teacher named Antonia Roper. It's quite unusual for us to hire someone with so little relevant experience. I'm sure you understand."

"Yes, of course," I said, trying to hide my disappointment.

"Just one more thing," Dr. Farber-Johnson said. "Regarding grading. Feel free to use your best judgment. You can choose to grade tough or to grade lightly, as long as you are scrupulously fair. All other things being equal, you will cause yourself less trouble if you choose to award mostly As and the occasional B. Of course it's wholly your prerogative whether you choose to follow that advice. Your mentor is away right now, at a field hockey tournament. For your first class, you should introduce yourself and do a few warm-up activities. I assume you can manage that much without help?" She cocked her eyebrow, and I thought about telling her that I hadn't the slightest idea even where to start, but this seemed to cast me in an unnecessarily incompetent light. I still remembered my own senior year vividly. Certainly, I could handle this simple assignment without advice.

"Of course," I said, mustering more conviction than I felt.

Suddenly, a vivid memory of Miss Pymstead came to mind; she was standing with her back to the class, staring out the window—talking so that her voice echoed off the glass and then came back to us.

"I pity you that you are born into an age when you are and will always be terribly, dreadfully, and completely ignorant," Miss Pymstead said. Up on the blackboard were the first lines of the poem "The Lake Isle of Innisfree," with all scansion noted, in her lovely rounded script.

And I remember knowing that it was true. There was not a girl in that room who could reliably recite a poem unless it was in the form of pop song lyrics. None of us had good penmanship. None of us could ever quite remember what a trochee and a spondee were unless it was right before a test. Miss Pymstead whirled around, and for a moment, the look on her face was one of pure, unadulterated anger. She flat out hated us right then, for our stupidity, for continually mixing up John Keats and William Butler Yeats, for the fact that at least once during every class somebody would raise her hand and ask, "Who cares about diagramming sentences anyway?"

We knew that Miss Pymstead believed that we were almost lost, consigned to a world in which lyrics memorized from album covers took the place of the great works of literature she had devoted her life to.

"Now, class, you may not believe me, but every girl in this class will learn this poem by heart."

Her voice led us in the recitation, and pretty soon, her tone gave over from anger to dramatics—her tremulous voice fluting up above ours, her eyes taking on that otherworldly quality, her hands floating in the air as though there was nothing in the world quite as lovely as to "live alone in the bee-loud glade." We made a study of being lackluster and resentful at first. Lissa slid off her ponytail holder, shook her hair out, and banded it up again. I made curlicues with my pen around the metal spiral of my notebook. Kat didn't look up. But after a while, we all just gave in to the force of Miss Pymstead's passion. There wasn't much else to do.

And she was right. We memorized it; and once learned, we never forgot. Ask me today, and I could recite the words of "The Lake Isle of Innisfree." I learned it by heart.

Now, it was my turn. I would teach Senior Honors English.

"I'm sure I'll be fine," I said.

"Honors English?" Jessica said while we were standing together in line with our lunch trays in Commons. "There is no such thing. Honors designations were dropped at the end of last year," she said.

"Why?" I asked.

"According to Farber-Johnson, it's an honor to be here."

I looked around Commons, deserted as usual. "I suppose."

Jessica looked around us and whispered, "But don't let Susan Callow get started on the subject . . ."

"Susan Callow?"

"Your department chair. She's *rather* strong-minded on most of the Farber-Johnson initiatives . . ."

"So, what are 'the Farber-Johnson initiatives'?" I asked after we were seated at a table near the window.

She laughed. "Well, some people just call them, 'the measures that are destroying our school' . . . but I'm a bit more neutral. I think some of the changes are for the better—but God forbid you should say that in front of the lumpen tweeds . . ."

I giggled. She didn't have to explain whom she meant by "the lumpen tweeds." I'd seen them all over the place.

"I like that, *the lumpen tweeds.*"

She frowned slightly. "That's what *he* calls them . . ."

I followed the direction of her gaze to a middle-aged man whose back was toward us, seated all the way over at the far side of the room.

"My husband," she said.

I cocked an eyebrow.

"We're separated," she said. "Or, rather, as separated as you can be from someone who lives and works in the same boarding school. We eat three meals a day together—just at opposite ends of the room."

"That's awkward."

She shrugged but didn't look happy.

"Faculty member?"

She nodded. "English."

"Oh." I looked at the man's back again, and, for the oddest half second, had the sensation that he looked familiar.

"You'll be meeting him soon enough."

Just then, a girl of about eight peered from around the man's side, caught sight of us, and charged across the dining room, dodging teenagers with trays like an old pro.

"Mommy!"

"Jane, this is my daughter, Molly. Molly, why are you home so early?"

"Half day today. Did you forget?"

I saw from the half-second hesitation that Jessica *had* forgotten. "Oh no, of course not, I . . ."

"Daddy picked me up . . ."

"That's great, honey."

"He's taking me apple picking . . . Bye, Mom."

"Molly! Don't forget your EpiPen . . ." Jessica looked back at me. "She has a peanut allergy. I worry because sometimes she forgets to take it with her when they go places."

I could see the pained look on Jessica's face. My guess was this child sharing was all new for her. I gave her a half smile; I was trying to convey how well I got it, but I'm not sure it registered. Jessica was watching Molly's back disappearing across the room.

I picked up a crust of sandwich from my plate, but the bread was unappetizing. I glanced at my watch. My first class was starting in fifteen minutes.

"Any words of advice to a novice teacher?" I asked.

"Grade easy," Jessica said. "You'll save yourself a lot of trouble . . ."

She jumped up and grabbed her tray. "Gotta run, kiddo. You'll do fine. Just remember, they're just kids. They don't know anything."

In spite of Jessica's encouragement, I was so nervous that I paused outside the classroom door before I screwed up the courage to enter. There were twelve students in all: eight girls and four boys. I only recognized

Kaitlyn Corsyn. All of them had fresh notebooks in front of them, and a small assortment of pens and pencils laid out neatly next to their notebooks. I could feel my heart skittering. I reached down, opened my bag, and pulled out my sheaf of yellowed papers. I turned to the blackboard, and I wrote a quotation from Salinger that I thought was certain to elicit some lively discussion.

When I finished writing, I turned around.

Nobody said anything. The students exchanged glances, and finally by some silent mechanism that I was unable to detect, Kaitlyn Corsyn was elected the spokeswoman for the group.

She raised her hand.

I nodded in her direction.

"Ms. Milton?"

"Yes?"

"We studied *The Catcher in the Rye* in ninth grade," she said.

"Well, good," I said. "Then you must already have formed some opinion of it." I waited, expecting that the students would have something to say.

A lengthy silence was finally supplanted by the scratching sound of ballpoints on virgin notebooks. That lasted about fifteen seconds, and then there was the stillness of expectant eyes upon me again.

I stood shuffling through my papers, prolonging the copying moment as long as possible, until the one girl down at the end of the table, the one with the slowest writing, had finished.

Finally, another girl a few seats over from Kaitlyn raised her hand and said, "Do we have to read the whole book again?"

"Never mind," I said. "We'll move along."

I turned my back to the class then, and made an elaborate business of selecting a colored marker from the tray in front of the whiteboard. For a moment, I closed my eyes, until the deadly silence was filled with the thundering sound of Miss Pymstead's voice, crowding my imagination.

I chose green. I took off the cap of the pen. I wrote:

> *Break, break, break,*
> *On thy cold grey stones, O Sea!*
> *And I would that my tongue could utter*
> *The thoughts that arise in me.*

I turned around to the class and stepped aside so that they could see it. The more assiduous among them had already started to copy even before I moved, their mouths clamped shut.

"Notebooks closed," I said. "Poetry is an aural pleasure."

The students looked at me, and then at each other, but none moved to close their notebooks. At least half continued to copy.

"Close your notebooks, please. We are moving to the oral portion of this exercise."

"An oral pleasure?" one of the good-looking boys said, and the other boys chuckled and exchanged glances.

"Yes indeed," I said. "Poetry is beautiful, and romantic, and sexy—and most of all, oral."

He grinned at me, and I felt the mood around the table relax. I had won them over, at least a little. \

"You'll read with me," I said.

I singsonged, and up-and-downed, and did every pantomime I could think of just to bring that poem alive. I caught a reflection of myself in the glass window, and I could see myself as they must have seen me—hair flying, eyes wide open, voice swelling up with words, nothing but words, but I didn't care.

As I looked around the classroom, I saw a variety of expressions; they ranged somewhere between tolerance and boredom for the most part, all expressions that were familiar to me—I had a fifteen-year-old son after all. But I could see them giving in, just a little, giving me half smiles for effort, softly murmuring the lines of poetry to themselves.

Except for Kaitlyn Corsyn, down at the end of the table where a shaft of light came in the window, illuminating the gold in her hair. She stared at me, a lock of hair folded over her French-manicured hand, notebook closed in front of her, her face a study in jaded loveliness. Her lips didn't move at all.

5

The phone rang fifteen minutes after curfew.

"Jane Milton?"

"Speaking."

"We have a report of students out after curfew in the vicinity of Wooten Boathouse. Can you check it out please?"

Had I been more experienced, I would have realized that I was not on duty. I would have thought to ask the caller's name. But I was exhausted and had fallen asleep as soon as my head hit the pillow, and so it was with a groggy sense of duty that I pulled on my jeans and tennis shoes, picked up my flashlight, and headed off across Siberia.

When I was halfway across the fields, second thoughts began with a vague prickling at the back of my neck. The thin beam of my flashlight cut a narrow trace across the dark expanse. I could see nothing beyond the confines of its light, but I knew, from past experience, that someone whose eyes were accustomed to the dark could easily see me. I froze for a second, thinking I heard titters, but heard only silence. I was possessed with an eerie sensation of double vision. One minute, I was myself, grown-up, walking across the playing fields—and a moment later, I felt like a student, seeing a dorm mother coming, and then scuttling away, lit cigarette cupped in the palm of my hand, the ember so close that I had to choose: open my palm, and I might get caught; close it, and I might get burned.

Though the boathouse was clearly visible from most places on campus, you had to cut through a path that snaked down a wooded hillside to get there. The path was narrow and rutted with roots. First, it passed between two wide-open meadows, then it narrowed as it plunged into the woods. I stepped carefully. Once, a tree root grabbed my ankle and I almost lost my footing, but I righted myself without falling. I listened for the sound of students laughing, but I heard nothing but the lapping of the river, now closer.

Then, all of a sudden, I was in a clearing. The boathouse was right in front of me. The night was dark, and the walls didn't look red but black. The smell of the river, faint up on campus, was strong here, earthy and immediate. Gravel crunched beneath my feet. I glanced up the hill behind me. There were scattered lights, but the campus was mostly dark. Now, the light of my flashlight seemed small. The outline of several tall poplars near the riverbank rose and stood out like dark webs against the sky.

"Hello?"

I realized I was on a fool's errand. If there were students here, they had had plenty of time to flee from the crashing sound of my footsteps through the woods, and the bobbing progress of my flashlight.

"It's after curfew—no students should be out." I heard the familiar words emerge from my mouth and almost laughed a little. I had often heard those words myself, while crouching somewhere half drunk, squeezed into a tight space, holding my breath, with Lissa and Kat crouching at my sides.

"All right," I said. I felt ridiculous. I stood perfectly still, listening, but heard nothing, then I did hear something: laughter, and running footsteps. Students, escaped already, high up on the hill.

Now, I was mad. I bit my lip and frowned. And yet part of me was relieved. It was just a prank, kids picking on the new faculty member, something we might have done. I felt again how tired I was. I took a step up the hill, another step.

A crash sounded, then the tinkle of breaking glass. My flashlight was knocked from one hand, blinking out, and I covered my face with the other. I stayed frozen for a few seconds, my heart pounding in my ears, but nothing else happened. Carefully, I groped for my flashlight among shards of glass. One jagged piece stabbed my finger with a sharp prick and I cried out, jamming the bloody digit into my mouth. I groped around, now more hesitant, and at last my fingers grasped the cylindrical form of the flashlight and switched it back on.

On the ground in front of me was a glass jar, broken against a rock. I pulled my finger out of my mouth. The cut was deep enough to bleed but not serious. On the ground, I noticed a folded-up piece of notebook paper, stained with three fresh drops of my blood. The note read: *We thought you would want to visit the boathouse, Ms. Milton.*

I stared at the words until they were swimming in front of my eyes. Could someone possibly know my secrets? But it couldn't be. It must just be students playing a prank on a new teacher. So, I picked up the broken pieces of glass, found a trash barrel over by the edge of the boathouse wall, and tossed them in, hearing the tinkling sound they made as they hit the tin on the way down.

I started along the perimeter of the boathouse, flashing the beam along the base of the building, where clapboard met late-summer mustard greens and Queen Anne's lace. As I rounded the bend of the building, the side that faced the river, my heart beat faster. I got up close, but all I could see was red paint, dry ground, and weeds, and I felt a sense of relief and closure. Of course the words could not have survived all these years. It was better this way.

Still, I couldn't leave without taking a look. Like an alcoholic who has to take just one more drink, I lay down in the dirt and shone my flashlight on the red-painted wall, just to prove to myself that words are ephemeral. My memories seemed as clear and crisp as a printed page, but weren't they more like the slowly disappearing typeface of an old book printed on acidic paper? Sure enough, as my flashlight cut a streak of light across the boathouse walls, I saw only paint. But then, the beam caught the edge, where the base of the building met the berm, down where a lazy painter couldn't reach with a roller brush even if he got down on his hands and knees. Underneath the line of fresh-enough red paint was a line of faded gray, and on the gray, faded more still, there were words: *A solemn thing it was I said, a woman white . . .*

I couldn't read any more. I didn't have to. I stumbled through the darkness up the twisting path, branches grabbing at my ankles again and scraping my legs. As I exploded out into the meadow above, my lungs were burning, but I kept running, across Siberia, and I didn't slow down until I was almost at the pathway in front of Cottage Row.

As I entered the well-lit cottage walk, I realized I needed to get hold of myself. I patted down my hair and slowed my pace, preparing to enter Abbott at a suitably housemotherly pace. But just as I reached the threshold, I heard a sharp voice call out from the doorway in front of Lane North, "Out after curfew, Milton?" and I recognized the voice of Abigail Von Platte.

Inside, all was quiet, the kind of too quiet that I recognized immediately as possible trouble, and when I reached the third floor, I had the distinct impression that Charlie had entered only a half second before me.

6

My faculty mentor, Antonia Roper, burst into the foyer of Gould Cottage, bringing with her the scent of cut grass. She held a field hockey stick in one hand and a clipboard in the other; she looked not much older than Charlie.

"Jane Milton?" she said.

I stood and stuck out my hand.

She looked from one of her hands to the other, and then awkwardly clasped mine with the one that was holding the field hockey stick.

"Hi, it's great to meet you. I'm Antonia Roper. Welcome to the Grove. You're going to love it here. Hey, guess what? I've got your son, Charlie, in my class."

At the mention of Charlie in relation to school, I felt as if my heart had taken an express elevator from my rib cage to my stomach.

"He's terrific," she said. "A very bright kid."

"Thanks," I said. I was warming up to her.

"I heard your first class was a bit rough."

"You did?" I could feel my face turning red. I thought it had gone okay. Had one of the students complained?

Antonia and I headed across Siberia. I had to half jog to keep up with her loping pace, and followed as she bounded up the steps to the library. Pencott was a tall stone building with ornate cornices and a tall clock tower. I vividly remembered its dilapidated interior, but as I followed Coach Roper inside, I found myself in a humming modern space, well lit, scented with clean carpet and printer ink. Antonia slowed her pace only enough to make her way through the maze of cubicles, desks, and chairs. She led me past a bank of computers to an open table near a large row of windows that looked out over Siberia.

"I can't imagine coming here not even knowing how to teach and being thrown into a classroom," she said. "That must make it really rough on you."

"I love books," I said a bit defensively. "I'm sure that will help."

Antonia looked skeptical. "The thing that helped me was practice teaching. You'll do fine though," she said. "You just need to make sure you have a lesson plan. And always use a rubric, so the kids know what you're grading them on."

Antonia proved a practical and patient mentor, and at the end of an hour I had a week's worth of lesson plans with clear instructions to follow. When she excused herself, I sat for a moment longer, looking around the space. In the old library, the reading room had a high domed ceiling that had been painted to look like the sky. It had not aged well, and by the late seventies, it had a greenish tinge, like a swimming pool filled with algae. Now, an ordinary dropped ceiling with squares of fluorescent lights hid the ceiling vault.

"Well then, you must be our new colleague . . . ?" I was interrupted by the sound of a gravelly voice with a pronounced Main Line Philadelphia accent. I looked up and saw that one of the lumpen tweeds stood next to me, only this one couldn't fairly be called lumpen. She was tall and thin, and her tweeds hung on her as though she were born to wear them.

"I'm Jane Milton," I said. "The new English teacher."

"You've never taught before, I understand . . . ?"

Susan Callow was looking down her patrician nose at me in a way that told me in no uncertain terms that she did not think highly of a middle-aged woman with no experience coming into her department.

"I'm a writer." I said. "Was a writer . . ."

"Ah yes . . . ," she said. "Didn't you write a little book about a cat, or something?"

I started to protest that my book had no cats in it, but there hardly seemed a point.

"I'm the department chair. Antonia Roper is the absolute newest hire. My least experienced teacher." She leaned in. "I don't know that she has completely integrated the departmental philosophy . . ." I looked at her, puzzled.

"But she's my teaching mentor," I said. "Dr. Farber-Johnson—"

She held up one hand, palm out. "Farber-Johnson is a technocrat. She's wonderful at crunching numbers. For the art of teaching—" She let out a theatrical sigh and started to turn away from me. "Sadly, there is no replacement for experience."

I tried to appear suitably contrite.

"We've recently lost one of our most experienced teachers, and I suppose you're supposed to take up the slack . . . ?" Her tone made it clear that she thought I was not likely up to the task.

"I'm certainly going to do my best."

Susan Callow looked skeptical.

"This job is very important to me," I added, wondering if I protested too much. "I'll do my absolute best."

"I understand that you are a Grove girl," she said. "That counts for something at least."

I was unsure if she really meant it as a compliment.

"How does it feel being back? It must be stirring up a lot of old memories."

Memories indeed. My bowels seemed to shrivel as I glanced out the window where the last rays of the sun were fading behind Wooten Boathouse.

7

"Hey, Mom."

"Yeah?"

"Can I have some money?"

"What for?"

"Everybody has been treating me to Starbucks for a week. It's getting embarrassing."

"Get used to it," I said. "You don't have any money. You can treat them to coffee in Commons."

"Nobody goes to Commons," Charlie said. "Kaitlyn says Commons is for scholarship students."

"Guess what?" I said. "You're a scholarship student."

Charlie looked as if this were news that was arriving slowly—as if by parcel post.

"How 'bout just five bucks?" he said.

I wanted to say no—I planned to say no—but his big brown eyes had a way of melting through my motherly resolve. Besides, I was not enamored of the idea of allowing him to be indebted to his female classmates. I scrounged around in my purse and eventually produced five dollars, partly in coins.

"This is the last time," I said. "But you need to go down to the library and see about getting a part-time job. I'm sure it doesn't pay much, but every little bit helps."

"I'll do it, Mom. I want to help."

I could feel my heart melting a little. He didn't deserve what we had put him through, and he was a good kid. I resolved, yet again, to get the hang of this teaching gig—and to not get too distracted by the ghosts of the past.

I had collected my first set of student essays and was preparing to grade them. The assignment was for the students to write an essay about a place on campus that they were fond of. The papers were stacked in a neat pile at my right hand. Charlie was sprawled on his bed in his room, a book open in front of him. Thus far, I'd had no complaints of him from his teachers. Charlie was a bright kid, but with all that had gone on in our life over the past year, his grades had slipped. Now, from what I could tell, Charlie seemed to be thriving as the lone male inhabitant in a girls' dormitory.

I picked up the first essay in the stack and began to read. In the spirit of fairness, I had folded the title pages, which included each student's name, away from me. Most of the papers were serviceable; some were amusing. There were paeans to dorm rooms, to Starbucks, to Commons, to the pool in Kiputh Gymnasium and the new student center. Someone wrote about Siberia at night after curfew. (I gave that one an A for courage.)

I remembered the cardinal rule: grade easy. I gave As and Bs . . . Most deserved it—I guessed. I looked out the window, down over the fields toward the river, and picked up another essay.

As I read the first two sentences, I felt my face flush:

> *To look at an image of the face of Chester Montgomery "Chestmont" Wooten, even in grainy black-and-white, is to know why he might inspire murderous passion. Wooten Boathouse sits on the banks of the Connecticut River like a passionate reminder of the final scream of a dying man.*

My hands were shaking when I finally forced myself to finish reading the essay. I flipped the page over to see the author's name, and when I saw it, I thought my eyes deceived me: Kaitlyn Corsyn.

I stared out the window at Wooten Boathouse and told myself to get it together. Hadn't her mother said she was interested in writing? The story that a Grove headmaster had once been murdered was common knowledge—it was part of the school's lore. Was it any surprise that the story would surface again and again?

I pushed my fingers up through my hair, flipped the pages over, and reread the last lines of the essay:

> *Sometimes, when I am somewhere, perhaps on Siberia, or maybe looking out the window of Lane North, and I catch of glimpse of Wooten Boathouse, I know that someday I too will leave the Grove, and what will remain is skeletons: the husk of the story of a half-forgotten murder, and an unassuming red building, housing boats that are called shells.*

I know that this student could not possibly be privy to the secrets of my past—but somehow, this piece of writing made me feel revealed. With my red pen, I marked a big red A at the top, and slipped the essay back into the pile of papers.

"So, how did you become a writer?" Jessica was asking. We were dawdling over mugs of tea in Commons. It was cold and windy outside, and there was hardly a soul in the place—just a little knot of old tweedy ladies over in the corner. All the students had already left.

"It was just something I always wanted to do," I said.

"That's really interesting. Are you writing another book?"

"Oh, I . . ." I hated this question. Jessica was looking at me with interest. "I don't think so," I said.

She cocked her eyebrow a little; she wanted to know the story.

"I guess when I say it was something I wanted to do, that isn't quite accurate," I said. "It was something I wanted to want to do. It was someone else's dream—only she never got to do it. I tried to do it for her. I just . . ."

I stopped talking and looked around Commons. It was hard not to see ghosts here.

"I spent five years writing that book—I had a writers' group and we all helped each other. We swapped chapters and we all edited them. I wasn't even the best writer in the group. Finally, I finished and I managed to publish it, somehow. I think it only sold five copies. I got kind of wrapped up in it—but it never really amounted to much. I was chasing after a lost dream. It was as if I were going after something that didn't really exist in the first place . . . but I don't think I'm making very much sense."

"Oh, I think you're making sense," Jessica said. "I know what it is to want something, only to have that thing be perpetually unavailable . . ." She stood abruptly, picking up her teacup and spoon. She smiled, with a trace of sadness, and left quickly, leaving me there alone.

A moment later, Abigail Von Platte walked by. She paused when she reached my table, and I thought she was going to say something to me, but she didn't.

Later, in class, my students seemed bored when I read bits of their essays aloud to the group. The boys were slouched back in their seats; the smart girls held their pencils at the ready—looking determined to find something to take notes on. But when I told the class that I was going to read an exceptional essay, I could hear the plummy thickness in my voice, just like the tone that Miss Pymstead could never disguise: praise in and of itself, and the students seemed to take notice.

Down at the end of the table, Curtis Lee, who had already asked me to write a letter of recommendation for Princeton, shifted in her chair, cleared her throat, and rearranged her pencils. Kaitlyn had tucked a lock of her smooth hair behind her ear, and she was sitting very still. I read on, the rich cadences of the writing carrying me along. When I was finished, the room was still, and as I looked around on some of the faces I could see it—the unguarded raw moment in which they recognized that they had been bested. And deep in the pit of my stomach, I was sorry. Not every student has equal ability, but learning that truth is hard.

Kaitlyn accepted my offering as though she were doing the rest of us a favor with her mere presence. She straightened up her books, smiled coyly, tucked another stray lock behind her ear, never catching my eye—as if to say, *You, teacher, are not important.* I felt it like bile rising up in my throat: I hated her. But that was as petty and venal as it was ridiculous. I pushed the feeling away.

"Good job, Kaitlyn," I said, forcing a smile.

"Right," she said, not smiling. She slung her bag over her shoulder and walked out of the classroom. Is this the way we had acted toward Miss Pymstead? I thought perhaps it was.

Later that night, one of the students, Mary Raschlaub, was seated at my kitchen table, wearing a fuzzy blue bathrobe. Her nose was red and running furiously, her narrow eyes were puffy with tears, and there was grease from the popcorn I had popped for her streaked across her chin.

I didn't have the full story—the full story was a convoluted non sequitur—a tangled mess of a dozen slights that when retold simply didn't retain the sting of the originals: "Kaitlyn said, *Why do you drink orange soda? Why do you use a washcloth? Why do you tell people 'Have a nice day'?"*

The popcorn in the bowl in front of her disappeared; the Kleenex box beside her emptied as the wastepaper basket filled up. I wanted to sit down beside her and tell her about girls' rules. I wanted to tell her that her only hope was to shed the fuzzy blue bathrobe, to toughen up, to develop a hard shell. I wanted to tell her that being nice would get her nowhere in the world of Abbott North—nice had never worked, not back then, not now, not ever. Mary Raschlaub should not tell Kaitlyn Corsyn to have a nice day, but there was no way for me to explain that to her.

The door opened, and Charlie walked in. Poor Mary Raschlaub squirmed in almost physical pain and studiously avoided his gaze.

"Hi, Mom," he said as he nodded in a good-natured manner to the girl, whose name he probably didn't know—she wasn't pretty enough to have gotten on his radar.

Mary rubbed her nose with her hand and tried to produce a smile, but she looked as though she wished the floor would swallow her up.

Charlie, tactful, or perhaps simply disinterested, ducked past us into his room.

Mary swiped the last few kernels of popcorn, then stood up, rubbing her oily hands on her bathrobe.

"Well, Mary, thank you for sharing what's going on with you. Please let me know if the problems continue . . . ," I said, aware that I hadn't really helped her at all.

She grabbed a final Kleenex from the box, plucked a stray piece of popcorn from where it had caught on the nap of her robe, and shuffled toward the door. I stood at the doorway and saw her out, feeling so unsure about how to help her. Would I ever get the hang of this job? In the classroom and as dorm mother, I felt as if I were groping my way along in the dark. The knowledge of how badly I needed the money spurred me on, but it was my growing realization that I was responsible for these girls—and that I did not know what they were capable of— that scared me more. After all, I remembered what my friends and I had been capable of, and the thought of it scared me silly.

8

On Saturday evening at the end of the first week of classes, I was invited to Antonia Roper's for dinner. Antonia lived in a second-floor apartment in one of the Victorian houses down on Walker Row. It was one part of campus that was unfamiliar to me—as unappetizing as oatmeal back when I was a student, the faculty housing that always looked out of place, with cars in the driveways, laundry on lines, potted plants on balconies. As a student, I was embarrassed to be that intimate with the smallness of my teachers' lives. Now, the row of houses looked appealing to me—connected to a life that was ordinary. I saw a child's muddy shoes lined up on a second-floor porch and an overturned tricycle, likely abandoned in the heat of play.

Antonia lived in Cross Cottage, a white Queen Anne–style clapboard, third down the line, that had a profusion of potted flowers growing on her balustrade.

I rang the doorbell, and Antonia answered, the scent of simmering garlic greeting me as the door swung open. Her flat was cozy, filled with soft, overstuffed furniture. While it lacked the spectacular vistas of my abode in Abbott, it more than made up for it in warmth and charm.

I saw Jessica seated on the sofa surrounded by some other women. I thought of the home I'd left behind in New Jersey, for a moment thought of all I had lost. But I didn't have time to dwell on it, because Jessica was patting a spot on the sofa beside her. Cheese and crackers beckoned on the coffee table, and Antonia was uncorking a bottle of wine.

The doorbell rang several more times and soon the room was filled with people. But the hubbub of adult voices in the room was pleasant, and Antonia poured me another glass of wine. I headed to the kitchen, where I started chopping tomatoes for the sauce she was preparing.

Antonia kept my wineglass filled, so by the time a dark-haired man separated himself from the crowd and came to the kitchen to help with the salad dressing, I was feeling a little buzz.

He held out his hand to me, but one of mine held a knife, and the other was covered with tomato glop.

"Jane Milton," he said, addressing me as if I knew him. I peered at him. He had the same vaguely familiar air of men I used to see around my neighborhood in New Jersey—half-forgotten dads from Charlie's old soccer teams and grade school classes.

I hastily wiped my hand on a dish towel and reached toward him, trying to hide that I didn't know who he was.

"Josh Miller," he said. "Hardley? I guess you weren't expecting to see me."

In a split second, the familiar face emerged from the unfamiliar, like a retriever shedding a dull winter coat.

"Josh Miller? You're here?"

"We're colleagues. I teach tenth- and eleventh-grade English." He paused for a sip of wine. "And Romantic Poetry."

Poetry. My sight clouded over and my heart thudded when he said it, but his own face betrayed no particular emotion. He probably didn't even remember after all these years.

"I'm afraid we did a half-assed job of welcoming you here." He picked up a bottle and poured some wine into a clean glass, topping off my own. "How's it going anyway? Pretty overwhelming to be thrown into dorm duty as a brand-new teacher . . . Don't know what Farber-Johnson was thinking . . ."

"How long have you been teaching here?" I asked.

"Fourteen years."

"I'm kind of surprised," I said. "I didn't think there'd be so many of us here . . ."

"Are you kidding?" he said.

"What makes you say that?"

"Just take a look out that window . . ."

I followed his gaze out Antonia's second-story window. Her view was modest. Just the upward sweep of lawn, edged by Grove Woods, where there was just the barest brushstroke of early fall color if you knew where to look.

"It is beautiful here," I said. "Even more than I remembered."

I felt the jostle of a child between us and looked down to see Jessica's daughter, Molly, reaching her arms up toward Josh.

"You still here, darlin'? Isn't it a little past your bedtime?"

"Mommy told me to come give you a kiss," she said.

I turned and saw Jessica.

"So, you two have met?" she said.

Josh gave Jessica a complicated look, too intimate for me to read. "Jane Milton of the Grove Academy for Girls? Yeah, I'd say we've met." He picked up his wineglass and took a sip. I thought he was going to say more, but a young guy clapped him on the shoulders, and Josh turned to say hello.

I caught a glimpse of Jessica's unguarded face, the corners of her mouth drawn down, with tight creases along the sides. "Guess you'll have some catching up to do," she said.

I shrugged, and then tousled Molly's hair. "Good night, Molly," I said. But after they had gone, my eyes sought out Josh's back, still broad and strong in a white T-shirt, now surrounded by a bunch of other people.

I was standing by the port wine cheese ball when Susan Callow cornered me. She was holding a glass of amber-colored liquid, and the scent of sherry on her breath was so strong that I was reminded, not pleasantly, of my old Grove headmistress, Miss Wetherby. But their resemblance ended there, as Miss Wetherby had been short and plump whereas Susan Callow was tall and slim.

"So, has Farber-Johnson turned her pressure hoses on you yet?" she asked me.

"I have no idea what you're talking about."

"She's always after the new ones to do her favors," she said. "Especially the ones like you."

"What do you mean, the ones like me?"

"The ones who seem weak."

She took a slow sip of her sherry and eyed me reflectively. I stared at her, hoping that a suitable retort would come to me, but none did, so I reached for a wheat cracker and shaved off a morsel from the cheese ball.

"I'll be sure to watch out for it," I finally answered, aware that my wishy-washy answer probably confirmed her worst suspicions.

She waved her empty glass in front of me. "Are you a sherry drinker? Antonia has got some out on the sideboard . . ."

"God no," I said. "I have a particular aversion to the stuff."

Fortunately, someone called her name from across the room and she turned away. Susan Callow was going to take some getting used to.

On Monday, I noticed that Kaitlyn was absent, and the class felt oddly sparkless without her. The smart girls didn't sit up as straight. The pretty girls absentmindedly wound their hair up into messy buns. The boys, normally stimulated by her proximity, seemed listless and kept glancing out the window, as though hoping to catch sight of her. The material, an excerpt from James Joyce's "The Dead," was laborious, even for me. It spoke to none of us, the words lying corpselike on the page, ready for the books to be flipped shut and consigned to their morgues of obscurity once again.

I read my notes and wrote on the board while the students copied. Today, I was waiting for class to be over. In my mailbox, I'd received a summons from Dr. Farber-Johnson. I still hadn't gotten over my fear that this position was going to turn out to be just like most other things in my life—something given then taken away, like a car repossessed. I had lost so much already: husband, house, life savings. This job was the last bulwark. But in addition to my fear of losing the job, an equally frightening prospect lurked beneath the surface. I could tell how people saw me now—middle-aged, motherly, somewhat hapless. But I knew the heart of the girl I had once been still beat inside me.

The words in Kaitlyn Corsyn's essay echoed back to me, eliciting a shiver: *I know that someday I too will leave the Grove, and what will remain is skeletons: the husk of the story of a half-forgotten murder, and an unassuming red building, housing boats that are called shells.*

I asked myself the same question that was thrumming behind my eyeballs like a dull headache. The question was: *How could she know?*

By the time I reached Gould Cottage, I had tucked in my shirt and smoothed my khakis. I ran my palms along my hair to smooth it and glanced at myself in the plate-glass windows. To teach in a school where you once were a girl is to come up abruptly and often against reminders of your own mortality. Within each reflection lurks the girl you once were, clouded, marred even, by the woman you have become. I wondered if Miss Pymstead had ever been disappointed. If the look in her eyes that we attributed to heartbreak was caused by nothing more than the glimpses of herself that she caught when passing windows.

One more glance and I patted my hair—since when had it taken on this absurd habit of flipping outward over my left ear—then opened the door to Gould Cottage. What could Dr. Farber-Johnson want next?

She was standing by the window, looking out over Siberia, when I arrived. Her office door was ajar. I knocked, not quite loud enough, hesitated, and knocked once more. Looking over her shoulder, she beckoned for me to enter and turned back to the window. I looked past her and saw that the girls' field hockey team was scrimmaging: red pinnies versus yellow, the colors bright as autumn leaves against the green grass. Antonia Roper was yelling. I couldn't hear her voice, but her face was red and her hair was whipping across her cheeks. She held her clipboard like a rapier. Dr. Farber-Johnson turned to me. "Our team is expected to win the New Englands this year."

"That's wonderful," I said.

She gestured toward the chair in front of her desk. For the first time since meeting her, I had been invited to sit down.

Before she began to speak, she took her time, arranging herself into the chair behind her desk, opening and closing a drawer, squaring up a folder. I waited in silence.

"It is fortunate for the Grove that there are things that can be counted on," Dr. Farber-Johnson said. "Field hockey has been very reliable for us."

I wasn't sure what she was driving at, but I was relatively sure that this was going to be a yin and yang kind of conversation, so if Antonia Roper and field hockey were the yin, I wanted to know what the yang was going to be.

"You have Kaitlyn Corsyn in your senior English class?" she asked.

This was such an abrupt change of subject that I was momentarily surprised. Dr. Farber-Johnson's face revealed nothing.

I nodded. "I do."

"A very gifted student . . . ," Dr. Farber-Johnson said as her eyes were drawn out the window toward the field hockey players, but then she turned back toward me. "Wouldn't you say?"

Was this the yang? It was hard to tell. I sensed that a trap was being set here, but I wasn't sure the nature of it.

"Yes," I said. "I would say so."

Dr. Farber-Johnson smiled. It was as understated as a pinstripe in a bespoke suit. "Her mother believes that Kaitlyn has a gift for creative writing. In your professional opinion, do you see such a gift?"

This was the first time Dr. Farber-Johnson had suggested that she believed any of my opinions might be considered "professional."

I straightened up in my chair a little. I thought back over the hours I had spent in my writers' "crit group," during which we had drunk wine and pored over each other's manuscripts. I had never been much of a writer, but I had always been the best reader in the group, the coveted editor, the one who could read things and tell people just where to move a comma or finesse a word. I had recognized right off the bat the one girl in our group who had real talent—the one who had gone on to write a book that hit the *New York Times* bestseller lists.

"Kaitlyn Corsyn is gifted," I said. "Her writing shows sparks of brilliance. She's young, of course . . ." What I had seen was quite uneven. There were passages that were lovely, interspersed with bits that were surprisingly pedestrian. Still, her writing was far beyond that of the average high school senior. Even far beyond that of most college students, I would wager.

"Interesting," Dr. Farber-Johnson said, "as her last teacher had a somewhat different view of her abilities . . ."

"Is that so?"

"Quite so."

I felt my stomach give a familiar flip-flop. Was this another situation in which I had overlooked the one essential thing that everyone except me had realized?

But wait a minute.

Didn't Dr. Farber-Johnson tell me that my predecessor was a lacrosse coach? Didn't she tell me that my predecessor had left to become a river guide? In Montana? In short, wasn't it possible that my predecessor was the one who was mistaken? Was it not only possible but also, in fact, *probable*?

I sat up straighter in my chair. "Dr. Farber-Johnson," I said more confidently, "I assure you that Kaitlyn Corsyn's work is indeed quite superior." For a second, I had a fleeting vision of Miss Corsyn herself, flipping that long, straight blond hair around in slow motion, the way popular mean girls in the movies always do, but I pushed it out of my mind.

Dr. Farber-Johnson's smile had widened. "She's—" But then she interrupted herself. "Are you a tea drinker? Can I offer you a cup of tea?"

"Tea would be lovely," I said.

Dr. Farber-Johnson poured the fragrant beverage into old-fashioned cups whose matching saucers were stenciled with the Grove school pattern; they were just like the ones that Miss Wetherby had used when serving tea in Underhill House.

Once settled over tea and cookies, I started to find out the true subject of our conversation.

"If only college admissions were as certain a thing at the Grove Academy as our standings in the New Englands in field hockey . . ." Dr. Farber-Johnson took a sip of her tea, crossed her feet at the ankles, and leaned slightly forward.

"There was a time," she said, "when the Grove was a solid feeder school to the Seven Sisters. Grove girls were all but guaranteed spots in the good women's colleges: Vassar, Smith, Mount Holyoke . . ." I nodded, blushed slightly, wondered to what extent Dr. Farber-Johnson might possibly be onto me.

"Then, for a while, when the men's schools opened up to girls— Harvard, Yale—they were happy to take Grove girls . . ." A line, just a slight pucker of a frown, marred the smooth surface of her face. "But those days are long gone. Our girls are competing on a wide-open playing field." My eyes darted out to the field, but the sun was setting, and the field hockey girls were clustered along the sideline, drinking water. "Good public schools, geographical diversity"—she leaned in, lowered her voice half a notch—"affirmative action . . ." She sat up again. "We do everything we can, but there aren't any guarantees. Not for our girls. Not for any girls. It's a brave new world."

She refilled my cup, offered me another cookie. I knew she was leading to something, but I still wasn't sure what it was.

"When we see a girl with Ivy League potential, we need to make sure we do everything we can on our end to help."

I was starting to understand the drift of the conversation. Kaitlyn Corsyn probably needed a letter of recommendation. Apparently, a former teacher, perhaps less versed in literary writing, had failed to notice her gifts. Dr. Farber-Johnson wanted to make sure I would be able to write her a good recommendation. This was going to be easy.

"You needn't worry. I can write her a good letter of recommendation without any hesitation."

Dr. Farber-Johnson laughed. "Ah, if only it were so easy."

I was surprised. "She's an A student, if that's what you're implying."

Now, *she* looked surprised. "I assumed that that went without saying. No." She stood up, walked over to the window.

"The Grove Academy is rich in history, but our endowment, like those of many girls' schools, is not endlessly deep. Women who went on to teach in colleges and found settlement houses and charitable institutions did not produce the same kinds of deep pockets that have lined the coffers of boys' prep-schools like Exeter and Andover—but you know all this . . ."

I tried to assume an expression that made it look as though I was well aware of it all.

I waited for Dr. Farber-Johnson, who was still gazing out the window, to continue. "The Corsyn family has been very supportive of the mission of the Grove."

It was beginning to become clearer.

"Look, Jane, I'm going to level with you." She turned away from the window and looked steadily at me. Her eyes were a cool gray, like a rainy New England day. "The Corsyns have made it clear that they are prepared to make a major gift to the school, but only if Kaitlyn is admitted to her first-choice college."

"Yale," I said.

She nodded.

"I assume she's abundantly qualified."

"She's well qualified. Excellent test scores and grades—she's a decent lacrosse player though not outstanding. If this were fifteen years ago, I'd say she was a sure thing, but in this day and age, I just don't know. She needs that something special to make her stand out."

"The writing," I said.

"Something objective to prove that her writing is truly something special," Dr. Farber-Johnson said.

"Like a letter of recommendation from a published author?" I said.

Dr. Farber-Johnson laughed again. "Don't be naive," she said. "These kids get letters of recommendation from senators, former presidents, you name it. Maybe a Nobel Prize winner who would make specific comments about her work would help, but probably not—letters of recommendation just don't count for much."

"What kind of thing were you thinking about?" I said.

"If she could publish a book this year—while she's still in high school . . ." Dr. Farber-Johnson smiled, her winning smile, the smile that she no doubt used to talk the parents into paying the fifty-plus-thousand-dollar tuition and making charitable contributions on top of that.

"Dr. Farber-Johnson," I said, "that seems like a long shot—even if she had the time to write a whole book, it's almost impossible to get a book published."

Dr. Farber-Johnson's face barely registered my outburst.

"Think about it. We desperately need a new boathouse. Wooten Boathouse needs to come down. Several of the shells were damaged over the winter. The Corsyns are willing to foot the entire bill for the construction of a new boathouse . . . as long as . . . we meet their conditions. I think of it as teamwork for the honor of the Grove. Not unlike what Antonia does for the field hockey team."

Dr. Farber-Johnson was showing me to the door, and I realized that she hadn't given me an opportunity to respond.

"I'm pleased with the work you are doing here, so far," she said. "But this—this would be a way for you to get on board at a whole new level . . . A level that would look a lot more like a permanent commitment."

By the time I left her office, it was getting dark. As always at the Grove, even in early fall, when the sun set, it got cold quickly. As I hurried up the hill toward Commons, I thought it over. On the one hand, I wanted nothing more than to keep my job, but on the other, what she was asking me to do sounded impossible.

Clearly, Dr. Farber-Johnson didn't know anything about the world of book publishing. I had spent five years writing just to see *A Chocolate Candy Sleuth* go in and out of print faster than you could blink an eye. A part of me wondered if I had contributed to our family's financial problems by going on the wild-goose chase of publishing a book instead of taking a normal job. I couldn't imagine that Kaitlyn Corsyn could find the time to write a book. Even if she did, and by some chance it was brilliant, I still didn't see who would publish her book. If my job security depended on such a crazy scheme, I really had something to worry about.

When I entered my rooms after dinner, I found Charlie hard at work at the kitchen table: he had an assortment of jars of various sizes filled with murky water arranged in groups, and he seemed to be studying them in some way. He barely looked up as I came in. He was recording notes and drawing sketches in a black marble composition book. I was afraid to seem too interested, for fear that my enthusiasm would immediately cut short his concentration, but I knew that he was doing his work for Jessica's class: field and stream biology. I had never seen him so motivated, and she had pulled me aside at lunch today to tell me that she was going to nominate him for an interschool overnight at an ecostation upriver. I edged around Charlie, muttering hello, and dragged my satchel of corrections into my bedroom, but one final glance at him told me the truth: this was a good place for him. The last couple of years had been hard on both of us. Here, he seemed more engaged in his studies, and at least that kept his mind occupied.

I carried my bag into my room, all the while thinking Dr. Farber-Johnson couldn't really have been serious, could she?

Settling down on my bed, I sorted through the piles of uncorrected essays until I found the one with Kaitlyn Corsyn's name on it. As soon as I read the first sentence, there was something so eerily familiar about it that the hair stood up on the back of my neck, and before I could keep reading, I closed my eyes, unable to continue, but then forced myself to read on:

> *Among three girls who are friends, there is always the one who wants everything, the one who has everything, and a third one, who is caught in the void in between.*

None of the other students could write like Kaitlyn. But I couldn't decide whether she really had a gift, or it was simply that I kept getting the feeling that she was retelling my own story.

Later that night, I was so convinced that Kaitlyn Corsyn must have copied her essay from somewhere that I approached Charlie.

"Hey, do you think I could borrow your laptop for a sec?" My hard drive died a few months ago. I didn't have enough money to replace it and had to use the computers in the library. "Isn't there some way to check a work to see if it might be plagiarized?"

He smiled, swung his legs around to the floor, and sat up. "Sure. Got a cheater in your class?"

"No . . . ," I said, trying to cover my tracks. "Not at all, it's just departmental policy," I fibbed. "We have to run each essay through some plagiarism sites just to be sure . . ." Why not let him think so? Keep him on his toes. Like when I told him that there would be a purple ring if he peed in the pool. I noticed that he always got out and went to the bathroom . . . not like some of the other kids.

"Just hand the stuff over—I'll show you . . . ," he said.

"I think I better do it myself," I said.

Charlie shrugged good-naturedly. "Whatever."

"Oh by the way, our first game is tomorrow," Charlie said.

I looked at him and noticed how happy he looked. His cheeks were pink and his eyes were shining. I don't think he would have made the school soccer team at home.

"That's terrific, honey," I said. "I can't wait. I'll be there with bells on."

I took the computer from him, but there was something nagging at me, an odd feeling that it wasn't going to be so easy. Every time I read one of Kaitlyn Corsyn's essays, I was hit by an eerie sense of déjà vu.

The essays didn't read like the work of a professional writer—more like the work of an excellent student—but why did they seem so familiar?

I tried to make the computer find the strings of words that Kaitlyn was using in her essay, but I came up with nothing. Finally, I shut down the computer, its blue light concentrating down to a pinpoint, and then nothing. I told myself that it was just being here at the Grove that made the writing sound so familiar, but I didn't sleep well that night. I awoke twice, looking out the window where the moon illuminated Wooten Boathouse. For the first time since leaving New Jersey behind, I slept the sleep of the damned.

9

The mood in the dorm started off calm, but now, as midterms approached, the atmosphere had been troubled by a series of small thefts, not of valuables but of items with sentimental value. The dorm inhabitants were edgy. I had weepy girls who were missing a scrap of security blanket, a threadbare teddy bear, or a favorite photograph.

One night, I heard frequent door slamming and lots of whispering in the hall—the sure sign of a brewing scandal, and I wondered what had been stolen this time. Usually, the bad news didn't get to me until there had been a plenary session of secret justice. It had to be bad though, because sooner than I expected, there was a knock on my door, and Soon Ji Shin, a quiet senior, stood before me, her face pale; a full phalanx of girls was grouped behind her. When I gestured for her to come inside, she scurried past me, not meeting my eye. I shut the door before any of those in the mob could follow.

I glanced up at Charlie's door, but he had discreetly swung it shut just as Soon Ji entered—I don't know whether he was naturally tactful or simply uninterested, but since he normally had headphones on, I didn't think he was privy to many of the girls' secrets.

I gestured toward one of the kitchen chairs. Soon Ji sat, but she perched at the edge of the chair, as though ready to spring.

"Would you like some popcorn, Soon Ji? Lemonade?" She shook her head, keeping her eyes firmly fixed to the floor.

I sat down across from her.

"Can you tell me what's the matter?" I asked.

She looked stricken but didn't answer.

I sighed a little. I knew that if I opened the door, there were at least fifteen busybody girls grouped outside in the hall who would be happy to tell me in great detail what had happened, but getting the details from Soon Ji would require patience.

"Is it . . . a problem of . . ." I didn't want to ask leading questions.

"My notebook." Soon Ji said in a voice barely above a whisper.

"Your notebook?"

Soon Ji didn't start to cry, but her eyes were enormous now—they took up half of her face, and they were so wet that it looked as if tears might spill over at any second.

"It's missing."

"Which notebook?" I said.

"My poetry notebook," she said.

"You misplaced it?"

"No, it's missing. It was in my room, and now I can't find it, and it has all my notes."

"And you think someone borrowed it?" I said. I hated that euphemism, "borrowed," but I had found it was better to tread lightly on the subject of theft—things seemed to float around the dormitory all too often, and most of the missing items did resurface after a while.

"I need it," Soon Ji said simply. "It has all my notes in it."

I knew that Soon Ji was reputed to be an excellent student, but I didn't think anyone would have stolen her notebook, and that didn't fit the pattern of petty thefts anyway. I was relieved that this seemed to be a fairly insignificant problem.

I stood up, moved around to Soon Ji's side of the table, and put my arm around her.

"What teacher do you have?" I asked.

"Mr. Miller."

I felt my stomach flop unexpectedly at the sound of his name. "Mr. Miller? I'll talk to him for you. I'll let him know that your notebook is missing. I'm sure you can get the notes from someone else, but I expect your notebook will turn up. Maybe you left it in the classroom."

"It was in my room," she said simply.

"It's almost lights-out. Don't worry. We'll keep on this in the morning."

Soon Ji looked unconvinced—as if she felt about me exactly the way I used to feel about Mrs. Dockerty—that I had no clue what was *really* going on. Except that Soon Ji was far too polite to demonstrate any of that in an outward manner, and so she stood up, and nodded, and said, "Good night, Ms. Milton."

After she left, I rubbed my eyes, yawned, and pushed Charlie's door open to say good night. He was lying on his bed, his face bathed in the glow of his computer screen.

"Charlie?"

"Yeah, Ma?"

"Do you think anyone in this dorm would steal a notebook?"

"I dunno. Depends on whose notebook."

"What about Soon Ji?"

"Soon Ji, who is probably going to be valedictorian? Maybe. To sabotage her. These girls are cutthroat. Trying to get into college is like an arms race around here."

I thought over what Charlie was saying as I brushed my teeth. Was someone out there so competitive that they would steal Soon Ji's notebook just to make things harder for her? Soon Ji had probably just misplaced it and it would turn up.

I climbed into bed and pulled the covers up to my chin, relieved that another long day was over, but no sooner had I started to drift off than there was a knock on the door. No doubt one of the girls had come to report another petty crime. If ever I was not in the mood to play the fair and impartial minister of justice, it was now. I shuffled toward the door, preparing to tell whichever supplicant stood there that she should look for the lost item more carefully—and that I would deal with it in the morning.

I swung the door open, a frown already set on my face.

To my surprise, there stood Kaitlyn Corsyn. With her hair clipped up, her feet in flip-flops, and her face scrubbed free of makeup, she looked younger. She held a stack of printed pages—maybe twenty or so.

"Dr. Farber-Johnson asked me to give this to you," she said. "It's something I wrote. She wants you to read it." She held the stack of papers out to me. "I'll bring you the rest later."

Her chin was tilted up; her expression was a little smug, or maybe just bored. I waited for that moment of understanding to pass, the artist's look, in which she would say, "I'm baring my soul to you here," and I would say, "Don't worry about it. I'll be kind . . ." That moment always came. It was a matter of trust. But Kaitlyn seemed entirely unconcerned. She might as well have been handing me a pair of shoes.

"Don't be nervous about it," I said.

She reached behind her, undid her hair clip, flipped her hair down, then bunched it up again. "Why would I be nervous?"

I remembered my conversation with Dr. Farber-Johnson. Kaitlyn Corsyn and her book might be my best hope to get a permanent position.

"Terrific," I said in a voice that was as cheerful as it was false. I tucked the papers up against my chest and bid her good night.

Once again, I climbed into my bed, but this time, I started to read. My eyes skimmed the page with disbelief.

The First Jump

It was my idea that we do the jump first. I knew all about the tree. My mother used to talk about it—she said that when you first let go, it felt like how death must feel. She told me that during the four years everyone had to do it once, but that most of the girls were scared and didn't do it until the end of junior year. It was unspoken that you couldn't start senior year unless you had already done the jump. When we first arrived on campus, that one poplar loomed up so large in my mind's eye that it seemed to block out all the sunshine. I couldn't live for three years with the terror of imagining it. I thought it would be better to do it first.

We climbed out a first-floor window of Lane and left it propped open with a big umbrella. We didn't tell anyone where we were going. I still remember how it felt to cross Siberia for the first time at night, under the stars. When we got down by the boathouse, the tree looked as big as the vine in "Jack in the Beanstalk." Luckily, Lilly went first. She climbed up, grabbed the rope, pushed off the tree, and almost before we could take a breath, she had dropped into the water and swum back to shore.

When it was my turn, I climbed up those wooden rungs, telling myself loud and clear that I better just do this and that once I did, I'd never have to do it again. I still remember the way it felt. One minute, my bottom was on the solid branch; the next minute, I was falling. The rope snapped with a hard jerk and the rope started swinging. Here's the thing. You had to let go the first time you went over the water, or you'd swing back and hit the tree trunk. It all happened so fast; the fall, the swift jerk, the water beneath, and then going against every single instinct and letting go.

Of course, June didn't want to do it. She sat on the tree branch for the longest time, and I thought for sure she was going to turn around and climb back down—betray us.

Then, without even warning us, she pushed off, swung, and fell in the river.

When she got out, I thought she was crying, but she said it was just water dripping off her hair.

With a rush, it all came back to me—the feeling of weightlessness before the rope snapped up the slack—and my heart started pounding as if it were all happening right now. I had seen the poplar trees along the banks of the river, but I could no longer tell which tree we used to jump from—none had hammered-in rungs, and none had a rope. How Kaitlyn had come across this story I had no idea.

10

When I awoke, it was past dawn, and the typescript piled up like snow-drifts around me. My neck was cricked, my shoes were still on, and my eyes were heavy, stupid with the effects of a poor night's sleep. The light in my room was burning, my door partway open. I slammed it shut, as though Charlie had seen me get drunk and pass out. But I was hung over only from words, their weight pressing down upon me as if I were a person who had stumbled in a snowstorm and was slowly suffocating under a frozen drift.

In the morning light, the pages looked so prosaic. I picked up one and scrutinized it. It was ordinary printer paper, white with black ink. The manuscript was a little like Kaitlyn herself, all smooth edges and glossy presentation. These days, student essays looked sleek and pretty—they no longer bore the traces of the anguish that had gone into their creation.

I thought about what paper used to look like back then: erasable bond, its slick, rippled surface never entirely free from smear marks. My own old typewriter, the one I had given to Kat when I had graduated, had a sticky *y* and a stubborn *t*—the *y* never printed its tail, and the *t* missed about every third or fourth cross.

I tidied up the pile of papers next to me on the bed. These papers were bland and anonymous. They were words without identity.

I still hadn't quite gotten used to the new Pencott, but at least I had staked out my territory in one of the carrels near the big new windows that looked out over Siberia, and down toward the boathouse and river. I knew which students were regulars—Soon Ji, Mary Raschlaub, and I always saw Kaitlyn holed up in one of the soundproof cubicles, typing away furiously. Usually, the library was reasonably quiet, but today, I was distracted by voices and looked up to see Susan Callow talking to a young woman who looked sort of familiar. The younger woman caught my eye and smiled.

"Oh, sorry. I think we're disturbing you," she said.

"That's okay," I said. "I just . . . you remind me of someone. Have we met?"

"Rebecca Doerr MacAteer."

That was it. She was the spitting image of Emma.

"Emma Doerr's sister?"

Rebecca nodded.

"She was in my class."

"Rebecca is a librarian at the University of Vermont," Susan said. "She has graciously donated her time to helping us archive some of the cataloged materials from the old library. I'm afraid it was a bit of a mess . . ."

"We found some fascinating things here . . . documents that had been saved over the years but never organized. It's a wonderful historical resource . . . ," Rebecca said.

"Sounds interesting," I said. "I love that kind of thing."

"I'm looking for a student helper. If you know someone who needs a campus job, I've got a small stipend."

"You know, I do know someone who needs a job," I said, thinking of Charlie.

"That would be awesome," she said. "I can use all the help I can get."

"I'm probably the only one," I said, turning back to Susan, "but I really miss the old library. Sentimental, I guess."

"My advice to you," Susan said, "is that if you want to teach here, you must let go of anything you are interested in for sentimental reasons. That's the only way for an old Grove girl to survive here in the long run."

Gazing over Susan Callow's shoulder, I saw Josh Miller pushing his way through the library doors, his soccer bag slung over his shoulder. I felt my breath catch.

Susan's warning already forgotten, I stepped forward to say hello, except that at that moment, from one of the book aisles, Jessica emerged with Molly in tow—and from the look on their faces, I knew it was better not to bother them.

❧

That night, about a half an hour after dinner, Mary Raschlaub knocked on my door. She had a laundry basket balanced on her hip.

"Ms. Milton, the candy machine just keeps taking my quarters and spitting them out."

From the blue and red smear on the palm of her left hand, I think she had already gotten the candy machine to disgorge M&M's once, but she was at my door with a woebegone look on her face and a fistful of change in her right hand.

"Well, did you try some different coins?" I asked. I was tired from my night spent crumpled up among the drifts of Kaitlyn's eerily familiar

ACADEMY GIRLS

pages, and I did not want to walk down to the basement to fix a candy machine.

"I tried," she said. "It spits out all the coins."

"Are you sure it's urgent?"

"I have a writing assignment," Mary said. "Candy helps me concentrate."

I sighed. I still wasn't sure how far I could step in with in loco parentis. I wanted to say, "Forget candy. I saw you taking double helpings of the German chocolate cake at dinner." But I held my tongue. "Well, I'll be down in a minute to see what I can do," I said. "I may not be able to fix it."

"Our old housemother used to call the company."

I knew that one way or another, Mary Raschlaub was not going to let me rest until I forced the machine to spit out candy—even if I had to break the glass and shovel it out myself.

"Oh really?" I said, trying not to let her see that she had succeeded in irritating me.

Kaitlyn Corsyn chose just that moment to walk by, flanked by two of her ladies-in-waiting, each a couple of inches shorter than she, not quite as pretty, and brunette.

"Yeah, Mary, she used to the call the company and rail on them for addicting you to sugar," she laughed, and the girls who were with her tittered.

"*Kaitlyn?*" I said, trying to look stern.

Mary swung around in a huff and grabbed her laundry basket by the wrong end, spilling some of her laundry onto the floor as she did so: a flannel pajama top, a pair of granny-style cotton undies, a beige bra that was none too clean all slid onto the floor. A blue spiral notebook plopped on top of the clothes.

Kaitlyn had stopped with exaggerated slowness to observe the spectacle of red-faced Mary gathering up her clothing, but when she saw the notebook on the ground, she said, "Now, what's this?"

73

We all looked at the notebook lying faceup on the floor. Across the front, in big, black block letters it said:

POETRY NOTEBOOK.

SOON JI SHIN.

Jessica and Josh were sitting together at lunch in Commons. I would have left them alone, but they gestured me over, and from the relieved smile Jessica shot me, I could tell I had interrupted a tense discussion. I set my tray down on the table and attempted to change the subject.

"We caught the Abbott thief," I said.

"Really?" Jessica looked up with interest.

"Caught red-handed, as it were—with Soon Ji's poetry notebook. She's down in Farber-Johnson's office right now." I winced a little in spite of myself. The poor girl would be no match for the headmistress.

"Who was it?" Josh asked.

"Mary Raschlaub," I said. "Do you know her?"

Jessica appeared startled. "Mary Raschlaub? Are you kidding?"

"Well, yeah . . . I'm not really that surprised. Are you?"

"Are you sure it's her?" Josh asked.

"The notebook fell out of her laundry basket." I picked up a lettuce leaf and laid it on top of my hamburger, and then covered it with the top of a bun. "I worry about her . . . She always thinks the other girls are picking on her, but it's never anything concrete."

"And are they?" Josh asked.

"I don't know," I said. "Probably. You know how girls are . . . but it's not anything overt that I can really pin down. It's hard to know how to handle it."

Jessica nodded. Josh looked less sure. "I wouldn't be so quick to assume you've caught the thief. It's been my experience that these situations can be tricky—and it never turns out to be the person you think at first, especially if that person seems like an obvious choice."

"Well, there is no doubt she did it," I said. "We caught her red-handed."

"I had Mary Raschlaub in my class last year," Jessica said.

I nodded.

"She's quiet, but she's very bright. To be honest, I'd be very surprised if it was her."

I shrugged. I remembered how she looked when the notebook fell out of her laundry basket—her shoulders were all hunched up around her face, her cheeks were bright red, and she seemed as if she wanted to drop right through the floor. My heart went out to her, but I didn't have any doubt that she was guilty as charged.

"Well, let's hope for your sake that it's her," Josh said. "Theft in the dorm always puts everyone on edge."

But I realized that Josh was right, and that somehow I still had my doubts.

Just then, Abigail Von Platte approached from the corner of my field of vision and addressed me.

"I have to leave campus for an appointment this afternoon. Do you think you could cover dorm duty for me until about five p.m.?"

Dorm duty wasn't too onerous—you just had to stay near the phone in case an issue came up. Still, I had been looking forward to having the afternoon off.

"Well . . . ," I said. "I *was* looking forward to my free time, but if you *really* need me . . ."

I was hoping she would take the hint. But instead, she just interrupted me with a raspy "Good," and quickly walked away.

"You should go easy on her," Jessica said. "Even if you don't like her, she's a wily one. She can do you a lot of damage."

"What do you mean?" I asked, blushing. I didn't know my feelings toward her were so obvious. "She was, uh, in my class," I stammered. "I've never liked her . . ." Of course I didn't want to say anything about the real reason she made me so uncomfortable. The presence of my former classmate was a powerful reminder that the mythic Grove of my memories and the place where I now found myself were actually one and the same.

"Just try to hide it better," Jessica said.

Josh didn't say anything. He had always tried to stay out of girls' wars, even back when we were in high school. I looked at his face, but his attention had been drawn out the window, where another flurry of leaves was falling.

I again felt the mysterious weight of the words from Kaitlyn's manuscript pressing down upon me.

I turned away from the window, and for a second, my eyes met Josh's—and I felt my stomach somersault. I jumped up from the table, trying to hide how flustered I felt in Josh's presence.

That night, I got an e-mail from Dr. Farber-Johnson stating that Mary Raschlaub had been suspended for three days, along with a terse warning that she expected that the dorm thefts would now cease. But then, just before lights-out, a teary-eyed freshman came to me sobbing because she couldn't find her special heart-shaped pillow. I remembered the sight of Mary standing in the hall, shoulders hunched, and thought of Jessica's reservations. Was it possible that Kaitlyn had set her up? But why?

That night, I tossed and turned, unable to get to sleep, and just before midnight, I heard a shuffling sound outside my door. When I got up to see what was going on, I saw that someone—presumably Kaitlyn—had shoved a pile of papers under my door. I swung the door open quickly to see who had done it, but whoever it was had already disappeared.

My hands were shaking and my mouth was dry as I read the first sentence. Then, my eye darted to the window, where it seemed that the blinds in Abigail Von Platte's apartment had moved. But the window was dark and still.

Bloody Murder

Mommy was a murderer. She murdered Daddy in cold blood. She tied a noose around his neck and hung him from the barn rafters in Vermont during the first big snow of senior year. I'd like to know if he went along with it willingly, if he stood on the corn crib and slipped his head into the twisted ropes, then kicked his feet away—that part I'm not quite clear on. I'd have liked to ask him that, I'd have liked to ask him a number of things, but I never got a chance. It was a plot all right, but they didn't trust me enough to let me in on it.

Mommy had been poisoning me against Daddy from the time I was the littlest girl, a steady corrosion, drip, drip, drip, like rust boring a hole through the side of a pipe. I loved Daddy, of course, who wouldn't love him? He was tall and slim, and as pretty as the water colors he painted. He wasn't a drunk like Mommy either. After dinner, the ice cubes in his glass started to tinkle, and his long, thin legs would sway in his soft chinos, back and forth, while he mumbled happy words . . . the fourteenth hole . . . the fairway . . . rounding the buoy . . . six-love, six-love. Everything was a game to Daddy. He always had a smile on his face. Most of the time, he wasn't home, but when he was there, I stuck by his side like a shadow, and he never seemed to mind.

She came for a visit on Parents' Weekend, and took me for a walk one day, just the two of us. It was a cold winter day, and we walked all around the Grove, circling down as far as the boathouse and to the highest point on the grounds up behind the chapel.

Mommy had hold of my arm. She was wearing her fur, and it was so cold that I was snuggling up against her. I remember thinking that if anyone had seen us from a distance, they would have thought we were the picture of the Grove—mother and daughter, out for a walk in the afternoon. The sky was white, streaked with pink and purple; the trees stood out against the horizon, up by the chapel; the view over the valley was heart stopping, breathtaking, but achingly cold.

We stopped there, at the crest of the hill, overlooking the drop-off behind the chapel. Mommy pulled me to face her, and I could see that her eyes were clear.

"You won't be seeing your father anymore. He's gone, and you should think of him as dead."

"What are you talking about?" I said. "That's not possible. Where is Daddy?" I was used to not seeing him much, but Mommy had never said anything like this—he came and went, like the swallows.

"Your father had no use for his old life. Let it be."

I tried to process what she was saying. His old life? Meaning, the one that included me?

My heart was beating so fast my voice came out like a whisper. "Where's Daddy? Is he okay?"

Mommy gripped my arm so hard it was starting to hurt. I could feel tears gathering in my eyes, like a storm about to break.

"Trust me, darling. There are things you don't know."

My parents did not give me enough credit. I knew a lot more than I let on. I saw them for what they were, both of them.

"The most important thing for you is to focus on your grades. You're either going to have to marry someone more suitable than you're likely to meet among the second-rate druggies at the Hardley School for Boys, or you're going to have to do it the modern way and get a career—if you want my opinion, I'd do it the second way."

This may have been one of the longest coherent philosophy-of-life statements my mother had ever uttered during the seventeen years of my existence, and I pondered it while I watched the pink streaks getting pinker and the purple streaks taking on an orangeish hue behind her.

"I think you girls have it much better than we had it. You know, I turned down that scholarship and I haven't ever regretted it . . ." Mommy couldn't fool me. I knew that it was the biggest regret of her life.

*"You should have just gone and gotten your stupid education!"
I said. "You never loved Daddy! You hate him, and you hate
me. You just married him for his money."*

*Mommy didn't answer right away. She just stared out at the
horizon, which had turned a murderous shade of red.*

*"Those were different times," she said. "You are going to get
an education."*

"Please, just tell me where he is . . ." I pleaded.

She shook her head resolutely.

*"No," she said. "May he rest in peace. He made his choices. As
far as we're concerned he's dead."*

"Can you at least tell me where he's buried?" I asked.

*"Absolutely not. Then you'd have the urge to go look for him,"
she said.*

11

The next morning, I was walking back from breakfast alone when I saw Josh pedaling up the hill. My heart skipped a beat, but I tried to act casual.

"Out for a bike ride?" I said.

"I'm going over to Hardley to check on the apple harvest."

"Hardley? Seriously? Why?"

"The Hardley campus was taken over by an English-language academy. We lease back some of the orchards for the farm project."

"I haven't seen Hardley since back when we were students."

"Why don't you ride over with me? Jessica's bike is in the bike rack outside Commons." He nodded toward the building I'd just come from.

"Where's Jessica?"

"Jessica and Molly are spending the weekend with her parents in Massachusetts."

I wasn't sure if this made me feel better or worse, but the sun was winking off the river and the sky was blue and the invitation was too tempting to pass up. Soon, I was speeding out the gates of the Grove, the wind beating against my face.

Straight across the river from the Grove to Hardley was only a couple of miles, but to get there by the road, the distance was closer to five. The fall foliage was just past its height, but still a palette of yellows, browns, and reds, and the river was by turns green, brown, and blue, depending on the mood of the passing clouds.

The Hardley School buildings were crammed together in a way that reminded me of a series of New England mills—this, in fact, reflected the school's heritage. Unlike its prep-school cousins including Exeter and St. Paul's, Hardley had been founded with a mission to educate the worthy sons of New England mill workers. Then, slowly over the years, it had become a second-rate prep-school—a place for boys who weren't quite smart enough, or well connected enough, or who had gotten kicked out of the first-tier schools.

As we pulled up to the front gate, I said, "Do you mind if we cut through campus?"

He shrugged.

"Do they care if we come on campus?"

"I doubt anyone is around. They usually take the students away on trips on the weekends."

In fact, the campus was deserted. There wasn't a soul about on the main quadrangle.

I looked at the various buildings. "Which ones did you live in?"

"Cavendish Hall, freshman and sophomore years, and Winslow Hall junior and senior years . . . There really are only two dorms, and they're wings of the same building." He pointed to the wings of the massive brick building that we stood in front of. "A lot of people called both of them Winslow-Cavendish."

"Wow, Winslow and Cavendish, I never thought of that . . . ," I said.

"Never thought of what?"

"Remember Kat? Her father's name was Winslow Cavendish Cunningham, and he was a Hardley boy."

"Whatever happened to her anyway?"

I touched his arm and turned him toward me. "Oh, I guess you didn't know. But then, how would you?"

He shook his head.

"She committed suicide. Ages ago."

He sucked in his breath and frowned.

"That's so sad," he said. "I like to think we're better at preventing it these days . . . though sometimes I wonder." We walked past a set of steep steps so worn from students' passage that they were hollowed out in the centers, past a bike rack with one bent-up bike missing its back wheel, past an abandoned Frisbee faded with age.

"Jeez, I haven't really looked at all this in a long time . . . Brings back memories," Josh said.

"Now you know how I feel every day over at the Grove."

"Well, I have to be honest, the main thing I remember about those days is ornithology."

"Ornithology?"

"See that water pipe that goes up the side of the building?"

"Yeah?"

"There was this kid named Brandon Barnes."

"You mean the dealer?"

"You knew him?"

"Are you kidding? Half of the Grove had him on expense account."

"So, there was this kid named Jimmy Holbrook, really smart kid but total pothead, never did anything except sit around all day and get wasted. So, one night, around two in the morning, he decides he needs some more weed, only problem is, the outside doors to Cavendish are locked and he can't get anyone on the first floor to wake up and let him in. So, he decides to climb up that pipe."

"*Up the pipe?*"

"To Brandon's room on the third floor. Only problem is, the pipe, as you can see even to this day, isn't very sturdy, so old burnout Holbrook gets up about two and a half floors, right outside my window, and the pipe breaks loose, and he starts swinging there and yelping for help . . ."

I laughed. I could picture it all too easily.

"I poke my head out the window and I'm yelling 'Shut up!' at him. So, the dorm supervisor comes out and says, *What the hell are you doing swinging from a pipe at two o'clock in the morning?* And you know what old Holbrook tells him?"

I shook my head.

"Ornithology."

"Ornithology?"

"Tells him that he's developed a passion for the study of the snowy owl. That he heard one hoot and tracked it across the courtyard and up the pipe in an attempt to catch a recording of it on his tape recorder, which supposedly he had tucked under his arm at the time—though what was actually under his arm was his bong. So, he has to go in front of a tribunal, and they get old Mr. Beckman, the biology teacher, who's a naturalist, to quiz him on the snowy owl. And Holbrook—see, he's one of the genius kids who never goes to class, just lies around and gets high and reads the encyclopedia—he answers all the questions right. Not only does he get out of trouble, but he gets out of biology and gets to do an independent study in ornithology . . . Long story short, that's how *ornithology* came to mean smoking dope at Hardley."

We had already passed through the far end of campus, so we turned onto a pathway that led toward the old playing fields. A padlocked chain was slung between two brick gateposts, blocking the path. Stepping over the chain, we entered the apple orchards. I followed Josh as he walked among the trees, clearly absorbed in his work.

"We should be able to start picking in a week or two," he said. "We make cider and sell it at the student store on Parents' Weekend." His eyes were sparkling as he spoke.

On the way back, the sun was in our eyes as we pedaled.

By the time we arrived at the Grove, the sun was setting behind the hills. As we rode up in front of Abbott North, he took hold of Jessica's bike.

"See you around," he said. My eyes followed him as he walked off, flanked by the two bicycles. For just a few seconds, I wondered if things could have turned out differently for us, but there was no use thinking about that now.

PART TWO
SENIOR YEAR

12

It was an ordinary night when we found the clue that set everything in motion. We had two mini bottles of peach schnapps that Lissa had somehow filched on the flight back from her last vacation in Cancun, plus two Budweisers from her boyfriend, Josh. It was early fall, but chilly. We snuck out after curfew and headed toward the river.

The founders of the Grove Academy had seen to it that Grove girls would be educated in splendid isolation, and even the Shangri-la of the Hardley School, whose lights we could see on the river's distant shore, was difficult to attain on a regular basis. Perhaps because of that, we were often drawn to the river's edge. At night, we would risk the long trek across Siberia, where our dark forms could easily be spotted from any dorm mother's window.

Wooten Boathouse was named after Chestmont Wooten, the headmaster of the school who was murdered in 1961. According to school lore, the boathouse was the site of the murder, and the red tones of the walls, a pleasant barn-red in daytime, seemed steeped in treacherous blood at night. Along the riverbank rose several tall poplars; one jutted out at a sharp angle toward the river, with several of its long branches extending over the water. Wooden rungs were hammered into the tree at intervals, and a long, thick rope was draped over the branch that stretched farthest over the water. Officially, the tree was off-limits, but unofficially, every Grove girl was expected to sneak out at night, climb the tree, grab the rope, jump off the branch, then let go and land in the river. Kat, Lissa, and I had dared each other to do it early in our freshman year and followed through. We were the first of the freshman class to jump, and it was that feat, more than any other, that had sealed our pact as a group. Lissa went first and Kat followed, but I hesitated up on the branch, too afraid to move. Silent tears dripped down my face as Kat and Lissa egged me on. All you had to do was hold tight to the rope and push off, but the first moment of faith, as my bottom slipped from the tree branch, felt like a taste of death.

We were anointed that night the moment we climbed through Katie Cornwell's first-floor window in Lane North after curfew, dripping wet—we were a team, and we had sealed our position as de facto leaders of the class.

By the beginning of senior year, almost everyone in the class had jumped—the tree, the rope, all old news. Now, as seniors, we were content to sit at the water's edge, masters of our domain.

The three of us drank the peach schnapps, pursing our lips around the tiny bottlenecks, then washed it down with the warm, soapy foam of the beer. Then, we lay on our backs and stared at the stars. The moon was out that night and the river was bright.

Kat was lying closest to the boathouse wall, and she discovered the words.

"Hey, look at this," she said.

We didn't see anything. We didn't carry flashlights with us, of course, when we were sneaking around after curfew. The night was bright, but faded letters on a wall in the moonlight are still very difficult to see, and at first, Lissa and I thought Kat was seeing things.

"I swear, there is writing here," Kat said. "You guys, I'm serious. It's down here so close to the ground that the painters probably never painted over it. I mean it. I think this might be a clue."

It was prickly down in the dirt and weeds, and we kept blocking each other's light, but soon we could see that, sure enough, there was writing on the wall. The words were down low, along a narrow band where the red paint stopped and there was a band of gray just above the ground.

"We'll have to come back," Lissa said.

"In the daytime," I said. "When we can see what it says."

"We can't," Kat said. "If we come back in the daytime, they'll see us. We need to come back another night and bring flashlights."

"Are you crazy?" I said. "If we bring flashlights, we're going to get caught."

A while later, we left, giddy with our newfound mystery. When we snuck back into the dorm, Kat and I were noisier than usual and our frumpy housemother, Susan Dockerty, popped her head out and said, "Girls? Do I hear a ruckus out there?" just as we clicked our door closed. We scrambled into my bottom bunk together with our clothes on and lay there perfectly rigid, finally falling asleep like that. The next morning, I awoke with a stiff neck, but also with a clear sense of purpose.

We all did.

That fall, it seemed as though Miss Pymstead was also on a mission—to teach us to memorize poetry. She started with a poem by William Butler Yeats called "The Lake Isle of Innisfree." Once we had memorized that, she decided we were capable of a little more than she had expected, as if it had never occurred to her that we *could* memorize things other than Beatles lyrics, when the reality was that we just hadn't heard the other stuff as often. So, Miss Pymstead decided that we weren't just going to read large chunks of the canon in English, but we were also going to commit them to memory.

One morning she was wearing a navy-blue suit with blue-and-white spectator pumps; her hair was drawn into a chignon fastened with a metal bobby pin that contrasted with her straw-colored hair.

She turned to the board. The other girls were copying, but I was fiddling with my pencil, wondering what made her dress like something out of a 1940s movie. Miss Pymstead was talking in that fluty voice of hers. "Girls, never think of Emily Dickinson as a frustrated woman, nor as unpublished, nor as a spinster . . ."

Her chalk made furious tapping sounds on the chalkboard, and the occasional squeak that made me grit my teeth. "No, never think of her as a gentle woman, as a poor thing, as a pathetic loner—no, never as just a lonely woman . . ." Miss Pymstead's voice was rising higher and higher as she wrote, though it was oddly muffled since she was talking not to us but directly into the blackboard. Finally, she stopped writing and turned around with a dramatic flourish.

"Girls, Emily Dickinson was, quite simply, a startling, independent, harsh, luminous, lit-from-within genius." Miss Pymstead held her arms up in the air as a preacher would in front of a Sunday revival, her shirt-front covered with chalk dust and her eyes illuminated with a feverish intensity that struck me as not without an edge of madness.

But the instant she stepped aside, revealing the words she had written, the three of us—Kat, Lissa, and I—could feel a current, like electricity, pass among us.

A solemn thing it was, I said, / A woman white to be . . .

After that, we were launched. What before had only been desultory speculation became the passion that haunted and obsessed us. For the words we had found written along the edge of the boathouse named for a murdered man were the same words of the poem that Miss Pymstead had chosen for us to memorize that day.

For the three of us, that was proof enough. We were ready to convict her of a crime and sit on her hanging jury. No matter that we hadn't decided what to accuse her of. Miss Pymstead was a woman alone, and we had already decided, long before, that she was guilty of passion. Once we had convicted her of that, we just needed one more thing to hang on her.

13

There was a single pay phone in the butt room in the basement of Lane North. Lissa, Kat, and I sat in a circle of scarred folding metal chairs listening to it ring. None of us moved. Our clove-scented smoke curled up and out the open casement window in purplish-gray strands. We exchanged glances: Lissa's bored, mine complicit, Kat's fretful. I was counting rings, 37, 38, 39, 40 . . .

Why answer the phone? Lissa was fighting with Josh. No one would call for me except my parents, and I didn't feel like talking to them. Kat—well, she never seemed to want to answer the phone . . . 41, 42 . . . Finally, footsteps started pounding on the stairs, first faint, then louder; a red-faced student appeared, hair wrapped in a still-wet towel from the shower. She grabbed the phone like it was the last life preserver on a sinking ship, and hollered breathlessly into it, "Hello?"

Lissa and I tittered. Abigail Von Platte.

"Kat Cunningham?" She looked over at us, hand cupped over the phone, face still all red.

Kat shook her head and made a throat-slitting gesture.

Indecision flashed across Abigail's face. To cross us or not to cross us? In her haste to get to the phone, she had pulled on a T-shirt without putting a bra on first, her saggy breasts showing through the damp cotton.

Lissa blew a smoke ring in her direction and mouthed the words "Don't you dare."

Alone, I wouldn't have been so mean, but with the power of three I felt invincible: I stared her down.

But Abigail was fingering the hem of her T-shirt. We could see the cogs turning behind her piggy eyes. "Kat Cunningham?" she said into the phone. Her voice was tight, pitched a half note too high. "Yes, she's *right* here. She's *smoking*."

Abigail let go of the handset and left it hanging there; it thumped once against the cinder block wall, then dangled at the end of its long twisted cord. Kat got up, stubbed out her cigarette, and crossed the basement, making it clear that she was in no hurry.

"Fatso," Lissa whispered.

Abigail turned, as if she was going to say something back, but she didn't have the guts. I watched her butt shake as she walked up the stairs. You could tell from how she held her hands real tight at her sides that she knew it was shaking, and that we were watching it. Lissa seemed to have no qualms about being mean, but it made my stomach churn in confusion—I thought that if I didn't side with Lissa, I might be her next victim.

Kat was twisting the coiled loops of cord around her fingers, playing with the change button on the phone, talking furtively behind a cupped hand. I think I knew, at some level, that Kat's life outside the Grove was more complicated than mine: the way she would sometimes disappear for a few days, the way the housemother, Mrs. Dockerty, would make allowances for her, telling me to pick up homework assignments with a worried nod that made me complicit in something that I didn't quite understand. Kat's grandmother, a tiny elegant woman with silvery hair and dark violet eyes, had died over the summer, but Kat didn't say much about it. She used to come visit Kat in a car that had a driver. I'd never seen a chauffeur before. Lissa told me one time that the grandmother was killed in a head-on collision less than a mile from her home, and that if she had left a will, no one could find it. I wasn't sure how Lissa knew these things. I had only the most shadowy impressions of the lives of my classmates outside the Grove.

Kat was old Grove, and despite her India-print skirts and worn-out Levi's with bandana patches sewn over the holes, she came equipped with a careless knowledge of things that all old Grove girls knew: field hockey, the words to Morning Prayer from the 1928 *Book of Common Prayer*, sailing knots, camp songs from Maine. She didn't seem to notice her own ease with these things, but still they gave her a certain panache. She fit in without even trying.

Once, sophomore year, Kat came back from one of her disappearances, pale and thin, her face wreathed in shadows. Her clothes smelled thickly of wood smoke, and there were silver ashes in her unwashed hair.

"My grandmother's old farmhouse burned to the ground. All we could do was stand there and watch. It got so hot—all the old family silver melted in the flames."

That was all she said about it. She didn't seem to care. She pulled on a pair of old gym shorts and an ancient Colby College sweatshirt that she always wore inside out, grabbed her backpack, and left Lissa and me behind.

"My dad says they're still loaded, but none of it's liquid," Lissa said after a while.

"What does that mean?" I asked.

"I'm not sure," Lissa said. "I think it's like being rich and poor at the same time. I think her grandma used to pay her tuition. Who knows who pays now? I bet nobody does."

I tried not to show surprise. I would have never guessed anything of the sort. I assumed that all the Grove girls went home to well-ordered but dull suburban homes like mine. I could not imagine what circumstances could make people like the Cunninghams into a charity case.

Besides that one conversation, I don't remember us often talking about money. There was nothing to buy at the Grove, nowhere to spend money, unless you went into town—and no way to get into town unless you stole off the grounds after curfew and then hitchhiked. Of course, after curfew, everything in town was closed except for one package store over in Brattleboro, unless you wanted to go all the way down to Amherst. In short, we didn't have much need for pocket money, except to buy pot, which came mostly from a boy at Hardley named Brandon, whose father was a diplomat stationed in Morocco—and who was willing to take credit to be paid on the days when parents showed up—Parents' Weekend, Sacred Concert, and Convocation.

"We need to learn absolutely everything there is to learn about the murder," Lissa said. "That's how we can figure out where to look for clues."

All three of us were on the top bunk, in Kat's and my room, and I had started a notebook: on the front, I had written *CLUE NOTEBOOK*.

That was about as far as we had gotten, though. Beyond that, we were having trouble deciding exactly what approach to take. We had, thus far, only three "facts." We knew that Chestmont Wooten had been murdered in 1961. We knew that there were lines of poetry, nearly obscured on the side of the boathouse. And we knew, or believed, that Miss Pymstead was implicated. But how? It was making that connection that seemed difficult.

"Could she be old enough to have been his lover?" I asked.

Lissa snorted and picked at her nail polish. "Could Miss Pymstead ever have been young at all?" she said.

"I think they were lovers," Kat said, "when she was a student. And then she got mad at him and shot him. And then she threw the gun into Echo Lake, and now, it's rusting there, at the bottom, with her fingerprints on it."

"I don't think a gun can have fingerprints on it for eighteen years at the bottom of a lake," Lissa said. She tended to focus on practical details. Kat was the storyteller; she got more caught up in the narrative arc.

"Do we know that a gun was the murder weapon?" I asked. I was holding the pen and notebook. I felt that we should be taking steps. If *A*, then *B*; if *B*, then *C*. If *C*, then—not that we had formulated a C yet. Having stumbled upon a clue quite by accident, we were certain the rest of the mystery should unravel with ease. But so far—since the discovery at the boathouse, followed by the revelation in the classroom—we were on a cold trail.

I looked at the notebook.

"Here's a summary of what we know so far," I said. But I got no further—both Lissa and Kat groaned. Lissa slid down from the top bunk, picked up Kat's Mason Pearson hairbrush from atop her dresser, and started to stroke it through her hair. Kat flopped over on her belly and grabbed her copy of *The World According to Garp*.

"This is getting boring," Lissa said, a fatal pronouncement. "I think I'm going to go back to my room. I have math homework I need to do." Lissa lived with Katie Cornwell, across the hall, but you'd have never known it for the amount of time she spent in our room.

I tried to hide my disappointment. This seemed to happen more often than not these days—I wanted to recapture the time when the three of us had been inseparable, when the stories we made up were the most exciting things happening to us. But I could feel both of them pulling away. For more than three years, the school had been our world, but now that we were seniors, we could feel the tug of the real world even inside this sheltered place.

Just then, out the window, up near the chapel, I saw Miss Pymstead, walking by herself. She was distant, but not so distant that I couldn't recognize her slim form hurrying along the pathway. Where was she going on the middle of a Saturday afternoon?

"I know," I said. "I think we should follow her. See where she goes and what she does. Try to find out more about her," I said.

Kat put her book down on the bed and looked up, interested again. "And we can write our observations down in our notebook, like Harriet the Spy."

Lissa finished with Kat's hairbrush. She picked up a bottle of Kat's hand lotion and started smoothing it on her hands and arms.

"You don't think you guys are getting a little lezzie about this whole thing? You want to stalk her?" Lissa said.

"Lissa," Kat said, "don't be so middle-class. We are serving a power higher than Eros, higher than Lesbos."

Lissa climbed up onto the bunk again, sat up, and held up her right hand as though she were holding a torch. *"The lamp is truth,"* she said.

"The light is knowledge," I said. Lissa and I were quoting the Grove school motto.

"I have a trig midterm tomorrow," Lissa said. "Can I borrow your blue sweater?" Without waiting for an answer, she picked up the sweater from Kat's chair and pulled it over her head and left.

Kat went back to her reading, but I was restless, so I grabbed the notebook and headed out of the dorm. I picked up the trail of Miss Pymstead up on Founder's Hill, behind the chapel. She was seated on the gravestone of the Reverend Elfred Winterston Clinch, founder of the Grove Academy for Girls, and she held a leather-bound volume whose title I could not discern from the distance at which I hid. The book was set aside, and she was looking out over the valley—her hair, which I had never seen unpinned, was loose behind her, and though sitting quite alone, she had a look upon her face that I can only describe as rapture.

I opened the spiral notebook and uncapped my Bic pen.

October 12th. Founder's Hill, I wrote. The first line of what would become our folly.

14

By early November, Miss Pymstead was breaking through to us: iambic pentameter started to seep into the usual free verse of our days. Snippets of sonnets popped into our conversation as naturally as television theme songs and jingles from the radio.

Then, on the Thursday before Thanksgiving break, Miss Pymstead wrote on the blackboard: *Je fais de la prose sans le savoir* . . .—Molière

"I hate to think who among you might have at least a passable accent in French . . ." She peered at each of us, as though expecting to be disappointed, and then finally settled on Kat.

Kat tended to grow more withdrawn as holidays grew near. This morning, her hair was unbrushed, and she had pulled her jeans and sweatshirt on right over her waffle-weave long johns. She looked pleadingly at Miss Pymstead. I knew Kat hadn't made it to Commons for coffee before class.

"I'm sure that your French won't hurt my ears at least," Miss Pymstead said.

Kat looked as if she wanted to crawl under a rock, but she looked up at the board and read the line flawlessly. Kat had all these hidden skills: fluent French, Olympic-level alpine skiing, concert piano. But you never knew about them, until that one time when she got high and snuck into Read Hall in the middle of the night to play Tchaikovsky for you, or the time she came back from a trip with her grandmother with a tag on her luggage that read: *Gstaad.*

The rest of us all took French or Spanish, about half and half, but none of us could toss off authentic Parisian like Kat.

"And that means . . ?"

Lissa was wearing a pink turtleneck with a pink crewneck over it, looking as dewy as Kat appeared warmed-over and stale. "Miss Pymstead. We can't be responsible for that. Not all of us take French. Some of us take Spanish." And Lissa, being Lissa—and unable to leave well enough alone—added, "Spanish is more practical."

I thought that Lissa's comment would set Miss Pymstead off on one of her tirades, but instead, she walked over to Lissa and laid both hands on top of her head.

"French or Spanish, it makes little difference to this one, because, you see, she's pretty."

She turned and erased the line from the blackboard.

"No French today. I've decided it is time for you to start reading prose. You will select a short story written by a writer of your choice. Read the story with care, then rewrite the story yourself, staying as close as you can to the original author's style. Only tell the story from a different point of view. Poetry is, by its nature, an oral form, and you can learn to appreciate it by reciting it aloud, but prose is a different matter."

Miss Pymstead looked around the room at each of us in turn. "Prose is climbing inside someone else's skin. The only way to do that is to get inside it, live with it, sleep with it, roll around and make love to it . . ."

Lissa elbowed me and rolled her eyes. Kat kicked me under the table. Katie Cornwell, down at the end of the table, giggled and received a stern look from Miss Pymstead in reply.

"Girls, this is no laughing matter. Try it. You'll see. It's not as easy as it seems."

The class was mildly interested by this new focus. For the past ten weeks, we had been memorizing the words of others—and now Miss Pymstead was asking us to produce some words of our own.

Then, there was a hubbub of housekeeping questions. Could we choose any author? How long did it have to be? Could the author still be alive?

Miss Pymstead plopped a thick copy of *The Norton Anthology of Short Fiction* on the tabletop.

"The story must be in here," she said. "And it must predate this decade, as I'm certain that no good writing has occurred since the year 1970. We'll consider that a given."

She shoved the fat book toward the middle of the table, but all of us were too reluctant to reach for it.

"Just one more rule," Miss Pymstead said. "No Salinger. The man is terribly overrated. I believe that he became a recluse because he was ashamed. I would simply die before I allowed any of you to try his ridiculous style on for size."

I felt caught out. Salinger was one of my favorite authors. After all, he had created Holden Caulfield, who had managed to pull off the one feat that had eluded the three of us so far at the Grove—getting kicked out of school.

I never went home for Thanksgiving break because my family lived in Michigan. This year, I assumed Kat would be leaving, but then, Tuesday noon came and went and Kat was still there. The number in Commons dwindled to just a couple of tables of orphans. The two gorgeous Iranian girls, Maryam and Parvaneh, spent most of their time huddled big-eyed around a radio. The rest of us paid them no heed. Then, there was a

Korean girl and Liz O'Meyer, whose father was in the Foreign Service; Kat and I; the fat girl, Abigail; and a few other girls we didn't know very well.

Lissa was spending a week in Barbados with her parents. I had assumed that Kat would leave too. When she didn't, I was secretly pleased. I preferred the company of Kat to Lissa, and now I wouldn't have to share her. But Kat herself had plunged into a stony and perpetual silence. I was afraid to ask her why she hadn't gone home.

I was lying on my bottom bunk, playing with the metal springs above me. Kat was on her bed, shifting from time to time, not saying much, so I guessed she was either sketching or reading.

"I've noticed that Miss Pymstead almost always visits the library between three thirty and four p.m."

Kat said nothing. The bedsprings shifted, but only slightly. I waited.

"She also attends chapel services. Even when they're not compulsory."

"Don't you think—" Kat's head popped over the side of her bunk, her ponytail hanging down. "Don't you think that you're getting a little obsessed with this?"

"Obsessed?" I said. I was glad I had her attention. I planned to play it for all it was worth. "With a case of murder?"

"We don't even know if Pymstead did it."

"Do you know how many poems Emily Dickinson wrote? Okay, I mean, if it was one of the really famous ones, like *I heard a fly buzz when I died* . . . I mean, everybody has heard of that one, but who ever heard of one about a woman white to be—and plus, I asked around, and none of the other English classes even studied that poem . . ."

Kat jumped down from the top bunk and landed on the balls of her feet. "We're Honors English. Did you forget that? I think one of the other classes is reading *Jonathan Livingston Seagull.*"

"They are not!"

"You'd be surprised. For all they go on and on about the Grove this and the Grove that, this is just a crap school these days anyway. Nobody wants to go to an all-girls school anymore. Nobody wants to go to boarding school at all."

"Nevertheless," I said, "it looks highly suspicious. And besides, we thought there was a tragedy in Miss Pymstead's past from the first time we saw her."

Kat looked at me. "I think the only tragedy is that she has to teach the likes of us."

"What's that supposed to mean?"

"She could teach college. She could be teaching at Harvard or something."

"Well, then, why isn't she?"

Kat bounced down on the bunk next to me, making its springs squeak. "Because . . ." She narrowed her eyes and lowered her voice. "Because she murdered Chestmont Wooten and tossed the murder weapon into Echo Lake, and she's afraid that if she leaves somebody will find it, so she stays here to confuse people, only she leaves clues in poetry, and nobody has ever noticed before until these three brilliant, talented, beautiful, insightful students . . ."

"The crème de la crème . . ."

"Exactly . . . came along . . . and started to realize what was going on and . . ."

I punched Kat's shoulder. "You're making fun of me."

"*Moi?*"

"Yes."

"*Jamais.*"

"So, why didn't you go home for Thanksgiving?"

Kat's expression clouded over. She stood up. "I'm going to go to the library and work on my story for a while. Do you want to come?"

"Who are you doing?" I wished I hadn't upset her.

"I haven't decided."

"I'm going to do Hemingway," I said. "It'll be easy . . . because of all the short sentences." I was not showing my hand. I cared desperately about trying to impress Miss Pymstead, but I didn't know if it was cool to care.

"Hemingway will be hard," Kat said. "Because he's a man. They think differently." She walked out of the room, shutting the door behind her with a firm thud. I was left alone with nothing but my notebook and a paucity of ideas.

That afternoon, instead of trying to get inside the skin, roll around, and make love to Hemingway, I tried to pick up the cold trail of Miss Amanda Pymstead.

It was a beautiful day, unseasonably warm, with just a few inches of slushy snow on the ground. But after three circuits of the campus with no sign of Miss Pymstead, the drama was getting a bit stale, so I returned to Lane North, hoping to roust Kat outside to glory in the day with me.

I found her chain-smoking in the butt room, hunched over a blue spiral notebook, with its cover folded back; she had a pen clutched tightly in her hand. The casement window was locked shut, and the pay phone was ringing insistently as I walked down the stairs.

From the set of Kat's shoulders I knew better than to think about answering it.

"Come out," I said. "It's warm."

"I'm working." She blew three smoke rings, then looked back down at her notebook. She was pressing hard. I could see that there were tears in the paper.

I tried to peer over her shoulder, but she shielded the pages with her hand. A dog-eared copy of *The Norton Anthology* was splayed, broken spined, at her feet.

The basement was chilly. Kat was perched on a metal stool, her feet tucked up underneath her on one of the rungs. She had the too-long cuff of her frayed sweater pulled over her left hand, and I could see that she had been chewing on it. Her lit cigarette rested on a Coke can that she was using as a makeshift ashtray; a long ash wavered on it, getting ready to topple.

Though we were both pretending otherwise, the phone hadn't stopped ringing. Its insistent bell cut through the air every few seconds.

"Kat, come on. Let's walk down to Echo Lake. Get some fresh air."

She picked up the cigarette. The ash wobbled and then fell, missing the can and falling to the cement floor.

She scratched something out, turned to look at me, her face blank. The air was thick with smoke, and the phone's bell clattered in my ears.

She shook her head.

"I can't." She looked down at her notebook, wrote another few words, and scratched a few more out.

"Of course you can," I said.

Mercifully, the phone let out just one more half ring before it stuttered to silence. I pushed on the one small window, propping it open with a broken stick. Now, the sun was low over Founder's Hill, the treetops stark against the sky. As I turned around, the fluorescent lights inside the butt room looked even more lurid.

Kat raised her gaze from her notebook.

"Come on," I said again.

I took hold of her sleeve, tugged on it.

She shrugged out of my grasp. "Please, can't you just . . . ?"

One of Miss Pymstead's lines, from Keats, popped into my head: *Heard melodies are sweet, but those unheard / Are sweeter . . .* I wanted to hear what she heard.

"I bet you're doing Sylvia Plath," I said. "That excerpt from *The Bell Jar*—I'll bet that's what you're doing your story on."

Kat didn't answer, just stared down at the notebook again, scribbled some more words, furiously, so fast that I could see her Bic boring holes through the paper as she wrote.

As I headed toward the basement stairs, the phone started ringing again. I counted the rings—four, five, six.

I was almost all the way to the fire door at the first-floor landing when she called out to me, "Jane!"

When I turned around, all I saw was the long, frayed sleeve of her sweater, dangling from the water pipe, swinging just slightly in the still air.

Kat was standing underneath, looking up to where she had tossed it. She was laughing.

"Sylvia Plath . . ." She tipped her head back and laughed. "How'd you ever guess?"

By Saturday afternoon, I hadn't yet caught sight of Miss Pymstead. I had grown bored of my lonely walks and had decided that it was time for me to work on my story for Miss Pymstead's class. Pencott Library was locked over the long weekend, and in my room, I kept finding things to distract me. So, with my *Norton Anthology*, pad of paper, and ballpoint in hand, I headed for the one building that I knew would be both empty and unlocked: Whittaker Chapel.

The chapel sat up high on Founder's Hill, overlooking the entire campus. Like all good New England schools, the Grove Academy had been founded on religious principles. But at some point, the Grove had taken a secular turn, and we were only expected to attend chapel four times per year: Invocation, Lantern Day, Sacred Concert, and Convocation. There were still a smattering of girls who attended weekly services, but the rest of the time, Whittaker Chapel served a variety of other purposes.

The Gothic chapel was constructed of stone and was most remarkable for its tall tower graced by a large rose window. Alvah Horace Whittaker, who had built the chapel to memorialize his daughter, Adelia—who drowned in the river one spring—had stipulated that the chapel always be kept unlocked, "for pilgrims who found themselves a moment's need at any time of day or night." There wasn't a Grove girl who had not memorized this line—or scarcely a Hardley boy either. Whittaker Chapel stood, doors open and empty, for a succession of pot smokers, late-night exam crammers, fornicators, drunken Amherst boys who couldn't find a ride off campus, and all other manner of pilgrims. If there were spiritual pilgrims among us at the Grove, I wasn't aware of it at the time; although as I carried my blank pages, pens, and thick paperbound fiction anthology to the topmost hill of campus that afternoon, it could be said that I felt the need of something akin to divine revelation.

Once inside Whittaker, I found a hush. First off, I settled in a left-hand pew, about a third of the way back, my anthology propped open by a blue hymnal as I attempted to read "A Clean Well-Lighted Place" and think about how I would go about writing the story from the point of view of the old waiter.

Fidgety from the hard wood of the pew, I decided that perhaps I'd be more comfortable at the pulpit, and so I approached the chancel, stepping up the three stone steps. I placed my clue notebook on top of the large leather-bound Bible that was kept on the pulpit, and over it, laid my open composition book.

I looked at the few sentences I had written. It was clear that though the sentences were short, they were also awkward and choppy, like hair shorn off by schoolgirl scissors. I had never been to Spain, but somehow, when Miss Pymstead had read a bit of the story aloud in class the other day, I could almost hear the feet of a thousand bulls thundering across Siberia. Now, though, in the cool dark of the chapel, I heard nothing. I set aside the notebook again, peered up at the rose window—the rays of light catching the individual panes, sending brilliant reds and blues cutting across the interior of the chapel—and without thinking, flipped open the clue notebook. But I flipped it shut again. I'd come to work, not to dawdle.

Perhaps if I tried to read a bit of it aloud. I pulled the notebook in front of me again, tucking our sleuthing notebook underneath it, and looked at what I had written. I opened my mouth to speak, but I did not hear Hemingway's bulls thundering outside, only the smallness of my voice in the big stone space. I cleared my throat. Coughed a couple of times. This was not going well.

My eye wandered to the Bible, lying open with a slender red ribbon marking the page that had a large illuminated *H* at the top. I lifted my notebook to get a better look. The Bible was just another one of those texts of which I thought I should know something but didn't. I glanced down at the open page, cleared my throat. The sound made a feeble echo in the stone chamber. I experimented with reading a line aloud: *"Hear my plea of innocence, O Lord; I give heed to my cry . . ."*

A triangle of light formed on the stone aisle as the nave door was pushed open.

"Carry on."

Miss Pymstead's head appeared from behind the door. She headed briskly down the center aisle toward me, her voice picking up where I had left off, ringing out over the stone. *"Listen to my prayer, which does not come from lying lips . . ."* She paused, as though expecting me to continue, but I said nothing.

"Psalm 17? My dear Jane, have you been accused of something?"

I was confused, not linking any meaning to the content of the words I had just read.

"Miss Pymstead, I just came here to work on my assignment . . ."

There was no prohibition against my presence in Whittaker Chapel, but still my cheeks burned.

She seemed not to notice my discomfiture but trod up the steps and came around beside me, where she saw the Bible, lying open to Psalm 17, and next to it, my notebook, labeled *A Clean Well-Lighted Place*, with the paltry few sentences written underneath. Fortunately, the clue notebook was still hidden under my English notebook. I took pains to cover the first paragraph of my essay with my elbow, but it was no use.

"Hemingway giving you fits, is he?"

I was surprised at her tone. I detected not scorn in it but warmth. She was looking at me with interest. Her expression was lively, and I might even have called it kind.

"It seems so simple, and yet, it's a bugger to imitate," she said. "At least one girl falls into the Hemingway trap every year." She made a motion, like scooping up fish in a net. "I'm surprised it was you though, Jane."

I felt a tingle along the back of my neck when she said it because I recognized the words as praise.

She arched her eyebrows. Miss Pymstead's eyes were a watery blue, but in the half-light of the chapel, the blue looked deeper. She held my gaze.

"Mettle," she said. "It's the quality I'm looking for when I look at you girls. It's a quality that seems to be harder and harder to find."

She studied my face intently and I stood quietly, submitting to her inspection.

"You seem trustworthy, Jane Milton. I shall remember that in case I find myself in need of a confidante."

It was not until after she left, that I realized I was scarcely breathing.

Three points on a compass, three stars in a constellation, gold, silver, and bronze—that was the way I had always felt in Miss Pymstead's class, flanked on the left and right by Lissa's robust beauty and Kat's intimidating brains.

There, in the empty darkening space of Whittaker Chapel, I had captured the flitting gaze of Miss Amanda Pymstead and held it transfixed by me alone.

I would tell no one. This was to be my secret.

15

On the Monday after Thanksgiving break, the twelve of us slapped our handwritten papers in front of Miss Pymstead in a haphazard pile, but you could tell that every girl in that room was hoping to find favor from her. It was one thing to be asked to memorize a poem, to mark scansion, to identify and describe passages memorized after late nights of study. But this time, Miss Pymstead had asked us to put a little of ourselves on the line, selves in which she had heretofore seemed uninterested. I knew that my "Clean Well-Lighted Place" was somewhat flawed, but I still held out hope. After all, I was Jane Milton, the girl who had shown the rare quality of "mettle." What's more, looking around the room, I wondered who could do better. After all, my only competition came from my two best friends—tortured Kat of the chain-smoking sessions in the basement, and Lissa, who had many virtues, but I did not believe creativity to be among them.

After Thanksgiving, things seemed to revert back to normal with us. Lissa broke up with Josh, and so she came back to us in 2B, looking for recreation. And whatever cloud had been cast over Kat's life seemed to drift away, leaving her sunny again. The weather, by contrast, had grown cold. A blanket of snow fell, and the sky lowered and turned a late-November gray.

"I don't think we've been taking the Pymstead matter seriously enough," Kat said from her perch on the top bunk. "A possible murderer is here in our midst, and we've done nothing. I think what's lacking is a concrete strategy."

I was sitting at my desk. Lissa was standing next to Kat's record player. It was a portable suitcase-style player, green on the outside. She slipped Fleetwood Mac's *Rumours* out of the paper sleeve and put it on the turntable, settling the arm over the vinyl. The speakers started to crackle and hiss. The vinyl dropped onto the turntable, the arm jerked up then across, settling down with a jump. The white hissing started, then the music.

"Turn it down a little," Kat said. "I can't think straight. Where's that clue notebook?"

I felt a small sense of betrayal, remembering my encounter with Miss Pymstead in Whittaker Chapel, her confession to me that she might need a confidante. I had not recorded that in the clue notebook. This was my first thrilling experience of what it might feel like to be a double agent.

I handed the notebook to Kat. She thumbed through it. "It's a bit thin," she said. "We'll have to do better than this."

"I think," Lissa said, "that we need to figure out how old she is. Face it. If Miss Pymstead wasn't around the Grove in 1961, it's going to be harder to prove that she had something to do with the murder . . ." Lissa was now sprawled out on my bunk, taking up all the space. I sat back down in my desk chair.

"We need to check the yearbooks. Find out what year she graduated."

"There are old yearbooks in Pencott," I said.

"Yeah, but we might arouse suspicion if we look at them," Kat said.

I was sitting astride my desk chair, thinking that this was so much like old times that I didn't want to do anything to wreck the mood. Just the three of us—Kat, Lissa, and me—that sense of camaraderie that, once gained, I had thought we'd never lose.

"Yeah, we don't want anyone to get suspicious," I said. I could hardly imagine old Mrs. Owen-Farrell, the stout librarian who could often be found napping in front of the fan in her office, would get suspicious if she found us looking at old yearbooks. But playing along seemed the best way to keep the momentum going.

"Well," Kat said, standing up, "I have a plan. I think we should spend the night in the library. We'll get ourselves locked in. Just like Claudia and Jamie in *From The Mixed-Up Files of Mrs. Basil E. Frankweiler*. You know, how they spent the night in the Metropolitan Museum of Art in New York City? We'll be just like them!"

Lissa rolled over on her stomach and propped her chin on her hands.

"Spend the night in Pencott?" she said. *"Party!"*

Kat shook her head. "No. This is serious. This is for research. We're going to look for old yearbooks and student newspapers—maybe the literary magazine, I don't know. And we're going to find out whatever we can about the murder, and whatever we can find out about Miss Pymstead."

As we spent a week laying in supplies—homemade apple cider from Hardley Farm Store and packets of saltines and graham crackers stolen one by one from Commons—I was happy that our friendship seemed to be working again.

Several days passed without further mention of our stories, but then, on Friday morning, when we entered class, Miss Pymstead had a gleam in her eye that told us immediately that something was afoot. The skies hung heavy over the Grove campus that day, and the temperature had dropped. There was a bitter chill in the air. I had to dig around in a box in my closet to pull out my heaviest winter sweater, which shrouded me in a faint scent of mothballs.

Miss Pymstead looked unseasonable for the weather. Her sweater was pale lavender, her slacks a light tan. Her hair was styled in a tight French twist, and I noticed that she looked almost ordinary, like somebody's secretary—the kind of person you might pass on a street in the city and hardly notice.

After all of us had filed in, shed coats and scarves, and settled around the table, Miss Pymstead pulled a manila folder from the canvas bag that was parked at her feet and plopped it on the table in front of her. My heart flip-flopped when I realized that the folder contained our stories. She looked around the table at us, and I imagined that her eyes settled upon me a bit longer than the others. I felt a momentary burst of hopefulness, but then her gaze passed.

"Prose is difficult," Miss Pymstead said. "Is there any among you, after this exercise, who would dare to contradict me on that?"

Katie Cornwell raised her hand to about half-mast, but the withering look Miss Pymstead shot at her made her quickly lower it again.

Miss Pymstead stood, flipped open the folder in front of her, and fanned the essays out on the table. "'The Lottery,' as told from the point of view of the one being stoned? Of that, I can only say *ouch*. 'A Rose for Emily,' as told by Miss Emily Grierson's ghost?" Miss Pymstead looked around the classroom to make it perfectly clear that she was not in the least amused. "Did it not occur to you that Mr. William Faulkner killed her *for a reason?*"

"However," Miss Pymstead said, "there is one girl who has achieved a level of mastery that rather surprised me."

Miss Pymstead looked across to our side of the room, and again, I thought I felt her eyes resting upon me, and I remembered the way that she had spoken to me when she said I had mettle. Maybe I had done a better job than I thought.

She reached among the papers and plucked one from the pile. As she started to read, I heard a quiver of something—pride or satisfaction—in her voice. I recognized it—it was also there when she read Tennyson to us, and Shakespeare, and Lord Byron. A small hitch, a throb.

"'A and P' by John Updike, as told by the plump one in plaid."

As she started to read, I ignored my eyes smarting with tears as I looked around the room, trying to figure out who had managed to impress Miss Pymstead. I knew it wasn't Lissa, who had tried her hand at a story by Virginia Woolf, nor Kat, with her Sylvia Plath. I listened to Miss Pymstead reading the words, stopping now and then to point out some aspect of the fineness of the craft; I looked around the room, furtively observing the expressions on the other students' faces. Some appeared impressed, others bored; on other faces, including Katie Cornwell's, I could detect a hint of jealousy. But as I gazed around the room, nowhere could I see the gleam of pride, nowhere, until I got all the way around full circle, to where Kat was not even looking up. She was sitting next to me, doodling in the margin of her notebook, as usual. I peeked surreptitiously to see what she was doodling. I realized that I was looking at the same pages she had been working on in the butt room—written in, then scratched out, then scribbled over to the point that the page was torn in places. At the top, she had scrawled a title: *A&P.*

It was the story of three girls who stopped at an A&P supermarket to pick something up for their mother—just a simple story, but it hurt hard down in the pit of my stomach as I listened to Miss Pymstead reading it, because it was clear that Updike's story could have been about the three of us: three points on a compass, three stars on a constellation: gold, silver, and bronze. It was like that in Kat's story too, only in her story, it was bronze who was talking, the one who was not quite as smart, not quite as pretty, the one who everybody knew was just along to make the other two look better.

I tried to stop myself, but before I knew it, I had rushed out of the classroom, and I was outside in the middle of Siberia, alone, under a leaden November sky.

16

I retreated to Whittaker Chapel to lick my wounds. The chapel was cold inside, gloomy and empty. For a long time, I sat curled up in the corner of a dusty pew, my arms drawn up around my knees, staring up at the rose window.

What was most infuriating was that I didn't like Hemingway—especially not "A Clean Well-Lighted Place." I didn't even understand it. I had no idea what the characters were talking about—Hemingway never seemed to have much to say about anything, as though he got to the end before he had even gotten started. But the thing is, I had never had the guts to come right out and admit it. If I couldn't see Hemingway's genius, surely that was my lack, not his.

Being here, in Whittaker Chapel, reminded me that I still had my edge. Perhaps Miss Pymstead had preferred Kat's story, but she had chosen *me* as her potential confidante. Kat had always had a way with words, but she was mercurial, anyone could see that—she wasn't someone who could be counted on. That was my job. Miss Pymstead had seen that about me.

By this time, I had settled back into the pew, lying with my head cradled in my hands. I was thinking, idly, that I was missing a French test right now and felt a flicker of apprehension about my grades, when I realized that I was not alone in the chapel. I didn't hear anything specific, but I sensed a presence. Since it was midmorning, most girls would normally be in class. Only a fellow truant would be in the chapel with me.

I listened intently but heard nothing. Still, I could perceive a vibration in the air. Since I was lying down, I knew that I could not be seen unless someone walked directly past my pew.

I lay flat on my back and looked at the narrow view my supine position afforded me: the back of the worn pew in front of me, a sliver of the aisle that ran along the side of the chapel.

I listened intently, and then I could hear soft breathing, quiet footsteps—the sounds made by a person who is trying not to be heard. I rolled onto my side, but that gave no further view, only stirred up more dust that tickled the inside of my nose, threatening to make me sneeze. Now, the sound of footsteps was more distinct, like whispers on the stone floor, then more assured as they reached the steps to the altar.

A moment later, the side door to the chapel opened with a distinct creak. From where I was lying, I couldn't see it close again, but I could hear it. I lay still for a moment longer, but I knew that I was once again alone in the chapel.

I sat up and peered anxiously around me, then stood and looked around once more. I approached the chancel, walked up the three steps—everything appeared the same: the pulpit, the communion railing, and the dusty rose-colored kneeling cushions below it. The large leather-bound Bible was still open to the same page—I could tell by the large illuminated *H* at the top.

It was only then that a folded paper caught my eye. It was thin blue paper of the sort used for airmail stationery, flimsy and light. I knew it hadn't been there the last time I had been in Whittaker Chapel—but a

Sunday had passed since then. Any number of people might have come and gone during that time.

I lifted the paper from where it was tucked between the pages of the Bible, next to its red-satin string, and started to uncrease it.

I could feel a prickling sensation; it had started somewhere down in my legs, but soon enough, it took over my neck and face.

I could not mistake Miss Pymstead's handwriting, that rounded cursive I so admired—I had been making a study of it since September. In blue fountain pen on thin onionskin paper, it only looked finer:

> *I heard a fly buzz when I died;*
> *The stillness round my form*
> *Was like the stillness in the air*
> *Between the heaves of storm.*
>
> *The eyes beside had wrung them dry,*
> *And breaths were gathering sure*
> *For that last onset, when the king*
> *Be witnessed in his power.*
>
> *I willed my keepsakes, signed away*
> *What portion of me I*
> *Could make assignable,—and then*
> *There interposed a fly,*
>
> *With blue, uncertain, stumbling buzz,*
> *Between the light and me;*
> *And then the windows failed, and then*
> *I could not see to see.*

I blinked as I read the last bit. It was growing dark in the chapel. I knew it must be getting ready to storm. I caressed the smooth paper with my fingers.

Kat's story about the A&P was nothing next to this. Miss Pymstead had chosen to confide in me. She thought me worthy of this and that I would understand. I wasn't altogether sure what the poem was supposed to mean. Frankly, Emily Dickinson's poems confused me. But I was certain that Miss Pymstead had left it for me. It was a clue, and as soon as I could figure it out, I could tell Kat and Lissa that I had solved the mystery.

At least I think that's what my plan was. I glanced again at the rose window, puzzled why it was getting dark outside when it couldn't have been much past noon—I hadn't even heard the lunch bells yet.

I folded the paper carefully into quarters, then thirds, then into a tiny little square, and stuck it in my pocket.

When I opened the door to leave the chapel, I saw it was snowing hard, a cold, blowing snow that bit my cheeks and blew into my eyes and mouth.

That day, the trek across Siberia brought to mind a journey across the real Siberia—the snow was already several inches deep, and the wind came in at a harsh slant. I could only see a few feet in front of my face, and there were moments when I almost became disoriented and had to turn around to catch sight of the tall tower of Whittaker Chapel to get my bearings.

As I staggered through the snow, I thought about my new clue, and I couldn't make up my mind: the thought of sharing it with Kat and Lissa was heady. But then, perhaps, I'd have a better advantage if I first followed the trail a bit myself. Just as I reached Cottage Row, I heard the first lunch bell ring. My jeans were soaked through above my boots, and my fingers were chilled right through my gloves. I ducked inside Lane North, grateful for the warmth. As I climbed the stairs, the girls flowed past me in twos and threes as they headed out of the dorm toward Commons for lunch.

As I reached 2B, I could see that something was amiss. Mrs. Dockerty stood in the doorway, looking toward the stairwell. "Oh, there you are," she said.

Mrs. Dockerty was a short woman, barely five feet tall. She held her hands clasped over the plump part of her belly, her wrists small and puffy. I remembered that I had cut French class and thought maybe she was coming to speak to me about that—though discipline at the Grove tended to be lax.

But the expression on Mrs. Dockerty's face was different—a kind of pained embarrassment that I wasn't sure how to interpret, and when I got closer, all she said was "Why don't you come on inside. "

Mrs. Dockerty motioned toward my desk chair, which had clothes strew over it.

"Sit down, dear. I'm afraid I've got some sad news to share with you—it's Kat . . . There's been a death."

The room stilled, got sharper edged.

I remember that the view out the window was completely blanked out with the almost-horizontal snow that was flying, and I had a vision of the frayed arm of Kat's sweater hanging from the water pipe in the butt room, swaying slowly in the clove-scented air.

"She's in Miss Wetherby's house right now," Mrs. Dockerty said.

I blinked slowly, trying to absorb this new piece of information. Miss Wetherby was the headmistress. She lived in Underhill House, a large brick house up behind Commons.

"The girls will be talking about it," Mrs. Dockerty said. "So, I wanted you to hear it from me first."

There followed a silence of an uncomfortable length while I thought about what I was supposed to say. Thank you? I'm sorry?

"I assume a family member will be coming to pick her up. I don't know exactly what the plans are. In any case, she'll certainly be gone for a while, but I'm not sure how long. A few days at least."

Up until this moment, I thought I had been following her, but at this last comment, I looked carefully at Mrs. Dockerty. "You'll have to collect up her homework for her," Mrs. Dockerty said.

"You mean . . . it wasn't Kat?"

"Oh, my dear, oh no . . . Kat's just fine—upset, of course, but that's to be expected. No dear . . . it's her father . . . Oh my, Jane, you must tell no one. It was not my place to tell you. If anyone asks you, say 'a death in the family' . . . Oh dear, Miss Wetherby will have my head . . ."

It wasn't until that moment that I burst into tears: wild, uncontrollable tears that could no doubt be heard well down the corridor.

Mrs. Dockerty seemed much put out by my newfound emotion. She muddled about me, patting my arm and handing me Kleenexes like a woman with a single bucket in front of a broken levee.

"Jane, please. You must get hold of yourself. For Katherine's sake. Now, please. It is your duty as her friend to see her through this." She handed me another Kleenex. I dabbed it at my eyes, but they were overflowing.

"She'll be coming back to get her things."

I thought of various ways to respond, but none seemed quite right.

"She's lucky that she has two such good friends in you and Lissa," Mrs. Dockerty said, patting my arm again. "Just keep a stiff upper lip for her, will you?" At that moment, I saw Mrs. Dockerty's eyes fill with tears, and she grabbed a wad of Kleenexes from the box. "Poor girl, the poor, poor dear . . ." And then she left the room.

A moment or two later, Lissa came in. "Killed himself, probably."

I affected knowingness. I had no idea what I was supposed to say in such a circumstance.

Kat came back from Miss Wetherby's to gather her things, stuffing some shirts and pants haphazardly into a laundry bag, but outside, the snowstorm had developed into a blizzard. Reports were trickling in that the roads were snowed in from here to Boston, and the road leading into the Grove remained empty. Even the butt room phone was stubbornly silent.

Kat sat on her bunk—arms wrapped around her legs, chin tucked down on her knees—and said nothing. Tears dripped down her face like someone had left a leaky faucet on, and she didn't bother to wipe them away. She didn't make a sound.

Early on, Mrs. Dockerty stopped by once or twice, rapping on the door so softly that the knock sounded insincere, stopping short of the threshold, calling out in a high, thin voice, "You girls making out okay in there?"

But then, as the hours passed, she stopped coming, and it was just the three of us. Lissa and I took turns going to Commons, folding napkins around bran muffins and buttered toast for Kat. The snacks collected untouched at the edge of my desk.

Finally, Lissa dragged me out into the stairwell.

"I'm calling my parents," she whispered.

"What good is that going to do?" I whispered back. Somehow, we knew that we needed to do something.

"I don't know, but her dad hung himself, and for all we know, he's still dangling from the barn rafters, frozen solid with his tongue sticking out, and Kat is sitting in there."

"Lissa!" I said.

"I'm serious!"

"Let's get Dockerty."

Lissa rolled her eyes. "And tell her what?"

"Tell her that Kat is catatonic," I said. I saw Katie Cornwell's door crack open a little. "Crap. It's Cornwell."

I knew that girls up and down the hall had figured out what was going on. I'd seen them meeting in Emma Doerr's room—2G. They were probably trying to get up the guts to send out a delegation.

Everybody knew that Kat hadn't been to a meal since the blizzard had started.

"I'm telling you, Lissa. We can't do anything."

Lissa stared at me with a look on her face that I had a hard time interpreting. Not anger, not even pity—more like dismissiveness. She left me sitting there in the hallway and walked down the stairs. I guess she must have called her parents, because the next morning, though there was close to a foot of snow, and the sky was still low and leaden, there was a silver-blue Mercedes parked outside Lane North.

Mr. and Mrs. Bronwen, dressed in matching outfits like they were on their way to a ski weekend in Killington, only stayed for a few minutes. I was watching out the window from 2B. I saw Mrs. Dockerty shutting the car door and waving the three of them off.

The next time I saw Kat was three days later. When she came back, she looked like her usual self, except that she was unusually pale. She was sitting at her desk when I came in late Tuesday afternoon after swimming practice; my hair was frozen from walking home while it was still wet. Kat's hair was drawn back in a loose ponytail, and she was working on something; there was a circle of yellow light on her paper, from the desk lamp. The rest of the room was dark. She looked up when she saw me, but she was deep in thought, so her expression was a little absent. Kat's eyes were a clear hazel. She looked at me without animosity, without joy.

"Jane," she said.

I remember wondering, right then, if I should say something to her—something about her father's death, or about how I was sorry for her loss. But I felt embarrassed. I was shy, unsure exactly what to say, and so I said nothing. After that, the time just never seemed right again.

17

The Pencott plan was simple. Kat would stay in the library after closing, hiding in the bathroom stall, "Just like Claudia and Jamie in *From The Mixed-Up Files of Mrs. Basil E. Frankweiler*."

It was Thursday night; we were in our rooms for study hall. We were planning the library lock-in for Friday night.

"How could you never have heard of that book?" Kat said. "It's one of the best books ever."

Lissa flipped her hair over her head and then flipped it back. "Look, can we get this over with? I want to finish my homework. If we do it, I'm going to invite Josh."

The mention of Josh got my attention. "I thought you guys broke up." I tried to keep my voice neutral.

She shrugged. "I broke up with him. We're still friends. He's coming for visiting hours. I don't think he's over me yet."

"Jane likes him," Kat said.

I felt my face turning red. "Who said that?"

Lissa gave me a withering look. "He hardly seems your type."

"I never said I liked him," I protested. Of course it wasn't true. I'd had a thing for Josh since the first time I saw him sophomore year. I'd been his friend before Lissa even knew him. But Lissa invited him to our Sadie Hawkins dance—and I pretended not to care. I told myself that she didn't know I liked him. It hurt most that she didn't even seem to like him that much—she kept batting him around like a cat playing with a mouse.

"We're just friends," I said, knowing she could hear the huffiness in my voice.

Kat was sitting at my desk with her books open in front of her. I was on my bunk with the clue notebook, making elaborate notes in the Plans section. My backpack was still zipped shut next to my chair.

"Soooo," Kat said, "back to getting locked inside Pencott Library."

"Just like Claudia and Jamie," I said.

"Does everything have to be just like something out of some book we've never even heard of?" Lissa said. I thought back to freshman year, when we had jumped off the huge poplar that hung over the river, "just like in *A Separate Peace*," and looked for treasure in empty tree trunks, just like Jem and Scout in *To Kill a Mockingbird*. That was before boyfriends, before taking our SATs, before really understanding that we'd be thrust back out of the gates of the Grove before we knew it—at that time, our imaginations had been enough.

"I read *From the Mixed-Up Files of Mrs. Basil E. Frankweiler*," I said. "It was good."

"That must have been while you were watching *The Brady Bunch*, Lissa," Kat said.

"Shut up," Lissa said. "At least we had a TV and I didn't grow up in some weird rural commune in Vermont with a bunch of trust-fund beatniks who can't be left alone with razor blades."

Lissa said it the way she said everything—very offhanded. She always gave the impression that she was born with a divine right to say whatever she wanted. I didn't move. I watched Kat; she was sitting at her desk, and I could only see the side of her head. This was the first time since she'd gotten back from wherever she had gone that any of us mentioned anything about it.

Kat was sitting very still—so still that she hardly seemed to be breathing.

She turned to Lissa really slowly and stared at her; a moment later, she started laughing. It was a tight, high-pitched laugh, like when you're with a bunch of people who are high and you pretend to be high too, but you aren't, and everybody knows it. Kat stood up on her chair, lightning fast. She was small and agile, like a gymnast, graceful and compact. With her two hands, she feigned making a slipknot, and then, pulling it up quickly, her head jerked, her tongue lolling out to the side.

I stared in horror.

She opened her eyes, mere slits.

"You mean you fell for that story?" she said.

Then, just as quickly, she sat down again, flipped open her French book, and started reading. I remember even now what she was reading. I approached her hesitantly and looked over her shoulder, so aghast that it was the only thing I could think of to do. She was reading the first few lines from the excerpt in our French textbook from Sartre: *Huis Clos. No Exit.* She studied her book intently, making it clear that our conversation was over.

I don't know how Kat amused herself in Pencott between Friday night closing at 8:00 p.m. and 10:30 p.m., when I snuck out of Lane North. Pencott was dark, and as I walked up the marble steps, I found myself doubting that Kat was inside. The double front doors were made of polished golden oak, inlaid with wavy beveled glass windows. The steps were icy; I grasped the brass railing. At the top, I waited, peering tentatively through the glass. I tried the doorknob. It was old-fashioned brass, heavy and solid, and it slipped inside my mittened hand, still locked. I pressed my nose up against the glass. It was cold and my breath doubled back, warm in my eyes. The glass fogged up. I blinked and drew my head away.

A white face bobbed up directly in front of me behind the glass. The face disappeared, then reappeared again, and the door opened.

"Where's Lissa?"

Now, I could see that it was Kat.

"You startled me."

"Sorry. Come on in."

"Why don't you just leave the door unlocked?"

"Are they coming?"

The way she posed the question, it made my arrival feel anticlimactic. I shrugged. "I guess."

Kat led the way into the dark interior of the library. When I entered the reading room, I saw that she had lit a torch—a large silver flashlight—and propped it in the corner of the room so that, like a party lantern, it cast a glow over the room. There was a yearbook lying open on one of the large tables.

"Did you find the yearbook with Miss Pymstead in it?"

"1961? No," she said.

In the open book, I saw rows of pictures, but as I got closer, I realized that they were portraits of sober boys lined up in coats and ties. Why boys? I scanned the faces for a trace of something familiar—it was an old Hardley yearbook, black-and-white photos, all the boys with their neatly parted hair and jackets and ties; they didn't look anything like Hardley boys now. I moved around the table and looked at the open page, studying the rows of portraits. That's when I realized what I was looking at:

Winslow Cavendish Cunningham '56
Drama I, II, Crew II, III, IV, Ivy Society III, IV, Bell Prize for Poetry

The face was narrow with fine features, fair hair that swept across a high forehead. His expression was sweet and very young-looking. I looked at Kat. Tears stained her face, glowing in the half-light.

"About my father," she said. "It's not what you think."

"Tell me," I said.

"He was in McLean," her voice was hushed, dramatic. I didn't know what she meant when she said "McLean" until she mentioned James Taylor. She was referring to the famous psychiatric hospital outside Boston.

"They were there at the same time for a while . . . ," she said. "I saw James Taylor once, during visiting hours. He looked awful. His hair was really short. It was after his breakup with Carly."

We sat down, side by side and alone in that dark library. Tears were dripping down her face, and her fingers were twisting in and out of each other.

I leaned in. I listened carefully. "But I thought . . ."

Kat could see that she had my attention now, so she leaned in closer, wiping a few tears from her eyes. "That's where he met Sylvia too . . . Before—the first time he was there . . ."

I fished down, deep in my pocket, and found an old Kleenex. I handed it to her. She swabbed away her tears, but a few more fell onto the table, where they glistened like rhinestones.

I hated it when I had to ask dumb questions around Kat, but my desire to seem knowing was outweighed by my desire to know. "Sylvia who?"

Kat slid the yearbook in front of her then, brushing her fingertip lightly along the page, resting when it got to the picture of her father.

"She was his first love . . ." She paused. "And it must have been true love, because the Thorazine made her drool, and it made her hands shake—and they cut her hair . . ."

"Sylvia who?"

Kat slowly turned her gaze toward me—away from the page in front of her, toward me.

"*Red hair? Eating men like air?*" she said.

"I beg your pardon?"

"'*Lady Lazarus*?'"

My puzzled look must have shown that I had no idea what she was talking about.

"Sylvia *Plath*," Kat said. "And you know, the thing about her is that people want to be just like her—win the *Mademoiselle* fiction-writing contest and get married to Ted Hughes—so much that they overlook the teeny-tiny little detail that she had to kill herself to gain immortality."

She rested her cheek on the smooth page of the yearbook and kept it there for a moment.

"Good-bye, Daddy," she finally said. I must have been looking at her oddly because she then kind of snapped at me. "Look, Jane, don't sweat it. You wouldn't understand."

I stood up and put my arms around her. "It's okay, Kat. Whatever you have to do." I felt very grown-up then.

Lissa and Josh arrived a few minutes later. They brought with them two large flashlights and the scent of pot. Lissa banged her army surplus bag on the table, and it tinkled with its cache of minibottles. The ambience started to seem more like a party. Josh was carrying a pillowcase, and when he opened it up, there was Kat's green portable record player and a stack of albums.

"Do you really think that's a good idea?" I said.

Josh was shining a flashlight around the room—up toward the high ceilings, where murals that depicted the story of *The Decision of Paris* surrounded an imitation night sky. The paintings were clouded and in need of repair, and the ornate ceiling was peeling and yellowed with age.

"Wow, you Grove girls have some pretty fancy digs here. Hardley's library is nothing like this," he said, making a sweeping gesture at the peeling domed ceiling, which may have once looked like the sky over Siberia but now looked more like the bottom of Echo Lake.

"Yeah, but it's falling apart," Lissa said. "They'll never have the money to fix it."

I noticed that Lissa was wearing Kat's most worn-out pair of jeans, the ones with the embroidered butterflies on the pockets. They were a little too small for her, which showed off the curve of her butt. Her hair was pulled up in a ponytail. She had taken out her contacts and was wearing glasses.

Josh was wearing a blue bandana twisted into a headband and tied in back; his hair was wavy and brushed his shoulders. He had taken off his blue down jacket—it looked just like Kat's and mine—and he was wearing a Head of the Charles T-shirt. His maleness seemed so out of place in the Grove library that I could almost see an aura around him, pulsating electric blue.

Kat started to flip through the albums one by one, then piled them on the table. *The Dark Side of the Moon* was on top, then *Pretzel Logic*. I saw Patti Smith, Dan Fogelberg, Queen, and Fleetwood Mac. Josh dug around in his army-navy rucksack and put an assortment of things on the library table: a pipe, some Zig-Zag papers, a smushed copy of *Walden*, and one dirty athletic sock.

Kat was shining a flashlight around, looking for an outlet.

I stood next to the table, flipping through the stack of albums. I held each cardboard sleeve between my hands. The decision seemed fraught with a thousand perils: choosing the right soundtrack would determine exactly how the night would unfold. Lissa slid *Rumours* out of its sleeve. Balancing it between the palms of her hands, she placed it on the silver nub of the turntable. The music started pounding, and Lissa reached into the rucksack, pulling out bottles and lining them up on the table.

We sat underneath one of the library tables. Josh carefully filled the bowl of the pipe, lit it, and passed it around. I sucked in the fruited smoke. My eyes watered and I coughed a little, and the next time the pipe came around, I let it pass. Lissa and Josh were sitting separately, not touching. I was trying to read what was up with the two of them. I couldn't tell if he was still into her or not. Lissa passed one small bottle around and then another. After a while, Kat stood up and changed the record. I heard Patti Smith singing. I tried not to seem like I was staring at Josh. He had a crooked smile and single dimple, and every time I caught his eye, he grinned. But after a few minutes, Lissa reached across and slipped her hand into his, and they stood up together. She leaned in, whispered something in his ear, and led him to the window seat below the big bay window. Soon, I could hear small *uffs* and sighs, and denim rubbing on denim. Kat was sitting cross-legged on the floor, hands folded loosely around a fifth of Jack Daniel's that had materialized from somewhere. Patti Smith was singing "Redondo Beach." Kat's head was bobbing, the flashlight's glow softly illuminating the curls around the nape of her neck.

I picked up the flashlight from the floor next to Kat and walked into the shadowy stacks.

The old Grove yearbooks were housed on dusty shelves under the big arched windows that looked out on the fields stretching down toward the river. It was a dark night—there were a few clouds and pinpoints of stars. I pushed open the heavy fire escape door to get a breath of fresh air. The air was a stiff metallic cold that bit my cheeks, startling me alert. From this vantage point, the only building on campus that could be seen was Wooten Boathouse, black as a bruise along the banks of the river. Beyond the river, I could see the Hardley campus: darkened shadows with scattered dots of light.

I closed the door, hearing it click softly, then turned the yellow beam of the flashlight toward the low, dusty shelves where the yearbooks were lined up, not quite straight. I ran my fingers along the spines. The older ones looked different from the more recent ones. There were several different sizes and styles. All of them were called *The Lantern*. I ran the flashlight beam along the spines, locating the 1960s. 1962. 1963. I saw that 1961 was missing, like the hole in a gap-toothed smile. I sat down in front of the low bookshelf. First, I shone the flashlight beam, set the light on the floor, and then poked my finger in the gap. I felt a presence beside me and turned, expecting to see Lissa or Kat, but it was Josh.

"What are you doing?"

"Where's Lissa?"

"She fell asleep," he said. "What are you looking for?"

I debated telling him. The flashlight beam glowed up from beside me, illuminating his face, lighting up his high cheekbones. His lips had a bruised, just-kissed look. My stomach flipped. I swallowed my saliva.

"Nothing."

He picked up the flashlight, shone it at the shelves. "What are these? Old yearbooks?"

He was balancing on his haunches and his knee brushed one of mine.

I shrugged, but it was dark, so he probably couldn't see me.

"Let me see . . ." The beam of the flashlight bobbed along the shelf; it caught the gap where 1961 should have been, but I doubt he even noticed. To me, it looked like a chasm.

I reached forward and slid out the volume with the embossed '60 on the spine.

He leaned closer to me. I could feel his hot breath tickling my neck.

"Are you looking for something?"

I shook my head, but I cracked open the volume anyway, settling down on my bottom and crossing my legs in front of me, shining the flashlight at the smooth pages, covered with black-and-white photos.

The Grove in 1960 looked no different from the Grove now, except for the girls. In 1960, they all wore the prim hairdos I associated with my mother. There were pictures of them walking in twos and threes across Siberia, their textbooks cradled in their arms.

"Did you know that the headmaster of the Grove was murdered in 1961?"

"Chestmont Wooten? Yeah, I've heard of him. He was headmaster of Hardley before he went to Grove. They never found out who did it, right?"

I closed the volume and then opened it again, leafing through the pages from the front. Three or four pages in, there was a full-page black-and-white portrait: *Chester Montgomery "Chestmont" Wooten, Deerfield Academy '37, Harvard College '42*

I felt a jolt of electricity. "That's him," I said.

I studied the picture. Josh leaned in a little closer, letting the tip of his index finger brush the page for just a moment. Chestmont Wooten was just as I had pictured him: dark haired and sober-looking. I thought of Miss Wetherby, with her yearly lectures on mental hygiene, her habit of inviting members of the Latin Honor Society to tea in Underhill House, at which she served sweet-onion sandwiches, with mayonnaise, on white bread. It would have been a lot different to have this movie-star handsome man as headmaster.

"What do you think of him?" I asked.

"I dunno," Josh said. "Jesus, I think I gotta go. What time is it?"

I shone the flashlight on my watch. It was almost midnight.

"I gotta hoof it out to the front gate. A kid from Hampshire is giving me a ride back to Hardley."

Josh was a little unsteady. He placed one hand on my shoulder to balance himself as he stood up.

Then, when standing, he leaned over and kissed the top of my head.

I looked up at him.

"What was that for?"

"For next time," he said.

I scrambled to my feet, but he had already slipped out the emergency exit and was walking unsteadily down the hill, his form submerging in the shadows. For half a second, I thought about running after him—but he had already disappeared.

I sat down again and flipped quickly through the pages of the yearbook. There was no Amanda Pymstead in the freshman class, no Amanda Pymstead in the sophomore class. The junior class was seated as a group on the lawn in front of Pencott on a sunny day, their skirts spread out around them, their faces no more than blurry dots. I scanned the names, below the group shot: Addison, L.; Whitcomb, E.; James, T.—and then there it was, Pymstead, A. So, if she was a junior in 1960, then she was a senior girl in 1961. I stood up and quickly flipped back to the full-page picture of Chestmont Wooten. When I held the book up to get a better look at his face, something fluttered against my leg and fell to the ground.

I bent over and shone my flashlight on the floor, but I didn't see anything. I set the yearbook down on the wide window ledge and got down on my hands and knees, shining my flashlight on the floor again, but I still didn't see anything . . . at first. Then, I noticed a thin piece of paper, creased and folded.

I grasped it with my fingertips and unfolded it.

"Kat!" My voice sounded loud in the empty library. "Lissa!"

I heard a shuffling and a bumping of tables and chairs, and a moment later, Kat was beside me.

The light from the flashlight shone through the thin paper so that the script was illuminated.

> *Delayed till she had ceased to know,*
> *Delayed till in its vest of snow*
> *Her loving bosom lay.*
> *An hour behind the fleeting breath,*
> *Later by just an hour than death,—*
> *Oh, lagging yesterday!*

Lissa was too busy feeling the aftereffects of the party to notice the paper. She started to heave, so I quickly pushed the emergency door open for her.

She vomited hard from the metal fire steps into the snow, and that seemed to revive her a little. Kat was little the worse for wear. She was examining the paper. It was onionskin typewriter paper, and the poem had been handwritten in ballpoint ink.

Of course, I recognized the handwriting: it was Miss Pymstead's.

Before replacing the yearbook on the shelf, I tore out the picture of Chestmont Wooten, leaving a jagged gap in its place.

We gathered up the detritus of our night—empty bottles, Josh's forgotten albums, the record player. I folded up the paper and put it inside the clue notebook, along with the picture of Chestmont Wooten.

I don't even remember climbing in a window to reenter Lane North that night. The parts of our rule breaking that had once seemed thrilling had gotten dull, but the murder of Chestmont Wooten was now so real to me that I could see it like a film reel spinning in my head.

18

I can't quite remember now if it was before or after Lantern Day when
I realized that Kat was spending time with Miss Pymstead outside of
class. In the late afternoons, Miss Pymstead occupied a carrel in the
reading room at Pencott. Lissa was on the basketball team, and Kat had
studio art, so I had taken to studying at that time. I would pick a spot at
the far end of the reading room, and I would observe her. There was a
small brass lamp with a green shade at the carrel where she sat. She cor-
rected student papers and paged through well-worn copies of the texts
that we used in class. I carried the clue notebook with me. I thumbed
through the meager collection of notes, reread the puzzling poems, and
sometimes, driven to boredom, I actually did my homework. Then,
one day, when Miss Pymstead stood and gathered her things, I waited
a suitable moment before following her.

Miss Pymstead walked at a brisk pace. The sun was setting behind
Founder's Hill, casting pink and purple reflections across the expanses
of brittle snow. It was almost dark now. Sports practices were in session,
and girls clad in thick sweats, with bandanas tied over their faces, jogged
past in twos and threes. When Miss Pymstead took the pathway that

headed toward Gould Cottage, I cut behind, climbing up the snowy hill toward Siberia. From there, I could see the front door and bay windows of her apartment, which was actually the back part of Gould Cottage but could only be reached by a separate entrance.

It was somewhat isolated, around the back—with no other faculty housed in the building. There were no pathways behind Gould Cottage except for the one that led to her front door, so there was little occasion to pass by her windows by accident—though sometimes we'd traverse the hill in front of them when out sledding on a winter afternoon.

Miss Pymstead reached into her bag and groped around for her keys, unlocked the door, then turned on the light. I watched as she pushed inside and laid her satchel on a table. I was crouching on snow, and though I had long underwear under my jeans, I could feel the cold creeping through, along with a realization my spying on her was veering toward odd—odder even than keeping watch in the library had been.

There was a large bay window at the front of Miss Pymstead's apartment. I looked on as she unwrapped her scarf, and took off her coat. The sky was darkening, the purple rays fading, the river shading from mauve to brown as I crouched there in the snow, my knees stiff. Miss Pymstead was lighting a fire. I could see her laying the logs in the hearth, crumpling newspaper, lighting a long match that set a bright blaze. At that moment, I startled, because someone was moving down the walkway. From my vantage point, I wasn't sure who it was: puffy North Face jacket, woolly hat, Bean boots—we all looked more or less alike at a distance.

Miss Pymstead opened the door, and even from a distance, I saw the look of delight on her face—a genuine smile, a smile of welcome.

As Kat walked into Miss Pymstead's apartment, I stood up, brushed the snow from my knees, and ran, stiff legged, down the path. The dinner bell was clanging before I made it all the way across Siberia.

Kat's mother, being an old Grove girl, came every year for Lantern Day.

"Oh, there you are, dear," she said. She was alone, sitting on my bed when I came in, and she jumped up, grabbing my chin with her knobby fingers and kissing me on both cheeks. Kat's mother was so thin, you could almost see through her, and she smelled like perfume, cold fur, and stale cigarettes.

"Hello, Mrs. Cunningham," I said.

"Oh, Jane dear, *please* don't call me *Mrs. Cunningham*—it makes me feel *dreadfully* old." She shoved her hand into her battered Hermès leather bag and drew out a pack of crumpled Chesterfields, tapping out a cigarette on the palm of her hand.

"Mrs. Cunningham."

"Jane, dear, if you could please just bring yourself to call me *Keach*. Just humor an old lady, would you?" She put the cigarette up to her lips. I could see a trace of a tremor as she did so.

"Mrs.—um, *Keach* . . . I don't think you should smoke up here. It's a fire hazard."

Keach Cunningham tipped her head back, laughed, and flicked her silver lighter, drawing hard on the cigarette, then blowing out smoke rings in a gesture that might have resembled Kat were she not so ravaged-looking, and were her lipstick not a bit crooked, and flecked on her teeth.

She winked at me. "Not to worry. Your secrets are safe with me, Jane dear. I'm not so old that I don't remember what it is to be young, after all. My roommate, Gail Cadwalader, and I used to smoke right out the bathroom window all during our senior year. And do you know who the housemother was that year?"

I shook my head.

"Miss Wetherby! She never said a word, just invited us over now and then to eat those disgusting sweet-onion sandwiches." She inhaled again, long and slow. "Soaked in vinegar and spread with mayonnaise," she said in a high-pitched mimicking voice.

I was trying to imagine Keach as a teenager—trying to imagine her pretty, and wondering if she might have looked anything like Kat. But it was hard. From a distance, checking her with a squint, Keach Cunningham looked good, but up close, her roots had grown out and her lipstick was two shades too bright.

"You know what I think?" she said, leaning in closer so that she now blew smoke right into my face.

"I think Miss Wetherby was just trying to make us fat, hoping that one of us would stay on with her." She winked at me. "You know what I mean? As a *female companion* . . . ?"

I scooted away from her a little. I glanced at the door, wishing that Kat would come, that Lissa would come. I was trying to think of something to say when the door swung open.

"Someone is smoking in here." Abigail Von Platte stood in the doorway.

Keach Cunningham stood up, stubbing out the cigarette with elaborate slowness on an empty soda can at the edge of my desk. She walked over to the window, grappled with the heavy sash, shoved it open with her matchstick arms, and tossed the can. The three of us could hear the faint rattling as it landed. She then sat on the window ledge, teetering as she pulled the window down. She brushed her hands together as if to say, *That's that.* The whole time, Abigail Von Platte stood like a tree stump, her feet planted in the doorway.

"There you are, no cigarettes. Are you satisfied now?" Keach said.

"It's against the rules," Abigail said.

"Young lady, it's against Grove rules to be ugly. Didn't anyone tell you that?"

Abigail's face crumpled in horrified surprise, and I felt my stomach churning at Keach's cruelty, yet I was reluctant to jump to Abigail's defense.

The ringing bells in Whittaker Chapel broke the silence—time for the students and visitors to assemble for tea with Miss Wetherby at Underhill House. Keach Cunningham waved her hand as though she had forgotten it no longer held a lit cigarette. "Now, run along. I've heard that Miss Wetherby is serving sweet-onion sandwiches in Underhill House."

Whether to save face or not, I didn't know, but at last Abigail said, "I like those onion sandwiches," and she shut the door, leaving me and Mrs. Cunningham giggling in something that felt like complicity.

Mrs. Cunningham rummaged around in her purse again and threw a fifth of Wild Turkey down on the bed.

"Have fun," she said. "And don't do anything I wouldn't do."

It wasn't until after she left that I realized I hadn't said a word about Mr. Cunningham. I wasn't quite sure what one said to one's roommate's mother about her semi-estranged, half-crazy husband who committed suicide by (maybe) hanging himself from the barn rafters in Vermont. And yet, it seemed like I should have said something. I wished I could ask someone for advice. I wished that it were me and not Kat who was being invited into Gould Cottage to sit near those crowded bookshelves next to that fire. I could ask Miss Pymstead questions then. Questions like, what do you say to your roommate's mother when you think her husband committed suicide but nobody is talking?

Old Grove girls were heading in twos and threes toward Whittaker Chapel. You could see them as they gathered under their lantern-shaped banners inscribed with their class years: 1920s, 1930s, 1940s. Grove girls got older, and thinner and grayer, but otherwise didn't change much. The serious among them had gone into teaching; the most brilliant proudly showed off the bare hands of Bryn Mawr and Radcliffe professors— their hands free of wedding rings, their brains stuffed with Greek, Latin, and chemistry. The beautiful ones had kept their perfect bone structure, their snow-white hair held by a few bobby pins into flyaway buns, their bright blue eyes dancing in the January sun.

Kat, Lissa, and I joined the throng of current students, shuffling along at the rear of the group. Kat was skipping, singing Patti Smith under her breath. She was wearing Chinese dime-store slippers, which had gotten wet around the edges, and pale pink ballet tights.

As we settled into the pews, the first rich notes of the organ filled the chapel, and I recognized the opening to the hymn "Jerusalem." I glanced over at Lissa. She had brought along her history notes and was studying.

From where I was sitting, I could see the hunched form of an old girl from the class of 1928, her feet, in brown orthopedic shoes, supported on the silver rests of her wheelchair.

After an interminable paean to Eugenia Wilcox—one of the school's most illustrious alumna, a missionary who had traveled all over Africa just after Stanley and Livingstone—had ended, Miss Wetherby explained that the student oration was an honor bestowed upon a senior girl by a senior teacher, and all the old Grove girls stirred in their seats in anticipation. "The Lantern Day student orator: Miss Katherine Winslow Cunningham. Chosen for Excellence in English Literature by Miss Amanda Pymstead."

I kicked Lissa. She looked up from her notes. She arched one eyebrow, shrugged. I studied her face for traces of envy but saw none, which infuriated me. I kicked Katie Cornwell on the other side of me. She shrugged too, but in a way that was much more satisfactory. She whispered, "Everybody knows that Pymstead has the hots for her—it's obvious . . ."

I mulled that over. That particular thought hadn't occurred to me until she said it. Did Pymstead have the hots for Kat? I remembered Kat slipping into her lodgings. It gave me an uncomfortable feeling—half thrill, half nausea.

I slouched in my seat and felt the hard back of the pew against my spine. Kat, whose hair was braided in one long plait, walked demurely up the three steps at the front of Whittaker Chapel. At first I thought that she was wearing a small white dress, but as I looked more closely, I realized that the dress was made out of a flour sack that said on it: *This flour is a gift to the Kingdom of Morocco from the United States of America.* I recognized the sack. It had been a door prize of sorts from Brandon Barnes, the Hardley hashish dealer. He passed them out to his biggest customers—it was chic to make them into shirts and dresses. Kind of an inside joke.

Our group tittered when we saw what she was wearing, and Ariel Steinmetz, the school's official Rastafarian, jumped up and sang a couple of bars of Bob Marley before Miss Benway, the field hockey coach, got in her face and silenced her.

Kat walked to the pulpit, self-contained and graceful, but I saw in her composure the look of a cat ready to pounce, and I noticed that the girls in our section had stilled in anticipation.

She had a notebook in her hand, and she opened it and laid it on the pulpit.

The old Grove girls sat in silent anticipation, waiting to welcome her into their world, waiting to hear what she had to say.

"It is an honor," Kat said, "to have been chosen to give the student recitation on Lantern Day." There was a smattering of applause around the chapel, and as though born to speak in front of crowds, Kat paused, looking around the room with quiet assurance.

"My teacher, Miss Pymstead, told me that I should choose to read something that best represents my experience here at the Grove. This was a difficult choice, as it is hard to represent one thing with another," she said.

Kat sounded older than her years. Her voice was sensible, her words well chosen. I wondered if I would have done so well. I burned that I had not been given the chance. "For the oration today, I've chosen to read a poem by Emily Dickinson." She began to read, her voice as bell-like as the pipes of the organ, which, according to school lore, were once the finest organ pipes to be found west of Boston. *A solemn thing it was, I said—/ A woman white to be . . .*

My breath caught when I realized that she was reading the poem that we had found on the boathouse wall. My eyes darted toward Miss Pymstead, who stood near the doorway with a half smile on her face, her expression impossible to read.

The Grove girls, young and old, sat silent for a full minute after Kat finished the last line, as though they were not quite sure she was finished. Then, a smattering of polite applause followed.

Kat waited until the applause ended, and then she said, "Thank you very much. I'd just like to say that I don't think that twenty years from now there will still be a Lantern Day. Eugenia Wilcox was nothing more than an imperialist. And you can't call the Grove a Christian institution anymore—lots of the students are Jews, Parvaneh and Maryam are Muslims, and even the ones who used to be Christians . . . Well, we're just playing at it. I say turn the chapel into a snack bar, you know—or something useful. Right now, all we do inside this chapel is either get stoned or make out with Hardley boys."

You could hear the surprised *Oh my, oh mys* circulating through the room until the sound of one person clapping took over. From somewhere in the back of the room, Miss Pymstead stood up. "Sometimes it takes youth to speak the truth, ladies. I say we say brava to the young lady for her courage."

I'll never know whether more of the old Grove girls would have decided to "say brava to the young lady for her courage" because Miss Wetherby was gesticulating wildly to the organist, and now the first bars of the Grove Academy song were playing. White hankies to wave came out of purses faster than you can say, "the Grove will stand forever," and soon the walls of Whittaker Chapel were ringing with voices young and old (but mostly old, because some of the young had never quite learned the words to the song).

> *Though she may quit these gates some day,*
> *In deep Grove's heart she'll always stay.*
> *If she graces halls of learning, or she toils in hearth and home,*
> *Wheresoever goes a Grove girl, the Grove is always home.*

At this last, hundreds of eyes filled with tears, and hundreds of heads—some snow-white, some silver, some salt-and-pepper, some brown—swayed back and forth as we waved our hankies and surrendered to the Grove. For me, it didn't help to blink hard. It didn't help to tell myself that I was surrendering to mass hypnosis, or to remember, as Kat was always telling us, that this was all just a big stage play to get the blue-haired ladies to part with their money. I just couldn't be as cynical as that. I was embarrassed to admit that I loved the Grove school song.

19

After winter break, everything changed. Suddenly, it seemed that we had turned a corner, and our days in the Grove, which had once seemed to stretch before us as endlessly as the winter-clad fields of Siberia, now seemed to narrow toward a definite point on the not-so-distant horizon. Just a few days after winter break, I was summoned to tea with Miss Wetherby at Underhill House. It was rumored that students sometimes received private invitations but there was something vaguely hush-hush about those occasions. So, when I found a large square envelope of heavy, cream-colored stationery inside my post office box, I pried open the wax seal and studied the Grove insignia on the envelope, wondering what lay inside. I didn't wonder long though, as Kat happened by.

"Oh, look at you. You're practically old Grove now . . . ," she said.

Even three and a half years into my Grove career, I still hated it when she let me know that a girl from Michigan still didn't quite know the code.

Underhill House was a square brick building with black shutters; I had always found it quite elegant. I stood before the door, hesitating. I was a few minutes early and I heard no sounds from within. I grasped the doorknocker, heavy brass in the form of a lion's head, and let it fall twice with a heavy thud.

In no time, Miss Wetherby swung the door open.

"Oh, hello there, Jane, right on time. Please come in."

Miss Wetherby showed me into the drawing room, but it wasn't until she had seated me in a wing-back chair near the fireplace and I saw that tea was set for two that I realized that this was to be a private conversation.

Miss Wetherby poured tea into Grove Academy china cups. I poured cream into mine and dropped in a lump of sugar. When I stirred the sugar, my spoon made a nice pinging sound on the delicate china.

"So, tell me a little bit about what interests you, Jane," Miss Wetherby said.

I stared down at my cup. The cream was so heavy that it had formed a swirling pattern. I disliked this kind of question, as I could never seem to come up with an answer. Right now, the only interest that was coming to mind was my curiosity about the identity of Chestmont Wooten's murderer. Here I was in the home that he had once lived in. I wondered whether he had perhaps taken his tea before this very fire . . .

"Jane?"

"Poetry," I said.

"Poetry." I saw from the smile that played on Miss Wetherby's lips that I had given a suitable answer.

"In particular, the poems of Emily Dickinson," I said.

Miss Wetherby was a small woman, rather petite in all her dimensions except for her rounded stomach and her breasts—and when I mentioned Emily Dickinson, those breasts began to heave in so overheated a manner that she reached down between them and pulled out a handkerchief, which she used to momentarily fan herself.

Once having regained her composure, she jumped up and said, "Oh, but my dear, my own passion for Emily Dickinson is absolutely unmatched. Oh, but I have a lovely edition of her collected poems here somewhere. Quite a rare edition. From a very small printing."

By this time, she had jumped up and was perusing a floor-to-ceiling bookshelf that ran the entire length of the wall on both sides of the fireplace and across the top of it as well.

I sat sipping my tea, wishing that I had thought of another topic of interest—French, perhaps, or Sylvia Plath. I was still unsure about the purpose of this meeting.

"I wonder if I have loaned it out and not remembered," she said. "Although it is such a prized volume of mine that I would think I would remember . . . Oh well, no matter. I'll keep my eyes out for it, and just as soon as I find it, I'll summon you back. But perhaps you could share with me which of the poems is your favorite?"

I felt like a fly under a microscope; I was unsure what to say.

"'I heard a fly buzz when I died,'" I said after some moments of silence.

"Really?" Miss Wetherby said, wrinkling her pudgy nose. "That is one of my less favorites. I do much prefer many of the others. In any case, Jane, Miss Pymstead has informed me that you are a gifted student. You know that we have a tradition of sending our students at Grove to the best women's colleges. Recently, there has been a trend for Grove girls to want to attend the men's colleges. I can't imagine why. Yale is full of a bunch of drunken frat boys who think the gentleman's C is the route to all the glory in this world. The women's colleges are places of serious purpose and scholarly study, much more suitable for a person of your talents." She looked at me thoughtfully. I sat up a little straighter.

"I'd like you to strongly consider my alma mater," she said. "Bryn Mawr. Bryn Mawr is, in actual fact, what Harvard and Yale pretend to be. According to Miss Pymstead, you have the makings of a scholar."

In spite of myself, I felt a small thrill.

Miss Wetherby opened a drawer in the table next to her chair and pulled out a pair of reading glasses, which she perched on the end of her nose. Then, from the chest behind her, she picked up a manila folder, which appeared to be a file that contained information about me, presumably my report cards and test scores and such.

She flipped pages while I sat in squirmy silence and watched her. Occasionally, she made small evaluative sounds: *hmms* and small grunts.

"Do you have a first-choice college?"

"Yale?" I said, my voice so small that I could barely hear myself speak.

"Speak up, my dear. A young woman should state her mind in tones as crisp as a ringing bell."

"Yale?"

Miss Wetherby pulled her glasses a little farther down the bridge of her nose. She perused the pages in silence for what seemed to be an eternity longer. Finally, she closed the folder, laid it back down on the shelf, removed the glasses, and put them back in the drawer.

"More tea, Jane?"

Without waiting for a reply, Miss Wetherby poured more tea into my cup, swished in some more cream, and dropped in two lumps of sugar, one at a time.

"Jane."

"Yes?"

"Yale admitted its first class that included women in 1969."

I nodded.

"That year, seven girls applied from Grove, and all seven were admitted."

I nodded again.

"This year, Yale's freshman class will probably be almost half girls. Those girls will be bright, talented, and have a variety of skills." I had nothing to say, so I kept my mouth shut.

Miss Wetherby pinched the bridge of her nose, rubbing the spot where her glasses had been. "It is likely that none of those girls will have flunked French in the fall term of their senior year."

My stomach flipped.

"However," she said, her tone bright, "you never know. Yale loves Grove girls, and you are still third in the class, even with that one little lapse in your grades, which have otherwise, as you know, been impeccable. The point is that you are the kind of girl that the Grove has traditionally sent to Bryn Mawr. We would be thrilled to see you go to Bryn Mawr. To see a woman of your talents end up among the do-nothings at Yale—quite frankly it would be—"

I could see that something over my shoulder had caught Miss Wetherby's eye, because she interrupted herself, jumping up so quickly that she knocked into her wing chair, which wobbled, threatening to upset the tea table.

"And then, here it is!" she said. "Ta-da!" Miss Wetherby grabbed the wheeled library ladder, pushed it so that it was directly in front of the fireplace, and climbed up the four steps. She stood on her tippy-toes, and I noticed that her skirt was dangling dangerously close to the open fire. But just in time, she grabbed a small, dark brown leather volume and brandished it in the air, shaking it in triumph.

As she did so, a single leaf of paper floated out of it and was sucked inward by the draft from the fireplace. I jumped out of my seat so fast that I upset the tea table entirely.

Miss Wetherby was so startled by my sudden movement that she teetered dangerously on the ladder, and I had to grab hold of her to keep her from falling into the fire. Once I had righted her, I rushed back to right the teapot, which was leaking onto the Oriental rug.

"Oh, I'm so sorry. I'm really, really sorry," I said, attempting to dab at the hot water with the sleeve of my shirt.

"But it is I who should be sorry, Jane. I was so awkward to lose my balance like that. If you hadn't grabbed me, I would surely have fallen into the fire."

I realized that Miss Wetherby was so flustered that she had not seen the escaping piece of paper.

I stayed about fifteen more minutes while she showed me the Emily Dickinson book. It was a nice volume, leather bound with fine printed pages. But the light was waning through the tall drawing-room windows; the fire had died down, and with it the liveliness of our conversation.

I was ready to leave, but I had the impression that Miss Wetherby was trying to draw out the visit by asking me more and more questions about schoolwork and my friends and activities. I watched with growing alarm as shadows overtook the room. By inches, I squirmed my way toward the front of the chair, studying Miss Wetherby's face to see if she had noticed that I was preparing to leave, but she gave no sign.

At last, I stood up and stuck my hand out.

"Thank you so much, Miss Wetherby, I think I must be going now."

"Of course, dear, you'll be late for dinner if you stay another moment longer." And sure enough, I heard the first clang of the dinner bell, muffled through the thick walls of Underhill House but still audible.

I rushed out without a glance back, escaping into the cold winter night just as the last dinner bell clang was reverberating in the air.

It wasn't until I was outside, safely away from Underhill House, in the light from a corner of the chapel, that I pulled the paper I had managed to retrieve from my pocket. I recognized the paper—thin onionskin, yellowed with age—but not the handwriting. This was not Miss Pymstead's handwriting. Another poem copied out:

There's a certain slant of light,
On winter afternoons,
That oppresses, like the weight
Of cathedral tunes.

Heavenly hurt it gives us;
We can find no scar,
But internal difference
Where the meanings are.

None may teach it anything,
'T is the seal, despair,—
An imperial affliction
Sent us of the air.

When it comes, the landscape listens,
Shadows hold their breath;
When it goes, 't is like the distance
On the look of death.

"Don't even tell me," Kat said. She was lying on her back on the top bunk, with her head tipped over the back, upside down. Lissa was sprawled on the bottom bunk, my bunk. I considered asking her to leave, but decided it wasn't worth the trouble. I sat down at my desk, pulled the paper out of my pocket, and commenced to study it in full view of the other two girls, wondering if either would notice what I was doing, but neither did.

I then opened the clue notebook and proceeded to copy the poem into it, detailing my observations—that the paper seemed similar to the other one, that the handwriting was different, that it had slipped out of Miss Wetherby's book. All the while that I did this, I cast glances at Lissa and Kat; neither was paying attention to me. I never thought of

Lissa as especially bright—she didn't have Kat's creativity—but of the three of us, she was by far the most diligent. When she set herself to studying, she studied, and it was clear that her mind rarely wandered from the task.

Kat was much more desultory, but right now, she seemed absorbed in her work. The less attention they paid me, the more assiduous I became.

There was something in the poem itself that repelled me. The slant of light described therein was now inseparable in my mind from my conversation with Miss Wetherby, and in fact, now the entire subject of Bryn Mawr College—which had previously been on my short list—was now bathed in an oppressive light.

Finally, I pushed aside the clue notebook. I was no closer to figuring out the puzzle of Chestmont Wooten's death than I had been at the outset. I opened my French notebook.

"So, what'd old sweetheart Wetherby want with you?" Kat asked.

"Not much," I said.

"I'll bet she thought you had too fine a mind to waste among those do-nothings at Yale . . . ," Kat said.

I spun around, so angry that my face was burning.

"Bunch of frat boys getting gentleman's Cs," she said. "Not worthy of a Grove girl . . ." She was laughing. "Only our failures get married . . ." Kat went on. She was a bit of a mimic, and as she spoke, her mouth and nose took on a rabbity cast. I tried to resist laughing, but I couldn't quite. The corners of my mouth started twitching.

"Did she teach you the Bryn Mawr cheer?" Kat said. "In Greek, of course . . . *Anassa kata, kalo kale* . . ."

Lissa hadn't joined in this exchange, but finally she set her book down.

"You know, the winner of the Eugenia Wilcox Prize gets a full four-year scholarship that can only be used at Smith, Mount Holyoke, or

Bryn Mawr. One of you two will probably win it. Then what will you do? Last year, Amy Manring turned it down to go to Princeton."

"What makes you think one of us will win it?" I said.

"Are you kidding? Who else would win? Senior girls only. Who would beat one of you? Abigail Von Platte?" She stared back and forth from one of us to the other. "Don't tell me you've never thought of this before? Jane? Kat?"

I looked at Kat, but now her face had shaded over.

She had flipped her braid over her shoulder and was picking some imaginary lint out of it. "The topic changes every year, and it's made up by the Eugenia Wilcox Committee—a group of little old ladies from the classes of the twenties and thirties. About every third or fourth year or so, it's creative writing, and I might stand a chance at that. The rest of the time, it's an essay of literary criticism—" She broke off, flipped the braid back around, jumped down from her bunk, and came over to where I was sitting at my desk.

"Working on the clue book, are we?" she said, suddenly changing the subject.

Kat's eyes were hooded, and I had a sudden sense that I didn't know if she was friend or foe.

I picked up the clue book and slid it into my desk drawer. "No," I said. "It's a cold case, and I've got too much homework right now."

Before I could stop her, Kat slid open my drawer and grabbed the notebook. The slender paper fluttered out as soon as she opened it—I swiped at it, but it eluded me, and Kat bent down and plucked it from the floor.

"Extra homework?" she said. From her tone, I knew that she had seen me copying all along, and that when I had thought she wasn't paying attention to what I was doing, it was just an act.

I shrugged. "Turns out we have another clue," I said. "I just didn't think you were interested."

The paper was folded lengthwise once, and Kat made a show of unfolding it slowly. Lissa had sat up on the bottom bunk and was watching her.

But when the paper was fully open, Kat's hand shook violently once, and then she stood silently.

Finally, she whispered, "Where did you get this?"

"It's a clue," I said. I was still angry. I was going to divulge the details of the find in my own time. I wanted to demonstrate some sense of power.

Kat turned to me, her face was snow-white, the freckles on her nose now stood out like dark blotches; her pupils were dilated. She looked as though she had seen a ghost.

"Where did you get this?" Still a whisper, but now hoarse, like a voiceless scream.

Lissa put her arm around Kat. "Whoa, it's just another of these freaky poems we've been finding. Calm down."

But Kat flung Lissa's arm off. She was trembling, her knees shaking so violently that she looked as if she might hit the floor.

Without another word, she threw the paper down on my desktop and strode out of the room, shutting the door with an angry bang, leaving Lissa and me behind in bewildered silence.

At five minutes past curfew, there was a timid knock on our door and Mrs. Dockerty stood outside.

"I wanted you to know that Katherine is unwell and she will be spending the night in the infirmary," she said.

"Unwell?" I said.

Mrs. Dockerty leaned in and put one plump hand on mine. "I don't think it's anything serious, dear. Stress. You understand, with the poor girl's family situation the way it is."

That night, I sat at my desk, staring at the poem penciled on the paper and tried to figure out what about it could have possibly upset Kat so much. The problem was, of our trio, Kat was the storyteller.

She was the one who could take seemingly disparate elements—a line of poetry on the wall of a boathouse, an English teacher, a long-ago murder—and make them seem to connect to each other.

I studied the Emily Dickinson poems we had found so far, and then I leafed through the book of poems I had checked out of the library. When I had first encountered the poems, they had seemed completely strange to me, but now, the more I read them, the more I seemed to understand them, as if someone had pushed the door open a bit to let some light into a dark room. Sometimes, I thought I could imagine myself many years hence, here at the Grove, like Miss Pymstead or Miss Wetherby, still surrounded by the same buildings and fields. Would I read Emily Dickinson then? Would my eyes light up like theirs did at the mention of her name? The idea sent a chill through me. Not me, I thought. I was planning to get away.

The next morning, when I entered Gould Cottage for English class, Miss Pymstead had written on the blackboard: *Eugenia Wilcox Prize for the Best Essay in English.*

"This is the most prestigious award given at the Grove Academy," Miss Pymstead said. "All the senior girls compete. It comes with a four-year scholarship that can be used at any of the Seven Sisters colleges that still functions as an independent entity."

Lissa's hand shot up.

"You have a question?"

"Harvard?"

Miss Pymstead wrinkled her brow a little, as though she couldn't imagine why Lissa was asking this question.

"Radcliffe has chosen to fold itself into Harvard. The Eugenia Wilcox Committee has decided not to support that choice with our endowment dollars. I have to say I support that decision."

"Smith, Mount Holyoke, Barnard, Wellesley, and, of course, Bryn Mawr . . . I can't imagine that the remaining schools don't provide adequate choices."

"Except for what's not on the list," Lissa said.

"Such as?"

"Harvard, Yale, Princeton, for starters," Lissa said.

"Men's colleges," Miss Pymstead said. "Vastly overrated."

"Vassar?" piped up Katie Cornwell.

Miss Pymstead shook her head. "Off the list since they went coed."

"That's completely unfair," Lissa said.

Miss Pymstead dismissed this statement with the barest brush of her hand. "Oh piffle, Lissa, your questions are so childish sometimes. In any case, you are headed for the university of matrimony, anyone can see that, and I'm sure you'll fare very well there. No doubt better than most. Now, back to the discussion of the prize . . ."

But she didn't say anything else about it.

Kat came back from the infirmary and made no further mention of the poem, so I decided not to bring it up. As for the prize, I had made up my mind. There was one difference between Kat and me that I did understand. Her financial situation was complicated and difficult, and mine was not.

After lights-out, when we were both lying in bed, sometimes I found it easier to talk.

"Kat?"

"Mmm." I could hear from her voice that she was almost asleep already.

"You know that Eugenia Wilcox Prize?" I said.

"Mmm."

"Well, you know how everyone says that one of the two of us is going to win?"

"Mmm."

"Well, I'm going to not do it," I said.

"Okay."

"What?"

"I said, okay." She was falling asleep. But my plan depended on her being awake enough to be grateful. I jabbed her bedsprings with my foot.

"Kat, wake up. I'm serious. I'm going to step aside. I'm going to skip the test. That way, you'll be sure to win."

I heard the bed creak. "What are you talking about? Are you nuts?"

"No," I whispered. "I'm serious. You might need the money for college, right? I don't need the money. My dad will pay for me to go to college."

"But the Eugenia Wilcox is a big deal," she was whispering louder now. "Amy Manring was wait-listed at Princeton, and then when she won, they took her."

"I don't care," I said. "You need it more than I do. If I'm not in it, you'll win for sure. I'm not saying I'm sure I'll beat you, but you know—it could go either way. We're the two best English students. Even Pymstead says so."

Then, I didn't hear anything for a while. Just silence and creaking bedsprings, and during that period of silence, I realized that I regretted what I had said. I should have kept my mouth shut. It's true I didn't need a scholarship, and after my meeting with Miss Wetherby, I was firmly convinced that I didn't want to attend a women's college. But through the curtain of pity I felt for Kat, I was starting to hear the siren song of glory in my ear. I wanted to compete because I wanted to win. Gold, silver, and bronze. Maybe this time, I could be gold. That's when I realized that the muffled sound I could actually hear was Kat crying into her pillow.

Then, the bedsprings creaked again, and she jumped down and flung her arms around me, burrowing her wet face into my arm.

"Thank you so much. You have no idea how much I want to thank you. I can't tell you how important this is to me . . ."

The rest of the night, I lay awake, thinking about how sorry I was I had ever thought of such a plan. Though I didn't need a scholarship, I realized only after volunteering to step aside how desperately I wanted to win.

20

As though in gratitude for my offer to step aside in the Eugenia Wilcox competition, Kat redoubled her interest in the Chestmont Wooten affair. Meanwhile, Lissa seemed to withdraw herself from the two of us a bit. She started to act as if she found us frivolous. She had met a new boy, Martin, a sophomore at UMass whom she had deemed a potential "keeper," and her interest in Emily Dickinson, rule breaking, Miss Pymstead, and even Josh Miller was starting to wane. Wonder of wonders, she was starting to spend more time with Katie Cornwell, whom she had decided "wasn't all that bad," and so Kat and I became more of a twosome.

In Miss Pymstead's class, we were reading *Dubliners* and had an essay due, but I was finding the combination of James Joyce and February weather to have a deadening effect on my nerves. No sooner would I seat myself at my desk than my eyelids would grow heavy and I'd want to lay my head upon my folded arms. To combat the soporific effect of Dublin and winter, I began a serious study of Emily Dickinson, Chestmont Wooten, the Hardley School, the Grove Academy, and, of course, Miss Pymstead.

But I found Emily Dickinson no more uplifting than James Joyce. In February, by four o'clock in the afternoon, the sky was dark purple and the light from the desk lamps in 2B barely seeped through the inky gloom.

"Emily Dickinson is obsessed with death," I said one especially dreary midwinter afternoon. "How am I supposed to find out anything about a specific murder when she just goes on and on about death in general?"

That afternoon, I had been staring at the poems until the slashes at the end of each line seemed as black and violent as knife marks on the white page.

A few minutes earlier, Emma Doerr popped her head in the door, looking for Lissa.

"Telephone in the butt room," she whispered, her eyebrows arching. "It's *Josh.*"

Kat shrugged. "I doubt she'll talk to him."

"I thought they broke up," Emma said. She was a gossip. I detested her for no particular reason.

"How should I know," I said.

"Tell him she's at the library," Kat said.

"Is she?" Emma asked.

"I have no idea," Kat said, shrugging.

"You know what the problem is?" I said when Emma had gone. "The problem is, we don't have a motive."

"Of course we do." Kat picked up the clue book and held it open to the spot where the torn-out picture of Chestmont Wooten was pasted unevenly onto the college-ruled page. He had black wavy hair, and his head was turned slightly in profile. It had gotten to the point that my chest squeezed whenever I looked at him. In the picture, it was hard to tell if his eyes had been gray or blue. He had a high, intelligent brow, a classic New England face. Oddly enough, he looked a little like Kat. I bit my lip.

"Look at him," Kat said.

"She must have loved him passionately," I said.

"Yeah, to blow his brains out . . ."

"So, what does Emily Dickinson have to do with it?"

"That's the part that's thrown in to confuse us."

The following afternoon, when I peered through the small glass window in my mailbox, I saw a large envelope. It was an invitation from Miss Pymstead. I was to join her for tea in her apartment in Gould Cottage.

At four o'clock on the designated date, I headed down the pathway that led behind Gould Cottage and knocked on Miss Pymstead's door.

"Welcome, Jane, please come right in." Miss Pymstead ushered me into Gould Cottage with a warm smile. The cottage was cozy and filled with light. There was a fire in the hearth, and everywhere I saw signs of comfort: watercolors on the walls, floral fabrics on the furniture, bright scatter rugs on the floors. Miss Pymstead's flat was so inviting—the dark blues and purples of midwinter seemingly held at bay.

The scent of baking spice cake filled the air. Miss Pymstead took my jacket, hung it on a peg by the door, and settled me on the sofa in front of the fire. She disappeared into the kitchen and emerged with two steaming mugs of cocoa topped with mounds of whipped cream. I sunk into the soft sofa. At the Grove, one got used to the fact that there were hard surfaces everywhere. The plush pillows and upholstered furniture here felt like a taste of the forbidden.

"How are you, Jane?"

"Very well, thank you."

I sat expectantly, waiting for Miss Pymstead to speak to me. She was watching me, but she said nothing. I reminded myself that this was my opportunity to look around her flat. There were bookshelves lining every wall, mismatched, mostly painted bright blue. They were stuffed with double rows of books: some looked like heirloom first editions, and others sported yellow *Used* stickers. If there was a bibliographic system, it was not readily apparent.

Miss Pymstead crossed to the window and stood before it.

"I assume you are wondering why I have brought you here."

I shrugged.

Despite the abundant comforts of the room, Miss Pymstead made me uncomfortable, and her demeanor here in her quarters was so like her demeanor in the classroom that I instinctively adopted my classroom demeanor as well: guarded.

"In general, Jane, you have done well as a student in my class."

I nodded. This was the kind of introduction that, coming from a Grove teacher, could easily move into either a positive or negative direction.

"Your critical faculties in English are quite well developed . . ." She paused, narrowed her eyes. "For a member of your generation."

She waited to see if I would say anything, but I said nothing. So, after another pause, she walked back and stood in front of me.

"I have learned to readjust my expectations. Given those adjusted expectations, I'd say that you have acquitted yourself well."

I remembered Miss Wetherby's comments to me during our meeting at Underhill House. I allowed myself a small smile.

Miss Pymstead stood up straighter; she was towering over me. She reached over and grabbed something from a shelf on the wall behind my head, which, too late, I recognized to be one of my papers.

"Until recently," she thundered.

I shrank down into the sofa, thankful for the thickness of the cushions.

Abruptly, she dropped into the chair across from me and threw the paper down on the table between us.

I recognized the heading for my paper: *Death and Dying in James Joyce's "The Dead," by Jane Milton.* The title was obscured by an enormous red *D*. I picked up the thick white mug and warmed my hands with it, then took a luxuriant sip, savoring the melted whipped-cream froth. I looked out the window. Miraculously, the sun had come out and its light was sparkling on the snow. A few sledders were careening down the hill behind Gould Cottage, their parkas bright against the white slope.

"Do you have something to say?" Miss Pymstead said.

I stared at her. In the warm room, her cheeks were flushed; her hair was straying from its bun, curling up in honeyed tendrils around her face. I had never noticed the fine lines around her eyes. I squinted a little, the sun beaming from behind her, trying to imagine whether she would have been pretty—she was so daffy-looking now that it was hard to imagine her pretty, exactly, although she certainly wasn't ugly either.

"Jane? You don't have anything to say for yourself?"

"I don't like 'The Dead.' I don't like thinking about 'The Dead.' I don't like talking about 'The Dead.' I find death depressing. I'm sorry."

Miss Pymstead didn't say anything. She just went over to her desk and rummaged around for a while in a messy drawer and then came back with a red marker. She scratched out the *D* and then next to it wrote a big red *F*.

"What's that for?" I said.

"For not reading the story," she said. "The people in the story are still alive."

"I read it," I said. "I just didn't like it."

"Speak up, Jane. I can't hear you. I don't know why we ever dropped elocution from the curriculum."

"I said I read it, but I didn't like it."

"James Joyce is one of the most brilliant writers of the twentieth century."

"He may be one of the most brilliant writers of the twentieth century, but I don't like him," I said. "'The Dead' is boring," I added. "It's dead. Just so you know, I also hate Hemingway."

Miss Pymstead narrowed her eyes and tilted her chin to the side. She looked out the window at the sledders, then through the doorway that led to her kitchen, then back at me. She lowered her voice and spoke with increased urgency.

"Who else don't you like, Jane? Tell me. What other writers do you hate with a passion?"

Now, I was stymied. Who else did I hate? I thought back over the books we had read this past year. The curriculum made no sense. We had been flipping back and forth in time, jumping from one period to another, from one form to another; if there were connections between the works we had studied, they were evident to Miss Pymstead but not to me. But most of the stuff I had found secretly thrilling. Except for "The Dead," which was dead. And "A Clean Well-Lighted Place."

"I'm going to tell you a secret, Jane. Your passion is surprisingly refreshing. What I'm finding among you girls is an astonishing degree of apathy . . ." Her eyes lingered on her overstuffed bookshelves. "When I was a student, girls were deeply passionate about literature, the loves, the hatreds—yes, hatreds, we felt them deeply. You girls, you seem to lack the same degree of—"

She leaned toward me, looking at me appraisingly. She said, "And what do you think of J. D. Salinger?"

I was just about to open my mouth to tell her that I loved J. D. Salinger and that *Catcher in the Rye* was one of my favorite books, but I was brought up short when I remembered Miss Pymstead telling us that J. D. Salinger was a pretender, a sham. She was still holding the red pen, rolling it back and forth between her fingers in a twitching motion. I had a feeling that if I gave the right answer, she might use that red pen once more, like a magic wand, and change that *F* magically into an *A*. Somewhere far off, in the distance, beyond the gates of the Grove, I knew that there was a place called Yale, a place that I knew I was supposed to be longing for with all my heart.

"Salinger?" I said weakly.

"Surely you know him?" I could hear the contempt that would quickly flood her voice if I didn't speak.

"I . . ."

"You've at least read *Catcher*—it's part of the ninth-grade curriculum—" The pen was twitching so violently in Miss Pymstead's hand that I thought it might fly across the room.

"I, uh, prefer *The Prime of Miss Jean Brodie* . . . ," I stammered out.

"Muriel Spark," she purred, now contented as a cat. "I agree with you completely. Salinger—he's vastly overrated . . . Besides," she said, leaning in to share a confidence, "he's a dirty old man. Recluse, my eye. Why, Grove girls have been making 'pilgrimages' to see him for years. And that is in the strictest confidence. You must say the Grove girls' swear."

Miss Pymstead uncapped her red pen, reached over, and crossed out the F, replacing it with an A.

"The essay was execrable. You will do more worthy work next time. Tell me, who is one writer you truly love?"

"Colleen McCullough," I said.

She picked up my essay and dropped it into the flames.

"Me too," she said. She walked over to her bookcase, reached to one of the higher shelves, and pulled off a well-thumbed copy of *The Thorn Birds*, to which she gave a loving thump and then replaced it on the shelf. "So, you do have very good taste, my dear."

I reached for my jacket on the peg by the door, but she held up her hand.

"I've asked you many questions, wouldn't you like to ask me one?"

I slipped my arm into the nylon sleeve of my jacket, my heart thumping as I wondered if I dared.

I was halfway out the door as I called back to her, "Were you ever in love with Chestmont Wooten?"

If I could say one thing about Miss Pymstead, it was that she never failed to surprise me.

She caught hold of my arm and held me there, one of those daffy smiles brightening her face.

"Oh, so you *do* like the dead?" she said.

I could hear the dinner bell clanging off in the distance. I hitched my backpack up on my shoulder. Miss Pymstead's face was shrouded in a deep blue shadow, and I couldn't read her expression. She gripped my arm so tightly that I could feel her fingernails through my down jacket and wool sweater.

Her voice, when she spoke, was oddly lower, gravelly. It frightened me.

"Leave it be, Jane. There's scum at the bottom of that pond. You don't want to be the one to dredge it up."

"I was just kidding," I said, trying to weasel out of it now, tugging my arm free. Her blue eyes were flashing almost black.

She grabbed my other arm and wouldn't let me go. "You weren't kidding, Jane. Don't try that juvenile ploy with me. You think I haven't seen you skulking all over campus following me? You think I don't know what you're up to? Well, you've been following a false trail all year."

"I didn't mean anything by it, Miss Pymstead," I said. I could hear the little-girl quaver in my voice, but I could see that she wasn't buying it.

"I'm warning you to let it lie," she said. "Chestmont Wooten was not a well-loved man. You want to look for suspects? You'll find plenty of them. But if you stir up the muck, there are people who could be hurt."

The dinner bell had stopped ringing, and Gould Cottage, tucked up against the hill as it was, was now completely plunged in shadows; they clung to the snowy hillsides like Spanish mantillas over whitened faces. Miss Pymstead's face was a sharp white too, her eyes as black as coals. Behind her, the light from the fireplace cast shadows out onto the snow.

"Somebody was already hurt," I said.

"You are a spoiled child who knows nothing. Especially about hurting people and being hurt. You are like a peach—one slight touch of a fingertip would give you a bruise."

I could still feel points of pain from where her fingertips had dug into the flesh of my upper arm, and inside I could feel a hot coil of anger winding up tighter and tighter as I thought of the cavalier treatment with the red pen—the D, the F, the A—as though she could conjure up and then dash my future with a single stroke.

"Well, what about you, Miss Pymstead? You're an old Grove girl too. Haven't you got anything better to do than waste your life teaching the likes of me?"

After the words were out of my mouth, I could feel my heart fluttering wildly in my throat, skipping beats. My breath came in short, shallow gasps. I knew I had crossed the line. The light was fading rapidly, and I couldn't quite make out her expression. I waited, expecting the worst.

But when Miss Pymstead spoke, her voice sounded tired. "It's getting dark. You need to get back to your dorm."

I looked at the darkening sky. One bright star shone above the outline of the chapel at the top of the hill, and the words of one of the poems Miss Pymstead had taught us came to my mind. I hesitated, but then I took a chance: *"The night was wide but furnished scant, / with but a single star . . ."*

Miss Pymstead sighed.

"If you quote Emily Dickinson to me, my life is not quite wasted after all, and you'll miss dinner if you don't skedaddle up the hill. But you'll not forget what we've discussed just now. Your schoolgirl nonsense is not worth the ruination of decent people's lives. I leave you with that as a parting thought. Now, good-bye."

PART THREE
NOW

21

I couldn't decide what to think about Kaitlyn Corsyn. Her essays were striking, certainly, but something about them seemed so familiar. I could not shake the feeling that I had read her words before. Each time, I collected her essay and ran it through an antiplagiarism website, it came up clean. But this time, I wasn't satisfied. I copied the first line and pasted it into Google just to see if anything would come up. *Bingo.* Google directed me to a blog page. The title at the top of the page said: *The Ghost of Abbott North.*

I stood up from my chair so quickly that it toppled to the floor. The window was open, and the sound the chair made was so loud that I thought I saw the pale face of Abigail Von Platte peering at me through her filmy curtains, which were still drawn.

Charlie poked his head through the doorway of his room.

"You all right in there?"

I swallowed twice to make sure my voice would come out okay.

"Hey, Charlie . . . can you look at this for a sec?"

Charlie lumbered out of his room. It seemed he had grown a couple of inches since we had arrived here.

Charlie leaned over and looked at the screen. "So, you found our blogger-in-residence, huh?"

I shrugged, hoping that I seemed as if I had known this all along, but my eyes were skimming quickly over the words. I could see that it was full of descriptions that were funny and biting. I paused when I came to this:

> *There once was young girl in Abbott*
> *They called her a thief gosh dagnabbit*
> *She stepped in a trap*
> *And got a bad rap*
> *But she's not the bad habit rabbit.*

"Who wrote this?" I asked.

"Been pretty quiet, last few days. Still, it's pretty funny—but hey, I really need my laptop back, if you don't mind."

I still hadn't replaced my busted laptop and had to rely on the computers in Pencott for my lesson plans. He reached over to pick up the laptop.

"Just a sec. How can you tell when this stuff was written?" I said.

"Oh, it has a date on it, see."

"And who is it?"

I peered at the white type, and saw the line from the essay. Kaitlyn's assignment, and I saw the date it was posted—the day before I had collected the essays.

"Who writes this blog?"

Charlie shrugged. "It's anonymous. Nobody really knows."

"Hmm," I said. "Any logical guesses?"

"Could be anybody."

If the blogger and the essayist were the same person, then there was a simple explanation. If they were different people, then one had copied from the other.

"Do most of the kids know about this blog?"

"All of them."

"What about the adults?"

"I doubt it. You'd have to find it by chance. Hey, how'd you find it?"

"I can't tell you right now," I said, putting my stern face on. "Now, go to bed."

"You done with this?" he said.

I wanted to say no, but the laptop was his, so I nodded. He picked it up and returned to his room, shutting the door behind him.

I couldn't get to sleep that night. I tossed and turned in my bed, which seemed to have grown hard and narrow. The moon pouring in the tall gabled window cast a blue light on my bedsheets. I knelt on my bed, pressing my forehead against the glass, looking out over the illuminated valley, down toward the purple splotch of the boathouse and the dark stripe of the river, blotted in irregular spots on both sides by trees. Beyond, the old Hardley School, now the Hardley International English-Language Academy, was mostly dark, just a few lights.

I got up, pulling my bathrobe from its hook and wrapping it around me, and stepped into the kitchen and living room without turning on the light. I stared across at Abigail Von Platte's apartment, where I noticed that a single light burned in her bedroom, the blinds were half pulled up, and her window was open a crack, but I couldn't see movement inside.

A moment later, I heard a knock at the door, but when I opened it, no one was there. Lying on my doorstep was a neat stack of typed pages.

nora carroll

Charity Case

My grammy died the summer before my senior year. After that, things got worse fast. When I returned to school for fall semester of my senior year, Mommy never gave me any money to buy books, so I did what I usually did—I put them on my tab at the student store, waiting for Parents' Weekend. Mommy came, dressed in her furs, but came empty-handed, nothing but a couple of bottles of Wild Turkey at the bottom of her handbag to try to impress my friends. But Grammy used to bring real money—money to pay my bookstore bill; she sent me things too—like winter coats, and plane tickets, and money to buy cleats and paintbrushes. The kinds of things that Mommy didn't think about.

So, once Parents' Weekend rolled around, I had a pretty big tab for books, and I'm not even talking about how much I owed for hash, except now there wasn't anyone around to pay for it. And all of a sudden, I realized that I had turned into a charity case.

Now, don't get me wrong. I was always a charity case at the Grove. As far as I could tell, Miss Wetherford owed us one. I think she must have had the hots for Mommy back when she was a student. I tried to squeeze it out of Mommy, but I could never get her to tell me—the most I ever got her to say was the secret Grove swear—which is not so secret because even people like Lilly and June know it.

But after I didn't pay my bookstore bill, it became public knowledge that I was a charity case, because Miss Wetherford

176

had to give me all the fifty-dollar checks that I needed to attach to college applications.

There are two kinds of teachers: the ones who want to be your friends, like Miss Wetherford. They want you to like them, and of course you don't because you are repelled by them. You notice all the repulsive things about them, like the way they have black hairs growing out of their chins. Then there are the ones who want to lead and inspire you—like Miss Pimsley. I think those are even worse. I became Miss Pimsley's project. Like her pet rock or something. She decided that she would feed me cookies and stuff my brain with knowledge and make it so that I would win the big prize that would pay my way to college. Thing is, I felt trapped into it—as trapped as any fly that has flown into honey. And Mommy just made matters worse. She kept telling me that there was not going to be any money from Grammy's will to pay for my tuition. She just went on and on about how I needed to study hard to win the big scholarship prize. It felt like a million billion pounds of stress were weighing down on my head. I didn't think it was my fate to win the prize—after all, I'd have to compete against June, and everyone knew she was the smart one. I was the crazy one. Lilly was the pretty one. I knew from studying Greek mythology what a bad idea it was to play with fate. I wish we had all thought a little more about that.

For a long moment, I closed my eyes, willing my heart, which was racing, to slow to a more normal pace. Miss Wetherford? Miss Pimsley? Lilly and June? My hands were shaking as I put down the pages.

The last time I saw Kat was on a windy street corner at 110th and Amsterdam a few years after graduation. We were outside the Hungarian Pastry Shop, and I was trying to talk her into going inside. I remember that it was freezing cold. The wind was whipping up through Morningside Park, blasting across the sculpture garden next to the Cathedral of Saint John the Divine. There was a blue plastic bag caught on a sharp spike of the fence, fluttering. I was pleading with her, "Come on, Kat, just come in, have a cup of coffee with me—let's warm up for a minute." She was holding a bunch of papers that I presumed to be her manuscript haphazardly in her arms; the pages looked like they might blow away at any minute. She was hatless and her head was all but shaved. She had dark circles under her eyes, and her lips were blue from the cold. She had called me the night before, telling me she had to see me, and so I had taken a day off work and come in from Connecticut to see her, come all the way uptown to the spot she had suggested—and now she was standing there, refusing to move, and I was getting to the end of my rope.

She thumped her hand on the top of the pile of typed pages.

"It's all in here," she said. "All of it. Every single word."

"What do you mean?" I asked. "All of what?" The wind was whipping up the street. I had to shout to be heard over the wind and the sounds of traffic on Amsterdam. "Why don't you come inside?"

She stood without moving.

"Just for a minute, Kat," I said, wheedling. "Let's have a cup of coffee. It's freezing out here."

"No," she said. "I have to go—I shouldn't have come."

"Kat? Are you kidding? I just came all the way up here to see you."

Just then, a couple of the pages broke loose and blew into the street. She took off after them, dodging a taxi and a city bus. I gasped, losing sight of her.

A moment later, she reappeared, clutching her papers in her hands. For some reason, I remember she was wearing Chinese slippers, just like the ones she had worn on Lantern Day.

"Kat, you're going to freeze to death out here. I'll buy you a cup of coffee." I was bone chilled and exasperated, but I tried to keep the irritation out of my voice. I stared at her uneven shorn-off hair. It looked as if she had cut it herself. As I gazed at her, I had a moment of realization: Kat, my roommate, whom I knew as intimately as a member of my own family, lived on, but only in my imagination. This woman—tiny, pale, scattered—was a stranger to me.

She wrapped her arms around the pages, clutched them tight to her chest, and backed away from me. "It's all here!" she repeated. "I told the whole story."

I held out my hand to her, but she kept backing up. She backed right into the street, not looking right or left, and then there was a loud honking sound—a city bus was bearing right down on her.

I gasped. "Kat!" But she had always been nimble on her feet, and she dodged. The bus passed, and she wasn't flattened on the road but had disappeared, off into the New York City streets—gone. I thought about following her, but the bus had blocked her from view. I could no longer see her. Then, I realized that she had dropped a couple of pages of her manuscript; they had blown back to the gutter in front of me, and I picked them up.

One of the pages was wet. I dried it against the nap of my wool coat and went inside the pastry shop and ordered an espresso. When the waiter brought my coffee, he jostled my arm, and three small drops fell like tears on one of the pages.

What was she going to do with our secret history? I didn't have to ever find out, because Kat flung herself into the Hudson a couple of weeks later. When they dredged her up, there was no bundle of sodden papers with her, and though I did eventually make a few inquiries about the possible whereabouts of a manuscript, apparently it was last seen at the corner of 110th and Amsterdam, clutched in the arms of my former roommate.

In my clue notebook, I had the first page and the last page—the ones she had dropped on the street that day. Now, as I read the pages in front of me, I knew that somehow the rest of the manuscript must have survived. There was no logical way that Kaitlyn Corsyn could have gotten hold of Kat's lost manuscript, but I was certain that the story was Kat's. For thirty-five years, I had wondered what had become of those pages—but how could they have possibly gotten into the clutches of Kaitlyn Corsyn, and why was she passing them off as her own?

Of course, the only profession I'd ever had, besides teaching, was writing mystery novels. There seemed to be a plot here—but I simply couldn't figure it out.

My night's sleep was shot. In the kitchen, I pulled open the fridge, poured myself a glass of milk, drank two sips, dumped the rest down the sink, and went back to my room. But as I climbed into bed, something out the window caught my eye. I pressed my face up against the glass again, staring out at the dark expanse of Siberia, but this time saw nothing. The moon was bright and the fields were illuminated, but there were shadows everywhere.

Then, there it was again—a thin flash, one then another, then another, darting in jagged lines across Siberia. If I looked closely, I could spot dark-clad figures—maybe two, maybe three; the lights were definitely flashlight beams. I tracked the figures across Siberia until they disappeared over the ragged edges where the fields ended at the wooded pathway that headed toward Wooten Boathouse. As I stood watching, I realized that I had no intention of doing anything. Leave this generation of students to their own nights of broken rules.

But, I couldn't stand the uncertainly. I got up, crept across the living room once more, and pushed Charlie's door open. The room was illuminated by moonlight and the air was unnaturally still. His bed was empty and his laptop was nowhere to be seen. Of course I knew where else to look. I'd seen Charlie and Kaitlyn Corsyn everywhere together the past few days—in Commons, at a table in Starbucks, sharing a carrel in Pencott, sitting on the rock wall outside the gym. Though it passed through my head that it might be better not to know, I ignored the thought. I stole down the hallway to Abbott 2C—Kaitlyn Corsyn's room. As I neared the doorway, I realized that if Kaitlyn wasn't in her room and her roommate saw that I knew, I'd be forced to do something about it; so I hesitated and contemplated returning to my room, but I couldn't. I pushed the door open a crack. Her roommate was asleep on the top bunk, but Kaitlyn's bottom bunk was empty.

I couldn't shake the feeling that someone was following me. Outside, the air was colder than I expected, and I started shivering. I took off across Siberia at a jog, headed toward the place where I had last seen the flashing lights. The fields of Siberia, though they appeared smooth from a distance, were pockmarked and pitted from sports practices that had slogged on even through the recent days of rain. I stumbled once, righted myself, then forged on, half jogging. I had no flashlight and the moon had ducked behind a cover of clouds.

I tried to hurry despite the darkness and uneven terrain, but about halfway across the fields, I set my foot down unevenly. My ankle wobbled, then gave way. My knee smacked the ground. I tasted dirt in my mouth, and hot daggers seared through my ankle. I listened to the silence around me, wondering what to do, but the pain started to lessen and I sat up. I looked around me—Siberia was dark, silent, and completely empty as far as I could tell. I tested to see if I could put weight on my ankle, and the pain wasn't as bad as I thought, but my nighttime adventuring was over. I had no choice but to head back to the dorm.

The trek up three flights of stairs on a sore ankle was agonizing, but my state of mind was worse.

Ever since the day I had driven back through the gates of the Grove, I had had the eerie, uncanny feeling that somehow someone had cast a net around me and was slowly, slowly drawing it closed. That would matter less if I had no secrets. But, of course, I did.

When I got back to our quarters, Charlie was in his bed, dead to the world, and his feet, which stuck out from under the covers, were clean and free from grass or other telltale signs of his recent outing. I leaned in close and gave him the mother's sniff: no trace of booze or pot that I could ascertain. No whiff of cigarettes. All I could smell was boy sweat, hair gel, and Old Spice shaving cream.

In the morning, I confronted him.

"Where were you?"

"What, are you crazy? I was asleep. In my bed."

"I went to check on you and you weren't there."

"What time?"

"What does it matter what time? I'm telling you, you weren't there."

"Mom, what are you talking about? I *was* there. I was asleep in my bed. Where do you think I would go?"

"I don't think where you would go—I just want to know why you weren't here."

"I don't know. Maybe I was in the bathroom. Did you check the bathroom?"

And here, I realized, was the one chink in my logic, because in my state of agitation, I *hadn't* checked the bathroom. I didn't respond, but as I looked around his room, I noticed that his computer was missing, and I thought I had him cornered.

"Well, then, where is your laptop?"

"My laptop? What are you talking about?"

"Where is your laptop?" I was mad. My best angry-mom tone. Charlie knew I was mad and he looked seriously worried.

"Mom, relax. Jeez. It's right here." He reached over to his dresser, and suddenly, I saw it, its slim white form under a couple of white T-shirts that had been there since the previous night, and I realized that it had probably been there all along and I just hadn't seen it.

My shoulders slumped a little. I realized that I was in the typical mom predicament, and I was probably never going to know the truth. Maybe he was out the previous night after curfew, running across the fields with Kaitlyn Corsyn, or maybe he was just in the bathroom and I didn't think to look.

I'd never know. That was the essence of being the adult. He knew it, and so did I.

22

My own dislike for James Joyce was reflected in my students' essays, which were, without exception, terrible. I was surprised to find that Kaitlyn Corsyn's essay was one of the worst—it reflected almost no effort. I did not want to admit to myself how much I enjoyed slashing the front of her paper with a large red F. When I returned the essays in class, I heard grumbling all the way around, but Kaitlyn's expression didn't change much. Alone among the students, she came up to me at the end of class and asked if I could explain what was wrong with the essay. I pulled up a chair next to my desk and she sat down across from me. She listened without expression as I read back her inanities.

"Michael Furey symbolizes everything that is dead about dead people . . . ?" I asked, my voice dripping with incredulity. "Is this the kind of work you expect to get you into Yale, Kaitlyn?"

The movement of Kaitlyn's shoulder was so slight I might have imagined a shrug. Her legs were crossed at the ankles. She was wearing a denim miniskirt and shoes that I couldn't identify by brand but that I knew cost hundreds of dollars a pair. Her legs had the unmistakable sheen of a salon waxing. How could those be the legs of a boarding school student? Did she pop off campus for spa treatments in between novel writing and her other Yale-worthy activities?

"This is not good. This isn't even close to good," I said.

Somewhere, deep inside, I knew that Kaitlyn's essay wasn't any worse than the other students' essays—instead, remarkably, it was ordinary. It just wasn't as good as some of the extraordinary work she had previously shown me.

I looked at her face. Her eyes were green with flecks of gold.

"Ms. Milton, I didn't enjoy this story very much."

Deep down, I knew that was a reasonable answer, but I was itching for a fight.

"School is not all about enjoyment. Sometimes you have to reach beyond yourself. Stretch yourself to uncomfortable limits."

Her expression was as blank as a turned-off TV.

"Do you have something to say for yourself?"

"Can I rewrite it for a higher grade?"

It was her implacability that drove me nuts. I could feel, gathering like a storm behind my breastbone, a desire to make her show some kind of emotion. It was a dark desire, and somewhere in the back of my head, a voice was telling me that it would be a far better idea for me to leave her alone. But I ignored that voice and pressed on.

"Rewrite for a higher grade? Can you give me a hope that you will have something more interesting to say the second time around?"

She hitched her purse up on her arm. It was one of those overpriced designer purses that all the girls seemed to use these days. I did a quick mental calculation of the price of her outfit. Even just half covered, she was wearing almost a thousand dollars' worth of gear—and that was not counting the French manicure.

"More interesting?"

"I presume you know what that means."

She narrowed her eyes slightly, but other than that, her expression didn't change much.

"Can you give me some specifics, Ms. Milton?"

I knew I wasn't being fair to her, but irritation was squeezing me around the chest.

"You'll need to figure it out for yourself, Kaitlyn," I said.

Now, her eyes flared slightly. I had a feeling no one had ever crossed her before.

She fiddled with a strand of hair, smoothing it behind her ear. "Do you mind if I ask you one question, Ms. Milton?"

"Not at all," I said. "Shoot."

"I'm guessing that if you could have done it all—write a novel at my age, get straight As, play a varsity sport, get awesome SATs, you know, be the perfect Grove girl and then some—then you would have gone to Yale yourself. And you wouldn't have ended up here, stuck at the Grove, teaching the likes of us. Isn't that right?"

That was when I heard the echo of my own long-ago question to Miss Pymstead being hurled back at me from across the years. The old twang of shame started to tremble inside me, setting up a note that became a chord and then grew like a crescendo. I pulled my shoulders up and blew out, getting ready to smack her down for humiliating me.

But when I looked at Kaitlyn, I saw that she was crying.

She grabbed her paper, crumpled it up, and threw it in the wastepaper basket under my desk.

"I hated that story," she called over her shoulder. "It was boring and stupid. I didn't get it at all. I just wrote the paper about what I found in the SparkNotes. I'd like to see you do better, Ms. Milton."

"Kaitlyn . . ." I called after her as she ran out the door. But I saw through the window that she had run into Charlie on the walk outside.

He had his arms around her and was consoling her as they walked along the pathway toward Founder's Hill.

"What do you have against Kaitlyn anyway?" asked my usually mellow Charlie later that evening. He so rarely made comments of an interpersonal nature that I knew I needed to take him seriously.

"What makes you think I have something against her?"

"Are you kidding? It's obvious. You treat her different from the other kids. Like you have it out for her. Her parents already go hard on her. She's under so much pressure to get into an Ivy League school. They act like the sky will fall if she doesn't get into Yale. Can't you be a little nicer to her?"

It had never occurred to me that I was treating her differently. I thought that the difference was radiating from her, but I realized that it was true. I hated her. I had from the moment I set eyes on her. And to me, the fact that I hated her had always seemed right and true and fair.

I could deny it to myself, but I didn't have to scrape hard beneath the surface to figure out why. She was Lissa reincarnated: my oldest friend, my benefactress, the person I hated most in all the world.

The next morning, I woke up early to see Charlie off on the bus to the ecostation trip upriver. Jessica was in her element, overseeing the kids as they loaded camping gear and observation equipment onto the bus. Charlie climbed aboard, and I noted the blond head of Kaitlyn, who was seated next to him. The bus rumbled and let out a puff of exhaust as it lumbered up the roadway toward the gates, leaving me in the silence of the early morning, alone with my ghosts.

It was such a beautiful October day that instead of heading down the hill, I walked up the pathway that led to Whittaker Chapel. The morning was clear except for a bit of haze that hung over the river, and the trees had erupted in splashes of bright red and yellow. From atop Founder's Hill, I could see across the campus and river to the spires of Hardley.

Here, at the only spot on campus with a panoramic view, someone had placed a teak bench. There was a small ornamental garden around it. The bench had a tarnished plaque on it, and I bent over it to read the inscription:

This bench was given in honor of
Miss Constance Eufenia Wetherby
Headmistress of the Grove Academy
From the members of the Class of 1961
Twenty-Fifth Reunion Gift

With my fingertips, I rubbed the ridged surface of the plaque. Then, I looked down over the valley, my eyes hesitating over Wooten Boathouse. From this distance, it looked like a barn, one of many that were visible from here, dotting the landscape. At the river's edge was a line of poplars, their leaves now yellow and red.

Here, behind Whittaker Chapel, the pavement bent in a hairpin turn around the chapel and the hill dropped off sharply. It was the highest point on campus. Below, in the distance, was the back of Gould Cottage, where Miss Pymstead's apartment had once been. As I looked at the steep drop-off, my stomach churned, and I thought I was going to heave up the coffee I had hastily swallowed. I was wearing one of Charlie's sweatshirts, and even though it had been laundered, I could just smell the faint scent of his deodorant lingering in the cloth, and it made me miss him. He was doing so well here. I wished more than anything I could set the ghosts of the past to rest.

I knew that only one thing would help: I needed to locate Kaitlyn Corsyn's manuscript and find out what lurked in the remaining pages. And I had to figure out where it had come from. Who had given it to her, and why?

If a student saw me letting myself into Kaitlyn's room, I would have to give a quick excuse, but as I turned the key in the lock, my mind was blank. As it happened, I was lucky. I slipped through the door before anyone passed and slowly clicked it closed behind me.

Inside, the room was stuffy, full of the smells of rumpled bedclothes and deodorant and cast-off clothes. Kaitlyn's roommate's bed was neatly made, her books stacked on her desk in a tidy pile, but Kaitlyn's things were strewn about, as though she expected that someone would come along and pick them up for her.

A pile of textbooks teetered on her desk, with stacks of papers littering the surface. I looked through the papers. They were all covered with math equations and scientific notation. None appeared to be essays. I shuffled them around a little, afraid to disturb them too much.

Kaitlyn's bed was unmade, but there was no manuscript piled on her bed or under it. There was nothing on her bookshelf. I opened her desk drawers and found them half-empty. There was nothing out of the ordinary here. Her laptop was closed on her desk, and I hesitated, fingers twitching, before I opened it. It was one thing to look around her room. As a dorm mother it was not such a stretch for me to enter her room, but privacy rules prevented me from looking at her computer without specific permission to do so.

I knew I was crossing a line. I looked out the window—nothing but a view of trees from here. But I didn't know where her roommate was or whether she was likely to return anytime soon.

My chest constricted uncomfortably, pinching me up under the ribs.

I heard footfalls in the hallway, and I recognized their heavy shuffling thump.

For a second, I was rooted to the spot, but then I grabbed Kaitlyn Corsyn's laptop, and slipped it up against my stomach, certain Charlie's bulky sweatshirt would hide it.

I heard the click of the key in the lock, and I found myself face-to-face with Abigail Von Platte.

"Jane?"

I had one hand clasped across my chest, holding up the laptop, and the other hand was on the doorknob of the room. My mind was spinning through a dozen reasons why I might be in a student's room. Then, I decided the best reason was to provide no reason and I took a step forward.

"Oh, did you get the message too?"

The message. Now, I was stymied. What message? And suddenly, the image of the bus with Charlie in it skidding across the road and overturning flashed across my mind.

"Is . . . everything okay?"

"Jane? Did you come in here to pick up Miranda's inhaler?" That was it. My excuse. "I couldn't find it," I said. "Doesn't she keep another one in the infirmary?"

Abigail looked over at the windowsill, where an inhaler was lying in plain sight. She reached past me.

"They said your phone was busy."

"I got a voice mail." I said, smiling brightly.

She picked up the inhaler and jammed it in her pocket.

"How are you going to get that to her?"

"I'm driving up there. I'm one of the chaperones," she said. "I just didn't want to go on the bus—the diesel fumes aggravate my sinuses."

"Is that so?" I said. "I didn't think of you as the campout type."

"Oh really? What type did you think of me as then?"

There was no answer to that question that wouldn't get me in trouble, and my arm was starting to ache from holding the laptop under my shirt.

"Have fun," I said.

Oddly enough, Abigail shut the door, leaving me standing in Kaitlyn and Miranda's room. I opened the door and stepped into the lighted hallway, Kaitlyn Corsyn's laptop still firmly pressed against my skin under my sweatshirt.

I didn't find the file I was looking for on Kaitlyn's hard drive. Hunched on my bed with her laptop on my knees, I clicked open file after file. My eyes smarted and my fingers burned, but I couldn't locate a manuscript. I just found typical stuff: iTunes, photographs, and homework. As I opened the photo files one by one, I was startled to find my son's face smiling back at me, his curly hair shining in the sun, the river throwing up glints of gold and silver behind him.

Throughout the night, I could hear a steady rain pouring outside my window, and at four in the morning, I got up, slipped into Kaitlyn and Miranda's room, and returned the computer to its place. Later that morning, the campers turned up, the trip cut short because of the heavy rain.

Kaitlyn Corsyn came to my apartment that afternoon and told me that someone had been in her room in her absence.

"How do you know?" I said.

"I can tell. A lot of my stuff is moved around."

"Like what?" I said.

"Everything. It looks like someone went through my drawers. My clothes are all pushed around, and I even think the person might have used my laptop," she said.

"Is anything missing?" I said.

She shook her head.

"I don't see how anyone could get into your room," I lied. "I'm the only one who has a passkey, besides Nate Hodges."

She fixed me with her clear blue eyes. "Someone was in my room." She seemed as if she was going to say more, but she spun on her heel and walked out.

23

I was only half engaged in teaching, distracted by the sight of Kaitlyn Corsyn, who was sitting near the window. She was wearing a blue T-shirt that brought out the color in her eyes, and the light from the window was setting off the highlights in her hair. Her skin was fresh and there was no trace of fatigue on her face—a little boredom maybe, but that was always there, the look that told me she found my class no more than an annoying way station on the road to fabulous things to come. I was transcribing a few lines from Joyce onto the whiteboard when Dr. Farber-Johnson popped her head in the door.

"I hope I'm not disturbing you?"

My heart pounded. Was this going to be a surprise classroom observation? Though I knew I was prepared for the class, I was feeling lackluster, fatigued from the previous evening's stressful escapades.

"Not at all," I said, forcing a smile. "What can I do for you?"

"I was just hoping I'd catch you," Dr. Farber-Johnson had plastered a smile on her face. She used it only in the presence of students, so it didn't get much use. "I wasn't sure what time your class ends . . ."

I glanced at my watch. "I can step outside for a moment."

She nodded. "That would be terrific."

At that moment, I realized that she must have been coming to tell me that Charlie had been caught breaking a rule. Why else would she interrupt me in the middle of a class?

But when I got into the hallway, she drew me a bit farther away from the classroom and then said, "So, any progress on the book front?"

"I beg your pardon?"

"Our meeting regarding giving Miss Corsyn some assistance with her creative writing? Surely it hasn't slipped your mind . . ."

I was surprised to find that this was the subject of our impromptu conversation.

Dr. Farber-Johnson leaned in and lapsed into a hissing whisper. In the semidarkness of the hallway, her expression was menacing, her gray eyes almost purple.

"Ms. Milton, I have solicited your opinion on a matter that is considered of utmost importance to the school. I take it that you received the writings . . ."

I nodded.

"And that you read them."

I nodded again.

"And?"

Dr. Farber-Johnson was staring at me with such intensity that I took a step back. I felt a chill creep up the back of my spine. Suddenly, here in the dark corner of the shadowy hallway, I started to feel like I had been backed into a trap. How much did she know about Kaitlyn Corsyn's manuscript? Was I being paranoid?

"Dr. Farber-Johnson, I'm in the middle of class. Now is not the time to discuss this. I haven't had time to read all the pages."

She put one hand on my arm and squeezed it. Her grip was tight and strong, as hard as any field hockey player's. "Jane, I need this to get done. I've got an entire budget that is on hold because I don't know

194

what to tell Mr. and Mrs. Corsyn. Read her manuscript. Tell me what you think of it. Come up with a plan. That's all I ask."

"I'll see what I can do," I mumbled without much confidence. "Now, if you'll excuse me, I have to get back to class."

After class, it was raining, and the leaves were falling off the trees in wet, lumpy drifts. I hadn't brought an umbrella; I let the cold rain drip down the back of my head and behind my ears. By the time I got back to Abbott North, I had managed to come to my senses: no matter how much I managed to convince myself that thirty-five years after the fact, Kaitlyn Corsyn was somehow channeling "our" story, her work was just the hallmark of a good storyteller who was tapping into universal truths. I should know since I was an English teacher and taught my students the basic premise every day: what makes a classic story different from just any story is the fact that it is universal. When you read it, you feel as if you are reading about yourself.

But that does not mean that you are, in fact, reading about yourself.

I steeled myself, then took the loose manuscript pages from their hiding place and started to read.

Rule Breaking

The first school rule I broke, I don't even know if it counts as "breaking" it, really, since I was invited to break it by the headmistress herself.

I hate these old buildings. I stood in front of her door. You know the kind—it looks like it has way too many layers of black paint on it, and you can see the old layers underneath. There's an old brass boot scraper by the door, and the door's knocker is shaped like a lion's head. Thumping on the door, it makes a dull sound.

When the creamy envelope with the invitation showed up in my mailbox, I thought a lot about not even going—I held it between my index and middle finger, right over the metal-grill trash can in the school post office, and almost let it flutter down. I didn't want to "come for tea with my mother's dear friend." I didn't want to be treated any different as the daughter of an old girl. I'd seen where all that had gotten my mother.

But I guess you could say that in the final analysis, I lacked for guts—so there I was, thumping on the door at four in the afternoon.

"My dear girl," she said.

I pulled away from her embrace, but not before I got more of a whiff of her perfumey boobs than I wanted in a lifetime.

I stuck out my hand to her. No dice. She bypassed my hand, grabbing my chin and examining my face, the way old ladies do.

"Uncanny," she said. "Such a strong resemblance. You're lovely," she pronounced. "Although, it's such a shame the way you girls get yourselves up these days."

Not that I hadn't heard that one before. I didn't think my jeans and fisherman's sweater were any less attractive than Miss Wetherford's ugly tweed skirt and peach blouse.

The house was filled with rooms that looked like no one ever used them. Miss Wetherford showed me to one that she referred to as "the drawing room," which just put me more in mind of a movie set. There were two stiff blue wing-back chairs facing each other near a window; a little table was set between them, with a silver tray bearing a cut-glass decanter and some crystal sherry glasses. Those I could recognize easily because I know all the etiquette regarding anything and everything relating to booze. My mother always said that it was better to drink than eat because it helped keep you thin.

Miss Wetherford showed me to one of the chairs and sat down across from me. She sat in that awkward way that fat ladies sit—where it's hard for them to sit in a skirt and still keep their knees pressed tight together. She poured some amber liquid into her glass, and then she poured the same amount into mine.

"It's Bristol Cream," she said, giggling a little, which quite frankly just made me want to puke right then and there. "It's sweet."

I knew it was sweet. My mother bragged that she used to pour a little into my milk when she wanted me to sleep, and frankly, it tended to gag me a little. But then, I giggled too, because I realized that I was getting a buzz on with the headmistress of the Up-Your-Butt Academy at four in the afternoon on the second day of school, which had to be against all kinds of school rules. I picked up the glass and took a big gulp. It was too sweet, but it still burned nicely on the way down.

Miss Wetherford leaned forward toward me with this stupid rabbit look on her face.

"Now, we're not going to tell anyone about this, are we? Old girls get treated a little bit differently sometimes, and the new girls might not always understand. You'll find that not all the girls will have your same level of . . . refinement."

"Don't worry," I said. "It'll be our little secret."

"Your mother and I . . . ," the rabbit said. "I don't know if she's told you much about me." I had decided to think of her as the rabbit. There was something about the way her nose twitched and the way her eyes were pink around the rims. "She and I share—"

From down in the folds of her bosom came an ample hankie, with which she blotted her eyes.

"A very special bond."

I had to think twice before I answered her, because I remembered what my mother had said about the rabbit, precisely. I knew that I was only here at the Up-Your-Butt Academy because the rabbit had gotten me full tuition aid.

My mother, in one of her more lucid moments, had said, "Be attentive to Miss Wetherford. You will find that she can be of use to you."

I looked at her twitching nose and watering eyes, and forced a smile onto my face.

"My mother has told me so many lovely things about you,"
I said. I knew how to trot out the old girl manners when
needed, but they were as false fronted as the rest of me. Then,
I watched in horror what looked like a change of seasons pass
across her face—fall-winter-spring-and-summer—before she
reached some level of composure again.

"Isn't it nice to know that I've remained in her thoughts," she
finally said.

24

I had been avoiding both Josh and Jessica, since they always seemed to be in the midst of heated discussions, but Josh sought me out at lunch in Commons, pulling up a chair to my small table, ignoring my pile of half-corrected papers.

He was wearing rubber boots and worn brown corduroys, and he smelled of apples. He told me that he had been supervising the boys who were working down at the cider press, making the fresh cider to bottle and sell to tourists out by the road. I was trying not to notice that I found him intoxicatingly attractive, bathed as he was in the scent of fresh cider and with a high pink in his cheeks, so I busied myself stacking and restacking the papers in front of me. I opened my tea bag, but tossed the wrapper instead of the bag into the cup; flustered, I stuck my fingers into the hot water to fish out the paper and burned them.

"Here," he said, smiling. He took my fingers between his and plunged them into his cup of ice water, but his fingers lingered there, holding my hand in the cup. My fingers throbbed at first and then went numb, but the rest of my hand continued to throb long after he let go of it.

"So, are you really not interested in staying on with us?" Josh asked. His question took me aback. "What do you mean?"

"We're interviewing your replacement for next year. We've seen one already. The second is doing his practice teaching this afternoon. I just assumed . . ."

"Interviewing my replacement?" I said, trying not to sound panicked. "I haven't even finished my probationary period. Won't they give me a chance to prove myself?"

"Do you want to stay on? I thought maybe you had other plans— maybe you wanted to write another book."

"Josh, I really need this job. You have no idea!"

"Tell me," he said, looking at me intently.

But where to begin? Even with the room and board, my pay was barely adequate—each month the IRS took almost three-fourths of my check. If Charlie and I weren't living here, we'd be on food stamps, and I was afraid that if I couldn't keep up with the payments, I could end up in jail like my ex, and then where would Charlie be?

But still, ever since the manuscript pages had bubbled up to the surface, I'd been suppressing my instinct to pack my bags and flee. For the past few days, every time I closed my eyes, I imagined that I saw a frozen hand, moving as I pushed open a car door. For thirty-five years, I had learned not to think about it, but now, it was back. Josh was still staring at me with a questioning look on his face.

"There's not much to tell," I said.

At the far end of the hall, I saw that Jessica had just come in but had not spotted us yet, and I felt, like I always did, that somehow I was betraying her.

"There's Jessica," I said, a little too loud, to cover up the feeling.

"Oh good," he said, turning. "I need to talk to her." Then, the feeling of betrayal was swiftly replaced by a flicker of something that I refused to label as jealousy.

My first eight weeks of teaching were over. I was graduating from Antonia Roper's tutelage. She clapped me on the back so hard I gasped for breath. "You learned fast, kiddo. I wish my kids took to field hockey that fast."

She was grinning at me, wide enough to show me her pearly teeth, a full lineup of the best that orthodontia had to offer. Antonia was as burnished as a crisp McIntosh apple, her cheeks pink, her eyes sparkling with health. I was going to miss our tutoring sessions in Pencott.

"Do you feel like you've got a handle on the lessons and assignments for the rest of the marking period?" she said.

I nodded. "I think so."

"If you want to meet again at the beginning of each quarter to map it out, just give me a shout . . ."

"I don't want to screw anything up," I said.

"Did you ever think of going out for the permanent position?" Antonia said. "I think you'd make a pretty good teacher for the long haul, if that's what you want to do . . ." She leaned in and gave me a pat on the shoulder that felt more like a smack. "Hey, I put in a good word for you with Farber-Johnson. She kinda likes me, what with the winning season, and all."

"You did?" I had to turn quickly because I could feel tears fill my eyes.

"It's nothing. You deserve it." She graced me with another of her flat-handed shoulder whams.

"Gotta run—practice starts in five minutes."

Now, if I could only figure out how to solve the thorny problem of Kaitlyn Corsyn and her manuscript, maybe I would feel like I was getting my groove. When I arrived back at the dorm, I found another installment in my mailbox.

The Confrontation

On the night that we decided to sneak into the library after closing, I got to the yearbooks first. It wasn't my idea to go and I would have tried to get out of it, but June insisted. It was spooky to be alone in the dark in the big library. The ceilings with the peeling murals were so high and filled with shadows.

I found the 1961 yearbook right away, on the shelf, right where it belonged. I can't really explain why I indulged June in her silly game of tracking Miss Pimsley. I knew that Miss Pimsley had nothing to do with the murder of Chestmont Wooten. She was our nicest teacher, the one who went out of her way to try to help us. Senior year, she invited me over for tea. Of all our teachers, I think she was the only one who realized how much I was struggling. She was in my mother's class, and my mother had always spoken of her bitterly, but she was harmless and kind, and I didn't see why my mother had animosity toward her. Miss Pimsley knew that we were having money problems, and she encouraged me in my efforts to prepare myself to sit for the Eugenia Wilcox Prize. I knew that June and Lilly were both smarter than me, but I also knew that I was more determined because I wanted to win for a concrete reason, called money, whereas they only wanted to win so that they could come out on top.

There was another reason I wanted to win. My mother had told me a hundred times that she had won the Eugenia Wilcox Prize her senior year, but she had decided to get married instead. But when I came to school, there was a big plaque hanging in the hallway of Loomis Hall. I looked at the plaque,

skimming along until I saw 1961. That's when I realized that
my mom was lying all along—she didn't win. Her classmate
Miss Pimsley won. And it figures, right? Miss Pimsley can
quote poetry and knows almost everything about every writer
who ever lived, and my mom, what does she know, besides
how to serve cocktails and drink too many of them herself?

I felt like somebody punched me in the gut when I saw that
plaque. I stood there, in the hallway, and June was standing
right next to me, not paying any attention, and she didn't even
notice that anything was bothering me. But to me, it was just
one more thing being taken away from me.

So, back to the night in the library. I went and grabbed The
Lantern *from the class of 1961, and then for good measure, I*
grabbed the Hardley yearbook from the class of 1956. I flipped
through the portraits of senior girls until I came to the photo-
graph of my mother.

I can't explain exactly how I felt when I saw her picture. It was
black-and-white, and she had her hair styled in some kind of
bouffant waves—nobody in our generation would ever style
their hair like that—but her eyes were clear and her expression
unclouded. I could see my own face in hers. I couldn't under-
stand how the young woman in the picture had turned into
my crazy addled mommy. But the part that took my breath
away was that underneath her portrait, there was a list of all
her activities and prizes—and printed beneath her picture, it
said: Eugenia Wilcox Prize.

After that day, I never felt the same about Miss Pimsley. Her kindness was suspect. She felt sorry for me. She took the prize from my mother, and now she was trying to make up for it.

The more time I spent poring over those poems and notes, the more sure I became that something bad must have happened to my mother. How else to explain why she had changed from that beautiful clear-eyed girl in the photograph? The best I could figure, Miss Pimsley and Miss Wetherford were lovers, just like everyone said, and Miss Wetherford connived to give the prize to Miss Pimsley instead of my mother. A hot coal of rage settled into the pit of my stomach and did not want to leave.

I hid the yearbook from June and Lilly. I was determined to figure out the mystery by myself.

25

Saturday morning, I was just leaving Commons when Josh caught my arm.

"Any chance you'd like to head over to Hardley again? I'm going to do some apple picking. I could use an extra pair of hands."

I was about to blurt out a yes when I thought better of it.

"Where are Molly and Jessica?" I asked.

"Away," he said.

"I don't know," I said.

"Come on," he said. "A little fresh air and sunshine . . . ?" My hesitation swiftly melted in the warmth of his smile.

We walked together down to the rack where his and Jessica's bikes were parked, and soon, we were zipping along the road and over the bridge that crossed the Connecticut River. We passed through the brick gateway. The quickest way to reach the apple orchard was to cut straight across the campus. At the far end of the quad, we hopped off our bikes and stepped over the chain that blocked the road to the orchard.

"Do you think about your student days much?" I asked.

"Not so much anymore. When I first got here, the old days kept bleeding through to the surface. I'd see a student and think it was someone else. There was this one kid who I swear was the spitting image of one of my old burnout classmates. Every time I'd see him, all I could think of was ornithology."

I snorted, remembering his story of "ornithology."

"Awkward, right? I had to keep reminding myself that I need to keep my history as a first-class burnout under wraps. Now, I'm supposed to be a role model."

"That stresses me out too," I said. "It's a big job to be responsible for these kids. I worry I'm not up to the task."

"Straight arrow, Jane Milton?" he said.

"Nobody is as straight an arrow as they seem," I said.

"You Grove girls knew how to party," he said. "Who else would party in the *library*?"

"You remember that?" I asked, blushing in spite of myself.

"Hell yeah," he said. "We were blasting music on a little portable record player . . . Weren't you guys obsessed with trying to solve a murder or something?"

"Grove's most famous unsolved murder."

"The headmaster."

"Chestmont Wooten. We were convinced we could figure it out."

"So, why were you obsessed with it?"

"I think I was looking for something to distract me from the fact that we were all trying to rip each other's throats out. We kept thinking we were finding all these clues, but we never actually got anywhere."

"Well, I do remember my dad telling me something once."

"Really? What did he tell you?"

"Actually, I don't know if you remember this, but it was one night at Bernigan's Tavern, when we ran into you and Lissa and Kat."

Of course I remembered that night vividly. I stiffened slightly but tried not to give any sign.

"My dad knew Kat's mom and dad. He knew her dad, actually, from Hardley. Her mom came over to say hello. Do you remember how weird she was? In the car on the way back to school, my dad was talking to my mom and I heard him saying something about how people said that she was implicated in the murder, but it was all very hush-hush."

"Kat's mom?"

"Now, let me see if I can remember this one . . ." He started to recite:

> Now, Ches enjoyed teaching's demands.
> For he said, with no buts, ifs, or ands,
> "All my lessons are such
> Hardley a boy's left untouched,
> If not by my speeches, then hands."

"Hardly a boy's left untouched? *That's* what they said about Chestmont Wooten?"

Josh laughed. "They pretty much said that about all the faculty members. I think we figured there was no possible reason for anyone to work at a place like Hardley unless they were hoping to get lucky. All-boys' schools are not healthy environments."

"Why didn't you tell us then?" I asked. "We would have been all over those limericks. We used to think that clues to his murder were hidden in poetry."

Josh sighed. "Not anymore. No kids writing limericks, no kids scrutinizing poetry."

I started to tell him about *The Ghost of Abbott North*. He was wrong. The limerick tradition lived on. But I decided that I needed to keep that information to myself for a while longer.

We parked our bikes and walked side by side, and as his arm brushed mine from time to time as we walked, I stopped thinking about the past entirely.

Soon, we were under a bower of branches so laden with apples that we had to bow our heads just to make progress between the rows of trees.

The light flickered through the branches, making a dappled pattern on the ground. Josh stopped from time to time to inspect the apples, but he didn't say much. There were barrels stacked at the far end of the rows.

"You want to pick for a while?"

I nodded. We took stepladders and worked our way down the rows, mostly in companionable silence.

From time to time, I watched Josh. Sometimes, I could feel that he was looking at me.

We picked all morning, until my back and fingers ached, and I could feel the imprint of the ladder rung in the soles of my feet. Finally, at about noon, the section we were working on was mostly stripped.

It had been a warm morning, but now, clouds were passing over the sun, and the breeze was cool. I was sweaty from the apple picking. I shivered a little and looked toward the east, where the clouds were amassing.

I pointed to the uppermost branches of one of the nearby trees. "Look, we missed a few . . ."

". . . *there may be two or three / Apples I didn't pick upon some bough. / But I am done with apple-picking now*," Josh recited.

I grinned. "Robert Frost."

Josh looked tickled. "No one ever gets my quotations," he said.

I felt a raindrop splash on my forehead, then a moment passed, then another fell.

"Maybe we better get going," Josh said.

I looked up at the sky but felt nothing, until another cold raindrop fell from one of the leaves and dropped onto my cheek. "*A drop fell on the apple tree, / Another on the roof* . . . ," I said, turning to Josh. "I bet you don't know who that is . . ."

Then, suddenly the sky let loose in a downpour. Josh pulled an orange-nylon poncho out of his backpack and pulled it over both of us. We huddled together under it, so close that our breath mingled. I could list all the things Josh Miller smelled like: apples, of course, and wet earth, Shetland wool, and Lifebuoy soap, Cheerios, coffee, peppermint, sweat, and somewhere, deep down, there was the hint of vinyl from LP records and clove cigarettes, a whiff of pot, Budweiser beer, because maybe the memory of suppressed desire is stronger than desire itself.

"I do know," he said. "It's Emily Dickinson . . ."

Just then, the heavens unleashed a torrent of rain that splattered on the poncho we were holding over us, and then cascaded down in front of our faces. Josh and I looked at each other and giggled.

"A drop fell on the apple tree / Another on the roof; / A half a dozen kissed the eaves . . . ," he whispered. The recitation ended as his apple-scented lips covered mine. But when we pulled apart, my heart was pounding from the intoxicating rush of his kisses. I climbed out from under the poncho and ran until I found a corner of a building to huddle under, and I sat there, shivering, watching raindrops drip off the end of a stone gargoyle's nose.

Eventually, Josh caught up with me. "Sorry," he said. "I guess you weren't ready for that . . ."

I stood up too fast, banging my head against the stone overhang, and swore under my breath.

"You're still married," I said.

"Jane, we're separated . . . ," Josh said.

I shook my head no. "Poetry has a tendency to cloud my judgment."

Josh had brought the bike to me, and I had no choice but to get on it. We rode back to the Grove in pained silence.

For the rest of the afternoon, it poured. I went to Pencott to grade papers. Over and over again, I started to feel the sensation of collapsing into Josh's kisses, and I had to blink myself back to the hard white edges of Pencott, the computer screen blinking in front of me, the papers in a pile at my elbow.

I couldn't keep my mind on the grammar quizzes; I kept lapsing into thinking about the things that Josh and I had discussed. I felt as if somehow I had fallen through a rabbit hole and landed back in senior year, plunged into my old obsessions.

I tried to imagine how Keach Cunningham could have been connected in any way to the murder of Chestmont Wooten. I wondered what had ever become of her. I had always imagined that she was dead, but I realized that she was probably still alive. My own parents were alive and well and living in Florida. I was sitting in front of the computer. I opened the Google screen and typed *Keach Cunningham*; I stared at the name, then put quotes around it and pressed "Enter." But nothing came up. I realized that Keach must be one of those girls' school nicknames— like Pookie or Muffy. Still curious, I typed in *"Winslow Cavendish,"* and this time, a number of hits turned up. I found pictures of a building in New York City that was destroyed by fire in 1858. I found pictures of an eighteenth-century farmhouse on Sheepshead Bay; it appeared that a large swathe of what is now Brooklyn once belonged to their family.

I remembered that night in the library, when I found Kat looking at the picture of her father in the yearbook. I could picture the open page before me, and I tried again: *"Winslow Cavendish Cunningham III."* Now, at the top of the screen, I see a new one. It's from the AIDS Memorial Quilt project. I clicked on the link to open the image, and I saw a blue square with white lettering in an arc across it. It read: *Goodbye, Winnie / We love you and miss you / Your Fire Island Boys / 1935–1985*.

I stared at the blue square until it becomes an ocean of blue with the white letters shimmering on its surface. I could feel that I was no longer on steady ground.

I was not going to grade any more essays that night. I gathered up my half-graded stack, shoved them in my bag, and headed out into the rainy night.

When I got back to my rooms, there was a bundle of papers inside a brown envelope sitting outside my door. The outside of the envelope was still wet with rain speckles. I picked it up and carried it inside.

Queens

My mommy's clever plan to kill off my father stayed secret exactly halfway through one bottle of Tanqueray that I bought her with the money Lilly gave me for the blue angora sweater that Grammy sent me the last time she was in Paris. I took the bottle home with me in early November, when I told them I had to leave "for emergency reasons." I think Mommy would have drunk nail polish remover in a pinch, but she had a special fondness for Tanqueray in that green glass bottle with the red seal and the silver metal cap. She took special care when she drank it, sipping instead of gulping, all ladylike.

I sat right down by her elbow and watched her, waiting until I saw the little signs, the slight drop in her shoulders, the looseness in the corners of her mouth that told me she was defenseless against me. Just to be sure, I took one of the big pink plastic water tumblers and swashed some more gin in it. When she picked it up and drained it—no lime wedge, no ice cubes, no Schweppes tonic—then I knew I could get her to tell me anything.

"So . . . ," I said. "Where's Daddy?"

She looked at me out of the corner of her eye, like I wasn't going to have her that easy. "Heaven," she said. "Or maybe Hell. Depending on whom you ask."

"And where exactly is Heaven?" I continued. I was unperturbed. I knew that I was going to get somewhere.

"Where exactly?" She looked at me suspiciously. "What do you mean? Everyone knows where Heaven is."

"Well, I don't know exactly where it is," I said. "I don't know where Daddy's part of it is."

"Hmmph," she snorted, reaching past me for the green glass bottle. I helped her along, pouring the strong juniper-scented liquid into the plastic cup. "Well, as a matter of fact, I do."

"Well . . . where?" I said. I knew I had her, but I didn't want to let on.

"Queens," she laughed, as though she had just said something hysterically funny.

"Queens?"

Her eyes got big as she got her own joke. "In more ways than one . . . !" My mommy doubled over on the sofa, laughing so hard she started gagging, and she had to wipe away her snot with the back of her hands. "Queens, yeah, couple of 'em."

"Mommy, come on. You gotta tell me. Where is he?"

"Heaven . . . ," she said, and then she got all serious on me.
"That's my last word on the subject."

PART FOUR
SENIOR YEAR

26

"Why don't you stop stringing Josh along?" Kat said.

"Why should I?" Lissa said.

"You never even talk to him, you're going out with someone else—basically, you're just torturing the poor guy."

"He doesn't have to let himself be tortured."

I was lying on my bunk, trying to stay out of it. The tension in the room, and around the dorm in general, had been hovering near the boiling point recently. The senior girls were to sit for the Eugenia Wilcox exam in two weeks. Even among those who pretended not to care, there was an increased sense of rivalry, and among Lissa, Kat, and I, it had been crackling around the room like static.

"He came to visiting hours and you weren't even here," I said, trying to hide the hurt in my voice. I was sitting alone at my desk when Josh had poked his head in. He smiled at me, and for the briefest moment, I had imagined he might stay.

"Can you guys just shut up? I'm studying," Lissa said.

"You have your own room," I said irritably. "Why don't you go in there?"

"With Cornwell? She never shuts up."

I shrugged and turned my attention back to my French homework. Lissa and Kat had been tearing their hair out studying for Eugenia Wilcox. But for the past couple of weeks, while the other girls had been cramming, I'd done nothing but pore over Emily Dickinson, line by line, trying to unlock the mystery that I was certain must be revealed in the verses.

Now, it was Friday night, and there were visiting hours for Hardley boys, but with Eugenia Wilcox looming, Lissa and Kat couldn't be budged from their desks. The problem with the Wilcox exam was that they could ask you almost anything. The question was pulled from something that had been studied during the four-year sequence of English courses. Every year, the question was different, although the committee seemed to favor questions about poetry.

Having decided not to sit for the exam, I didn't need to study, but I had no date for visiting hours, so I headed to Pencott Library. Mrs. Owen-Farrell, the librarian, had agreed to get out the boxes of microfilm where the old copies of the *Grove Bell*, the school newspaper, were stored.

The microfilm reader was in a dusty corner of Pencott, around the back of the circulation desk; the space was not easily seen from the main reading room. Mrs. Owen-Farrell brought a misshapen old shoebox, its blue color faded on one side.

The light felt like a heat lamp on my face. Sweat started to bead up on my forehead, and I had to pull off my sweater. The box was filled with tightly coiled plastic rolls. I had asked the librarian to bring me the year 1961. I had no idea there would be so many rolls. I pulled one out at random, attached it to the wheel, and started to scroll through, looking at the tiny pages as they flashed by on the screen.

I wasn't sure when the murder had taken place, but I had a hunch that it was winter, so I scrolled through some early fall issues, changed the roll, and tried again.

Now, I was into some later fall issues, scrolling quickly through the headlines until suddenly I stopped. There was a picture of a group of girls standing on Siberia in front of Loomis Hall, and something caught my eye. I looked at the girls in the picture. They were dressed in light-colored skirts and white button-down shirts with Peter Pan collars; their hair was drawn back into buns. Two of the girls had fair hair, but one was dark. It was the dark-haired girl whose face drew me in. She was fine featured and very pretty, her waist slim in the skirt. She cradled her schoolbooks in her arms.

I looked at the caption on the photograph: *Senior girls enjoying the unseasonably warm weather wait outside for class to begin.* Did I know her? I felt sure that it wasn't Miss Pymstead, who was fair, and the face was different—more elfin, less elongated. No, Miss Pymstead would never have looked like that. Perhaps Miss Pymstead could have been one of the other girls in the picture. One of the blond girls—their faces were not clear enough to discern their identities. I lingered a moment longer, but still, I couldn't place the face, and so I scrolled forward, then replaced the roll, and continued scrolling, through Lantern Day, through Christmas Vespers. Finally, in the paper dated February 17, 1961, I found what I was looking for. Just one paragraph. An obituary. Nothing about the cause of death. I shifted in my seat. The only thing I had ever heard was that he had been murdered, or shot. But had he really been shot? How had he been killed? I sat staring at the page on the screen, the heat blasting out from the lamp, the light searing my eyes.

An ice-cold hand gripped my shoulder. I gasped, jerked my head around. I found myself looking in a face as white and flat as a china plate.

"Abigail? For God's sake. Take your hand off me. You scared me half to death."

"Somebody is looking for you," she said.

"Who is it?" I whispered. I could still feel the outline of her hand on my shoulder, and the feeling of its imprint gave me the shivers.

She shrugged.

"Who is it?" I repeated. But I could tell she wasn't going to answer. She was peering over my shoulder, looking at the image of the newspaper that was still blazing on the viewer in front of me. Up close, she had a pungent body odor, as sharp as soiled cat litter. I leaned away, flicking the switch so that the light on the viewer went off and the image of the newspaper faded away.

"They say somebody shot him," Abigail said. "And the blood froze all around him in the snow."

"Shot who?" I said, my eyes narrowing with suspicion.

"Your man," she said. "Wooten. The blood froze in the shape of a heart. You better hurry up. Somebody is waiting for you. Outside. By the sugar maple. I wouldn't keep him waiting. It's colder than a witch's tit out there."

Abigail turned and walked away, leaving a trace of her stink behind.

I was unable to sift through the various things she said, not least of which was how it was she had come to figure out that Chestmont Wooten was "my man." I popped the microfilm off the reel and shoved it into the box, which I carried to the front desk. Out front, I slipped on the ice of the marble steps of the library, barely managing to right myself by grabbing the brass railing with my mittened hand.

The day had gotten warm enough to thaw the surface of the ice, but now it was frozen again, and each of my steps made a brittle cracking sound. Somebody in Levi's and a puffy down jacket was leaning against the tree. I saw longish brown hair, a green-and-white Dartmouth scarf—and I felt my rib cage breaking open like a pair of hands.

"Josh?"

"Kat told me you weren't studying."

"I don't want to go to a women's college," I said.

"Oh." Josh looked puzzled. And cold. He looked very cold. He had his hands jammed in his jeans pockets. His breath was coming out in snowy bursts. He shifted his weight from one foot to the other and stamped.

I realized that the conversation wasn't going well.

"Well, what are you here for?"

Cold or not, he had a smile to melt glaciers. I felt mine melting; it was melting so fast that the snow I was standing on might melt away, leaving me floating on nothing but air. The ground itself might melt. I might fall through to China. Even in the snow-lit night, I could see the blue in his eyes.

"Well, I thought . . ." Josh stopped. Looked at the ground. "Um, I . . ."

Then, like one of those time-lapse photography films, I felt my melted glacier start to freeze up again.

"It's Lissa, isn't it?" I said. "She's busy—she's studying."

"I know," he said. "It's not that it's—" He held out his hand to me palm out, the way you hold out your hand to a dog that you're afraid might bite you.

"Why don't you stop following her around like some lovesick groupie," I said. "It's pathetic."

He jammed his hand back in his pocket. He stood there for a minute, just looking at me. Hands in pockets, he stamped the ground a couple more times.

"Is that what you think I'm doing?"

I nodded.

"Then I want to tell you something. Lissa is the kind of girl that you forget if you aren't looking straight at her."

Josh turned and started walking toward the roadway that led toward the buses that took the Hardley boys back to their school at the close of visiting hours.

"Josh—"

At first, I didn't think he was going to turn around.

"What?"

"What kind of girl am I?"

"The kind Byron was talking about!" he called as he jogged across the icy grass toward the front gate. At least that's what I think he said. I couldn't quite hear him over the loud crunching sound his footsteps made as he ran.

27

All of a sudden, without our quite noticing it, it was the first of April. I uncovered no further clues in the Wooten case. The clue notebook lay untouched on the corner of my desk as if it were an adolescent crush I had outgrown.

One day, Katie Cornwell came into Commons with an unexpected bounce in her step, seeming to radiate a newfound light. Katie had never had the ability to make people look up when she passed through the door of Commons. Only a few people had that—Lissa, of course, Kat, me, but only when I was with them. But now, we were all looking up at Katie. She was holding something in her hand, something that we would all soon learn to recognize as a fat admissions envelope.

Katie Cornwell had been admitted to Yale, and her acceptance letter had arrived in a well-stuffed envelope, folded and crammed into her Grove PO box that day, two weeks before the "official" date when letters were supposed to be mailed out.

Back in our room, Lissa was atwitter with the news.

"What do you expect?" she said. "She's a Vanderbilt on her mom's side. Do you know that at Yale there's a special room in Vanderbilt Hall, and if any descendants are in the freshman class, they get to claim it. If not, then it goes by lottery."

"That's outrageous," I said.

"Who wants to be a Vanderbilt?" Kat sniffed. "Everyone knows they were robber barons."

"Better to be a robber baron," Lissa said, "than to have to beg for your college tuition."

Kat reached across and slapped Lissa on the cheek so fast that for a second I could see the imprint of her small hand across Lissa's high cheekbone.

"How dare you?" Kat stood with her heels pressed together, perfectly still, like a ballet dancer in first position. Her eyes narrowed. Rose-colored blotches appeared on her cheeks, but her face was otherwise deathly pale.

Lissa opened her mouth to say something and then shut it again, and I felt a small flame of satisfaction knowing that she had been bested. Finally, she banged her books together into a stack and flounced out of the room.

It started to warm a little. The ice melted during the day, and then froze again at night. The morning of April fifteenth dawned clear and bright and a little warmer. I could smell the spring thaw in the air.

The Eugenia Wilcox exam was to be held in the large lecture hall in Loomis Hall. I hadn't seen Lissa, but Kat got up in time for breakfast. We sat in Commons together. Kat sipped her black coffee, not saying much. Her hair was pulled back into a neat ponytail, and she had three sharpened pencils and three blue Bics lined up in a row next to her.

I brought her a slice of toast. She nibbled at the corners, then at her bitten-to-the-quick fingernails.

When she got up, she gave me a quick hug and whispered in my ear. "Most people wouldn't do something like this. I'll never forget it," she said.

She walked all the way down the length of Commons, threading her way through the tables and chairs. Then, she pushed open the double doors at the far end and disappeared in a flash of light. Up until that moment, I had believed that I was going to do the right thing. I was going to sacrifice my own chance for glory to help out a friend in need. But just a moment after she left my sight, I realized Jane Milton was not that person. I was going to betray her.

I looked at my watch. After ten minutes had passed, I got up and hurried in the same direction. By the time I got to Loomis Hall, most of the girls were already there, hunched over their blue books, their pencils scratching on the pages. I saw Kat way up toward the front, bent over her work. I didn't see Lissa but thought she must be way up in front. I ducked into one of the back rows, taking care to sit directly behind Kat so that I would be out of her line of sight.

Miss Pymstead looked up when I came in, and I saw the expression on her face: studied neutrality, but it masked something deeper. Her eyes were a deep navy, and they locked onto mine.

"You are late," she whispered, her voice barely audible.

I nodded, my eyes downcast.

She picked up a blue book and walked down the aisle toward me, setting the pages of the exam and the blue composition book in front of me.

There were two white pages stapled together, on the first page, it said: *The Eugenia Wilcox Prize for the Senior Examination in English.*

I turned to the second page. Inside, it said: *Explicate the following poem.*

I felt gray, then white, then little black dots flash in front of my eyes as the words of Emily Dickinson appeared on the page:

Remorse is memory awake,
Her companies astir,—
A presence of departed acts
At window and at door.

Its past set down before the soul,
And lighted with a match,
Perusal to facilitate
Of its condensed despatch.

Remorse is cureless,—the disease
Not even God can heal;
For 't is His institution,—
The complement of hell.

There was light streaming in the tall Palladian window, striking the white page. I had the sensation that the typewritten words were popping off the paper, glowing with an orb of light around them.

I could hear Miss Pymstead's voice ringing in my ears as it did the first day that she had introduced Emily Dickinson to us in Gould Cottage: *Girls, never think of Emily Dickinson as a frustrated woman, nor as unpublished, nor as a spinster . . .* I had spent the past three months poring over the poems of Emily Dickinson, searching for clues. At first, her poems had seemed completely opaque to me. I could never seem to see what she was getting at, but the months of solitary study, which had gotten me no closer to solving the murder of Chestmont Wooten, had given me a deep appreciation of the poems. I was going to win the Eugenia Wilcox Examination, and I was so sure that I could feel the hair standing up on my forearms and the blood pulsing in my ears.

I rolled the new number-two Ticonderoga pencil between my fingers and folded back the composition book, making a smart crease in the blue paper cover. An hour later, I was done. I closed the blue book, walked to the back of the auditorium, and placed it facedown in the small cardboard box next to the back door.

Kat never knew I was there.

That year, April 15, the day of the Eugenia Wilcox exam, fell on a Saturday; the rest of the Yale admissions envelopes arrived the following Monday, Black Monday. That day, when I looked in my PO box, I saw a skinny envelope. Yale had placed both me and Lissa on the waiting list. Kat had been admitted.

28

As though to remind us that she wouldn't let us go so easily, winter dumped two feet of snow on the night of April 17. The daffodils bowed their heads in submission; the crocuses were buried. But for those of us who had felt the sting of the Black Monday of college admissions, we welcomed the return of winter. It made us feel that perhaps the Grove wasn't planning to cast us out those gates so soon.

Kat swore she hadn't breathed a word of her Yale success to her mother, but the ancient Range Rover pulled down the freshly plowed main drive the next morning. Keach looked a bit less bedraggled than usual, her knobbiness covered in a white mink. She tapped up the stairs of Lane North like the Pied Piper, collecting a following of Emma Doerr, Abigail Von Platte, and Katie Cornwell.

She pushed open the door to Kat's and my room and stood at the threshold, her arm extended in front of her.

Keach loved nothing more than an audience, so she plucked a bottle of Wild Turkey from her bag and tossed it onto my bunk while the other girls looked on, eliciting just the sort of hushed gasp I'm sure she was looking for. Then, she gave them her most winning smile. "Now, darlings, if you'll just excuse us for a moment . . . ?"

The three girls backed up, murmuring politely, and Keach nudged the door shut with the tip of her finger.

She looked around at our cramped quarters, the bras hanging on the bedsteads, the crumpled socks gathering dust.

She held her hand out in a theatrical gesture. *"Sweet hours have perished here / This is a mighty room . . ."* Perhaps she was waiting for applause, but when her words were met with stony silence, she added, "That's Emily Dickinson, you know."

"What are you doing here, Mom?" Kat hadn't even gotten up. She stared at her mother morosely, upside down from the top bunk.

"But, darling, I'm just so proud of you—I've come to take you three out for a celebration."

"There's no reason to celebrate. I don't want you here. Just go away."

"Now, sweetheart. What way is that to treat the mother who drove all the way here through a snowstorm to see you?"

"I didn't ask you to do that."

"And, Jane darling, how are you? Aren't you happy to see me, and where is that lovely Lissa? Are you girls going to Yale too?"

"I'm not going to Yale," Kat said.

"Oh, whatever nonsense are you talking about? Of course you are going to Yale."

Kat jumped off the bed and lunged at her mother so fast that Keach recoiled and stumbled against my wooden desk chair, twisting her ankle and breaking the heel of her shoe.

"Ow, now look what you've made me do! What on earth is the matter with you?" Keach shook her purse open and fumbled around in it until she found her pack of Chesterfields. "Well, in any case, we're going to celebrate. I'm taking you out to Bernigan's Tavern, so don't make any plans. Tonight is a night to celebrate."

"You're going to *pay* for it?" Kat said skeptically.

"Of course, darling. I'm *inviting* you."

Kat rolled her eyes.

"*You'll* come, darling, won't you?" she said to me, giving me what I assumed was supposed to be a winning smile.

I was too polite to say no to someone's mother, even if that mother was Keach, so I nodded my assent.

Throughout the day, the weather got colder, and by the evening, the temperature had plummeted to the upper teens. It had been snowing off and on all day. At about a quarter to seven, Kat pulled on her Bean boots, white cap, and a thick fisherman's sweater, calling out over her shoulder, "If Keach is looking for me, tell her I'll be right back."

"Where are you going?"

"Underhill House."

"You're going to see Miss Wetherby?"

Kat shrugged and shot me a challenging glance. I didn't respond. By the time Keach came to get us, Kat had returned. I noticed that her pants legs were damp from her walk through the snow, and I guessed, since she hadn't been gone more than ten or fifteen minutes, that Miss Wetherby hadn't been home.

Keach wanted to start in the bar, and so we did. The bartenders would overlook the drinking age for Grove girls if the parents ordered, so we ordered whiskey sours and Keach got a gin and tonic. Our drinks were watered down, but just being off campus for the first time since Christmas felt heady enough.

Keach downed three gin and tonics in rapid succession, and though her behavior didn't change in any significant manner, I did notice a certain slackness around the corners of her smile. When she was halfway through her fourth gin and tonic, a waiter came to show us to our table. We were making our way through the dining room when I caught a glimpse of a blue blazer, a ring of wavy hair curling over the collar—Josh.

He had his back to me, but I could see that he was with his mother and father. His father was black haired and solemn-looking. His mother was pretty, and she was listening intently to something he was saying. Josh looked up, and caught sight of us. "Hey," he said softly, as if expecting us to stop—but then the waiter led us across the dining room in the opposite direction.

When Keach got up to use the ladies' room, the heel of her shoe, which she had glued back in place, had come loose again. She half limped across the now-crowded dining room, pushing herself past a group that was waiting to be seated. I watched her, hoping that Josh Miller and his parents would not notice her. But to my dismay, as she approached their table, I could hear her voice rising into a shriek. "George *Mi*-ller. Can that really be *you?*"

Keach took her time coming back from the ladies' room, and when she returned, she was wearing the mink, had her purse tucked under her arm, and wore a fresh coat of lipstick.

"Girls, I'm just going to leave you here for five minutes while I run out and do a little errand. I'll be right back." She turned quickly and hop-walked out.

I glanced at my watch in confusion.

"Packy closes at nine," Kat said. "She'll be back. If she doesn't skid off the road and kill herself. Pretty icy out there."

"Kat," I gasped in spite of myself.

"*Jane,*" Lissa said, licking chocolate icing off the tines of her fork. "Relax."

We waited a long time for Keach to come back, so long that the waiter started to get a little antsy. Finally, Lissa asked for the bill. She slid a slim green American Express card out of her wallet, waving it at him between her index and middle finger.

"Do you take these?" she said.

I had never seen anyone with a credit card except for my father. I looked at Kat, waiting for her to put up a fuss since it was her mother who had invited us out for this celebratory dinner.

But Kat gave the impression that she wasn't paying attention, and the waiter took the credit card and came back with a black leather folder containing the slip for Lissa to sign.

It wasn't until a few minutes before closing that Keach returned. She gave no explanation for where she had been, nor did she inquire how we had paid for our dinner.

Outside, the air was bitter cold and the night was dark but clear, the stars bright pinpoints. It had been snowing steadily since we entered the restaurant, and it didn't look as if the snowplow had come by.

Keach drove fast. I gripped so tight to the side of the door that I was losing sensation in my fingertips. My feet pressed into the carpeted floor. Each time we hit a bump, there was a clinking of bottles from the back.

Nobody said a word.

Just as we entered the stone gates of the Grove, the car started to skid. I saw one of the stone pillars veering toward me, like in a carnival ride, but then the tires got traction and the car straightened as it passed through the gates.

If I thought Keach would slow down when she crossed into campus, I was wrong. She careened down the long roadway, through the woods, past Echo Lake. With each too-fast turn, I could feel a sickish skid-out moment, and then the tires would grip the road again.

Kat was slumping against the window in the front seat. I couldn't see her expression. Lissa was sitting beside me with her face pressed up against the window and one hand gripped tightly around her seat belt.

Keach gunned the accelerator, and the wheels spun out on the ice, then the car leapt forward. We were heading for the sharp turn that went up behind Whittaker Chapel.

There was a bump. A thump. Another big bump, and then the car did start to skid, sideways and zigzag, and front to back. The skidding seemed to last forever, until abruptly the car jerked to a stop, flinging us all forward, then back hard against our seats.

Nobody made a sound.

"What the hell just happened?"

"I don't know." I had banged my head, and I wasn't sure that we had stayed upright. I looked around. Lissa was next to me. Kat in front. Out the window, everything was white. Not only was the car upright, but miraculously, we still seemed to be on the road.

"Girls? You all right back there?" Keach's voice sounded unsteady. "Everybody okay? I think we skidded a little."

"Skidded. I think we hit something, Mom. It felt like we hit something."

"Hit something?" Now, she sounded tentative. Was it possible that she hadn't noticed the bump?

I peered through the window, but there was nothing on any side of us, except the empty roadway.

"Why don't we just get going?" Lissa sounded petulant. "I really want to get home. I have a calculus test tomorrow."

"Maybe it was a flat tire?" I said. "A blowout, or something. Would that feel like a bump?" Nobody said anything.

"Do you want to get out and check, dear?" Now, I could hear the bending tones in her voice, and I could feel my heart battering against my rib cage. It felt just the way I remembered a bird's heart felt beating against my fingers when I picked one up that had broken its wings.

"Me?" I said, but my voice caught in my throat.

I cursed myself for wearing good leather shoes instead of my snow boots. With my Bean boots, I could have just gotten out of the car and walked back to Lane from there, but there was eighteen inches of snow, it was freezing, and we were still clear on the other end of campus from Cottage Row.

I popped up the lock button and tried to push the door open. I met resistance and pushed harder. The door didn't want to open. I put my shoulder into it.

Then, suddenly, the door popped open, and the interior light flashed on.

Before I knew what I was doing, I screamed and drew back to the far side of the backseat, pushing up hard against Lissa.

It was an arm, in a blue wool sleeve, and a white hand, fingers and thumb curled half-open, protruding into the car. Kat had turned half around and was screaming too. Then Lissa or I—accidentally or on purpose—pushed the handle and the door flew open, and we fell backward into the snow on the other side of the car. The shock of the cold riding up under our shirts in the back made us stop screaming and gasp for air.

Kat opened her door and got out, on our side of the car. The safe side.

"What was it?" she whispered. "It looked like—*a hand.*"

"I can't open my door. Girls . . . *Girls!* Come around to this side. I can't open my door. Something is blocking the door. I can't open it."

I could see Keach inside the car, ramming her shoulder against the door with more and more force, making little grunting sounds now. "Girls! I'm serious. Help me get out."

"What should we do?" Kat said. "She has claustrophobia. She may freak out."

"Leave her there for a sec," Lissa said. "We need to see what's . . . over there . . ."

"I'm not going. I don't want to look. Let's go back to the dorm and tell them that we found a body up on the road and that somebody needs to come."

I could feel my heart doing an odd staccato, like a piano playing the "Flight of the Bumblebee." I had gotten one look at that hand, but one look was enough. I knew that hand belonged to a dead person, and I didn't want to see it again. I wanted to get as far away from that hand as possible and let someone else take care of it.

"Girls! Girls, let me out . . ." Kat's mom was letting out weird-sounding sobs now. Like a cat stuck in a tree.

"Mom, shut up."

"Doesn't she know she can get out the other side?" Lissa whispered.

"Shut up. Don't tell her," Kat said. "That'll just make it worse."

"We need to go get someone. Miss Dockerty, or Miss Wetherby, or someone," I said, turning to leave. I would just have to walk down to campus in my Pappagallos since this was an emergency.

"Jane, don't go anywhere. Wait a second."

"Kat, you let Mummy out of this car right now. Right now. You understand me. I can't stay in here." Keach leaned over and started banging on the door again. With each bang, the Range Rover rocked a little.

"Guys, we need to think."

"Why do we need to think?"

"Because . . . ," Kat said. "Because, let's say there is a person over there . . . What if we did run into someone. We can't just leave them there. We need to see if they need help."

I thought about that hand, and I knew deep down that whoever it was, he or she was beyond help—but I also knew Kat was right.

Lissa, Kat, and I joined hands and slowly made our way around the side of the car. There was almost no light, just the little illumination from the car's interior light shining on the snow.

At first I was relieved. There was no hand there. There was nothing there. Just the roadway, some snowdrifts.

I felt the terror slip out of me as I studied the mounds of snow, the bushes, the rocks that lined the side of the road.

Then, Lissa's and Kat's nails dug into the soft flesh of my palms.

Pushed up against the driver-side door was a pile of snow. Emerging from that snow was a woman's torso with an arm extended. Her head was hidden under the frame of the car. But even with the snow-covered torso and the hidden head, it was not difficult to recognize the woman. We had just run over Miss Wetherby.

Lissa went back around to the passenger-side door and grabbed a flashlight from the glove compartment, ignoring Keach, who was now slumped at the steering wheel, babbling nonsense to herself.

The three of us crouched down near the mount of snow and peered under the car. The beam of the flashlight revealed the worst. Miss Wetherby's hair stuck straight out behind her. What I could see of her head appeared intact, but there was a black smudge on her forehead. Her eyes stared wide open glassily. Her lips were parted.

"What do we do now?" I whispered. My lips felt cracked.

"We check her pulse," Lissa said. "Then we administer mouth-to-mouth breathing if necessary."

I stood up, but I felt myself swaying, so I quickly crouched down again.

"Take her pulse," Lissa said to Kat.

"I don't know how. You do it."

"I don't know how either."

They both looked at me. She took hold of the extended arm and pushed it toward me. "Do it."

I put my hand on the arm. Shivers that felt as alive as snakes crawled up my skin. I dropped the arm and it thudded, stiff as a piece of firewood.

Lissa picked it up and thrust it back into my mittened hand.

"Take your mitten off."

But I couldn't get any landmarks. I pushed up the sleeve a little. Miss Wetherby was wearing a watch. I could feel it ticking. I touched the surface of her skin, which felt slick, frozen.

"There's no pulse."

"Are you sure?" Lissa said.

I wasn't sure. I was hardly an expert, but I didn't think a living person should be that cold.

"She's wearing a medical bracelet," I said, then read the words on it aloud. "In case of chest pain, administer nitroglycerin?"

"Okay," Lissa said. "Let's try that."

"Lissa, look at her—she's frozen solid."

Lissa looked at her, shining the flashlight the length of her and then finally prodding her, first with a finger and then with the toe of her shoe.

She flashed the light beam up and down the length of the body, then into the cab of the car, where Keach was still slumped over the steering wheel, if not passed out, then close to it.

"She's dead," Lissa said. "But we didn't kill her. She must have fallen out here, and it's so cold that she froze."

But there was something that didn't make sense.

"Then how come we didn't run over her on the way out?" I said.

"Maybe somebody else ran her over," Lissa said. "Could a body freeze this solid in the four or five hours since we left?" On this point, we were unsure.

"Look, she's half covered with snow."

Lissa started to dust the powder off the body with her hand.

"I think you should leave it," I said. "It might be evidence."

Lissa ignored me and continued, brushing the snow that was covering Miss Wetherby's belly. I could see what she was doing. It was clear that there was a piece of paper clutched in her right hand—the one that hadn't protruded against the car door.

Kat made a sudden movement. She leaned forward and grabbed it. Lissa tried to get it from her, but Kat was too quick. The paper was wound into a tight scroll. Kat unwound it, and Lissa shone the light on it, but Kat held it away from her, so Lissa couldn't see it—but I could.

Kat met and held my glance, then the three of us turned toward the Range Rover, where Keach let out a loud moan.

"Give me that," I said. "It might be a clue." I took the paper from Kat and shoved it into my jacket pocket.

Kat bent and grabbed one of Miss Wetherby's legs. "Come on now, you've got to help me pull her off the road."

"What are you talking about?" Lissa said.

"We can't pull her off the road. We need to leave her here so that when the police come, they can see how we found her. We'll walk down the hill. Just leave your mom in the car . . . ," I said.

"Are you crazy?" Kat said. "We can't leave my mom in the car. She's drunk. They'll say she killed her."

"She didn't kill her," Lissa said. "Anyone can see that. She must have been dead long before we got here. We'll just explain what happened."

"If she was lying in the road for a long time, how will we explain the fact that we didn't run over her on the way out?" I said again. My teeth were chattering, and all I wanted to do was get off this hill and inside someplace warm.

Lissa shone the light into the Range Rover again. Keach hadn't changed position, though she was awake and muttering gibberish to herself.

"Jesus Christ," Lissa said.

"I can drive," Kat said. "Let's just . . . move the body so that I can drive the car down the hill. Please, please. Come on, guys. Please. She's dead anyway. What difference does it make?"

Our only other alternative was starting to seem less and less appealing: we'd have to traipse down the hill, go and alert someone, Mrs. Dockerty presumably, and have her come up here and try to explain about Keach and the Range Rover and how Miss Wetherby was already dead when we hit her.

My teeth were chattering so hard it was like having rapid gunfire inside my head. I looked at Lissa; she looked at me. We looked at

Keach, who had starting moaning again, and then our eyes followed the flashlight beam that Lissa had trained on Miss Wetherby's frozen white face.

Lissa went over to her, unburied one of her feet, and gave it a tug. She nodded to me, and I grabbed hold of her other foot and tugged as well. We braced our feet in the snow.

"One. Two. Three. *Pull.*" Lissa said. We tugged on Miss Wetherby's stiff body. At first she didn't move at all—then all of a sudden, she did.

I remember in the brief moment that I felt the body jerk free, I was so startled that I let go. Maybe Kat and Lissa did the same. I don't know. What I do know is that her frozen body tobogganed right off the road and sped down Founder's Hill, the steep hillside that sledders favored. In the dark, we couldn't see where it ended up, but after four winters at the Grove—including many afternoons spent sledding—we could imagine that Miss Wetherby most likely came to her final resting place somewhere in the environs of the backside of Gould Cottage. Her body probably stopped in the vicinity of Miss Pymstead's front door.

The three of us—Kat, Lissa, and I—stood in stunned silence, but then Lissa set to brushing the snow to cover the footprints we had made, and Kat and I followed suit. My hands were bare, and the cold snow was stiffening and numbing my fingers. When my palm struck something hard, at first I thought it was a rock. But by chance, Lissa flashed the light toward me and I saw the glint of something metallic—a gold earring or ring—attached to a leather thong. Kat noticed it at the same moment. Her hand darted out; she scooped it up and then quickly shoved it into her pocket, muttering, "there it is" under her breath.

"What was that?" I asked, my teeth chattering so hard I could barely get the words out.

"Not now!" she whispered, pulling open the car's driver side door. "We need to get out of here."

Kat shoved her mother away from the steering wheel to make room for herself and climbed into the driver's side of the Range Rover. Keach had toppled over into the passenger seat and was, apparently, passed out.

When we got back to the dorm, it was a couple of minutes before ten thirty, which was lights-out, but the door was already locked.

"Good thing I was just unlocking for somebody else so you didn't have to wait for me—it's freezing out here," a male voice said.

Nate Hodges came around from the back of the building, seemingly out of nowhere.

I looked up quickly to see if he had noticed that Kat was at the wheel of the Range Rover, but she had already pulled it around to the side parking lot.

He unlocked the door of Lane North with a loud rattle of keys. I remember that he was wearing a red-plaid hunting jacket but his hands were bare despite the cold.

I was so exhausted by then, overwhelmed—and maybe still tipsy from the two whiskey sours—that it seemed to take a long time to get to the top of the stairs. Then, partway down the hallway, the blasting heat from the radiator got to me. I leaned over and vomited on the floor, barely missing the shoes that were sitting on a square of newspaper, surrounded by a puddle of melting snow, right outside Abigail Von Platte's door. By three in the morning, when I awoke in a cold sweat, Keach had driven away; the spot where the Range Rover had been visible from the window of our room was empty.

I like to think that the thud of certainty with which I awoke fully later that morning was similar to the thud with which Miss Wetherby's feet knocked upon Miss Pymstead's door the night before. It is said— and I like to believe that it's true—that she heard what she thought was a knock at her door, that she then pulled on her dressing gown and went to look through the peephole in her door. But when she saw nothing, she stayed up for over an hour, drinking tea and reading Swinburne, before she felt calm enough to return to bed.

29

In the morning, the campus appeared serene; the snow was already throwing back her bedclothes, showing rumpled sheets of green here and there beneath the sodden drifts. As I pushed through the doors of Lane, my eyes darted across Siberia and down toward Gould Cottage. Its back was completely obscured from this angle, but I saw no unusual activity.

At breakfast in Commons, there was a brief announcement that Senior Honors English would be cancelled, as Miss Pymstead was ill. I glanced worriedly at Lissa. Was this related to the frozen corpse of Miss Wetherby that had no doubt landed in the vicinity of Miss Pymstead's doorstep? Kat had not come to breakfast, but then, that was unlikely to arouse attention. I was so nervous I couldn't eat a bite.

As I was leaving Commons, Nate Hodges waylaid me and said I was wanted in Loomis Hall, the administration building. Just then, I saw Kat approaching up the hill in the company of Mrs. Dockerty, and as I started up the hill, I saw that Lissa had come out of Commons and was being taken aside by Nate Hodges as well.

The trip up the hill seemed interminable. The high walls and stern façade of Loomis Hall looked like a prison, and as I walked, I mentally measured the distance from the walkway to the woods and contemplated the possibility of fleeing. Out of the corner of my eye, I watched Kat and Lissa. Lissa was smiling and chatting with Mrs. Dockerty, but I couldn't hear what she was saying over the thundering in my ears. Kat's expression was neutral, and she was looking down at her feet as she walked.

There were a number of people milling around, most of whom I didn't recognize. Mrs. Dockerty showed us to a drawing room and seated us on a stiff sofa.

A tall, slender man whom I recognized as Mr. Treadway, the headmaster of the Hardley School, came into the room, and the three of us stood up like jack-in-the-boxes, but he motioned us to sit back down.

"Thank you so much for coming, girls," he said, giving us a smile that though genial struck me as forced. His eyes were light blue, and his hairline was receding. I had already taken a dislike to him, but I attempted to plaster a smile on my face. An innocent smile. My knees started to tremble, and I pressed my arms against them on both sides to try to get them to stop.

"I'm sure you're wondering why we've called you here," he said.

The three of us nodded solemnly. I glanced sideways at Lissa. She was wearing Kat's blue angora sweater. It flattered her, bringing out the blue in her eyes. She was smiling.

That was when I noticed that there was another man in the room, and though he wasn't wearing a uniform, I could pretty much tell he was a policeman. There was something about the way his pants were creased and his shoes were shined, and the way his sweater bunched up over the belt and the front pocket area. Hardley and Grove men didn't look like that. Plus he had a clipboard and a pad of paper.

Maybe Mr. Treadway noticed the look of fear that passed over my face, because he said, "Please, girls, I don't want you to be worried about anything. We just want to ask you a few simple questions. It just so happens that you were the only girls who left campus yesterday evening. I'm afraid that there was an accident yesterday. We were just wondering if perhaps any of you might have seen anything. That's all."

"An accident?" Lissa said.

"Yes, I'm afraid so," Mr. Treadway said. "It's very unlikely that you would have seen anything, but Nate told us that you were out to dinner last night, and we thought just on the off chance—"

The other man looked up. "Do you mind if I jump in—?"

"Girls, this is Detective O'Connor."

"How do you do?" Kat said.

"He's just going to ask a few questions."

Lissa smiled and flipped her blond hair around. "Go right ahead."

"What time did you all leave campus last night?"

Kat, Lissa, and I exchanged glances, and then Lissa spoke up. "Around five."

"And where did you go?"

"Bernigan's Tavern."

"Just the three of you?"

"And Mrs. Cunningham," I said.

"And what time did you get back?"

Lissa spoke up without hesitation. "At 10:28. It was just two minutes before lights-out."

"That check out with you?" Detective O'Connor asked Mrs. Dockerty.

"That's correct," she said. "The girls got in just under the wire. I had already locked the door. Nate had to open it."

"Did you see anything unusual coming in or going out?"

I had walked into Loomis Hall that morning expecting to tell everyone exactly what had happened on the hillside the previous night. After all, we had done nothing wrong; we had nothing to hide. So, what reason was there not to tell the truth?

But as I heard Lissa making no mention of Miss Wetherby's icy hands, as we sat in the warm room, I felt my courage failing me. I consoled myself with the fact that Miss Wetherby was already dead when we found her and that however she got that way, I didn't have anything to do with it. But each time I thought of that icy hand, I couldn't help but squeeze my eyes shut. I remembered that as I pushed open the door, it had appeared to move. Wasn't it equally possible that we had killed her? I waited for Kat or Lissa to confess, but neither did. I kept my mouth clamped firmly shut.

We weren't in Loomis Hall for more than about ten minutes. We were given hot chocolate with whipped cream and thanked for our time. Lissa and Kat left together, but I stayed to go to the bathroom, and just as I was coming out into the hall, I heard Mr. Treadway and Detective O'Connor speaking to each other in the drawing room.

"It benefits no one to do a full investigation, Mr. O'Connor," Mr. Treadway said. "The poor woman is dead. We know she had a weak heart."

"With all due respect," Detective O'Connor said, "the *location* of the body raises questions. We just want to make sure that justice is served. There is also that smudge on her forehead. Doesn't fit with the rest of the picture. I might just need to bring your English teacher down to the station for questioning . . ."

"Miss Wetherby took a walk around campus every evening between nine thirty and ten o'clock. Even in inclement weather. Ask any member of the faculty."

"With a loaded pistol in her pocket?"

"I'm sure that was a completely unnecessary precaution, given the safety of our campus, and its rural location. I'm also sure it was just a personal eccentricity."

"Well, seeing as it was her pistol . . . ," the officer said, sounding not fully convinced.

"And no shots fired," Mr. Treadway said. "I see no reason it should raise any suspicion."

I emerged from the hallway. I felt reckless. I wanted to make them know that I had heard them. But I noticed that the two men paid me little mind. Still, I kept thinking about what I had heard about bringing Miss Pymstead *in for questioning.* What if we had gotten ourselves off only to point the finger of blame at Miss Pymstead? It was guilt, but just a flicker. At age seventeen, I was willing to let her go down to save my own skin. I had proven to myself, at least, that Miss Pymstead was entirely mistaken about my character. If there was one thing I seemed to lack, it was certainly mettle.

30

The memorial service for Miss Wetherby was held in Whittaker Chapel at 4:00 p.m. on Friday afternoon. We settled into the pews, greeted by puffs of dust, a lot of suppressed throat-tickling coughs, and a feeling that nobody was going to tell us the whole story.

Officially, Miss Wetherby had died of a heart attack, but unofficially, it was known that she was found dead on Miss Pymstead's doorstep. This, of course, had given rise to any number of stories about how she had been on her way to or from a lesbian tryst. While we listened to Mrs. Tarkington-Luce, the president of the board of trustees, extol the virtues of Miss Wetherby, there was a scribbled ditty making the rounds among the girls that was garnering its share of suppressed guffaws:

> *There once was a lady Pymstead*
> *Who loved our headmistress in bed.*
> *Then one day they fought,*
> *For she loved her for naught,*
> *So she shot the dear lady quite dead.*

That was funny enough for a while, and then I saw Kat balancing a scrap of paper on top of a *Book of Common Prayer*, and pretty soon a second limerick was making the rounds. You could see the wicked little gasps, like the mouths of fishes opening eagerly as this one floated by, obliging us to respect her, if only for her wickedness:

> An unpious Mistress of Head
> Traded Sundays in church for her bed.
> She would skip out on hymns
> For a mouthful of Pyms,
> And God struck her wrathfully dead.

By the time we had sung the Grove school song and shuffled out of Whittaker Chapel, we were already talking of other things, and as soon as it was over, no one even talked about it. I could understand how the other students saw it. She was old. She died. We attended a mandatory chapel service. The end. I could see that, dead or not, Miss Wetherby was never going to achieve the kind of immortality that had been bestowed upon Chestmont Wooten.

I felt isolated in my twisted emotional state, and desperate to try to seem as if everything was normal. But in reality, two desires, one to cover up and one to confess, writhed inside me. I imagined the feeling like the two intertwined snakes of a caduceus. Deep down inside, I knew that when our car crazily skidded along that icy road above Whittaker Chapel, we had bumped into something nefarious—much more fraught with complications than just an old woman with a weak heart—but as usual, I couldn't link the pieces together. I worried that we had accidentally cast blame on Miss Pymstead, but I didn't dare come to her rescue for fear I'd end up taking the fall. I looked at Kat and Lissa in an entirely new light now. Could both be counted on to keep the secret? Kat did not want her mother involved, but Lissa—I had no doubt that if we were accused, she would happily throw me and Kat under the bus. Were we accomplices to murder? I simply didn't know.

At off hours, I crept back to Lane North and stared at the clue book. The murder of Chestmont Wooten and the death of Miss Wetherby had to be connected. I could see the faint dotted line that traced through the years and across time. I redoubled my efforts trying to figure out the puzzle—I was certain that at any moment, I would be summoned again to Loomis Hall, and this time, Detective O'Connor would put me under arrest. Indisputably, there was one link between the two deaths: *Emily Dickinson.*

Miss Pymstead was out of class for a week, and during that time an exceedingly dull teacher from Hardley came to take her place. Each day, when I entered the classroom in Gould Cottage and saw her missing, I thought about what we had done. I imagined Miss Pymstead wearing handcuffs, hunched up in a jail somewhere. Then, one day about two weeks later, she reappeared, offering no explanation for her absence. Her appearance was markedly changed—she was paler and thinner, a wraith of her already-ghostly self. As she resumed her place in front of the chalkboard, her much-changed aspect jangled me like an accusation. Like the bedsheets that blew on the lines outside the faculty apartments on Walker Row, I flapped in the wind, twisting, turning, knotting and unknotting. I could scarcely sit in Gould Cottage and listen to Miss Pymstead without feeling chills traveling up and down my spine. She stood at the blackboard inexplicably dressed in a heavy sweater and tweed skirt, as though it were still winter. Her face was as pale as unmelted snow hidden under a bush. Each day, I thought about confessing, and yet, every day the sun set upon my silence. But as the days passed, the whole thing started to slip away from me. Nothing happened. As my eyes took in the green expanse of lawn outside Gould Cottage's window, as we flung open our own windows to let in the soft spring air, the events of that icy, wintry night seemed to fade like the scenes of a gripping novel read long ago.

The Grove was heavy with spring, weighed down with trees in bloom, flowers swollen with pollen, and lilacs hanging their scent upon the air. But we were lighter, shorn of jackets and boots; we tripped along in shorts and flip-flops, as though the lightness of our footsteps upon the pathways foretold our impending departure.

Miss Pymstead had announced that in lieu of a final exam, she was giving two equally weighted assignments: a take-home essay exam on a topic of her choice and a final essay on a subject of each student's choosing.

"For the take-home exam, I will select a different topic for each student," she said. "But be forewarned—I plan to quiz each of you on something you might rather not be quizzed on . . ."

"I'm sorry . . . ," Lissa said, rubbing her forehead in an exaggerated manner. "I'm not following you, Miss Pymstead. Can you explain the take-home exam again?"

"What I mean," Miss Pymstead said, "is that each student's take-home exam will have a different essay question. I will choose a topic for each of you that I suspect may give you a little trouble. I want you to be forced to write about a piece of literature that I know you do not find easy to like."

"But that's mean," Emma Doerr said.

"It's the essence of what I believe literature is for," Miss Pymstead said.

31

"Lissa." I heard a male voice and then a scatter of pebbles pinging against the window of 2B.

I had just pulled on my nightgown, easing it over my sunburned neck. It was Picnic Day, and the boys from Hardley had been at the Grove all day, playing Frisbee and eating and hanging out on Siberia.

I was tired and sunburned, and my nerve endings were alive from the thousand brushes of fingertips and elbows and shoulders with Josh Miller throughout the course of the day.

"Tell them to go away." Kat was in a peevish mood. She rolled over on her bunk, flopping harder than she needed to, and pulled the covers up over her head.

"Lissa!" The rattle of pebbles came again, harder this time.

I shoved up the window and looked down and saw Banger, one of the druggier Hardley boys, standing below my window in a circle of light. I leaned out.

"This isn't Lissa's room," I said.

"*What light through yonder window breaks . . . ?*"

"Banger! Shut up!" I whispered. "You're going to get us both in trouble."

"Jane, I missed the bus. *It is the east, and Juliet . . .*"

"Banger," I said, "shut up . . ."

I popped my head back inside the window, pulled on a tank top, and ran outside.

When I got downstairs, I pulled Banger into the shadowy recesses behind the bushes. "Are you nuts?"

He giggled, and I realized he was high. When something moved behind us, I spun around and gasped.

"Josh?" He was standing in the shadows, the hood of his navy-blue sweatshirt pulled up over his head. He gave me a crooked grin.

"Romeo was shy . . . ," Banger said.

"What are you guys doing here?" I asked.

"Trying to get kicked out . . . ," Josh said.

"He's freaking nuts," Banger said. "Only you'd never know it to look at him."

"Yeah, I'm a freaking murderer, man," Josh said. "One of those guys that nobody ever guesses, 'cuz he's so freaking nice."

Josh was grinning that loopy grin of his, and my heart was banging away like a middle school drum majorette's.

"Guys, can we move away from the building? Somebody is going to hear us."

Just then, the door to Lane pushed open, and I took a step back, preparing to run from Mrs. Dockerty. But it was Lissa.

"Hey . . . where's the party?"

Banger was skinny, and he had thin blond hair that hung to his shoulders and flipped under in soft waves. He stood on the balls of his feet like a cat. "Party? Banger's the party. Right this way, ladies, right this way." He reached into his pocket and pulled out a flask, which he handed to Lissa.

Lissa and Banger tripped ahead, out across the dark expanse of Siberia, but halfway across, Josh grabbed my arm and stopped me.

"Look," he said.

"What—what is it?"

It was a dark night with no clouds, the stars hanging low in the sky. Up on the ridge, the buildings of the Grove were lit up in peaceful patches of glowing yellow, and off in the distance, the lights of Hardley twinkled.

"My dad said the Grove at night was the prettiest place in the world."

I drew up close to him. Close enough to feel his breath on my face. He slipped his arm around my bare shoulders.

"Yeah, nights are beautiful," I said, blushing hot as I remembered the one kiss, that night in front of the library. I moved in closer, tipping my face to his.

"I wish I could see it, but to me it looks haunted."

I could see the outline of Wooten Boathouse, like a black blotch in the distance. The hair stood up on the back of my neck.

"*Haunted*? Why?"

"You wouldn't understand,"

"Try me . . ."

There was a pause, as if he was thinking over saying something but couldn't quite decide.

"Guys!" Lissa was calling from up ahead, and so Josh grabbed my hand and pulled me forward and we started running; then we were crashing into the woods, down to the boathouse.

One look at Lissa told me that she was getting pretty wasted, and a little warning voice told me that I should really be thinking about getting her back to the dorm, before things got out of hand.

Banger had lit up a joint, and he was sitting Indian style on the riverbank, staring out at the flow of the water.

Josh had drifted away from me, over toward Banger so he could get a hit from the joint.

I cast about for something to draw him back to me, and I remembered—our secret.

"Josh, come here. I want to show you something . . ."

"What is it?"

"Come here."

I pulled him over to the grass and lay down next to him. But neither one of us had a flashlight. I took hold of his hand, put my fingers up to the wall, and traced the place where I knew the letters were, and I said, "There's poetry here."

He rolled onto his side and traced the outlines of my face.

"Here too."

I looked up and saw the dark sky, studded with countless white stars.

His face neared mine until I could feel the buzz of electricity passing in the space between our lips.

"Josh!" It was Banger. "Guys, you better get over here."

"Yeah?" Josh rolled over.

"Don't," I said. "Not yet."

"Dude, Josh. Get over here. I need some help." Banger's voice was coming from somewhere up the hill, and he sounded worried.

"Jane," he whispered, "don't move. I'll be right back." Then, he pushed up and ran up the hill, leaving me staring at the side of the boathouse—facing the wall where there was a line I knew by heart.

I lay there for a long time, a very long time, until finally I started to realize that Josh wasn't going to come back. When I stood up, stiff, and went back up the path, trying to find Banger, Lissa, or Josh, all of them had disappeared without a trace. I climbed in a downstairs window back at Lane, and when I trudged past Lissa's door, Katie Cornwell popped her head out and whispered, "Where's Lissa?"

I shrugged. "With Josh," I said, trying to seem like I didn't care.

At 7:00 a.m. the next morning, Abigail Von Platte woke me up with a harsh rap on the door. My head felt as if it were going to split apart.

"Phone."

"Go away. I'm dead. You can come to my funeral."

"It's *Josh*."

Despite the pounding in my head, I remembered the sweep of Josh's hand across my bare shoulder. I felt the wave of twinkles traverse my body. But the twinkles were immediately swept away by the memory of waiting for him to come back and finding out he'd taken off with Lissa. What on earth could he want now?

"Hurry!" Abigail said. *"He said it was an emergency!"*

"Okay," I said. I ran down the three flights of stairs to the basement, feeling a jarring in my head with each step.

I grabbed the phone.

"Jane."

"Mmm-hmm."

Josh's voice sounded ragged. "Listen, I have to ask you for a favor."

I smiled—I smiled to myself, to the wall, to the ugly butt room, and to the faint scent of cloves that made me want to vomit at seven o'clock in the morning. Smiled even though he had betrayed me, just at the sound of his voice.

"A favor?"

"Listen, it's Lissa."

"Lissa?"

There was a faint metallic taste in my mouth. "What about her?"

"She's here with me. She's pretty wasted." I heard a chuckle, muffled, the battle scar of a hard-fought party. "She's mumbling something about a take-home exam."

"She's where?"

254

"She's—look, it's a long story, but basically she was pretty messed up, and I couldn't just leave her there, so I brought her back here."

"Here? Josh, where the hell is *here*?"

"Winslow Cav—She's in my—" He broke off, dropped his voice to a loud whisper. "Look, Jane, I can't talk right now . . . She's in my dorm room. She's going nutso on me. I've got to keep her calm or someone is going to find her. She's saying something about a mailbox, and a take-home. Due by four. I can't let her out until she's making a little bit more sense . . . Can't you just . . . ?"

"Can't I just, what?"

"You know . . ."

"No, I don't know."

"Jesus, Jane. It's just a take-home. I'd do it for one of my buddies. Is it really that big a deal?"

I paused long enough for him to understand that I did think it was a big deal.

"Look, I'm feeling like—" He broke off again, and then again, the whisper. "Look, you know why she was so wasted? Banger spiked the Jim Beam with bennies—thought it was funny. She didn't have a chance. I feel responsible for what he did. I'd do the exam thing myself, but it's just that . . ."

"It's just that what?"

"It's just that I'm kinda tied up here . . . I'm scared to leave her alone." A pause. "I'd owe you one."

"You already do."

Then it was his turn for silence.

"You want me to cheat," I whispered.

"Look, at Hardley we call it standing together as brothers. Don't you Grove girls have something like that?"

"I wouldn't know—they have the Grove sisters' swear, but they only teach it to the old girls . . ."

"Look, Jane, I'm begging you . . ."

My head was throbbing. I leaned against the cool cinder block wall, and then banged it once just for good measure.

"You know, Lissa and I are both on the wait list at Yale. Why wouldn't I just let her blow it and hope that I'd get the spot instead of her?"

"Because that's not the kind of person you are."

Before I slipped Lissa's take-home exam out of her intercampus mailbox, I could not have possibly imagined a set of circumstances that would have conspired to make me do what I was about to do. Grove had an honor code, and I never even thought about cheating. I didn't need to. Most of the time, I was the smartest person in the room.

But when I took the pages out of her box and carried them up to my dorm room, there was something of the inevitable about it. As I sat down in front of my typewriter, and threaded a paper through the black roller, I realized that I, Jane Milton, had become the sort of person to whom rules did not apply.

I flipped back the cover sheet to expose the topic on the page underneath, written in Miss Pymstead's unmistakable handwriting. The instructions read: *Compare and contrast the following poems.* Below that, two poems by Emily Dickinson were listed.

My head ached, and the essay that I wrote was serviceable but not brilliant. I still had the ideas I had expressed in the Eugenia Wilcox exam fresh in mind, so it wasn't too difficult to come up with an adequate response—not my best work but Lissa-worthy, I figured. I listened to the keys strike the paper, their rhythm as erratic as the memories of the evening before that flickered through my head: Josh's face so close to mine. I typed quickly, the words appearing before me in sentences that seemed to make sense. By now, all my ideas about Emily Dickinson seemed hashed over and stale.

Once finished, I slipped the exam into Miss Pymstead's box, and then returned to my own mailbox, as now I had my own exam to complete. Mercifully, several cups of coffee and a few aspirin pilfered from the bottom of Kat's sock drawer had started to take effect.

Back in front of my typewriter, the fog had lifted for me. I turned the cover page of the exam to my own essay topic, fully expecting to see the dreaded question about "The Dead." Only now, I had to laugh to myself, because Miss Pymstead had given me a quotation from *The Catcher in the Rye*, the one that said that Pencey Prep was full of crooks. The question that followed read: *What was Salinger getting at here, if he was getting at anything at all? Explain.*

Mr. Treadway and Mrs. Tarkington-Luce summoned me three weeks before the end of school. It was late May; the blossoms were gone, and the new leaves were starting to unfurl. For the past few weeks, I had been thinking of only agreeable outcomes that might be in store for me: announcements of honors about to be bestowed, perhaps early news of the Eugenia Wilcox Prize; maybe I'd get off the waiting list and get accepted to Yale. The trees canopied above me; the valley spread out before me. The Grove had taught me that I was born with a natural immunity to all ills. My recent history had driven this point home only too well.

Mr. Treadway and Mrs. Tarkington-Luce both stood when I entered the drawing room at Loomis.

I sensed from their expressions that there was something somber about this occasion, but I brushed that concern aside. As I crossed the room, I heard only the sound of my flip-flops slapping my heels.

Mr. Treadway gestured me toward a chair. It was a black Hitchcock chair, knobby and uncomfortable, stenciled with a Grove insignia. I sat down, feeling the cool surface on the backs of my thighs. I was starting to think that something was not right.

After a portentous pause, Mrs. Tarkington-Luce spoke. "I'm sure you're wondering why we brought you here?"

There was no one else in the room. No one who looked like the police officer from our meeting after the "accident." Still, I had a growing sense of unease.

"I'm afraid that we have caught you in an infraction of a very serious nature, " Mrs. Tarkington-Luce said.

"An infraction the nature of which is not consistent with the standards to which we hold Grove students," Mr. Treadway said.

"An infraction which, unfortunately, can be punishable by means up to and including expulsion," Mrs. Tarkington-Luce continued.

I saw my life start to collapse in front of me—graduation, college, my entire future. Would I be arrested? Put in jail?

The whole scene came back to me—the car skidding, the icy road, the hand. Ever since that night, I was haunted by the feeling that when I had pushed the Range Rover door open, the hand had moved. We didn't call an ambulance; we didn't alert anyone to Miss Wetherby's whereabouts. Kat and Lissa had been so sure she was dead, but shouldn't I have stood my ground?

"Academic integrity is one of the fundamental pillars of the Grove Academy," Mr. Treadway said.

"*The* fundamental pillar," Mrs. Tarkington-Luce said.

"Academic integrity?" I said. I was completely confused. I might be an accomplice to murder, but I was no cheater. And then, it seemed that the room spun in a half circle as I suddenly remembered the take-home exam.

Lissa must have gotten caught for handing in the take-home exam that I had written for her. The only small satisfaction that I was going to have in this matter was that Lissa and I were going to end up in the same boat. She had asked me to cheat for her, and I had done so. It looked as if neither of us was going to get off that waiting list for Yale.

"Do you have something to say for yourself?" Mr. Treadway asked.

I shook my head.

"Fine," Mr. Treadway said. "So, you admit wrongdoing?"

I was so relieved that I probably didn't look suitably contrite.

"Cheating? Sure," I said. They had no idea that I was actually getting away with murder.

Mr. Treadway and Mrs. Tarkington-Luce exchanged a glance, and I could detect a note of relief in it, as if they had gotten off easy.

"Good. These are your consequences. You are hereby disqualified from competition in the Eugenia Wilcox Examination. You will not be allowed to graduate with your class."

"But—!"

"Hear me out!" Mr. Treadway said, frowning.

"You can walk with the class, but your folder that would normally hold your diploma will be empty. You must fulfill a community service requirement in order to receive your diploma—you may do that between now and graduation, but you will still not receive your diploma with the class," Mrs. Tarkington-Luce continued.

"But what about Lissa?" I asked.

"You worry about yourself—we'll worry about your classmates," Mr. Treadway said. I should have realized that his answer was a dodge.

"We'll get back to you within twenty-four hours with the community service assignment," Mrs. Tarkington-Luce said dismissively. I realized that they were gesturing me toward the door.

"But wait, wait," I said. "I don't understand. Why are you disqualifying me from the Eugenia Wilcox exam? What does that have to do with anything?"

Mrs. Tarkington-Luce was a tall woman, and thin, which made her appear even taller. She drew herself up to her full height, and arched her eyebrows.

"I've been the president of the Eugenia Wilcox Committee for the past sixteen years, and this is the first time, to my knowledge, that a Grove girl has *ever* resorted to dishonesty on the Eugenia Wilcox Examination. Eugenia Wilcox has always represented the best, the very best of what it means to be a Grove girl. To sully her name with this kind of action . . ."

I held up both of my hands. "But Mrs. Tarkington-Luce, Mr. Treadway, I *didn't* cheat on the Eugenia Wilcox exam." Even as I said it, I could hear that my words carried a ring of weakness. I had just admitted that I was a cheater.

Mr. Treadway sighed. With exaggerated slowness, he picked up a manila folder that was lying on the desktop in front of him. He opened it and fanned out three papers. One was my answer to the Eugenia Wilcox exam. The other was the answer that "Lissa" had written for the take-home exam. The third was Lissa's answer on the Eugenia Wilcox exam. There were a number of passages that were underlined in red ink in all three of them. The passages were remarkably similar, enough so to make it clear that all must have been written by the same person—or that copying was involved somehow. As I looked at the three essays side by side, I could imagine the terror of an animal that stepped into a trap and discovered that there was no way to escape.

I tried to imagine the inside of the lecture hall in Loomis when we had sat for the Eugenia Wilcox exam. I remembered how I had arrived late and sat in one of the rear rows. I could picture the back of Kat's head, how I had carefully positioned myself so that she wouldn't see me. But where had Lissa been? I scanned my mind's eye and couldn't remember where she was sitting. I wasn't looking for her because I was so intent on covering up my betrayal of Kat. Lissa must have been sitting behind me. She must have copied from me. I don't know which startled me more—that my friend would do such a thing, or that she obviously knew all along that I had lied to Kat.

When I had written Lissa's take-home exam for her, without real-izing it, I had used a number of the same ideas and turns of phrase as I had used in the Eugenia Wilcox exam. Instead of realizing that Lissa had been the one cheating, they had assumed it was me. Maybe I could have explained it to Mr. Treadway and Mrs. Tarkington-Luce—but I had already confessed, and I could see their faces set in conviction.

I looked back and forth, from one face to the other. I blubbered and cried and protested. I tried to explain—one way then a hundred ways, then a thousand ways—that it wasn't the way it seemed. But by the time I left that meeting, I had a brand-new identity: Jane Milton, cheater.

PART FIVE
NOW

32

A few days after my outing with Josh to the apple orchard, I was at the library, working on the computer. When I noticed how quiet it was and that nobody was around, I tapped in the URL for *The Ghost of Abbott North*. I checked it every few days, but it had been quiet for a while.

But today, I saw that there was a new entry:

November 11

There once was a mother of Abbott
Who solo her bed did inhabit
She seemed to quite like
The man on the bike
So perhaps they will someday cohabit

A memory of the afternoon a few days earlier that Josh and I had spent in the Hardley orchard flashed in front of me. Was I really that obvious? I could feel my face getting hot, and I looked around to make sure that no one was watching me.

It continued from there, a bit of gossip about some of the girls, some complaints about the ravioli in Commons, then this: "Ms. Rectitude was seen apple picking last Saturday in the company of Lord Byron himself. The Ghost of Abbott North finds this a surprising match."

I quickly x-ed out of the blog and went back to my work, but it kept bugging me. Who was watching me? Who knew that I had been out with Josh?

On my way out the door this morning, I'd found more manuscript pages stuffed in my mailbox. I hadn't had a chance to read them yet, but just knowing that I had them made my stomach churn.

I decided to see if Rebecca MacAteer was around, and I found her in the back room, seated at a broken carrel that I recognized as one from the original library. She was sorting a stack of old papers, with a cardboard box at her feet. She looked up and then smiled when she saw me.

"You've come to help me?" Rebecca said.

"Actually, I was wondering if you could give me some help. You mentioned that you've been cataloging old papers. I've got a student who I think may be plagiarizing. I know it's a needle in a haystack, but is there any obvious place I might look? Is there any way she could have gotten hold of student essays from previous years?"

Rebecca scratched her head, and I noticed that there were dust motes trapped in her curls. I fought off the urge to sneeze.

"You know, I'd probably start with the Internet. Most of these kids would rather die than touch paper. I can't imagine them looking here . . ."

"I've Googled the heck out of these documents. I don't know. It's something, just a hunch, I guess. This is probably going to sound silly, but one of the essays she handed in—well, I would almost swear it was written by my old roommate . . ."

She shook her head. "You know who you should ask? Charlie. There was a stash of old papers and he's been filing them for me. You want to take a look?"

I nodded, feeling the futility of my pursuit.

Rebecca stood up. "Follow me . . ."

Lined up in neatly labeled bins, not far from where the old yearbooks were shelved, I found exactly what I was looking for: a bin labeled *Senior English Essays*. Inside, there were a series of manila folders, each labeled *Senior Honors English*, followed by a year. With a start, I recognized the handwriting: Miss Pymstead's. I spotted shiny onionskin papers, clipped together, old student essays slightly yellowed with age. Flipping through the pile, I soon recognized the typeface of an old manual typewriter that skipped the crosses on the *t*'s and dropped the tails of the *y*'s.

"Happy hunting . . . ," Rebecca said.

I was hardly listening. I had just found what I was looking for.

Lucky enough for me, Kaitlyn Corsyn was alone in her room. I knocked but didn't wait for her to invite me inside, just pushed past her, then swung the door shut behind me. If she was alarmed by my behavior, she didn't show it. I couldn't tell what she had been doing before I entered. She was seated facing away from me, at her desk—her computer had a screensaver on; her desk had some books and notebooks on it, but they were all closed.

"Blogging about matters of a personal nature is against school policy," I said.

"Accusing students of doing stuff they didn't do is also against school policy," Kaitlyn said.

"Don't mess around with me."

"I have my father on speed dial. You'd be messing around with him."

"You plagiarized an essay."

"I have no idea what you're talking about."

What I hated about Kaitlyn—what I had hated about her from the moment I set eyes on her—was her look of dismissal. If she had appeared worried, upset, or even angry—okay. But she never did. It was that slight curl of her lip. I could almost hear the mocking tone she might use to describe me to one of her friends. I knew that if I were halfway out of earshot, she would call me Ms. Rectitude.

"Of course you know. Don't lie to me. You copied your Joyce essay from a paper in the archives, just like you planted Soon Ji's notebook in Mary Raschlaub's laundry bag."

Kaitlyn uncapped her Burt's Bees lip gloss and started smoothing it over her lips, looking in the mirror that hung on the wall above her desk. She pressed her lips together and gave herself a satisfied smile.

"Prove it. And you'd *better* prove it, because tomorrow morning, my parents are going to be sitting in Dr. Farber-Johnson's office complaining that you've been harassing me."

"I am not harassing you," I said.

"Your own son thinks you are," she said.

Her back was to me. I was looking at her reflection in the black computer screen.

"Leave Charlie out of this," I said, but her comment had hit the mark. He had told me this himself.

Kaitlyn slipped a pink fuzzy band off her wrist and used it to tie back her hair. "Now I can see what Charlie means about you," she said, then slipped her feet into shearling scuffs.

My jaw dropped. I couldn't help it. Did Charlie complain about me? *To her?*

"So anyway, how much is Nate Hodges charging these days for passkey services?"

She turned her head just slightly. At least now I had her attention.

I lowered my voice. "Do you still have to throw in a few kisses for the tricky assignments?"

"You'll never get me to admit to anything," Kaitlyn said.

I reached underneath my shirt, where I'd been holding my trump card. I unfolded a copy of her essay, "The Dead: Joyce's Hidden Fury."

Folded up inside it was another essay identical to it. I had found it in the archives, just as I'd expected to. I had recognized the typeface of my old manual typewriter, which Kat had used to type her essay.

"They'll never believe you," she said.

"They don't have to," I said. "I have proof."

I hoped that she couldn't see my hands shaking.

She narrowed her eyes and stared at me. "Nate Hodges is repulsive. I got Charlie to open the door for me."

"Someday, you'll know that it was better for you to get caught and have to pay the consequences now."

Kaitlyn's eyes widened, and then she smiled at me, so wide that I could see the perfect whiteness of her teeth.

"'Pay the consequences'? Are you kidding? I'm not going to pay any consequences. You will though."

I felt a few pulses of pity. She was so unscathed. But now that had come to an end.

"I think you'll soon find that academic integrity is a very serious matter . . ."

"Believe it if you want," she said. "We'll see who's right."

I might have found some more choice words in retort except that Kaitlyn's roommate returned.

"Oh, hi, Miranda," Kaitlyn said, her voice not betraying the slightest trace that anything untoward was going on.

"Hi, Ms. Milton. Is anything wrong?"

"No, nothing's wrong. I was just having a nice little chat with Kaitlyn," I said. "I'm just on my way out."

The summons was inevitable. It came from Dr. Farber-Johnson at nine the next morning. When I reached her office, I half expected to find

Mrs. Corsyn's Escalade parked outside Gould Cottage, but at least I was spared that horror.

If I had thought I had previously seen Dr. Farber-Johnson not amused, I was wrong. I was greeted by an icy silence that was only broken by a loud plop—the sound of a thick spiral-bound manual smacking the smooth surface of her desk.

"This," Dr. Farber-Johnson said, "is the Grove Academy Faculty Handbook, otherwise known as the bible."

I nodded.

"This," she said, tapping on a manila folder, "is the lamentably slim contents of your faculty file. In it, I find neither academic credentials nor earned accolades. I do find, however, a signed copy of this notice."

She held up a photocopied piece of paper and dangled it in front of my nose.

"Do you see this?"

A rhetorical question.

"This is your signature, stating that you have received a copy of the Grove Academy Faculty Handbook, and that you are familiar with its contents."

After a freighted pause, she continued. "Section 3.4.5 clearly states the following: *Any suggestion of wrongdoing on the part of a student concerning violations of the honor code, regarding A. Academic Integrity, including plagiarism, cheating, and copying, and B. Dishonesty, including, theft, stealing, and breaking and entering, must be dealt with in strict accordance with the policies laid out in the faculty handbook.*"

She looked up. "Am I making myself clear?"

"She plagiarized an essay," I said. "I have copies of both. She was raiding an old class archive."

"These are sensitive issues, and there are procedures that have to be followed. You can't storm into a student's room and start throwing around wild accusations."

"And, what's more, I think she stole something else."

Dr. Farber-Johnson narrowed her eyes. "Pray tell?"

"Her book manuscript."

Elaine Farber-Johnson drew back her chin and pinched in the corners of her mouth. "I hope that you're very sure about this, Ms. Milton. You found an original written by someone else?"

I shook my head.

"How then?"

I tried to figure out the best way to put it.

"I recognize the story."

She stared at me. "You *recognize the story*?"

I nodded.

"And you have a copy of the original book?" She looked concerned.

"No," I said. "Not a book. She's copying from something unpublished—a manuscript."

"Where did you find the original?"

"I don't have the original—well, not all of it," I said. "But I recognize the story."

Dr. Farber-Johnson put her hand up to her forehead, and then drew it down over her face.

"Jane."

"Yes."

"Look. I don't know how to put this less bluntly. Just because you are a cheater doesn't mean that everyone is. Lissa Edelstein was candid with me about your . . . *history*. I'm going to be frank with you, Jane. There is one thing and only one thing right now that is probably going to keep the lid on this whole situation and prevent me from having to fire you right on the spot—and do you know what it is?"

I didn't know. Then, all of a sudden, I did.

Charlie.

Kaitlyn, of course, would beg for them to show me mercy for fear I would leave and take my son with me.

The words "I quit" were pushing so hard on the tip of my tongue that I had to bite the inside of my cheek to silence them. I pictured the Subaru in my mind's eye; I remembered the trip up here, when I'd had hardly enough money to buy gas—and I begged the wiser part of myself to stay silent.

"I can't transfer her out of your class, but outside of class, you are forbidden to speak to her unless another adult is present."

"You can't do this to me."

"Of course I can."

"Don't be ridiculous."

"Well, if that's how you feel about it, I'll have Nate pack your bags." She paused, and let that settle for effect. "And, of course, Charlie's."

That was it, her trump card, and she knew it. I shook my head.

"One more thing," she said. "You know, your teaching is not bad. The girls in the dorm like you. But you are a typical old girl. I know the grounds, the buildings, even the girls, remind you of yourself at that age. It's an obstacle to your success."

I said nothing.

"Good day," she said.

It was late, and when I heard a knock on my door, I was expecting a sick or troubled student. I could not have been more surprised when I saw Susan Callow standing in the hallway outside my flat.

From the way she stepped inside quickly, I got the impression that she wasn't eager to let anyone know that she was there either.

I had never seen her not dressed in her tweeds. Now, she was wearing a black-velour pantsuit of the Talbots variety. She looked slightly less formal—only slightly.

"Would you like to sit down?" I asked, still wary and unsure of the purpose of her mission.

"Let me not waste words," she said. "You have got your back very far up against a wall."

I nodded.

"Farber-Johnson brought you here to be her ally."

"Her ally?"

"If you cease to be one, she will show no mercy."

"Susan, how about some nice peppermint tea . . . ?" I didn't wait for an answer but started to fill the electric kettle.

"I'm not joking about this, Jane. Look, you've probably got a sentimental attachment to the honor code, but this is a brave new world. Do the girls cheat? Yes, they cheat. If you have a concern, you bring it to Farber-Johnson. Do you realize that the tuition, room and board at the Grove Academy has now topped fifty thousand dollars for one year? Who can afford that? The parents who can expect to be treated accordingly. If you want to stay here, you have got to learn."

"The girl is claiming to have written a novel. There's no way that she did."

"So what if she didn't? Does it really make a difference? It's not like she killed someone."

I felt as if she had taken a knife and twisted it in my gut. "You have no idea what these kids might be capable of," I said.

She gave me a wry smile. "Oh, trust me," she said. "They scare the bejesus out of me. I just feel that, well, you are new here, and I do like to encourage an old Grove girl, *on principle*. But I fear greatly that you are unwittingly stepping on too many toes. Keep a lower profile and you may just do well here. There are many who think that Farber-Johnson is setting her cap for Choate—she may be gone in five or six years . . ."

She stood up, set her mug on the counter.

"Susan, I really need this job. I'm doing my absolute best. I guess I just don't know the ropes quite yet."

She patted my arm. "It's an open secret that I'm aiming for the head of the school position if and when she does leave. I've looked around the department and I don't see too many likely candidates for English chair. Many of our faculty members are older. Among the younger ones, they're all just *unbearable* Farber-Johnson hires, what with their teaching degrees. You're old Grove and passably well-spoken. I've got my eye on you. The only other contender is Josh Miller." She smirked. "I'd prefer that a woman held the post."

I saw her to the door.

"You'll do fine," she said. "Just back down and this will blow over."

"Josh."

I was not supposed to be away from Abbott North at that hour, but I was standing on the threshold of Walker House, tapping softly on the door because the doorbell didn't seem to work. I didn't want anyone to see me. I glanced at my watch. It wasn't late. Maybe he was in his flat with the TV on and couldn't hear me.

I crept back outside and threw a handful of pebbles at a window that I thought might be his bedroom. The night was cold. I stood in the moonlight, my sweater sleeves pulled down over my hands, about to turn and go back up the hill. But then, I saw the window crack open.

"Hey?" he said.

"Josh."

"Jane?"

When he opened the door for me, he was rumpled from sleep. He wore flannel pants tied at the waist and an old white T-shirt. I was distracted by the smell of him, hot from the bedsheets, but I tried to stay focused.

"Jane, what are you doing here?"

"Were you asleep? God, I'm so embarrassed."

"No, you're not bothering me. It's just—what time is it?" He ran his fingers through his hair and glanced at the clock.

"I'm really sorry."

"Don't worry about it. I just turned in early. Come on in. What's going on?"

Josh pulled on a sweatshirt and handed me an afghan to throw over my shoulders. It was chilly in his flat. He walked over to his stove, in the kitchenette off the living room. "Tea?" he asked. I nodded gratefully.

His feet were clad only in socks; the sleep creases on his face were adorable.

"Mint okay?"

The cup of tea felt warm in my hands, though the touch of his hand as he passed it to me had felt even warmer.

"So, what's on your mind?"

"I just . . . need some advice, I guess. I caught Kaitlyn Corsyn red-handed, cheating. She copied her essay from an old cache of essays in the library. I confronted her. She admitted it. But now, Farber-Johnson is telling me that I didn't follow the faculty handbook, and Kaitlyn's facing no consequence. I'm not even allowed to talk to her unless another adult is present or she's in class. Can you believe it? Susan Callow came to see me and she told me the same."

"You have to follow the guidelines, Jane. You should have taken it to Farber-Johnson. You shouldn't have tried to handle it yourself. Try not to personalize this stuff. It has nothing to do with you."

"Ohhh, but it does."

"No. No, it doesn't. It has nothing to do with you. We're just here to follow the rules. We've got no particular stake in things."

"But how can you say that? After what I went through?"

Josh turned away from me, opened a cupboard, and took out a bottle of brandy.

"I was wrong. You don't need tea. You need something stronger." He poured out a generous amount and gave it to me, and I felt it warming me on the way down.

"Listen, all that crazy stuff we did when we were younger—most of it wasn't all that bad. I don't know what your particular demons are, but you need to get it clear in your mind what happened back then, and then set it to rest."

I hadn't gone there to be angry, but I could feel frustration tightening in a hot coil around my throat.

"What are you talking about, Josh? How can you stand there and say you don't know what my demons are when the whole thing was your fault?"

Josh took a step back.

"Whoa, Jane. Slow down . . . You're losing me here . . . I hardly know you. I haven't seen or heard from you in more than thirty years."

"You're trying to tell me that you didn't know I never graduated from the Grove?"

"You *what*?"

"You don't remember when you asked me to take Lissa's exam for her?"

Josh stood up and paced the room. He rubbed the palms of his hands against his pants. He turned around.

"Jane. I'm sorry. I never should have done that. I still feel terrible about that. Honestly, I do."

"Well, I'm glad you feel terrible. I got caught cheating, and they wouldn't let me graduate with my class. They said I had to do community service—I did about half, and then I found out the college that I was supposed to go to—Connecticut College, withdrew the acceptance. So, I just bagged the community service. I didn't want the Grove diploma. I thought it was tainted."

Josh was listening with his brows knitted together.

"I don't get it. If you were cheating for her, then what happened to her? That doesn't make sense. Wasn't Lissa valedictorian?"

"It's because they didn't know she cheated. They thought *I* cheated. I guess I used the same turns of phrase or something as I had on the

Eugenia Wilcox exam, and Lissa had apparently copied off me, unbeknownst to me. It made it look as though *I* was the one who had cheated—but it was her."

"She got off scot-free?"

"Yup."

"And without even a smidgen of guilt too, I assume."

"No doubt. I guess since we're on the subject, I might as well ask you," I said. "Why did you tell me you'd meet me that night and end up with Lissa in your dorm, asking me to cheat for her?"

His shoulders slumped. "I'm sorry, Jane. I really am. If I could go back and change it, I swear I would. Maybe a lot would have turned out differently." He looked at me searchingly.

"But why?"

I waited for him to answer. "Josh, please tell me. Please. I know it was a long time ago. But it's important for me to know."

"I can't tell you."

"What?" I stood up, furious again. "What do you mean you can't tell me?"

"I just . . ." Josh wrapped his arm around me, and I felt my anger slipping away in spite of myself.

"Listen. You came here to ask my advice, so here it is. You're going to have to let that stuff go, hard as it is. Those old stories aren't real anymore. They're like those images that resurface on paintings after they've been painted over . . . what they call pentimento."

Then, more than anything, I didn't want to leave. I wanted to stay right there, where I was, next to the warmth of his beating heart. But I was AWOL from the dorm, and there were seventy-four girls whose parents believed that I was under the eaves of Abbott North with only their daughters' well-being on my mind.

"I've gotta go," I said.

I stepped back outside into the cold, no closer to an answer. My memories of senior year remained vivid. There was only one way for me to get past this—I needed to find the manuscript.

33

The next day, I vowed to myself that I would figure out how to do better. If only I could find the missing manuscript, I could bolster my case against Kaitlyn. And maybe, I reasoned with myself, if I could just figure out what was going on, it would set my mind at ease.

I figured that somewhere in Pencott, there had to be an old *Lantern* yearbook with the picture of Chestmont Wooten torn out of it. I tried not to appear too eager as I asked the librarian where the old yearbooks were kept, then spirited myself away to the hidden corner of shelves where, I noticed gratefully, I could look at the books at my leisure without being easily seen.

I ran one finger along the aging spines until I saw the volumes for the 1960s, each spine embossed with one year of the decade, lined up in an even row, with no volumes missing. I pulled out the 1960 *Lantern*. It was easy to find the page where Chestmont Wooten's picture had been torn out. I wondered if anyone had looked at this volume since the year we pulled it out.

I flipped through the pages, unsure what I was looking for. I saw the torn page. I looked at the other pages. There were rows of girls with bouffant hairdos. There were pictures of parties where Grove girls in white gloves danced with young-looking boys who had wet-looking crew cuts and wore Rogers Peet blazers. I slipped the volume back into its place and found the row of Hardley yearbooks. I traced with my finger until I found the spine embossed with '56. This was the one that I had found Kat weeping over in the library. Wouldn't she have known that her father wasn't really dead? I thought back to the night when Mrs. Dockerty told us about his death. Did her mother call the school to inform them, or was Kat the source of the story? I wasn't sure.

On the page where the boys' last names started with *C*, I saw his face with the name below it. He was handsome and so young-looking too, not much older than Charlie. He had a thin, pretty face with fine features, sandy hair, and a gentle expression. It saddened me to think of him so long dead. I flipped through more pages, and saw the same kinds of images as in the other volume: football games, sports teams, dances with Grove girls. I turned the pages slowly, conscious that I was looking at a lost world.

My eyes traveled over the picture once more, studying Winslow Cunningham's winsome face. It seemed pretty clear that Winslow Cunningham had grown up to be Winnie Cunningham, one of the Fire Island Boys.

I heard footsteps; a couple of students crossed behind me but didn't disturb me. I tipped the musty book shut and slid it back into its place, then turned to the row of Grove *Lanterns*. I traced the dusty spines with my fingertips and tipped out the '61 volume with my fingertip.

My legs were getting stiff from squatting, and the library was quiet, so I decided to carry the volume to a carrel at the end of the aisle. It was more comfortable and better lit but still secluded. I laid down the book, observing the embossed lantern design on the front, then slowly opened it and began to turn the pages.

I had a feeling that Kat had hidden this volume from me back then for a reason. I looked with interest to see what that reason might have been.

Just then, a group of girls walked by.

"Hi, Ms. Milton."

I turned my head and saw Soon Ji Shin and Mary Raschlaub.

"Hi, girls," I said.

They walked past and I returned my gaze to the book in front of me.

I leafed quickly through the candid shots, not really looking at them, until I got to the pages of the senior portraits. I looked through the *P*'s until I found the picture of Miss Pymstead. *Amanda Vining Pymstead.* She looked exactly the same as when I had known her, except that her thinness was less accentuated. I looked at the list of her activities: *Dramatics I, II, III, Literary Magazine I, II, III, IV, Field Hockey I, II, Yearbook III, IV Plans for the future: Smith College. I hope to teach English someday.*

Having seen Miss Pymstead's portrait, I now knew precisely no more than I had before. I flipped through some more pages. Then, I saw the picture of Chestmont Wooten. It was a formal shot, ringed in black. His birthday and death date, with the quotation, *"The true teacher defends his pupils against his own personal influence."*—Amos Bronson Alcott.

I leafed through the rest of the volume, stopping when I got to the picture of the Literary Society. Suddenly, I realized that I was looking at a picture of a young Miss Wetherby—same round face, same protuberant eyes. There was a small group of girls gathered around her, among whom I recognized Amanda Pymstead. I scrutinized the photo and saw another face that looked familiar: a pretty dark-haired girl with elfin features. I leaned closer to the page and looked below the picture, where the names were listed: *A. Pymstead, B. Abbott, K. Noel.*

I sat up and blinked several times. Where had I seen that face before? B. Abbott. K. Noel. I used my index finger to mark the page and then flipped back to the pages where the senior pictures were lined up in rows. Barbara Abbott. That was the blond girl on Miss Wetherby's right; she was unfamiliar to me, but my gaze lingered over the girl on the left. K. Noel. She was a pretty girl with a heart-shaped face. Her dark hair was pulled back. She was smiling. She looked familiar because she looked a lot like someone I had known very well at that age. I looked at her name. *Katherine Mallory "Keach" Noel.* Her activities included: *Dramatics, Field Hockey, Literary Society, Eugenia Wilcox Orator III, IV, Winner of the Eugenia Wilcox Prize. Plans for the Future: Bryn Mawr College. Quotation: "The man's world must become a man's and a woman's world. Why are we afraid? It is the next step forward on the path to the sunrise, and the sun is rising over a new heaven and a new earth."—M. Carey Thomas.*

What on earth had happened to Keach Noel? How had the beautiful girl in the picture turned into the skinny, drunken, chain-smoking Keach Cunningham that I remembered?

I returned my gaze to the picture of Miss Wetherby, and stared until it seemed she had emerged from the photo and floated holographically above it. It seemed that the new prefab walls of Pencott Library fell away, the lights dimmed, and the old library reemerged like an old friend—and the faces in the old yearbook seemed to dance and sway around me in the half-light.

I imagined that I could see the old murals that used to ring the rotunda below the painted impression of the night sky. They depicted scenes from the story of the Decision of Paris. I remember sitting in the library, the old desks battered from a century of students tapping with their pencils and hammering with fidgety heels, staring up at Paris holding the red apple. I used to contemplate the expression on his face. To whom should he give the apple? The three beauties stood together: Athena, the goddess of wisdom, had pale brown, curly locks;

Hera, the goddess of marriage and domesticity, was raven haired; and Aphrodite, the goddess of love, was blond. Paris looked at the three of them and tried to choose. I used to imagine that the goddesses were secretly pinching each other, hard enough to hurt.

The image of Miss Wetherby floated in front of me, her eyes as glassy and frozen as they had looked when she had taken her eternal rest. I looked down at the picture of K. Noel and A. Pymstead grouped around her in the 1961 yearbook, and I knew that something had gone terribly wrong that year—just as something had gone wrong our year.

Eighteen years later, pretty and accomplished K. Noel had evolved into Keach Cunningham, the caboose at the end of a train-wreck marriage to Winslow Cunningham, the gayest Hardley boy in the class of 1956.

As I stared, the horrifying holograph of Miss Wetherby receded, the lights brightened, and the customary businesslike hum of Pencott returned to my ears.

I returned the volume to its slot among the old yearbooks, slipped outside, and hurried down the hill to Gould Cottage. I went inside and walked along the hallway where the trophies, class portraits, and plaques that commemorated the Grove were hung, and as I reached the end of the hall, sure enough, there was a large mahogany plaque. At the top, there was a brass plate inscribed: *Winners of the Eugenia Wilcox Prize*. I followed the prize down the rows of winners until I found the class of 1961. The engraved name was not *Katherine Mallory "Keach" Noel*. It was *Amanda Vining Pymstead*. Something had changed between the time that the yearbook was printed and when the plaque was engraved. I knew that yearbooks had to go to the printers early back in those days. So, Keach Cunningham must have won the prize and then given it up, so it had passed to the runner-up, Miss Pymstead.

I remembered sitting in Commons on a spring day, so long ago, and hearing that Lissa Bronwen had won the Eugenia Wilcox Prize—not me. I had been disqualified. I could almost feel the competition, the conniving, the cheating, and the jealousy percolating up through the years.

The next morning, I headed to Loomis Hall, to the Office of Alumni Records. I wrote a name and class on a piece of paper and handed it to the secretary. I waited for her to ask me for something—identification, proof of my need for the information—but she just smiled and said, "Certainly." A moment later, she was writing something on the scrap of paper and handing it back to me. I looked at the paper in my hand and saw that Katherine Mallory (Noel) Cunningham '61 had a current address in Vermont, not more than fifteen miles from the Grove Academy.

PART SIX
SENIOR YEAR

34

My career at the Grove ended the moment I walked out of my meeting with Mr. Treadway and Mrs. Tarkington-Luce in Loomis Hall. There were still a few weeks left of my senior year, plus final exams and graduation. And I was eventually assigned to twenty-hours of kitchen duty, working the dishwashing machine in Commons as penance to the Grove community. But from that day forward, I knew that my familiar life of the past four years was over. The friendships that had sustained me for years were also finished. Lissa and I were barely speaking to each other. Kat was distant and withdrawn.

At lunch on Friday, we were informed that the winner of the Eugenia Wilcox Prize would be announced at dinner, and when I walked out of Commons, I found Kat vomiting in the bushes.

That night at dinner, Kat still looked ashen faced. When it was time to make the announcement, Miss Pymstead got up and walked to the end of the dining room. There was a microphone set up there that they used for making special announcements. Miss Pymstead turned it on and tapped it twice.

"Good evening, girls," she said. "I'm here to announce the results of this year's Eugenia Wilcox Examination. As you know, this is the highest honor bestowed at the Grove Academy. It carries with it a four-year scholarship to one of the Seven Sisters colleges."

There was the sound of anticipation and shuffling feet.

"This year's winner is an outstanding student who excels in every area, including English literature. The Eugenia Wilcox Committee, in judging her essay, said, 'Her attention to detail, refined analysis, and understanding of the nuances of language separated her essay from those of her peers.' I am proud to announce the winner of this year's Eugenia Wilcox Prize is Elizabeth Anne Bronwen. Congratulations, Lissa."

Back in my room, there was a knock on the door. It was Abigail Von Platte. She stank as usual. She was scowling at me.

"I don't know what she's going to do," she said, her face impassive.

"What?"

"She's hiding in there. She seems pretty upset about something. I think you better go."

"Abigail, for God's sake. I have no idea what you're talking about. Can you leave me alone for one second? I'm busy."

She shrugged. "Sure." She started to walk away. "I mean, it's just since suicide runs in her family and all . . ."

I grabbed her arm and whirled her around. "What the hell are you talking about?"

"Kat."

"What about her?"

"She's in the boathouse. I think she might be getting ready to kill herself."

I ran as fast as I could, cutting across Siberia and ducking down the pathway through the woods, I was completely winded when I reached the boathouse.

"Kat!"

I paused, straining to hear above my breath. I was panting from running so fast.

I circled to the front of the boathouse; its garage door opening was shut tight and padlocked. I wondered if Abigail had been pulling a prank, but she didn't have much of a sense of humor.

I ran around to the back of the building; there were no doors, but I saw a small casement window at about eye-level that was propped open. It was not very big, but Kat was small, and agile. I pushed on the window and peered inside, but it was dark.

"Kat?"

I stood on tiptoe and tried again to see inside, but all I could make out were the long, slender shells turned upside down and stacked on tiered metal hangers. Not much else.

"Kat?"

Hoisting myself up, I slithered through the narrow opening, but my shirt snagged on the splintered window frame and cobwebs caught in my hair as I passed. Catching hold of the metal boat hanger, I pulled myself into the cool interior of the boathouse.

Inside, it was damp and still, the air scented with winter earth, varnish, and grease. At first, I could hear nothing, but then I heard muffled sobs. As my eyes adjusted to the dim light, I realized that Kat was seated not far from me, her back pressed up against a wall stacked with tiers of shells. Her arms were crossed over her knees, and her head pressed into them. She looked upset, but hardly suicidal, and I wondered how Abigail Von Platte had even known she was in here.

"Leave me alone," Kat said. "Go away."

I crouched down next to her and put my hand on her shoulder. "Kat, even if Lissa won, I still think you're smarter than she is. Don't let it get to you."

She stared at me red eyed. "You think that's what I'm upset about? You think I just wanted to win for winning's sake. That's not me—that's *you*, Jane. You're the one who's always so obsessed with being the best."

"God, I'm sorry, Kat. I wasn't thinking. It's the money, isn't it? I should have realized."

Kat slapped my hand off her shoulder so that it banged up against the metal boat hanger hard enough to leave a welt, and I felt tears gather in my eyes.

"Jesus, what did you have to do that for?" I said, my sympathy rapidly dissipating.

I rubbed the welt on the back of my hand, and my lungs filled with such a murderous rage that I thought if I didn't get out of the boathouse right that very minute, I might kill Kat on the spot—and then there would be two murders associated with Wooten Boathouse.

That night, Kat looked exhausted. She was hunched over her desk, poring over the clue notebook. I recognized the paper she was looking at. It was the one I had found clutched in Miss Wetherby's frozen hand. The paper was stiff from having been wet and then dried. It was furred on the outside, and the ink had run but was legible:

> *I died for beauty, but was scarce*
> *Adjusted in the tomb,*
> *When one who died for truth was lain*
> *In an adjoining room.*

Kat's face was sallow and she had dark circles under her eyes.

"Look, I'm sorry," I said. "There's got to be another way to pay for college. You can take out loans or apply for financial aid."

Kat didn't even answer. Her eyes continued to study the words in front of her.

"It makes no sense," she muttered. She traced the lines with her fingertip. "I don't get it."

"Don't get what?"

"The handwriting," she said.

"I know, it's weird," I said. "It's the only poem not in Pymstead's handwriting. It must be a clue."

"I know whose handwriting this is," she said.

"Who? Whose is it?" This was the first time we had any kind of break in the case.

"It's not a clue," she said. "And I'm not going to tell you."

I could not convince her to say another word.

After that, it seemed as if Kat became as obsessed with the clue notebook as I had once been. When I came into our room, I found her puzzling over the poems, muttering the words to herself as if she could somehow force herself to ferret out the solution. She kept asking me to go over the events of the night of April 17 with her again and again—the bump with the car, the hand, the snow over the body, the blackish mark on her head. Every time she brought up the events of that night, I put on music, stuffed a towel in the crack under the door, and pleaded for her to lower her voice. What had happened had happened. I did not want to discuss it anymore.

One day, I returned to the room and she was poring over the clue notebook, concentrating so much that she didn't even look up. I was startled to see that she had an old *Lantern* yearbook on her desk.

"Hey, where'd you get that?" I asked. I was startled to see the date embossed on the spine—it was the missing yearbook: '61.

"Where did you find this?" I asked again as I reached toward it and flipped the front cover open. Inside, there was a stamp that said: *If found, please return to Pencott Library, Grove Academy, 1 Lantern Way, Eakin, Vermont.*

"You stole it from the library?"

"I borrowed it," Kat said. "I'm going to return it." She grabbed it from her desk and shoved it into her backpack.

"Well, what did it say? Anything interesting?"

"Nothing," Kat said. She stopped and stared at me, as if she was considering saying something else, but then she changed her mind and rushed out of the room.

"Kat," I called after her. "I think you should just let it go."

But she wouldn't let it go. Each day, she seemed to become more withdrawn, more obsessive. One day, I came in and found that she had copied out another poem:

> *Success is counted sweetest*
> *By those who ne'er succeed.*
> *To comprehend a nectar*
> *Requires sorest need.*
>
> *Not one of all the purple host*
> *Who took the flag to-day*
> *Can tell the definition*
> *So clear, of victory,*
>
> *As he, defeated, dying,*
> *On whose forbidden ear*
> *The distant strains of triumph*
> *Break, agonized and clear!*

Kat had marked the last four lines with a pink highlighter and penciled in the words: *This must be it!*

The atmosphere in our room started to get claustrophobic. I began to study in the library. One night, upon returning to our room after study hall, I found Kat deep in concentration—arms clasped around her knees, chewing on a pencil, her brow furrowed. The clue notebook lay open on her desk in front of her.

But as soon as I entered, she slammed the notebook shut, strode across the room, and jammed it back into the drawer in my desk, where I usually kept it. I almost reached past her and pulled it out again, but I didn't want to antagonize her. Besides, I was tired of everything—clues, poems, mysteries. I wanted to put all of it behind me.

But Kat wouldn't, or maybe *couldn't*, leave it alone.

A couple of nights later, I found Kat balancing a volume of *The Collected Poems of Emily Dickinson* on her lap. She was muttering to herself, reading the poems aloud under her breath.

She looked up briefly when I came in, before returning to her reading. We had a half hour between the end of study hall and lights-out. I went about my nightly routine, but Kat didn't budge from her bed.

"Are you going to bed?" I asked.

"I'm close," she said. "I've almost got it."

"Honestly, Kat, you should forget about it. The whole thing was dumb anyway. What did Pymstead ever do?"

She looked so wild that it almost scared me. "Obviously, you have no idea what people are capable of."

"I guess I don't," I said, edging past her. "I just don't understand why you're wasting your sweet hours on this . . ."

Kat's eyes widened.

"Wait a minute. What did you just say?"

"I said I don't see why you're wasting your sweet time on this."

"No," she said. "You didn't say 'sweet time.' You said, 'sweet hours' . . . *Sweet hours have perished here; / This is a mighty room; / Within its precincts hopes have played—/ Now shadows in the tomb.* That's it!" she said. "I got it!"

I was completely baffled now. This wasn't one of the poems that we had found on campus, not one of the poems we had studied in class.

Kat hunched over and scribbled the lines down on the paper.

"Look, Jane. Don't you see? *Sweet hours have perished here? This is a mighty room. Within its precincts hopes have played—now shadows in the tomb.*"

"I'm sorry, Kat, I don't get it." I was tired. I just wanted to go to bed. Shortly after I'd come inside, a heavy rain started. The sound of drumming rain and the scent of loamy springtime ground came through the open window.

"How can you not get it?" she asked. "Just look around!"

I glanced at the scene she was pointing to—the cramped confines of our double room, crammed as it was with a bunk bed, two dressers, two desks. There were field hockey sticks propped up in a corner, laundry bags bulging from hooks on the inside of our half-open closet door. Our single bookcase was stuffed full of books; our desks were piled high with papers and notebooks.

"*Sweet hours have perished here* . . . Right?"

Had we wasted time here? Absolutely. Nursed dreams that had never come true? My thoughts first flashed to Josh, swiftly followed by the familiar stab of despair each time I remembered my disastrous academic situation.

Could Emily Dickinson really have been writing about boarding school?

But as far as I could tell, the only real mystery was why we cared so much. The unsolved puzzle of Chestmont Wooten was fading from my mind. In spite of myself, I was looking toward the future that was hurtling closer whether we wanted to go out and meet it or not.

But I didn't think I could explain any of this to Kat. I picked up my toothbrush and soap box, and headed out the door to the bathroom down the hall.

When I came back, Kat was gone. I pulled open the drawer where I usually kept the clue notebook, and I noticed it was missing. I tried to remember the last time I'd seen it. Not since a few days earlier, when I had seen Kat returning it to the drawer. What could she possibly want with it? I had already figured out that it was Kat who had left the poems for me, in the chapel and in the yearbook in the library. Kat, who had poems written in Miss Pymstead's handwriting given to her during their study sessions. Our sleuthing was fun and amusing for a while, but now it was over.

I lay awake for a long time, after lights-out, listening to the pouring rain outside the window, waiting for our door to open. The next morning, I saw her clothes from the previous night in a heap on the floor, soaking wet, and muddy around the hem of her jeans. Kat had already gone out.

Protruding from the jeans' pocket, I saw the knot of a leather thong. I pulled it it out, and found that it was attached to a Grove class ring. I listened for any sound in the hallway, but heard nothing, so I slipped it into my pocket.

That morning, Nate Hodges stopped me as I was entering Commons and told me I was wanted in Loomis Hall. The rain had stopped sometime during the night, and the high windows in Loomis's draw- ing room were filled with a pleasant morning light. Mr. Treadway and Mrs. Tarkington-Luce were both wearing summer-weight chinos and seersucker shirts. Only I had changed. I was Jane Milton, the cheater. Jane Milton whose hands were chapped from dishwashing: a Grove china plate, but one with a chip in it. I could see it in their expressions that said, "You again . . . ," hear it in the slight brusqueness in Mr. Treadway's tone as he said, "Sit down."

The same black, shiny table sat in the middle of the room that had been there before. Only now, in the middle of the table sat my clue notebook.

"Your roommate, Katherine, has made some very serious accusa- tions. She says that you will be able to corroborate them."

I could see how doubt flickered in Mrs. Tarkington-Luce's eyes when she used the word "corroborate." I realized that Kat did not know that she had taken a risky gamble using me, a tainted source, as her only witness.

Mr. Treadway opened a manila folder, not unlike the folder he had shown me with the Dickinson essays inside, but in this one, there was a piece of paper with a scribbled limerick on it. I'd seen the limer- ick before. It was one of those that had made the rounds during Miss Wetherby's memorial service.

"Do you recognize this handwriting?" Mr. Treadway said, pointing to the limerick.

I nodded yes.

"To whom does it belong?"

"Kat," I said.

"And what about this?"

He flipped open the clue notebook, showing me an Emily Dickinson poem that had been glued into the book.

"Miss Pymstead," I whispered, so softly that it must have been inaudible.

"I can't hear you," he thundered.

"I said that's Miss Pymstead's handwriting."

"And where did you find this poem?" he asked.

I didn't answer.

"You need to answer these questions."

"Why?" I asked.

"What do you mean, why?"

"Well, why do you want to know?" I said. I could hear my voice shaking, and it was barely audible.

Mrs. Tarkington-Luce gestured as though to quiet Mr. Treadway. She seated herself beside me. "Were you aware that Kat sometimes visited Miss Pymstead in her apartment in the evenings?"

I nodded, yes.

She smiled a little.

"And, what do you think she was doing there?"

"Kat told me Miss Pymstead was tutoring her."

"I see. And why would she do that? Kat was an excellent student."

I decided to say nothing about the Eugenia Wilcox exam. "She said it was something to do with her mother, but she couldn't say why because she swore the Grove sisters' swear."

"Did Kat ever tell you that some of the attention that Miss Pymstead paid her was unwanted?"

"What do you mean?"

"Did she tell you that she wished Miss Pymstead would leave her alone?"

I was trying to think about it. I didn't remember Kat saying too much about Miss Pymstead. "I don't know."

Mrs. Tarkington-Luce was smiling kindly now. It was a kinder smile than I had seen from her in the past. She patted my hand. "Let me ask you another question. Do you have any reason to think that Miss Wetherby was jealous of Kat's relationship with Miss Pymstead?"

I think I was feeling a little dizzy. They had summoned me to Loomis Hall before I had even had breakfast. It felt hot and stuffy in the room. The sun was now blazing in the windows, the air felt close, and my clue notebook, which I had so carefully kept hidden, looked pitiful, exposed there on the table.

Now, Mrs. Tarkington-Luce reached over and slid it toward us, flipping it open.

"Kat told us that she has been keeping a record since earlier this year, but she was afraid to come forward until now that the year is almost over."

Mr. Treadway was shaking his head and staring at the floor. I followed his eyes to the pattern on the Oriental rug. I noticed white fluff on the black parts of the pattern. The rug needed to be vacuumed.

"I think we're overwhelming her, Elliott," Mrs. Tarkington-Luce said. "Jane dear, I understand that this is a very, um, delicate matter. What we need you to do is just confirm what Katherine has told us."

The change in their demeanor toward me was shocking. The last time I was here, they were accusing me of cheating. This time, they were gentle and kind. Whatever it was they wanted from me, they obviously wanted it very much.

I lifted my eyes from the rug and looked into Mrs. Tarkington-Luce's eyes. "But I don't know what she told you . . ."

It occurred to me in that instant that adults never seemed to understand how infinite the possibilities were for lies; like a handful of pebbles tossed at the ground. I took a quick survey of the possibilities: Miss Pymstead the murderer of Chestmont Wooten, Keach Cunningham the murderer of Miss Wetherby—Kat and I were possibly accomplices, sleuths, cover-up artists, or good storytellers, and the people around us were perpetrators, bystanders . . . The only thing I was sure about was that if I let the chips fall as they may, they might not fall in my favor.

Mr. Treadway took his index finger, placed it on the paper where the smutty limerick was scribbled, and moved the scrap about on the polished surface of the table. He cleared his throat a few times as though preparing to say something he did not especially want to say. I tracked the paper with my eyes, as it moved in and out of a ray of sunlight that was dappling the table. At that moment, I realized the ditty was written on a scrap torn from the front of the *Book of Common Prayer*.

Mrs. Tarkington-Luce was flipping through the clue notebook, pausing each time she came upon one of the Emily Dickinson poems. Only now, I noticed Kat's handwriting penciled in underneath, where before there had been nothing. Now, there were written lines. I read one silently: *Her declarations of undying love make me squirm inside. Her caresses feel like the tongue-lashings of snakes . . .*

Mrs. Tarkington-Luce flipped a page and I saw another. Where yesterday, there had been only the line: *I died for beauty*, now, there was Kat's handwriting, in pencil: *Constance is jealous. She knows Pym has spurned her for me. Mandy threatens to kill her, but I have begged her not to.*

As I said, Kat was a storyteller. She had carefully doctored the clue notebook, purging my mentions of Chestmont Wooten, and managing to twist the clues into a well-constructed narrative of Miss Pymstead's wrongdoing.

As I slowly flipped through the pages, I couldn't believe it. This was not about murder. For reasons I could not fathom, Kat was trying to ruin Miss Pymstead, and the only one who could protect Miss Pymstead was me.

Mrs. Tarkington-Luce and Mr. Treadway were watching me. I thought of everything I had lost recently—my diploma, my chance to win the Wilcox award, and worst of all, my dignity.

I didn't know what I was going to say.

35

I left Loomis Hall with just enough time to make it to Gould Cottage for English class. I was nervous about seeing Miss Pymstead, afraid I would not be able to meet her eye.

When I walked in, I was startled to see a poem written on the chalkboard. I couldn't be sure, but it looked like Kat's handwriting.

> *Success is counted sweetest*
> *By those who ne'er succeed.*
> *To comprehend a nectar*
> *Requires sorest need.*

"Where's Kat?" Lissa whispered.

"I don't know," I said. "Did you see her last night? She was out after lights-out."

Lissa shook her head. "No, I have no idea."

Miss Pymstead was often a little late, but as the wait grew longer, we began to shift in our seats and look at our watches. Our whispered conversations turned to louder ones. We were talking about summer plans and colleges. This final class was only a formality, and apparently Miss Pymstead was not even going to show up.

After about twenty minutes, Katie Cornwell stood up. "I guess she's not coming."

"I guess not," echoed Emma Doerr.

I thought about Miss Pymstead and I felt terrible. Of all my teachers at the Grove, she had been the most passionate, yet we always seemed so ready to pounce on her. What exactly had we found lacking in her? I think it was just the idea that it seemed that her swelling heart and outsized passions had led her only here—to this room, to us.

One by one, girls picked up their backpacks and slid their feet back into their flip-flops and headed out the door without even a look back.

I was the last to go.

At lunch, there was an announcement. *Emergency all-school meeting in the chapel at 2:30 pm.* We all started whispering immediately. The all-school meetings were reserved for only the most dire circumstances. The last time we had one was sophomore year when one of our classmates was killed in a car accident over spring break.

My heart started pounding furiously. I hadn't seen Kat all day. I had no idea where she might be. Lissa and I exchanged a look.

"She went out last night in the pouring rain," I said. "I know she came back, because I saw her muddy clothes in a heap on the floor. But she was up and out before I woke up. That's not like her!"

"Chill out," Lissa said. "What would happen to her?"

What would happen to her? I realized that all year I'd been just waiting, thinking that something might happen to her. I tried to calm myself.

At two fifteen, the bells of Whittaker Chapel started chiming and we all filed up the hill in groups of twos and threes. All the doors to the chapel were open and light was streaming through the rose window. Even so, the interior was dim.

My mouth was dry and my heart was pounding. I could feel tears pricking at my eyes. I was convinced now that we were going to receive bad news about Kat. I steeled myself.

But as my eyes adjusted to the gloomy interior, I picked out Kat, sitting alone in one of the pews near the back. I rushed forward and sat down beside her.

"You're okay?" I said. I felt as if I were seeing a ghost. She stared at me, then turned her face away.

A moment later, the rest of the crew came in—Lissa, Emma Doerr, and Katie Cornwell. My emotion changed on a dime from fear to an undercurrent of drama. Knowing that my own little crew was safe, my worry had changed to curiosity.

A hush fell over the room when Mr. Treadway walked through the door and approached the pulpit. I could see that his face was much changed from this morning. He looked pale and shaken.

The chapel was now dead silent. Nobody moved.

He cleared his throat.

"I'm sure you are all wondering what precipitated this emergency all-school meeting," he said. You could see everyone looking around at the students in the pews and the faculty gathered around the perimeter. Who was missing?

"With great sorrow, I am here to announce the death of our beloved teacher, Miss Amanda Pymstead."

At first, the chapel was absolutely still. Then, a moment later, a torrent of whispers filled the room.

Miss Pymstead. No, it can't be. We were just waiting for her. We didn't even wonder where she was. We erupted into astonished chatter, not even

302

sure what to feel. I looked at Lissa, who frowned back at me, then tried to catch Kat's eye, but she was looking the other way.

"Her death was a tragic accident," he said. "I'm so sorry. We will announce details of the memorial service at a later date."

All the girls sat in stunned silence for a moment, but soon enough, people started to shuffle and pick up backpacks and cough and restart conversations. Only the seniors sat frozen and silent. Unsure what to say or do. But after a few moments, Emma Doerr grabbed her backpack and the rest of us followed suit.

"So sad," Katie Cornwell whispered, her eyes big.

"She was my favorite teacher," Emma said.

"I wonder what happened to her," Lissa said.

Only Kat said nothing. She stood up and bolted toward the door.

By dinnertime, everyone knew the story. Miss Pymstead was found crumpled on the riverbank, just underneath the giant poplar behind the boathouse. The jump tree. It was presumed that she had jumped to her death. Nate Hodges found her around 11:00 a.m., when he went to unlock the boathouse, but from her mud-stained clothing, it was presumed she had died sometime during the night. Before the end of the day, a limerick was making the rounds:

> *Now, Pym took The Jump and she's dead*
> *So she can rejoin our dear Head.*
> *They've gone straight to hell*
> *And they like it quite well—*
> *It's hotter than Hades in bed.*

Kat was not in our room, and Mrs. Dockerty popped her head in to tell me that Kat was in the infirmary with a high fever.

I was left alone with my own conscience.

36

Graduation day dawned over the valley like a bright storm. The for-
sythia stood out against the buildings, and the lawn mower had left
shirred swathes upon the lawn. Parents milled about—fathers in their
Brooks Brothers, mothers in linen dresses in ice-cream colors; there
were tents up here and there, all of them muting our presence. On the
vast campus where we normally felt like giants, the presence of our
parents seemed to shrink us.

I did what the others did: I marched on damp turf; I sat on a folding chair set up on Siberia, feeling it tilt as the metal legs settled in the
wet ground; I winced at static when they tested the microphones; I
heard Lissa's voice, amplified, echo back and forth between the stone
walls of Whittaker Chapel and the brick walls of Kiputh Gymnasium.

Lissa's valediction was as dull as a piece of corn on the cob and at
least fifteen minutes too long, and Abigail Von Platte tore off a piece of
the program, hastily scribbled up a ditty, and passed it around, which
did lend a bit of levity to the moment:

There once was a girl with blond hair,
And some people thought she was fair.
She told many lies
And stole her a prize—
And now she is going to Yale.

When it was my turn to walk to the front of the crowd, I'm sure that I extended my hand, and shook the hand of Mrs. Tarkington-Luce—and received the empty case that did not hold a diploma—but all I can remember is the words that were running through my head:

A solemn thing it was, I said,
A woman white to be,
And wear, if God should count me fit,
Her hallowed mystery.

A timid thing to drop a life
Into the purple well,
Too plummetless that it come back
Eternity until.

The schedule was tightly packed; there were meals and assemblies to attend, and our rooms had to be packed up and vacated on a strict schedule. Once they were done with us, they were done with us. The weekend passed in a blur that felt like exiting a commuter train during evening rush hour, a one-way push from which there was no hope of turning back.

Since the incident with the clue notebook in Loomis, I had not had a moment alone with Kat; the administration had allowed her to stay in the infirmary, secluded and talking to no one. Now, with the press of people swirling around, I thought I might see Kat and have a chance to speak to her, but the chance never presented itself. So finally, I scribbled a few words on a luncheon napkin, wadded it up, ran upstairs to Lane North, and slid the note into the crack in the closet.

My message was short: *Why did you betray Miss Pymstead?*

Our room was stripped bare now; nothing left but my suitcases lined up next to the door. Kat's trunk was already gone. I couldn't be sure she would come back for the note. I hesitated, thinking it would be better to try to speak to her instead, but then I left the note and ran, not wanting to have to explain my absence to my parents.

After lunch on Saturday afternoon, I slipped away from my parents once more. First, I ran up the stairs of Lane North to 2B, where my note had not been touched, then pell-mell down the hill toward Gould Cottage. I ran so fast that the strap to one of my Capezios broke, and for the rest of the weekend, I had to tuck in the buckle and walk carefully to keep it from flapping. I stood on Miss Pymstead's doorstep, and I imagined the moment when she saw Miss Wetherby's frozen corpse on her stoop—and the way her mouth must have fallen open in shock when she was falsely accused of molesting a student she had tried to help. I pulled off my corsage and laid it on her doorstep. I muttered the words *"I'm sorry."*

PART SEVEN
NOW

37

She knelt with her back toward me, her hands busy with an urn overflowing with dark crimson mums. Her hair, pulled back into a ponytail, was that indiscriminate color between gray and blond. She turned when she heard my footsteps and stood up, clapping her hands together to knock the soil off her gardening gloves.

The sight of her startled me so much that I forgot my manners and said nothing, just stood there, mouth agape, trying to gather my thoughts. This woman who stood before me looked scarcely older than I was. Her face was unlined, her manner modest and slightly subdued.

She took a step forward, a tentative smile on her face. "Can I help you?"

For a half-moment trick of the light, I thought I was seeing Kat.

She tilted her head to one side, a trace of worry washing across her face.

"Oh, I'm sorry. I was just so startled to see you—you look so much like Kat . . ."

Her eyes widened, and then, I saw recognition. "Jane Milton?"

She opened the door and ushered me inside her home—half of a Victorian house that was light and bright, with high ceilings. There were well-tended houseplants everywhere. Keach offered me a seat in her living room and busied herself preparing coffee in the kitchen. In a few moments, she returned with a tray.

Even from this brief encounter, it was clear to me that Keach was not a drinker anymore. Her eyes were clear, her demeanor calm. I had never realized how young she was—but as a member of the class of 1961, she was eighteen years older than I was, and with her impeccable old Grove breeding, she had an ageless air.

"You live nearby. Do you return to the Grove often?" I said.

Keach poured coffee into my cup and then into hers. She took a sip and smiled a small, rueful smile.

"Oh no, I'm afraid I haven't been there in years. I send off a check every year, for faculty salaries and financial aid . . ."

"That's kind of you."

"I don't know if you are aware of this, but Kat attended the Grove on a full scholarship—" She looked up and studied my face.

"I'm terribly sorry for your loss," I said. The words, of course, were inadequate, but I felt at last a tremendous relief for having been able to say them. Whatever memorial there had been for Kat back then, I knew nothing about it. At the time of her death, I did not feel that I could stick my toe into the swirling waters of the Cunningham darkness without risking being swept away.

Keach looked out the window and took another slow sip of coffee.

"One never expects to outlive a child. It was I who was headed on the path to destruction. It has been hard to be the one who survived. I've tried to live right as a way to make it up to her."

"I guess part of why I'm here is that I've always blamed myself, and I thought maybe if I understood what happened back then a little better . . ."

"Your fault? Jane dear, why on earth would it be your fault? Kat went through a lot—and I'm afraid—" She broke off, but restarted. "I'm afraid that I made some bad decisions. I'm sure she was suffering from clinical depression—there's a strong family history of it. People were just not as knowledgeable in those days."

"She really wanted to win the Eugenia Wilcox exam, and I told her that I wouldn't sit for it so that she would win . . . But I lied, and I took it anyway . . . although I didn't end up winning—Lissa did."

"Look, Jane, I'm going to level with you. I'm sure you know I had an alcohol problem back then. Kat's grandmother, Dorothy, her father's mother, died just before the start of her senior year."

"I remember that."

"Shortly before that, her big old house had burned to the ground, the one that had all the old family things—that family had money that dated back ten generations, back to Dutch New Amsterdam . . ."

"The fire . . . Kat was very upset . . ."

"Everything was lost in that fire, including all of the family papers. It wouldn't have made any difference—I'm sure she was planning to have the papers drawn up again, but then she was killed in a car accident."

I nodded. I wasn't sure what she was getting at.

"So, when she died, she had no will. She had sizable assets, but all of that money was tied up in trusts and land, and it was very compli- cated. Win and I—Win was Kat's father . . ." I nodded. "We didn't have much money of our own. I didn't work, and Win was a 'painter' . . . Occasionally he sold something, but the rest of the time, we subsisted on the handouts Dorothy gave us whenever she felt like it. Then, all of a sudden, she was gone and our source of income just dried up."

Keach looked pained to tell me this, as if she were telling me the story of a wayward sister instead of talking about herself.

"I remember all of this," I said. "Sort of. Kat didn't talk about it much. But I remember when her grandmother died and she seemed to have money problems."

"She had a full scholarship to the Grove, but that was on a more informal basis—Constance Wetherby had worked it out for us without having to go through all of the humiliation of the paperwork and forms. But Miss Wetherby had explained that for college, we would have to go through the official channels—and then when Kat's grammy died, there was the matter of Win's inheritance."

Keach paused and looked at me, obviously hoping that I was going to understand without her explaining it any further, but for a fleeting moment I felt that old sensation of not knowing. "I'm sorry, I . . ."

Keach sighed and put down the cup. "You've heard the phrase 'poor little rich girl'? That was Kat. We had no money to pay for college, but Win's family had sizeable assets and she was not going to qualify for financial aid. Dorothy would have paid for it, but now, Dorothy was gone. I was pressuring Kat to win a scholarship because I didn't know where we were going to get the money for her tuition."

Keach grabbed a tissue and dabbed at her eyes. "In the end, I needn't have worried about it. Win's brother was a stand-up guy. He agreed to sell off a property so that Win could pay Kat's tuition. We were so proud that she was going to Yale. I feel really bad about it. Kat never knew that her father paid her tuition."

"Because he died?"

"Oh, he was very much alive. Win was gay," she said. "Closeted, of course. He fell in love with a fireman he had met in a gay bar in the city. He moved in with him, but he didn't want Kat to know. Things are so much different today. But in those days, being gay was a big shameful secret. Win and I both thought we needed to shelter her from the truth. I told her that she should think of him as dead. I didn't think she would take it so literally."

"You thought it would be less traumatic to lose her father than to know he was gay?" I was incredulous.

"You come from a different generation," she said. "It was so different back then. Things have changed for the better, and I'm glad."

I could see tears in her eyes.

"She was so heartbroken that I desperately wanted to tell her how to get in touch with him, but I promised Win that I wouldn't. I was planning to tell her—honestly, I was, but I never got up the courage. I kept thinking I'd wait for her to get out of college. I was determined that she get an education and not end up trapped, depending on a man, miserably unhappy—like I did. She was doing well in school and I didn't want to rock the boat. Deep down, I knew how fragile she was."

I couldn't think of what to say.

"Then he got sick and died of AIDS. In a way, I'm glad she was spared knowing about that. She was so incredibly fond of him, even though he wasn't such a great father. But I've always worried that keeping his secret might have been the thing that pushed her over the edge."

"Do you mind if I ask you a question?"

"Not at all."

"Of course you knew Amanda Pymstead."

I saw a look come over Keach's face, the first look that was more discomfiture than sorrow.

"She was in my class."

"Were you aware that she took a special interest in Kat?"

Her eyes darted away from me. She picked up the coffeepot, offered me some more coffee, then poured some more for herself. "Yes—no . . . What do you mean?"

"Kat told me that Miss Pymstead was tutoring her for the Eugenia Wilcox exam."

"That wouldn't surprise me. I believe that Amanda took a special interest in Kat because Mandy felt that she owed me something. I resented it at the time—I shouldn't have. It was small-minded of me.

Mandy knew what shape I was in, and she had a good heart—always looking out for her students. Kat needed all the help she could get."

"Did you know that Kat, Lissa, and I thought that Amanda Pymstead was the one who murdered Chestmont Wooten, the headmaster? We had a kind of weird obsession with his death."

Keach stood up. "What? You thought what? Where did you get a crazy idea like that? Are you telling me that Kat talked about that?"

"All the time. The three of us did. I think we were just bored, or something. We fixated on Chestmont Wooten, and we thought Miss Pymstead was the one who killed him."

"Well, she didn't." Keach said with an air of authority. "What else did Kat say about Chestmont Wooten?"

"Nothing."

"Did she know that he was her father?"

"What?"

Keach sat down again.

"Chestmont Wooten got fired from the Hardley School because there was a nasty rumor going around about him that he was overly fond of boys. They called him—"

"I know—*Hardley a boy* . . ."

"Yes, yes, that's it . . . *Hardley a boy* . . . They sent him to Grove as a punishment. I guess the idea was that he would be safe around girls. Ironically, he hadn't the slightest interest in boys—it was girls he had an eye for. He was very good-looking, and twenty years our senior, and at first we girls were entirely swoony for him."

"I've seen his picture," I said.

"I was the special protégée of Miss Constance Wetherby. Every year she had a 'special girl,' nothing inappropriate, you know, just a lot of those sickening sweet-onion sandwiches and long soulful talks about Emily Dickinson . . . When Wooten came along, she hated him—hated him with a passion you could cut with a knife. For one thing, she had been the clear favorite for the headmistress position when they decided to give it to him."

"That must have stung. Hardley's reject becomes head of the Grove . . ."

"I'll admit, I was quite besotted with him, and flattered that he was flirting with me. I used to sneak out at night to meet him. He recited poetry to me, and I pretended not to notice when he slipped his hand onto my knee. One night, he slipped me a flask of Johnnie Walker, mixed up with Hardley's fresh-pressed apple cider. Before I knew it, he was dragging me off the path, back behind the boathouse . . ."

The light was fading outside the window, and she and I both kept our gazes fixed on the view outside the window.

"I won the Eugenia Wilcox Prize that year—the topic was Emily Dickinson. But it turned out I wasn't going to be able to go to college at all. What had looked like gates flung wide open to the whole world for me suddenly opened to a path that got narrower and narrower . . . but I told myself I didn't care."

"Pregnant?" I asked.

She nodded. "I had to drop out of school. They ended up giving the prize to the runner-up: Amanda Pymstead. I found myself back home, here in Vermont, with a swelling belly. My parents looked around among the people of our social set to try to find someone who was willing to marry me in the condition I was in, and there was Winslow Cavendish Cunningham. He was a lovely Hardley boy, with just the right everything, and he was searching for a wife who would look nice in company. Turns out, he was also trying to find someone desperate enough to overlook the fact that he was queer as a two-dollar bill and feckless enough to be likely to use up the last of his family fortune for his own entertainment."

I sipped my coffee.

"There's this one poem by Emily Dickinson, I don't suppose you know it? *A solemn thing it was, I said, / A woman white to be, / And wear, if God should count me fit, / her hallowed mystery. / A timid thing to drop a life / Into the purple well, / Too plummetless that it come back / Eternity until."* She recited from memory.

I startled. "As a matter of fact, I'm quite familiar with it," I said.

"I had in mind to go to Bryn Mawr, and then maybe become a war correspondent, or go off and travel and see the world, but I developed another plan. I decided that I would retreat inside my domesticity—I would be a woman in white, I would *throw* my life inside the purple well—a martyr . . ." Keach laughed; it was a rueful laugh. "It all seemed very poetic to me. Seventeen and wrecked by poetry. Seems utterly crazy, doesn't it?"

I smiled. "If anyone could understand, it would be me."

"Didn't quite turn out that way. It was cold and dark and lonely inside that purple well in a drafty barn of a house in Vermont with a cranky toddler and no one for company except for Winsome Win. He was utterly charming but used to disappear entirely for months on end. And there I was, surrounded by diapers, spit-up, play toys—didn't take me more than a year or two to realize that I wasn't cut out for that life." She looked at me intently. "I was too young. I was a bad mother. It's my biggest regret."

"I have a son. He's a terrific kid, and I do my best, but I worry constantly. We do the best we can with the tools that we have. It's not always enough. I think Prozac would have helped Kat."

Keach folded and unfolded her small bare hands in her lap. "I guess you're right. But I wish I had done better."

I saw a look of indecision flutter across her face, but then she stood up, crossed the room, and slid open a drawer in a wooden dresser that was painted a lovely robin's-egg blue. She pulled out an old Morocco folder, slipped out a piece of paper.

She handed it to me. I could see that it had once been creased and folded, and had then been pressed smooth. It looked like an old sheet torn out of a Mead spiral notebook, and I recognized Kat's handwriting, complete with the scribbled-out patches. It started: *I died for beauty, but was scarce / adjusted in my tomb . . .*

I looked at Keach and saw the pain fluttering there, at the corners of her mouth.

"It was her suicide note," she said simply.

The dark waters of the Hudson River.

I clasped her hand in mine.

"I'm sorry," I said.

There were a few moments of awkward silence until Keach smiled and squeezed my hand. "Jane, I do thank you for taking the time to come see me. It's lovely to see you again."

"I'll come again," I said, and I meant it. Because I knew that our shared memories were the only way to keep Kat alive. "But, Keach, I haven't asked you the question I came here to ask you . . ."

She was so small and slight, and with her fine bones, graying hair, and blue eyes, she looked just like any other old Grove girl standing with her class under a lantern-shaped banner on Lantern Day. I felt at ease with her. I found myself wanting to like her. I was letting down my guard.

"Ask me anything you like, dear."

"The night that Kat got into Yale, you came and took us to Bernigan's Tavern."

I waited to see a trace of something pass across her face, but nothing did.

"Do you remember that night?"

"I was so proud of Kat for getting into Yale . . . Of course, I'm sure it helped that Win and his father had both gone there, but still—what an accomplishment for a young woman . . ." She was smiling.

"Do you remember that night?"

Her face fell just slightly.

"No, I . . . not specifically, no. Did I say something . . . ? I'm sorry if I said things when I was drunk that may have caused you pain. I've been a member of AA ever since Kat died . . ." She looked at me searchingly.

"No, nothing." I said. "It was nothing . . ." I bent forward and kissed her on the cheek. "Good-bye. I hope you'll come to Lantern Day."

"Oh no. I couldn't. I don't think so. Too many painful memories. I try to stay away from the place."

"I guess that's understandable," I said. "But if you change your mind, you're always welcome."

Two days later, I received a note from Keach, just a few lines on a simple card, thanking me for the visit. As soon as I saw the envelope, I recognized the handwriting, but when I slipped the note card out, I was even more sure. Another piece of the puzzle solved. It was the handwriting of the poem that I had found in Miss Wetherby's house—and the handwriting of the poem that Miss Wetherby clutched in her hand at the time of her death. I could now easily imagine an earnest young Keach sitting in Underhill House, dutifully copying out Emily Dickinson poems as Miss Wetherby fanned herself with her handkerchief. I could picture poor Miss Wetherby holding the papers with Keach's handwriting, perhaps holding them up to her nose to catch a lingering trace of her student's perfume, then folding the pages and placing them reverently in her brown leather volume of Emily Dickinson poems to keep.

38

About a week after my visit to Keach, my phone rang near midnight, waking me from a sound sleep. Dr. Farber-Johnson's voice was crisp. There could be no mistaking her meaning.

"Charlie is in my office in Gould Cottage. You must come and get him at once. He was found sneaking out of the library after hours. He had a copy of the passkey with him. I'm afraid this is grounds for immediate suspension."

Charlie looked contrite. I felt a momentary pang—but just momentary, because I was furious. What confused me was that I was expecting to see his cohort in crime, Kaitlyn, but he was alone, completely and totally alone, and looking about ten years old and scared to death.

"He was sneaking out of the library," Dr. Farber-Johnson said. "After it was closed . . ."

I steadied myself on the arm of the Hitchcock chair, but I didn't want her to see any weakness, so I remained standing.

"I'm sure there must be some explanation."

I turned to my son. "Charlie?"

"I was . . ."

Dr. Farber-Johnson held up her hand. "I suggest that you save your story for the discipline council. For now, he'll be sequestered in the infirmary."

I thought I'd be able to ask him what happened when we got home, but obviously that was not going to happen.

I looked at Charlie, but he wouldn't meet my glance.

When I returned to Abbott North, I lingered as I passed Kaitlyn's room. I stopped outside the doorway and heard voices within. Obviously, the girls were not asleep. It was past one in the morning.

Back in my own bed, I couldn't sleep, and then I thought I heard footsteps. I opened the door to an empty hallway, but at my feet was a stack of pages.

Freak Snowstorm

When the fat envelope had arrived from Yale, I had carried it around for several hours before I even opened it. I couldn't stand the thought of going back to my room, where June would certainly be snooping all around, prying, trying to read over my shoulder. It had reached the point where I simply couldn't bear her anymore. I was starting to count the days until we would be free of each other.

I managed to get from the post office all the way across Siberia and down to the empty boathouse. As I passed the sidewall, out of habit, I stooped to look at the writing on the wall, the dark shadows of the letters falling away to the dirt.

A woman white to be . . . I lay down on my side next to the letters and saw that lying on the ground would be the perfect angle at which to have written the words in the first place. I stared at the odd scraggly letters as they trailed along the pale strip of white and disappeared into the dirt. There was an anthill not far from the edge of the building, and I watched the ants for a while, coming and going from the hole. That's when I noticed that there was something else there. Something was sticking up from the dirt near the anthill.

I prodded it with my finger and dislodged it.

It was a small gold class ring with a Grove insignia. I picked it up and brushed the dirt off. Inside, there were initials: CEW. I stuck it in my pocket and stood up. There still didn't seem to be anyone around, but I didn't want to open up the envelope outside. I tried the boathouse door, but it was locked, so I slipped in a side window. Inside, it was as quiet as a tomb, and ripping the envelope sounded like a small explosion.

I already knew that both June and Lilly had been put on the waiting list, but I held in my hand an acceptance letter from Yale. I had been going around telling everyone that I wanted to go to Bryn Mawr, but it wasn't true. I'd had it to death with going to an all-girls school. I imagined it being full of the "moles-on-their-eyelids" of the world like Miss Wetherford. Going to a women's college portended a future of cream sherry, sweet-onion sandwiches, and special tutoring sessions with favorite girls.

I told June and Lilly and anyone who asked that my daddy committed suicide, but it wasn't true. Mommy told me to think of him as dead, but I couldn't understand why my daddy would leave without telling me anything about it. Didn't he understand that I needed money for college? Every time I brought it up, Mommy just said, "Study really hard and win the Eugenia Wilcox exam." She kept explaining that it might be hard for them to come up with the money to pay for college because of Grammy's will. After I thought about it for a long time, I decided that must be why they were pretending he was dead. Maybe she thought that if Daddy were dead, I would get a scholarship.

I decided that the best thing to do would be to talk to Miss Wetherford. I didn't want to tell anyone that I wanted to go to Yale if there wasn't going to be a way to pay for it.

I pulled on my white stocking cap and my white fisherman's sweater, and when I looked in the mirror, I thought about the poem on the boathouse—the woman white to be, which reminded me of the ring that I had found. I slipped a leather thong through the ring and tied it around my neck. Maybe it would bring me good luck.

I took a shortcut up the hill, and the snow was almost over my knees. Instead of April, it felt like mid-January.

As I trudged up the hill, Underhill House reminded me of a large ship on the night sea, like the ones I used to see from the sleeping porch of Grammy's house in Portsmouth.

When I got to the top of the hill, Miss Wetherford's path was neatly shoveled.

I almost turned back. Each time I thought of her rabbity eyes, her puckery mouth, how I always wanted to retract my hand when she clasped it, I knew that she was the last person I wanted to get involved in my problems. But I had nowhere else to turn.

I tapped on the door with the big brass lion's head. It made a dull thudding sound that mirrored the sound of my heart.

"Hello!" she said warmly. Her eyes lit up like the little push-pins in a Lite-Brite set at the sight of me. "Dear me, you must come in out of the cold."

"I can only stay a minute. My mother is here. I just need to tell you something."

A pucker of a frown passed across her forehead—as reliable a signal as the Grove dinner bell: she doesn't like my mother.

"Well, step out of the cold, dear. If you want to speak to me, you must at least come into the foyer. I imagine you're here to apologize for missing tea."

"I'm here to tell you that my father isn't dead. It's just a hoax cooked up by Mommy to help me get financial aid. She

thought if he was dead, then it would take them so long to figure out my inheritance that I'd end up with a scholarship. Or something like that. I'm kind of guessing, because she won't tell me. I got admitted to Yale and I want to go, but I need you to help me with financial aid."

Miss Wetherford's face was usually reddish, but not in a healthy way—the upper parts of her cheeks were a waxy yellow, but the lower parts were a mottled, veiny red. Suddenly, her eyebrows shot up and the blood just drained away from her face—it was waxy and pale all over.

"What's that?" she said.

"What do you mean?" I asked.

One hand shot out as she steadied herself against the door molding, and with the other, she reached slowly toward my chest. She grasped the ring that was hanging around my neck, fingering it slowly on the leather thong.

"Where did you get this?"

"I found it."

"You found it?" Her voice was unsteady but wheedling. "I'd love to see it. May I take a closer look?"

I shrugged, and reached up to slip the thong over my head.

The ring twirled and dangled between us, as though she was afraid to look at it more closely. But then, she grabbed it and looked at it, holding it up to the light so that she could see the initials carved on the inside.

"Did someone lose it?" I asked, my voice cracking a little. I knew since I had found it half buried that no one could have lost it recently. Besides, the style was unlike that of the class rings that people had now; this one had a plain gold seal—the Grove class rings looked slightly different.

"Your mother gave it to you," she said. It was an accusation, not a question.

"No," I said. "I found it. I swear. She didn't give it to me. She doesn't have one. Or if she does, I've never seen it. I don't know whose it is. Those aren't her initials—C. E. W. Her name starts with K. I don't know whose those are . . ."

Miss Wetherford looked kind of sick. I'd never noticed it before—her protuberant eyes, her yellowish skin.

"Constance Eufenia Wetherford. C. E. W.," Miss Wetherford said, "Your mother told me she lost it and I believed her. She convinced me that she had lost it. If your mother was lying, then a grave injustice may have occurred."

There was a thin sheen of sweat covering her forehead and her upper lip. This meeting was not going the way I had planned it at all, and I needed to get back to Lane before my mother came and found me here. Stupid ring. Of all the unbelievable luck, I had stumbled across the lost ring of Miss Wetherford.

"But my mother is a terrible liar, Miss Wetherford. She is a liar. That's what I came here to tell you. Weren't you listening to me at all? Nobody will tell me where my father is. I'm supposed to pretend that he's dead."

I left her there, in the foyer, holding the unearthed ring dangling on the end of the leather thong. I don't know what was going through her mind. What was going through my mind was that she was no more help than my mother. I might as well hand both of them spades and let them start digging my daddy six feet under.

The thing that really got to me was that I heard her calling out to me, "Sweetie, my sweetie-cums, my sweetest little peach. I've got a spot of my angina—if you could just bring me my medicine from the medicine chest."

I was not her "sweetie," or her "sweetie-cums," not her "sweetest little peach"—and the sound of each of those roiled in my stomach like a single squish of mayonnaise with sweet onion on white bread.

I didn't go back.

Okay. Call me a murderer. But I didn't go back to her. Face it, would you have?

The apartment seemed stifling to me, so I opened the window a crack, feeling the frigid air coming in.

I looked across the valley, at the bulk of Commons, the student center, and library, the expanse of playing fields, and the gym in the distance. I looked across at Abigail's windows. I could see the blue square of her computer screen, her head a dark blob next to it. But I knew that if I left and went outside, within a few minutes, I'd see her there. Just like in the old days, when she always seemed to pop up in the wrong place at the wrong time. She was born to be a dorm mother, always watching, always noting the smallest details. That's when it hit me. Abigail Von Platte. I don't know how on earth I never thought of it before. The shoes.

The night we came in, the night that Miss Wetherby died. That night, when Nate unlocked the door for us, he said that he had just unlocked the door to let somebody else in. But later, during our interrogation, we were told that we were the only ones who left campus that night. Who was out past curfew and allowed to be let in with a key?

My sweetie-cums. My little peach.

I remembered vividly the moment when I was standing upstairs in the hot hallway vomiting and looking at Abigail's shoes that were crusted with melting snow.

A few minutes later, I knocked on Abigail's door, already weary with a sense of the doomed aspect of my mission. When the door swung open, my heart sank even more, if that was possible. Her mouth was set in a grim line. Her face was a frozen block. She held her hands clasped at her waist. There was a faint unpleasant odor in her apartment, a lingering trace of old fried onions.

She stood immobile, staring at me, and I thought she might slam the door in my face—and during that exact moment, I realized, too late, how richly I deserved that, for hadn't I done the same thing to her many times before? Abigail was the head of the school's disciplinary council. Right now, my son's future at this school rested in her hands.

But she didn't shut the door, and I pushed past her, into her small common room, so that she wouldn't have the opportunity to change her mind.

"Why were you out past curfew the night that Miss Wetherby died?" I asked.

"Well, well," she said. "And I thought the subject might be your son Charlie and his discipline council . . ." She glowered at me.

"You aren't answering my question," I said.

"I haven't the slightest idea what you're talking about."

"Oh, I think you do . . . *Little peach.*"

I saw her start and then regroup, conjuring up a mask of indifference.

"So what if I was? I was hardly the only one. I wasn't even her favorite . . ."

I could see, plain in her face, that Abigail was nursing old grudges, keeping them fresh across the years. "You three were always the favorites. No matter what you did, you could do no wrong."

"I regret that I wasn't always as nice as I could have been . . . if that helps any," I said, "but that doesn't excuse the fact that you killed Miss Wetherby. Did you refuse to give her the medicine, or were you wild with jealousy when Kat showed up?"

She glowered at me, her eyes smoldering like coals that have heated to ash. "I didn't kill her. I couldn't stop her from going out into the snow that night. I told her she was a fool to take a walk in the snow when her heart was bothering her. She wouldn't listen. She just put one of those heart pills under her tongue and pulled on her coat."

"I don't believe that," I said. "You're trying to tell me that she walked all the way up the hill in the snow at night with a bad heart?"

"Miss Wetherby never missed an evening constitutional. Everyone knew that."

"Even on a night when there was a foot of fresh snow on the ground?"

"Something Kat told her that night made her crazy. She started rambling on and on about how she had made a big mistake, a grave mistake—she had been duped, and some terrible harm had been done. She went rummaging around in her library, talking to herself. Finally, she pulled on her coat and walked out the door."

"A 'terrible harm'?"

"That's what she said."

"What did you do?"

Abigail didn't say anything, just turned and went inside her bedroom; I could hear some scraping and shuffling sounds, as if she was looking around at the bottom of a drawer. She came back carrying an amber-colored glass bottle.

She held it up and I squinted at it.

It was an old prescription bottle; the faded label read: *Nitroglycerin*.

"I stayed there alone in the house," Abigail said. "I drank an entire bottle of Bristol Cream sherry, flushed the rest of her heart pills down the toilet, and then I went back to Abbott. Not that it mattered. She never came back from that walk. That's the last I ever saw of her. I purposely waited until after curfew to come in because I wanted to get caught. I was hoping to get in trouble—maybe get kicked out. I just wanted to get away from the Grove. But Nate, when he saw me, just winked and said, 'Late night with Miss Wetherby?' And he gave me one of those foul, sloppy kisses of his. When they called the three of you down to ask about Miss Wetherby's death, they didn't even call me . . . Do you remember that poem Miss Pymstead taught us by Emily Dickinson?"

"Which one?"

"The one that goes: *I'm nobody! Who are you? / Are you nobody, too?*"

I nodded.

"I carved the words *I'm nobody* into the inside of my forearm that day with the broken end of a Bic pen. You can still see the marks if you look in the light." She pulled up her sleeve, and I saw a spidery tracing of scars on the inside of her forearm. It didn't look like words to me, but I felt the hair stand up on the back of my neck all the same.

"She had a gun with her that night," I said.

"Oh, Miss Wetherby never went anywhere without her gun." Abigail shrugged. "Didn't you ever see it?"

I shook my head.

"I thought she showed it to everyone."

"Obviously not," I said. "I wasn't in Miss Wetherby's inner circle. She creeped me out. I only met with her once, when she wanted to advise me not to go to Yale." I laughed. "Not that she needed to worry about *that*."

"You know where I went to college?" she asked.

I didn't. Since leaving the Grove, I had never given Abigail Von Platte a second thought.

"Smith," she said. "On a full four-year scholarship, courtesy of the Eugenia Wilcox Committee."

"You?"

"Lissa won, but she didn't want it. She didn't need the money, and the second she got off the waiting list, she chose Yale. You were disqualified—they told me you had the highest score. Lissa was second and I was third. I see you snooping around, but I know everything. You should just ask."

"You're the Ghost of Abbott North, aren't you? You're our mad blogger. I should have known it all along from the limericks."

Her eyes narrowed. "I'm flattered, but no. You'll need to look among your own girls for the cyberpoet. Though it's true that I've got a pretty good idea as to what goes on over there. Nobody ever pulls down their blinds . . ."

"Very titillating, I presume . . ."

"Your son's discipline council is riding on my good humor. You'd best be watching what you say to me."

I nodded and bid her good night, hoping against hope that she wouldn't hold her dislike of me against Charlie.

"Jane!" she called after me.

I spun around. "What?"

"Don't worry. Your son's a good kid."

I looked at the woman standing in her doorway, and I realized that she and I were in the same leaky vessel. We were neighbors, colleagues, long-ago classmates—and by rights, we should have been friends, only I had never realized it before.

"Thank you," I said, trying out a smile.

39

Winter in Vermont had set in with a vengeance. The temperature was plunging and there was a blanket of snow on the ground, but upstairs in my flat, the radiators were furiously clanking and I pushed my window open, hoping for a breath of cooler air. Charlie was still suspended and staying in the infirmary, awaiting his disciplinary hearing, and I was restless with an odd feeling that something wasn't right. I looked in Charlie's bedroom, which seemed oddly empty without him, then spied his laptop and decided to borrow it to check in on *The Ghost of Abbott North*. The computer flickered on, and the black screen floated in front of me. I stared and blinked as the words rose up, not believing what I was seeing:

December 12

A solemn thing it was, I said,
A woman white to be,
And wear, if God should count me fit,
Her hallowed mystery.

A timid thing to drop a life
Into the purple well,
Too plummetless that it come back
Eternity until.

At the end of the lines of poetry there was a blank space. Then, it said: *I have a date with a purple well. This means good-bye.*

One of my girls was in trouble.

I knew beyond certainty that behind one of those closed doors, someone was missing. I only hoped it wasn't too late.

As I pulled my own door open, I saw another pile of papers lying at my feet. I hastily scooped up the pile and put it on the table—and then sounded the alarm for a door check. Soon, I had a houseful of pairs of sleepy girls standing at their doorways. One girl was missing.

A series of quick phone calls got the Grove emergency system activated, but I had a sick feeling that there was not a moment to spare. I took off at a run across Siberia, headed for the boathouse. As I ran, I knew that I might be wrong, or even too late, but I also knew that in case I was right, it absolutely had to be me who went there—I was the one who was going to have to make amends.

The temperature had been dropping steadily all afternoon; now, in the middle of the night, the air was brittle with cold. All was quiet at the boathouse. Under the light of the half-moon, the snow on the ground cast up a ghostly light, and the banks of the river were crusted with ice. I had left Abbott North so quickly, I hadn't pulled on gloves. So, I jammed one hand deep into my parka pocket, with the other feeling frozen to my flashlight.

"Hello? Is anybody here?"

The river ice creaked once nearby, a harsh sound. I approached the boathouse warily. I saw no lights. It was locked up tight. I passed around to the side where the door was. Still no movement.

I jiggled the door handle; the door was locked. I then peered through the window but saw nothing amiss.

The ice creaked again. I heard a sharp staccato, like gunfire. I spun around and froze, arcing my flashlight beam around, but I didn't see anything unusual.

"Hello?"

"You're too late." Her voice was shaky but defiant. "I've already made up my mind."

I stood still. Her voice was coming from somewhere near the river.

"Kaitlyn? Where are you?"

"Turn off your light."

I hesitated, afraid to make one false move.

"I said, turn out the light." Her voice was shrill, hysterical.

I pushed the button, and the light faded away, leaving me plunged in darkness.

"She died." Kaitlyn said, her voice now eerily calm.

"Who?" I asked.

"The girl who wrote the book," she said. "I asked after her." Now, I could hear that she was crying. "I was stupid enough to think I could get in touch with her. I got this crazy idea that she would understand me. I made up some lie about why I needed to get in touch with her. I asked about her in alumni records. But she was dead—a long time ago. I'm sure she killed herself. She always wrote that she was going to."

Her silhouette was beginning to emerge from the darkness. She had climbed into a tree at the river's edge and was on a branch that hung over the water. The night was so cold that the river was frozen about a third of the way out, but the water still ran through the middle. If she jumped in, she would last five minutes in this weather. My knees were shaking and my teeth were chattering even though I had my big parka on. The sound I'd heard must have been a frozen branch breaking off as she climbed the tree. There was no rope here, no rungs, no big strong branches—the jump tree had been taken down years ago. Her perch, from what I could see in the dark, appeared flimsy.

As she was talking, I was creeping forward. But now I could see that she was doing the same, inching farther out on the frozen branch. The limbs looked brittle, and as she pushed off one with her foot, it snapped off—and the entire branch swayed and looked as if it might crack. I could see her eyes, the whites almost luminescent as they widened with fear—but she made no move to back down.

"Kaitlyn?" I said. "Why don't you just come down? We can talk about it down here?"

"There's nothing to talk about."

"There's always something to talk about . . ."

"You, you're worse than any of them," she said. "You should feel lucky I don't want to kill *you*." She inched a little farther along the branch so that now she was out over the ice.

I stepped onto the ice. I could feel it creaking under my feet. "No, Kaitlyn, come down."

There was a branch above her, and she stood so that she could grasp it to pull herself farther out on the limb.

I could see the limb bending, and it was making a sick, splitting sound. "Stop."

She grabbed the branch above her, but then her feet slipped on the ice. In a moment, she was hanging, seven or eight feet above the icy river.

Without thinking, I rushed onto the ice so that I would be beneath her. I got there just as she fell; we plunged through the ice together.

The water was excruciatingly cold. My arm was wrapped around her waist. Right next to us, an ice shelf crumbled. I jammed my shoulder into it, trying to prevent us from being swept downriver.

The ice was thin, and it gave way. The water was up to my shoulders, and for a second I lost hold of her. I grabbed first only water, next hair, and then I wrapped my arm around her waist again. Under my toes, I could feel river bottom, though my feet were almost completely numb. I dragged her across the bank and up to the boathouse, breaking the window to get inside. There, I found stacks of folded blankets, several of which I used to wrap us up.

After a few moments, I tried the boathouse phone, but it wasn't working, so we huddled under the blankets, waiting for someone to find us. Kaitlyn seemed sleepy—kind of dazed. I talked to her to keep her awake.

"How did you find the book?" I asked.

We were both shivering. Kaitlyn's teeth were chattering so hard she could barely talk.

"I'm not the Abbott thief," she said.

"I believe you," I said.

"You don't."

"I didn't," I said. "But I do now."

We fell silent. Kaitlyn shivered and I held the blanket tighter around her.

"Just tell me where you got the book," I asked again.

"Leave me alone, Ms. Milton. *Please*. I'm not going to tell you anything. I wish you didn't find me."

"Okay, okay," I said, retucking the blanket around her. "Don't worry about it. We don't have to talk about this now. I'm just glad you're okay."

Right then, that's when it hit me. I almost didn't get there on time. A split second or two, and things would have been very different.

"Kaitlyn, listen to me . . . Please, just listen . . ." My voice sounded shaky, and my teeth were chattering too. "If you're not here, you don't get to tell your own story."

It was almost dawn when I finally reentered my flat, shivering and too jangled to sleep. I picked up the pages that had been left outside my door.

Sore Loser

Let me just start by saying that I didn't win the Eugenia Wilcox Prize. But the thing that really teed me off more than anything was that June lied.

"I'm going to skip the test. That way you'll be sure to win." She was so stuck-up about being smart, so sure that she was going to win! And even so, I cried and thanked her for being so nice. I wanted to go to Yale, but I didn't know if I'd have enough money. My next best hope was to win the prize—so I thanked her even though what I really felt like doing was stabbing her in the heart. Then, instead of sticking to her word, she snuck into the lecture hall in Loomis a few minutes late. I didn't see her but Lilly told me. After that, I could barely stand the sight of her. She was such a liar. When she got caught for cheating, I thought it served her right. Miss Pimsley pulled me aside the night before the results were announced and told me. She said that June was disqualified and Lilly came in first. I was so relieved I gave her an enormous hug, but she disentangled herself from my embrace and pushed me back.

She was staring at me and I knew whatever she said was not going to be good.

"I can't tell you any more," she said. "I shouldn't have said this much, but I just wanted you to know that if Lilly turns it down, the money will go to the next highest scorer—and that isn't you."

I can't really explain how I felt right then. My whole body started shaking and I could see that Miss Pimsley was talking to me, but I couldn't even hear the words.

Then, all of a sudden, I could hear my mother's voice saying: "She took something that was rightfully mine." All this time, I thought Miss Pimsley stole someone's affections; I assumed that my mother and Miss Pimsley had quarreled over love—how banal, how ordinary, how female that would have been. But now I could see the truth—it wasn't love they were fighting over; it was their futures. Miss Pimsley had stolen the prize.

And an entire lifetime of possibilities had been taken from my mother, like a big heavy door thudding shut.

"My mother won the Eugenia Wilcox Prize—not you."

"That is true," Miss Pimsley said. "I had hoped so much that you would win this year. I thought it would help to make things right."

"Because you felt guilty!"

"I suppose so, yes. Your mother and I were friends. But she was the brilliant one."

"But you stole her prize."

"I didn't steal it. It passed to me when she relinquished it."

"But why?" I said. "Why would she give it up if she wanted it so badly? It makes no sense."

Miss Pimsley looked sorrowfully at me, as if she was trying to decide what to say next.

"Tell me why and I'll leave you alone. It had something to do with Chestmont Wooten—didn't it?"

Miss Pimsley's brow puckered. I could see that I'd hit a nerve.

"Tell me, child. What do you know?"

"I know everything!" I screamed. "Absolutely everything. You have no secrets from us."

I pulled Miss Wetherford's gold ring out of my pocket and showed it to her.

"Wetherford was in love with you, and she wanted the prize to go to you. But Chestmont Wooten found out and tried to stop it, so you had Miss Wetherford kill him. To pay for her silence, you two became lovers."

Miss Pimsley didn't answer. She picked up her kettle from the kitchen counter and put it on to boil.

"I'm going to make tea," she said. "And you're going to calm down. These are wild accusations you are spouting. You are not making the slightest bit of sense."

I wasn't going to calm down. I had seen several storms flit across Miss Pimsley's face. Maybe I didn't quite have it right, but I could see that I was close to the mark.

When the Earl Grey was ready, she poured out two mugs and set them across from each other on her compact kitchen table.

"I understand that you were counting on this award, but there are other ways for you to pay for college. I will help you figure it out."

I couldn't believe that she was simply changing the subject after I had divulged to her that I knew she had participated in a conspiracy of theft and murder.

"For the record, I did not steal your mother's prize. She relinquished it. You seem not to know the precise reasons for her decision. But I suggest that you ask her, not me. Perhaps I will regret saying this, but I do want to say one thing. I know that she loves you very much—and I know with all my heart that it was worth everything she gave up to get you. She's so proud of you."

"That makes no sense," I said. "She didn't give anything up to get me. She didn't have to get married!"

"Nowadays, I believe you could matriculate in a family way, but in those days . . ."

I stood up. "What are you insinuating?"

"Those were different times. What your mother did was a reasonable solution to a thorny problem."

I stepped away from her. "What are you trying to say?"

I tried to read her expression, but it was a puzzle to me—she looked confused, embarrassed. "I'm sorry," she said. "I think I've said too much."

"My mother and father got married in June, right after high school graduation. I was born in December. I was premature—I was so tiny. Tiny enough to fit in the palm of her hand . . ."

But it was too late—I could see the look on her face. I had never questioned my mother, never counted up the months, never thought about it at all. I hated her for marrying young and for choosing a man she obviously didn't love. I hated my father for running off.

At that moment, I realized that I had been wrong all along. The person I should have hated was myself. Me. I was the one who had caused all the problems. But it was too late *for me to save Miss Pimsley. I had already lied about her and betrayed her. I had already turned her in.*

"I hate you, Miss Pimsley!" I shouted at her.

I shoved the chair and it clattered to the ground, then I ran out the door into the pouring rain.

40

"I'm terribly sorry to bother you," I said. I had been thinking about phoning Keach all day. Now, I was hoping that I wasn't calling too late.

"You're not bothering me," said the voice on the other end of the line.

"There's just something I've been thinking about, and . . . I just wonder if you might be able to clear it up for me."

"Jane, please. Feel free to ask me anything you want."

"Do you remember when I told you that Kat, Lissa, and I were obsessed with the murder of Chestmont Wooten, during our senior year?"

"Yes."

"Well, I didn't tell you how it was that we got interested in it."

"No . . . no, you didn't. I just supposed that people still talked about it."

"Well, one day, we were down at the boathouse, at night, and somehow, one of us noticed something odd."

"Did you?"

"Yes, we noticed that there was actually just a tiny fragment of poetry . . ."

There was a gasp on the other end of the line—enough of a gasp for me to know that I had hit it head on . . .

"Seventeen years later, it was still there?"

"Believe it or not, you can still read it faintly, if you know where to look . . ."

"I was a virgin when he dragged me there, and I was so drunk, I didn't know how to say no. I do remember that it hurt like the devil and that I was bleeding. His fountain pen fell out of his pocket—good old India ink. I opened it up and squeezed the ink onto my fingertip . . . something to mark the spot. Something unsullied and pure to leave behind . . ."

I heard a rueful laugh. "I was so young that I thought language had that kind of power."

"This might sound like an odd question, but did you ever have Constance Wetherby's ring?"

"Well, now, how on earth did you guess that? But to answer your question, yes—yes, that was Miss Wetherby. Every year, she picked the best senior girl in English, and that girl got to keep the ring all year. She said it was for outstanding devotion to study . . ."

"You've gotta be kidding?"

"I kid you not. I lost it that night. She was furious at me—she kept accusing me of having given it to another girl. I'm telling you, she was a little batty. I got so mad at her that I blurted out the real reason why . . ."

"You told her that Chestmont Wooten raped you?"

"I believe my exact words were 'he took advantage of me' . . ."

"Mmm-hmm."

"Well, the poor old lady, she turned almost purple with rage. I've never seen anything like it. Her hands were quivering. Her voice was shaking . . . For a minute I thought she was going to hit me, until I realized she wasn't angry with *me*. 'The bastard,' she said. I was shocked, of course, to hear her utter a word that wasn't used in polite company. She had this crazy look on her face . . . almost as if the wrong had been done directly to her."

"Was she . . . in love with you?"

"You know, she never laid a finger on me. She just had all this emotion fluttering around inside her. What was it she used to say . . . *A something in a summer's noon / An azure depth, a wordless tune / Transcending ecstasy* . . . All that Emily Dickinson verse inside her and nothing to do with it . . ."

"Well, thanks, Keach."

"It's no problem Jane, except . . . Except, if you want my advice, you'd be better off letting it go."

Letting it go. I stared out my bedroom window, looking out over the snowy fields, the river, the dark outlines of buildings. Wasn't I already an expert at letting go? What else did I have to give up? Wasn't that what everyone did all along, every year, every moment? My marriage had ended, my money was gone, my child was growing up. I held tenaciously to the past, to my memories, to my versions of my stories. After all, what else did I have?

But at least I had more than my old friend Kat. Tired of feeling sorry for myself, I switched off the light and went to bed.

41

There were four lines scribbled on the folded piece of paper that had been shoved under my door:

> *She walks in beauty, like the night*
> *Of cloudless climes and starry skies,*
> *And all that's best of dark and bright*
> *Meet in her aspect and her eyes . . .*

A line underneath the poetry said: *Meet me at the boathouse, at midnight.—Josh.*

I ran to the window and looked out at the boathouse—it had turned a dark crimson in the setting sun. I spent the rest of the evening debating with myself about going, but at five minutes to midnight, I slipped into the hall. Outside, there was no moon and the sky hung low. The stars were bright points. There were a few bare gray scrims of cloud. All the way down the path, as I picked my way through the drifting snow, I was furious—furious at him for playing this game with me, but doubly furious at myself for going along with it.

I tried the door to the boathouse and found it unlocked. There was no light and no motion within.

"Hello?"

All was silent. The only thing I could see was the illuminated orange numbers on a digital clock: 12:04. There was a faint smell of oar grease and varnish.

Then, up high in the rafters, there was a rapid fluttering, rushing sound. Startled, I shone my flashlight upward but caught only motion and the rafter beams.

I heard the sucking inward gasp of my breath. Felt my hair stand up on my forearms.

There was something moving up there. Something swinging. I strangled a scream. My flashlight couldn't seem to penetrate the darkness. It cut a swath across something that looked like a body. It was—

But it wasn't. It was an old rain poncho with a Grove logo, flung over one of the wooden beams. Now, I could see it. My pulse banged against my throat.

"Jane."

I swung around, almost screamed again—then I was melting against him, a meeting too long delayed.

"You scared me to death."

"I'm sorry," he said, grasping my chin and then closing his lips over mine. I heard a faint thud when my flashlight dropped from my hand.

"Why did you bring me here?"

"Unfinished business."

"Couldn't we have unfinished business someplace warmer?" I was so close that his breath made a hot circle on my face.

He had a blanket with him, and he pulled it around my shoulders. "There's another word that is kind of like *pentimento*," he said. "Do you know what it is?"

I shook my head.

"It's *palimpsest*. Back in the Middle Ages, it was so hard to make parchment that they used to recycle it. They used to boil down the parchment to get rid of the old writing to reuse the paper for illuminated manuscripts. There are some ancient texts that are only preserved as ghost writing—you can see it if you use special lights to look underneath what was written over it. That's palimpsest."

I nodded.

"Life is like that, but here, I think you just notice it more. It's as if each year is a new sheet of parchment. At the end of the year, you erase it and start over. The old stuff is still there—you just can't see it very well."

"I can see it," I said. "In living color."

"That's because you just got here," he said. "Over time, it fades."

"Has it faded for you?"

"It had. Until . . ."

"Until?"

"Until you got here."

I shivered. It was freezing, even colder here inside the cavernous boathouse than outside.

Josh put his arm around me and led me over to a workbench. He sat me down and wrapped the blanket around both of us, leaning in to give me more warmth.

"There's something you don't know," he said.

I turned in the darkness and looked at him. "There's a lot I don't know," I said.

"Yeah, but this is something that matters."

I leaned back against Josh's chest so that I could hear his voice rumbling through my body.

"Senior year, during the worst storm of the winter, my parents decided to come up to see me and take me out to dinner. My parents were nuts. My dad was from upstate New York, and he never let a little snow faze him. At dinner, we ran into some Grove girls—my ex-girlfriend, and the one that I secretly had a mad crush on but could never get to pay me the slightest bit of attention."

I turned to look at him, but in the darkness, I couldn't see his face.

"On the way back, my father, who was a Hardley boy, wanted to drive through the Grove campus and show my mom how beautiful it looked at night in the snow. He was quoting poetry: *She walks in beauty, like the night* . . . My dad loved poetry. I think I got my love of poetry from him. My mom wasn't that into the idea, but he insisted. When we drove in, the Grove roads were unplowed. Then, not far inside the gates, before the campus proper begins, there was something blocking the roadway. We stopped and got out of the car and realized that it was a woman who had fallen. She was unconscious but breathing, and my father noticed that she was wearing a medical alert bracelet for a heart condition."

I gasped. "Miss Wetherby!"

"Since we couldn't get past her, we decided to go back out toward Bernigan's Tavern to call for help. But the road was narrow there, and icy, so when my dad tried to turn around, he went off the road and got stuck in the snow."

I nodded.

"So, he asked me to get out and give a push, only I wasn't strong enough. My dad was a big guy, and real strong. Then, he asked me to take the wheel."

"Okay."

"So, my dad gives a real big push, and I floor it . . ."

Josh stopped talking.

Finally, I broke the silence. "Yeah?"

"I ran her over."

"You what?"

"There was this big mother-fucker of a thump, and my dad hollered, *Shit-pardon-my-French!*—and I slammed on the brakes. Then I skidded and jumped out of the car, and there's my dad standing there, hat in his hands, and he's saying, *Son, she's gone, and it's not your fault.*"

I turned around and stared at him even though I couldn't really see him in the half-light. "You've gotta be kidding me?"

"I wish I were kidding you, Jane. But I'm not. We're standing out there on this icy-cold road with a corpse. She didn't look any different. I didn't really run *over* her—she skidded away from the car on the ice, I guess. But she had a black smudge on her forehead— probably a tire mark. My mom and dad were arguing about whether it was worth endangering my bright and shiny future by reporting that I killed someone, who was probably already a goner, while trying to be a Good Samaritan. My mom—she'd had one too many pink ladies anyway—was throwing a fit, saying that I looked like a hippie and we were out-of-towners and it was just better not to get involved with these small-town police. But my dad, it didn't sit right with him. He couldn't bring himself to just get in the car and drive away. So, finally, he says, *I'm sorry, we've got to do the right thing*—and my mom, reluctantly, she gives in."

"And?"

"Well, up to then, I've been dealing with the situation, but as soon as my dad says 'police,' I start freaking out and you can probably guess why."

"Other than the fact that you just ran over Miss Wetherby?"

"No, actually not. I'm freaking out for the same reason any self-respecting Hardley boy would be freaking out. Ornithology."

"Ornithology?"

"The snowy owl?"

It was starting to dawn on me. "Oh, I get it, your parents were in town and . . ."

"'Fraid so. I'd just paid my bill with Brandon Barnes, I've got an ounce of Morocco black in my pocket, and all I can think about is *Midnight Express*, which had just played at the Hardley School cinema for the forty-ninth time. I'm sweating and shaking—you remember how long my hair was in those days, and I'm wearing my rattiest jeans and that blue kaffiyeh wrapped around my neck and that T-shirt that said *Keep on Tokin'* . . . Which I had pulled a blazer over, to go out with my folks."

"Yeah . . . I remember . . . ," I said. "Nice formal dress for a dinner out with your parents."

"So, I jammed my hand in my pocket with the baggie in it. I don't want to get rid of it because it's some good stuff and I just paid for it, and I'm going, *Oh shit, I better think up something good to say.* So, I offer to hike down the hill myself, since I'm the only one wearing boots. And my parents say okay. I tell them to get back in the car, and turn on the heater and wait. I walk halfway down the hill, hide behind a tree, wait awhile, and come back up and tell them the police are on their way. While they're inside the car, I kick a bunch of snow over the body to make it look like it had been there for a while."

"And then . . . ?"

"Well, we sat there in the car, with the heater on for about forty-five minutes or so, until my dad started worrying that we were getting low on gas, and it was such a snowy night. Finally, he just says, *We just can't wait any longer—we'll have to go.* And that was it. We drove away. And I guess my parents started rationalizing it all away in their minds. They never mentioned it again. It wasn't until later that I thought of the fact that you guys would be driving down that same road, and that you'd probably run into her too."

"Don't you think your father knew you never called anyone? I mean, really?"

"I don't know. I thought about asking him a lot of times, but he was a reserved man, and I could never think of a way to bring it up. What do you say . . . ? Hey, Dad, remember that night we did that hit-and-run . . . ? Maybe that was his way of appeasing my mom and letting his own conscience off the hook. I didn't want to hurt him, you know, in case he didn't know."

"Don't you want to ask him?"

"Not gonna happen. He died of colon cancer four years ago."

"Oh God, I didn't realize . . . I'm sorry."

"Not your fault, Jane. You had no way of knowing. I lost my mom a long time ago too. Drunk driving."

"She was hit by a drunk driver?"

"No, she . . ."

"Oh . . ." That sat in the air for a while. I snuggled down closer to him, pulling the blanket around both of us.

"So, you knew about what happened with us?"

"I knew."

"Since back then."

"Yes."

"I guess it helps a little to know what happened to her, but I still don't understand why you had to bring me to the boathouse at midnight to tell me this."

"Because I never knew that one thing led to another, which led to you not getting to graduate . . . It's why I took Lissa back to Hardley that night."

"Miss Wetherby's death?"

"Banger had slipped her a couple of downers, and she was so drunk she could barely stand up. She wasn't making a lot of sense, but the part that did make sense was that she was saying that you guys had killed Miss Wetherby. Yelling it, out loud, to the night sky."

"Oh Jesus. And I thought we were so good at keeping it quiet."

"I knew you didn't kill her, but if she started confessing all over the place, the only way I was going to be able to get you out of trouble was to confess myself."

"Which wasn't exactly what you had in mind . . ."

"The only thing I could think of to do was to drag her off to my room in Hardley. I knew my buddies wouldn't rat me out, and I could let her sleep it off."

For one wild moment, that long-ago night came crashing back to me, and I was trapped inside an overheated car that was careening on ice and filled with gin fumes. All of a sudden, I whirled around and was pounding him on the chest as hard as I could, pounding him, pounding him.

"I hate you," I said. "I hate you, I hate you. I hate you."

Then, he had his arms around me so tight that he was almost crushing me, and he was whispering in my hair, "I love you. I love you, I love you, I love you"—and stroking the back of my neck.

"Every step I've taken, since one stupid night when I put my foot on the gas pedal too hard by accident, has driven a wedge between us, but that doesn't change the fact that when I close my eyes and imagine perfection, I still see your face."

42

I was grading papers in the library when Jessica hurried toward me; her face, flushed with worry, signaled that something was wrong.

"Jane! Have you seen Josh anywhere? I need to find him right away. Molly's really sick. I'm on my way to the hospital. Please tell him to call me on my cell phone if you see him."

"Oh dear, of course. I hope she's okay," I said.

I didn't see Josh until two days later, when he rushed past me, looking haggard, as though he hadn't slept since I'd last seen him.

"Is everything okay?"

"Oh, Jane. I'm sorry."

"Josh, what is it? What's going on?"

"It's Molly. She got hold of a cupcake at school that must have had a trace of peanuts in it. She had a severe reaction . . . She couldn't breathe . . ."

I put my hand on his arm.

"Oh my God, Josh. Is she okay now?"

"She's going to be okay, but they had to put in a breathing tube. A few more minutes and she wouldn't have made it . . ."

He was crying.

I put my arms around him, but I felt him stiffen, and he muttered, "Not right now, okay?"

"I understand," I said. "Give my love to Molly and Jessica."

We were well into the heart of the marking period. No more time for fun and games, the class had to read two Shakespeare plays and *The Adventures of Huckleberry Finn*. The mood on campus turned, the weather settled in, and I was inundated by requests for letters of recommendation for college. Kaitlyn had been sent home on medical leave. I ducked out of Josh's sight whenever I saw him.

The sky darkened and seemed to press upon us; the colors, now all browns and purples, seemed to wrap themselves around us like a thick winter cloak. Charlie was barely speaking to me.

"You put too much pressure on her," he said, almost crying, the day after Kaitlyn left school. "It's too much. Who can do that? Get straight A's, perfect SATs, excel at sports, and then on top of everything, write a novel. It's crazy. You, her coach, Dr. Farber-Johnson—you all pushed her over the edge."

I couldn't think of what to say to him. I could see he was right. I had misjudged Kaitlyn greatly. I had missed every clue.

"I tried to help her," he said. "But it just backfired."

"No, Charlie! Don't blame yourself!"

He just stared at me with hurt in his eyes and didn't answer.

My relief at having rescued Kaitlyn was tinged by the fear that I had entirely misread her, guilt that I had played a part in her desperation, and the nagging doubt that continued unabated—where had she found the pages?

Some days, I convinced myself that I was crazy. No matter how much I felt exposed by the manuscript, wasn't it perhaps just my own hubris that made me think that Kaitlyn's story was about me and my friends? Wasn't it, in fact, probable that her story had nothing to do with mine, that I was only imagining it? I had broken my own code of ethics, and the school rules, and secretly searched the poor girl's room—and I had come up empty-handed. I had seen her countless times inside one of the soundproof study carrels in the library, typing away at lightning speed. I had imagined her plagiarizing her essays only to find that she was *The Ghost of Abbott North*. The sole essay she had plagiarized, the one about "The Dead," was also the only paper of hers I hadn't liked. And worst of all, I had misjudged the girl. I had been convinced that she was shallow and vain, when, in fact, she was struggling mightily beneath her cool exterior. I had no choice but to come to the conclusion that I knew far less than I thought I did, and this thought scared me silly. Me, of all people? Shouldn't I have realized that it's hard to know what teenage girls are capable of? I watched the other girls with concern, trying not to stereotype them in my mind. Charlie continued to push me away.

Still, I couldn't stop thinking about the manuscript. I ticked through the people who spanned both generations—Abigail Von Platte and Nate Hodges, how would either of them have gotten hold of the manuscript that I last saw in Kat's arms on the Upper West Side of New York? Finally, I had an idea. Maybe Kat had published the book somehow. Maybe a copy of it was sitting in the library.

I hurried to Pencott and sat at one of the computers. I saw Charlie behind the circulation desk with Rebecca MacAteer. He was working.

I went into Pencott's online catalog and typed the name *Katherine Winslow Cunningham*. No dice.

I looked up at Rebecca, and Charlie was no longer standing there, so I walked over.

"Do you have any books in the collection that are not in the catalog?" I asked.

"Not in the catalog?" Rebecca looked puzzled.

"I mean, for example, if there were a book published by a Grove alumna, maybe in a private edition?"

"Is there any particular book you have in mind?"

"No, uh, it's just a general question," I stammered.

"To my knowledge, all books are cataloged. Of course there are the archival papers that Charlie is working on. Not all of those have been indexed yet. But there are no books to my knowledge—just papers, ephemera, old letters, and such."

That's when it hit me, plain as the nose on my face. The answer had been right in front of me all along.

I pushed Charlie's door open and stepped over the clothes strewn across his floor. There was nothing in his drawers, inside his desk, or on the shelf of his closet, but when I lifted up a corner of his mattress, there it was: a weathered padded mailer. On the outside, a typewritten note was affixed with a large binder clip. The mailer was addressed to Pencott Library, with a return address from West Eighty-Sixth Street in New York.

The note read:

Dear Librarian,

I found the contents of this envelope on a park bench in Riverside Park, in Manhattan. These appear to be

important to someone, but the only address I could find
was the library address on the inside flyleaf of the Lantern
yearbook, 1961. I am hopeful that if I send these items to
you, you can return them to their rightful owner.

Underneath, there was a penciled note: *Contents of envelope: Lantern*
yearbook, reshelved: Manuscript: untitled, unknown author, to be archived.
The note was on top of a pile of typed pages—erasable bond, yellowed with age. I recognized the typeface immediately from the missing tails on the *y*'s and skipped crosses on every fourth or fifth *t*.

43

Abigail Von Platte presided over Charlie's disciplinary hearing and reported to Dr. Farber-Johnson that Charlie, as a first-time offender, should be given a warning. Now, when I passed Abigail on the pathways or in Commons, she smiled at me, and we regularly swapped notes on the students, exchanging the million routine concerns of dorm supervision.

When Kaitlyn returned from medical leave, I suspected that she had been put on an antidepressant, as I saw her heading down the hill to the infirmary every morning; because medical records were confidential, I didn't know for sure. In any case, I felt slightly wary around her—more likely to try to look past her surfaces, less content just to take her coolness at face value. I invited her up for popcorn from time to time, and asked her, discreetly, to fill me in on Abbott gossip.

I had sat in on a meeting with her parents, feeling so sorry for her worried mother, who kept blotting her eyes with a tissue throughout the meeting and who hugged me and thanked me for helping Kaitlyn on that awful night. We all agreed that her quest to gain admission to Yale should be abandoned, and the insane idea to publish a book before graduation should likewise be dropped. Kaitlyn was going to work with the college counselor to draw up a new list of colleges. Because of the circumstances, her attempts to plagiarize would be forgiven. Later, Dr. Farber-Johnson pulled me aside and said that the Corsyns were so grateful for our interventions on Kaitlyn's behalf that they had made a major pledge to the school, and that work on the Corsyn Boathouse would begin over the summer.

Mornings spent teaching, afternoons in the library, evenings spent correcting papers—my days had settled into a comforting routine. The dorm too seemed to have settled, and the students were mostly on an even keel. During a routine room inspection, I found the cache of small stolen items in the room of a homesick freshman from California. Upon being caught, she seemed relieved that getting expelled meant she'd be sent home.

I thought back on my hasty rush to judgment about Mary Raschlaub. I had learned so much since then. After further reflection, Soon Ji had remembered that she had left her notebook in the laundry room; it had most likely been swept up accidentally, into a pile of Mary's clean clothes. There was a bit of embarrassment, as the school had to issue a formal apology and expunge the three-day suspension from Mary's record, and I'd had to endure a lengthy lecture from Dr. Farber-Johnson on the importance of certainty in these matters. For her part, Mary Raschlaub had been a good sport about it. I was learning the ins and outs of being a dorm mother, and I felt a growing sense of pride in my abilities. I doubted I'd make that rookie mistake again.

I had been keeping my distance from Josh since our conversation about Molly. I had seen Jessica and him sitting together with Molly in

Commons at dinner. Molly looked pale, and she had a small Band-Aid at the base of her throat.

Finally, after about a week, Jessica threaded her way through the throng of students to join me. She threw her arms around me, and I could feel the ribs through her shirt—she had dropped at least ten pounds and there were bags under her eyes.

"How *are* you?" I said. "And more importantly, how's Molly?"

"She's much better," Jessica said. "But it's so hard. I feel like I just can't relax. These peanut exposures, each one is more serious than the last. If she has another exposure, she might not make it."

"I can't imagine what that must be like," I said.

She shook her head, and I could see that she was blinking back tears.

"Josh has agreed to go to counseling," she said. "Molly needs us both to be there for her right now. I think this forced us both to reexamine our priorities . . ."

"I'm happy for you," I said.

She hesitated, scrutinizing my face. "Are you?"

I squeezed her arm. "I am, Jessica. You can rest assured. I really am."

The manuscript had sat untouched inside the envelope in my room. I told Charlie that I found it in his room and he quickly confessed. He had discovered it by chance in the library while working on the archives and thought that maybe Kaitlyn could pass it off as her own—he was trying to help her. She spent hours holed up in the library, retyping it piece by piece, taking care to alter the names of the main characters. When she finally finished, he snuck into the library to return it to the archives. That was what he was doing when he got caught.

As for me, I had started to dare to imagine that I was going to stay on. I'd had an encouraging conversation with my lawyer a few days earlier. The IRS had agreed to a settlement that would reduce the garnishment on my paycheck, giving me a little breathing room. The weather grew colder; we were immersed in the work of second semester; and then, suddenly, the campus crews were busy buffing and polishing everything in sight. It was time for Lantern Day.

I was embarrassed to admit it to myself, but I had changed clothes three times that morning. I had settled on wool slacks and a navy sweater, a blazer, and pearls. I slid on my black flats. I pinned on my name badge, the act of doing so rendering me an outsider again. Today, I was no longer Jane Milton, English teacher. I was Jane Milton, alumna.

Those bearing lantern-shaped-banner bearers lined up on the pathway outside Whittaker Chapel. There were a few brave souls from the 1930s, and then, with each decade through the 1950s, the crowds got bigger. It took me a moment to find the banner for our class because the banner bearer wasn't holding it up; she was leaning on it, still furled up, while she bent over to fix her daughter's shoe. But after a moment, she held it aloft, and I noticed that it was a little wrinkled from where it had lain on the ground.

Soon, a sprinkling of women joined the group. At first, I thought I wouldn't see anyone I knew, but then, in a burst of shouts and hugs, I saw a short woman with a pixie haircut, smiling and saying to me, "Emma . . . Emma Doerr . . ." And pretty soon, we were a group. Katie Cornwell was there with her twelve-year-old daughter. And, of course, Lissa came with her two towheaded children, and Maria, her nanny. Some of the girls looked like housewives from suburbia and some looked like city girls; some looked corporate and some looked liked artists. Maryam and Parvaneh were there, both gorgeous as ever in fur coats, adding a little class to the occasion. I looked around at the group and tried to decide if we looked like old Grove now . . . But I didn't get a chance to decide if we did or not, because the procession started moving, and I could hear the chords of the organ inside.

A hush fell over the crowd as Dr. Farber-Johnson stood to announce the student who would give this year's Lantern Day Oration.

"A truly outstanding student," Dr. Farber-Johnson said. "She excels in all of her subjects, but she has shown a special ability in English and creative writing. I'm proud to announce one of our most accomplished students, Soon Ji Shin."

Soon Ji rose slowly and tucked a strand of hair behind one ear as she walked to the front of the chapel and up the three steps. She spread a paper out on the podium in front of her.

"Today I have chosen to discuss a poem by John Keats."

I turned around and smiled at Josh—he would be pleased that she had chosen one of the romantics. Soon Ji's words floated in the air of Whittaker Chapel, joining so many other words that had passed before—the words themselves not as important as the fact that they were being said.

At the close of the ceremony, the organ struck up the chords of the Grove school song, and white hankies were pulled from purses.

"And she will come and she will go, / but never will she leave no more."

I waved my hankie, I mumbled the verses I didn't remember by heart, and I surreptitiously blotted my tears. It turned out Kat had been wrong. The traditions had been strong enough to go on. *"Though she may quit these gates some day, / In deep Grove's heart she'll always stay."* All around me women warbled, tapping into their younger selves.

I glanced over my shoulder to try to catch Josh's eye again, but this time he wouldn't look at me, and I could see that he was also a little teary. Finally, he glanced at me, and I could see a reflection of my own feelings in his eyes, and then he looked away.

When we left Whittaker Chapel, snow was falling in big, fat flakes, dressing up the campus in a dusting of lace. Josh caught up with me as I rounded the back of the building. He was wearing a black overcoat and had a blue-green woolen scarf around his neck. My breath caught in my throat when I saw him, the blue of his scarf, and the same blue in his eyes, a spark in the rapidly whitening landscape around us. He slipped his arm around my shoulders, and I thought I caught a faint whiff of apples.

"Pentimento," he said. "Do you remember what it means?"

"When old images that have been painted over resurface," I said.

We were on the pathway walking down the hill, but when he spoke, I turned and headed against the wave of alumnae headed toward Commons, up near the top of Founder's Hill. I glanced over my shoulder and saw that he was following.

A moment later, we were alone, where the pathway curved behind the chapel. The teak bench with Miss Wetherby's memorial plaque was already covered with a light dusting of snow, so that her name was obscured. Below us, the valley spread out. The buildings' lines were softened; the fields were a pattern of stubble and white; the river was slate colored, and the Wooten Boathouse was brown. Off in the distance, we could see Hardley's dark buildings against the white sky.

It was cold. Josh stamped his feet, and his breath came out in cloudy bursts. There was a lock of hair that fell over his eye, and I reached up with my mittened hand and smoothed it away.

"Jessica and I are going to counseling," he said.

"She told me."

"When we almost lost Molly . . ."

"You don't have to explain."

"But I want to," he said. "We're going to be seeing each other all the time, and I don't want you to think that this is easy for me."

"Josh, I know it's not easy."

"I mean it, Jane. You'll always be the painting underneath, bleeding through to the surface, the text hidden underneath the top layer of words . . ."

There was a snowflake caught in one of his eyelashes. He blinked, and it melted away. There was a bright red patch, right at the knob of his cheekbone on each side of his face.

"Josh, please . . ."

"I told you I held an image of you in my mind's eye," he said. "But the one I see now . . ."

I was afraid to look at him, so I gazed past him, out at the valley, but then my eyes were drawn back to the familiar contours of his face.

He reached up and his mittened hand cupped my chin. *"Thus mellow'd to the tender light / Which Heaven to gaudy day denies."*

Then, his arms were around me, and my nose was pressed up against the rough surface of his cheek, and I felt as if he would never let me go.

But just as suddenly, his arms fell away.

I thought of Jessica, her friendly smile; she was the first person who had welcomed me and treated me like a friend.

"Josh," I said, "you know the palimpsest? The words that have been written over?"

He nodded, shaking snow from his eyelashes. I fought the urge to reach out and touch his face.

"Remember what you told me. It fades."

He turned and walked away from me, down the pathway, then called back over his shoulder.

"It doesn't. I was lying about that part. That's the thing about it. It's always there. Under the surface. You can't see it. But it never goes away . . ."

And at least I had that. Because when I closed my eyes, I saw not middle-aged shoulders, slightly rounded, retreating away from me down a snowy pathway. I saw the face of a seventeen-year-old framed in tousled shoulder-length hair, looking at me with a loopy smile, and he was calling out to me, "I'll be right back."

But before I had a moment to think, the marchers came around the corner of the chapel, carrying their lantern-shaped banners, and someone had thrust our class banner into my hands. I was carried along the pathway, jostling for space with my Grove sisters.

Emma Doerr slipped her arm around my shoulders. "So, you've pulled a Pymstead on us, huh? I have to admit I always thought she had it pretty good." She reached down to adjust the scarf that was slipping off one of her daughter's shoulders, then tugged at the other one, who was trying to run ahead.

"I always thought so too," I said.

I looked out over the valley and beheld the wintry landscape, and I smiled, knowing that I had found a place for myself here.

That night, alone in my room, I slid the faded onionskin papers out of the envelope, startled to see our real names—Lissa and Jane, Miss Pymstead and Miss Wetherby—typed into the original manuscript. This was Kat's version of the true story. I was ready to learn how it ended.

The Second Jump

I don't know what I was thinking when I ran out the door of Miss Pymstead's house. I didn't have a particular destination in mind, but the entire campus of the Grove slopes downward, toward the river, and so I ran down, across the soaked expanse of Siberia, down the path to the boathouse. I tried the boathouse door, but it was locked.

I decided to climb the tree.

Beyond the rain and the wind that was rushing in my ears was the sound of my own stupidity. All of these mysteries we had tried to untangle and the only mystery was my own ignorance. My mother was pregnant and she gave up everything to have me, and now I had let her down. I felt so betrayed remembering all of the times she had told me how I was born premature—how I'd been so tiny she could hold me in the palm of her hand. I had believed her.

I slid across the slippery riverbank toward the giant poplar tree and grasped the bottom rung.

My shoes were muddy and the rain was streaming down. I put one foot on the rung and started to climb. About halfway up, the slick, muddy bottom of my Top-Sider lost its purchase and I dangled there, my shoulders almost wrenched from their sockets, but I kicked around and settled my foot back on the wooden rung.

At the top, I heaved myself onto the branch and scooted my bottom along the wet surface. Rain was still pouring down. My jeans and T-shirt were soaked through, and my hair was dripping water down my face. I felt as if I had jumped and was already in the water.

The night was noisy—all river current and crashing rain. I grasped the rope and held it in my lap; it was wet too, and I stared into the blackness. I wanted to jump—to feel it again: the deathlike drop, the sickening snap, the letting go—but I was scared. The rain-clouded dark was thick, and the sound of the river below was wild.

I was a mistake in this life—the cause of my own mother's misery, and a disappointment to her and to everyone. I had accused Miss Pymstead of doing things she had never done; I was trying to get back at her for stealing my mother's prize. So, here I was, both a chump and a traitor. I seemed to destroy every life that I touched.

Only one thing was on my mind, and that was the jump. I wanted to feel that plunge, like a taste of death.

But then, through the crashing rain and roaring river, I heard another sound—a voice calling my name, and soon, I could hear Miss Pymstead.

"Kat? Where are you?"

"I'm up here," I said.

"Kat, come down and let's talk. It's cold out here. You don't belong up in that tree."

"Leave me alone. I'm going to jump," I said.

Miss Pymstead had a flashlight, and its thin beam cut a trace of light through the shadows. She pointed it up toward me and the beam caught me in the eyes.

"Kat, I'm so sorry. I was out of line to say what I said."

"Leave me alone," I repeated. "I'm going to jump." I held the rope in my hands, twisting it in my lap.

"No!" she said. "Wait, I'm coming up."

"Don't come up, Miss Pymstead. It's slippery, and besides, you can't stop me."

She ignored me and put her foot on the lowest rung.

I knew that the rungs were slippery. I wanted her not to chase me. I willed myself to jump off the branch. I gripped the rope. But my stomach was in my throat, and my bottom refused to budge even though I was desperate to get away from her.

She came, up, up, up. Her flashlight making jagged flashes as she climbed.

She reached the top, and still I hadn't had the courage to jump.

She reached out to slip her leg over the branch I was sitting on. Her flashlight beam went straight into my eyes, blinding me momentarily.

That was the moment I chose to jump. I pushed off from the branch and felt the sickening sudden drop. The last thing I saw was her outstretched hand.

The current was so swift that it swept me a ways down the river before I was able to get my bearings and scramble out. Sopping wet, but proud and exhilarated, I shoved through the weeds on the riverbank, my feet sliding in the mud. Back in Lane North, I got out of my muddy clothes and fell into a deep sleep.

Early in the morning, I slipped out of our room before Jane woke up and went to Miss Pymstead's house to apologize, but she wasn't there. I walked around for a long time, and finally I decided to come clean. I headed toward Loomis Hall, preparing to explain to Mr. Treadway and Mrs. Tarkington-Luce that it had all been my fault. That Miss Pymstead had never done anything wrong at all, and that evidence in the clue notebook I had handed them two days before was just a fabrication. But I was only halfway up the hill when I saw an ambulance parked down next to the boathouse, and on a stretcher was the pale body of Miss Pymstead; they were just covering it with a cloth.

I know what you're thinking. You're wondering if I pushed her out of that tree and then walked right past her on the muddy bank, ignoring the grotesque twist of her pale neck, and the strangled scream that lingered on her lips. I think back to that moment in the tree when her hand was outstretched. She was trying to help me. She had been trying to help me all along.

When one who died for truth . . .

I swear, I never saw her. And that's all you're going to get from me.

44

As a member of the English department faculty, I was invited to submit a recommendation for the English Department Prize to be awarded to the outstanding student at Class Day, but as it turned out, it was unanimous anyway. Three other teachers had nominated Kaitlyn Corsyn. In February, at Susan Callow's request, I had taken over the editorship of the *Signs* literary magazine.

"Keep your eye out for Kaitlyn's work," she said. "I think she may have the makings of a real writer."

On Class Day, it rained, and so we sat on folding chairs inside tents, the rain dripping off the canvas tarps, making a steady dripping sound. After the ceremony, I tried to catch up with Kaitlyn, but I didn't see her, and I started to wish I had caught her earlier, instead of waiting until the last minute. But then, I decided to duck my head into her dorm room, and I found her alone. Her suitcase flipped open on top of the ticking-striped mattress, she was jamming the last few items into the already-bulging valise.

"Kaitlyn. Oh good. I'm so glad I caught you."

She rewarded me with one of her genuine smiles. I couldn't believe I had ever found her aloof. Hers was a face that was alive with emotion and quick intelligence, her eyes bright with inquisitiveness.

"Ms. Milton. Hi. What's up?"

I was holding a small brown volume; its leather cover was worn and soft from years of use. I had found it in a used bookstore in Brattleboro.

"Before you leave, I want to give you something."

She looked at it, but when she saw the lettering on the cover, her face clouded, suddenly as turbulent as a frozen river in midwinter. I had marked one of the pages with the faded silk ribbon, and I let the book fall open.

> *Dare you see a soul at the white heat?*
> *Then crouch within the door.*
> *Red is the fire's common tint;*
> *But when the vivid ore*
>
> *Has sated flame's conditions,*
> *Its quivering substance plays*
> *Without a color but the light*
> *Of unanointed blaze.*

"Do you know what this poem is about?" I said.

Kaitlyn scanned the lines. She nodded. "I think so."

"Passion," I said. "You have it. Every generation, there are a few who do. Take it. Don't squander it. Use it. Use it wisely. And above all, Kaitlyn, take care of yourself."

I flipped the book shut. I pressed it into her hand.

"Knock 'em dead, girl," I said.

She took the book, threw it inside the suitcase, and then, with one enormous shove, she jammed the suitcase closed and sat on it while she locked it shut.

"Oh my God . . . I'm late. I gotta go. Thanks, Ms. Milton. You are so sweet. I gotta go now. My dad's coming to get this later."

She ran out the door and left me alone in the room, the dorm now strangely silent, ready for summer. Out the window, I could see that the rain had stopped. In a moment, I could see her again, running down the hillside toward Siberia, hair flying in all directions, jeans and hot-pink T-shirt out of place among the ice-cream colors of the parents in their cottons and linens. She darted in and out of the crowds until she disappeared, unquestionably, vibrantly, and wonderfully alive.

45

The year was finished. Abbott North was silent. The last fathers and mothers had dragged overloaded trunks down the stairs; the last weepy students had shared hugs and good-byes before climbing reluctantly into their parents' waiting cars. As I signed yearbooks, helped locate missing possessions, and hugged my girls, I realized how profoundly the Grove had become my home. Now, there was a brief lull, but soon enough, the dorms would fill up again with summer students, and before long, fall would bring the girls back to me, suntanned and full of stories of their summer exploits. I would enjoy the break, but I would miss them while they were gone.

Today, I felt content as I sensed the building's emptiness. My windows were propped open; outside, I could hear the lazy sound of a light breeze ruffling through leafy trees. The final note that Kat had left for me, wedged behind the coatrack in our old room, lay unfolded on the surface of my bare desk.

One who died for truth. Perhaps I would never really understand what had happened to Kat.

Here's what I knew about myself. During my second trip to Loomis Hall, from the way Mrs. Tarkington-Luce warmed up to me and gave me encouraging smiles, I got the firm impression that I might save myself if I were willing to bring Miss Pymstead down.

"Did Kat ever tell you that some of the attention that Miss Pymstead paid her was unwanted?"

To this day, I can remember the way her voice sounded when she said it. She slipped one hand over mine and gave it a little squeeze. She peered into my eyes, filled a small plate with cookies, and pushed it toward me, even though my mouth was as dry as sawdust, and my stomach was weighted down with lead.

"You can trust me," Mrs. Tarkington-Luce purred. "If you tell us the truth, nothing bad will happen to you. We understand that you've been through some difficulties recently. If you tell the truth now, we will credit this in your favor."

Her eyes were the blue of a New England sky in early summer; I peered into them, trying to read my future there. I had already told this woman the truth, several times, and no good had come of it. Now, I could hear the insistent sweet song telling me that lying might work better. *Say yes*, it sang. *Say yes, say yes.*

"Do you think Miss Pymstead was in love with her . . . ?" Mrs. Tarkington-Luce said, and I could read it in her eyes, *Say yes, say yes.* I could read it all there—my diploma, maybe even the Eugenia Wilcox Prize. All would be forgiven.

"Do you think she had an . . . ahem . . . unhealthy attraction to her . . . ?" Mr. Treadway added, clearing his throat in the middle, as though the words were so loaded they stuck there.

Right then, I was looking out the window at the large, spreading sugar maple. I could remember when it was dropping red leaves as big as dinner plates in the fall, and when it was bare and black in the winter. Now, it was floppy, with big green leaves that fluttered idly in the faint breeze.

"I think Miss Pymstead loves poetry," I said.

"Yes, I'm sure she loves poetry, but we are talking about something of a more . . ." Mr. Treadway folded his hands on the table, lowered his voice a notch. "I'm not trying to shock you, my dear, but we are referring here to . . . sapphism."

The first day, senior year, the twelve of us came into Miss Pymstead's class and seated ourselves around the battered wooden table. Senior Honors English was the only class that met in the Gould Cottage seminar room, and the trek across Siberia and down the steep hill made us feel as though we were heading somewhere important. We scattered ourselves around the table in groups of twos and threes. It was warm still, and so we were clad in the cutoff jeans and halter tops of summertime. Miss Pymstead, though she wasn't old, seemed to come from another era. Her hair was pinned up in a bun, and I remember that her attire was oddly dated: a white sailor suit with a dropped waist and navy-blue piping at the sleeves and hem.

I sensed her unease with our informality: Emma Doerr was braless underneath a Jimi Hendrix tank top. Kat was wearing a man's suit vest over a white embroidered peasant blouse.

Miss Pymstead stood before us saying nothing, and so we chatted a bit among ourselves, waiting for her to give us a sign that she was ready to begin. But she gave no such sign; she just waited, her face as implacable as a board, her wide eyes unblinking. Under her steady gaze, we fell silent, and into that pause, Miss Pymstead spoke.

"The subject of this course is literature. But the *real* subject of the course is to recognize the truth when you see it. That is an enterprise which is both more difficult and easier than you think."

Miss Pymstead stopped talking and looked at all of us. I remember that on that first day, we were just settling in. Lissa was unzipping her pencil case. Abigail Von Platte was flipping open her notebook. Emma Doerr was fiddling with her backpack.

Miss Pymstead made it clear that she wanted our full attention.

"Great literature speaks the truth," she said. "You will recognize it because it is impossible not to recognize it. It sings its own song—it hums with the power of righteousness . . ." I remember distinctly that at that point, Lissa cocked one eyebrow and gave me a look.

Miss Pymstead whirled around. Her gestures were always theatrical.

"These are the words of the great poet Emily Dickinson. She wrote them in a letter to T. W. Higginson, a mentor, who, it may be noted, never once recognized her greatness but overlooked it because he was so hemmed in by the prejudices of his time."

The room was silent except for the erratic tapping sounds of Miss Pymstead's chalk on the chalkboard. Then, she stepped aside and began to recite without looking at the board—clearly from memory: *"If I read a book and it makes my whole body so cold no fire can ever warm me I know that is poetry. If I feel physically as if the top of my head were taken off, I know that is poetry."*

She let us sit in a silence long enough to rival a Quaker meeting, long enough to allow us to become shifty and uncomfortable, to let us fear that we had missed the point, to wonder if we were supposed to say something, to squirm in our chairs and fidget with our fingers under the table.

"Poetry is truth. Learn it and you'll learn truth," Miss Pymstead said.

"Jane!"

I saw a frown flicker back across Mrs. Tarkington-Luce's face. I knew that I had given up my one chance.

"So, you are saying your roommate is liar?"

"She's good at telling stories," I said. "Sometimes the things she makes up are not very nice."

"You will not corroborate her story. You believe that it is completely untrue."

I hesitated for only a moment before I spoke out in a clear tone.

"I do."

Mrs. Tarkington-Luce was staring at me, the disappointment bare upon her face. If a moment before she had looked friendly and helpful, now, I could see that the window of possible forgiveness had slammed shut.

"Well, liars love company," said Mrs. Tarkington-Luce. "You may run along. I'm sure you have community service you need to get done."

It took me fifty steps to get out of that door, and with each step I waged a battle not to turn around and lie my way out of trouble. With each of those steps, I realized how easy it would be to lie, how high the stakes were for me, how foolish I was to stick to my guns. I wondered then, and have for many years since, what it was that made me stand up for Miss Amanda Pymstead. I didn't know that I was especially fond of her, and my obsession with her had ruined my senior year. Unbeknownst to me, she was already dead as I defended her, crumpled at the foot of the jump tree. I will always feel some level of responsibility for what happened to her, but at least I know that when the time came, I refused to let the words of the poems she so loved be twisted and used against her.

Now, as I step into Miss Pymstead's shoes, I vow to myself to honor her memory. I will teach literature as if all our lives depend on it. Because they do.

EPILOGUE

A death-blow is a life-blow to some
Who, till they died, did not alive become;
Who, had they lived, had died, but when
They died, vitality begun.

—Emily Dickinson

The Pearl-Handled Pistol

If you've read all the way to the end of this book, you must be wondering about the mystery of what actually happened to Chestmont Wooten. It has occurred to me, more than once, that the only true mystery is human nature itself. Why Jane felt the need to run all over campus trying to find the answer to the question of who killed Chestmont Wooten when the real answer was right in front of her, I'll never know.

Jane never seemed to have a clue. She wore her naïveté wrapped around her like a big white cloak. It looked so soft and warm that I used to wish I could climb under it with her, only I realized right away it wasn't big enough. That's the thing with that kind of a cloak: once you climb out from underneath it, there's no going back.

So, there was no way to tell her that I already knew who killed Chestmont Wooten. Poor old Miss Wetherby blurted it out to me practically the first time I met her.

It came out in dribs and drabs—sly little giggles. "Oh, you'd be surprised what skeletons I have in my closet, my dear. You'd be very surprised. More sherry, dear? Why, some say I even killed a man . . ."

"Killed a man?" I said. "Sweet little Miss Wetherby?" I knew how to pluck her like a chord. I could get her all aquiver, as easily as strumming a guitar.

"I'm not as sweet as you think, my dear. Cross me and my blood runs cold. Deep down, I'm as tough as ice."

"I don't doubt it," I said. "I have no intention of crossing you."

One evening, I just flat out asked her. "Grove sisters' swear," I said. "But tell me, was the man you killed Chestmont Wooten . . . ?"

She giggled a little and her eyebrows shot up. "Oh, I couldn't possibly tell you that. But, to satisfy your curiosity, I'll show you something."

She walked over to the secretary at the end of the room and slid open a drawer. I think there might have been a secret drawer or something, because she flipped up a hidden switch and slipped her hand inside, then she pulled something out, and I saw that it was a little pistol with an inlaid pearl handle.

"See this," she said. She pointed to the place where there were engraved initials: CW.

I looked at her.

"Nothing like using a man's own folly to bring him down," she said.

"I don't understand."

"I told him I greatly admired him, and could he give me some pointers on how to become a better teacher. I said I'd heard that so many people at Hardley were moved by his speeches, and I said that I hoped that I myself would be headmistress someday. He laughed when I told him that. He said he hoped I'd be headmistress too, as he had no intention of wasting too much more time in a school for girls.

"I expressed a fascination with firearms, and so, the poor man, he brought his pistol to show me. I let him think he'd have his way with me, but instead, I was able to shoot him in the head."

"How did you shoot him in the head?" I whispered. "Wasn't he much bigger than you?"

"Ah, but I bored him . . . I lured him out into the snow, and I began to read him the poems of Emily Dickinson. I remember

that he was drinking Johnnie Walker Red Label, no doubt in an effort to stay warm, and then, he had a moment's fatal inattention. You see, I just wasn't pretty enough to interest him that much. He dozed off, and I slipped the pistol out of his jacket pocket, held it to his head, and I pulled the trigger. His blood made a heart-shaped pattern in the snow."

"Then why didn't they think it was a suicide?" I said.

"Because I couldn't part with the pistol," she whispered. "I like the thrill of it . . . I like taking it out and feeling the chill in the palm of my hand."

"But aren't you worried I'm going to rat you out?" I said.

"Oh, but you won't," she said. "That's why I picked you to tell. I know your kind. You prefer the thrill of the secret."

I told myself then and there that I'd go back and tell everyone—I'd tell Jane and Lissa, and they'd spread it to everyone else, and pretty soon the whole dorm would know.

But by the time I was halfway down the hill, I knew she had me. She was right. I would never tell. Because if I told, the story would change as it made its way from girl to girl—it would take on new details, and get fuzzy, and lose its power. This way, it was mine. Just mine, and I would always remember it. I would take it to my grave.

I remember she said, "I don't believe it hurt him much, what with the cold, and the scotch, and the snow." It was just as

Emily said it would be—cold, stupidity, and of course, letting go.

Appearances are deceiving.

We were looking for passion and mystery, to have Botticelli faces and dress up in party clothes, but there was passion right there, staring at us, with rabbity eyes.

ABOUT THE AUTHOR

A former obstetric nurse, Nora Carroll now writes full-time. She lives with her husband, four children, and a madcap golden retriever in Southern California.